D0209376

The Deal,
the Dance,
and the Devil

ALSO BY VICTORIA CHRISTOPHER MURRAY

Sins of the Mother
Lady Jasmine
Too Little, Too Late
The Ex Files
A Sin and a Shame
Grown Folks Business
Truth Be Told
Temptation
Joy
Blessed Assurance (contributor)

The Deal, the Dance, and the Devil

Victoria Christopher Murray

A Touchstone Book
Published by Simon & Schuster
New York London Toronto Sydney

Touchstone
A Division of Simon & Schuster, Inc.
1230 Avenue of the Americas
New York, NY 10020

This book is a work of fiction. Names, characters, places, and incidents either are products of the author's imagination or are used fictitiously. Any resemblance to actual events or locales or persons, living or dead, is entirely coincidental.

Copyright © 2011 by Victoria Christopher Murray

All rights reserved, including the right to reproduce this book or portions thereof in any form whatsoever. For information address Touchstone Subsidiary Rights Department, 1230 Avenue of the Americas, New York, NY 10020.

TOUCHSTONE and colophon are registered trademarks of Simon & Schuster, Inc.

Manufactured in the United States of America

ISBN 978-1-61129-789-8

This book is dedicated to two very special people whom I lost the very same week in 2010.

My uncle, Elmer Yearwood. Second to my father, there is no man on earth who had a greater impact on my life. From my earliest days he cared about me, nurtured me, and loved me so that I would grow into the woman I am today. I pray that I made him proud. I will always love you, Uncle Elmer. Rest in God's hands.

My agent, Elaine Koster. Until her death in August, Elaine was the only agent I'd had. From the very beginning, she believed in me, told me that I had amazing talent, and said that she hoped to build my career to "the greatest heights." (She said that at least once a year.) Her belief in me helped me to believe and I will always be grateful that God chose her to help build my career. Thank you, Elaine. RIP.

The Deal, the Dance, and the Devil

Chapter 1

Five million dollars.

All I could do was stare at the check. To be sure, I counted again: Seven figures, two commas. Yup, this was definitely five million.

I could have stared at those numbers all day, but I had to look up and at my boss, Shay-Shaunté.

My eyes asked the questions; she explained, "That's for you," and then she leaned back in what I called her throne—a snake-skinned upholstered executive chair with a back that was six feet high. She smiled as if she gave out seven-figure checks on the regular.

That's when I started laughing—hard. There had to be a joke in here somewhere, and I figured I'd get a head start before Shay-Shaunté filled me in. But she didn't laugh; she didn't chuckle, she didn't even blink. Just smiled, as if she was waiting for me to get it together.

That's when my heart started thumping. Could this five-million-dollar check made out to me, Evia Langston, be real?

The thought made me weak. Made me fall into the leather chair in front of her desk.

Okay, keep breathing, I told myself. First, I inhaled, then I did just the opposite. Deep inside I knew this was one of those too-good-to-be-true moments, but for a second I pushed aside the question of why anybody would give me five million dollars and thought instead about how desperately Adam and I needed this money.

"Oh, my God!" I said under my breath. "This will save our lives."

I didn't mean to say that out loud, but I guess I did, because Shay-Shaunté said, "That's what I was thinking."

My eyes burned; tears were on the way. But just when I was about to get down on my knees and thank God and Shay-Shaunté, that ringing in my heart started.

Oh, no! I wasn't trying to hear that. I tried to shake it away, but it trilled all the way down to my soul.

When I was a kid, Big Mama told me that all God's children had His voice inside them. Well, I didn't have a voice; what I had was more like an alarm clock, but however it sounded, my grandmother told me it should never be ignored.

"It's the love of the Lord, warnin' you when somethin' ain't right. Never turn your back on the Lord, chile, or you'll find yourself knee-deep in the devil's trouble."

From the time I was ten till now, Big Mama's words had been nothing but the truth. Every time I heard that alarm, I sat down and thought things through. But I didn't want to do too much thinking about this. It wasn't that I didn't want to listen to God; it was just that I didn't want Him to do too much talking right about now. 'Cause I was sure that if He spoke, it could mess up this whole five-million-dollar thing that I had going on.

"What is this?" I spoke with a calm I didn't feel. The check was still clenched in my palm; my plan was to never let it go.

My boss tossed her auburn-streaked hair away from her face. "I'm assuming you're not really asking me what that is, since you know it's a check." She stood, did one of those model-sway strolls toward me, perched her butt on the corner of her glass desk, and stretched out her long legs. "Let's call this a fee . . . for services rendered."

What kind of services would have to be rendered to get a five-million-dollar fee?

I knew it; this had to be a joke.

I'd worked for Shay-Shaunté for six years as one of two executive assistants. Basically, I was her right hand, in charge of numbers and anything else she didn't want to handle in her hair care empire. In that role, I'd done lots of things—including putting together all the investor reports (since I'd been an accounting major in college) and working on other stuff till the clock ticked way past midnight sometimes. Occasionally, I even traveled with Shay-Shaunté when Rachel Stone, the other executive assistant, couldn't.

But even with that plateload of responsibility, in the more than two thousand days that I'd been employed by Shay-Shaunté and her company, Ferossity, I'd never done anything that came close to earning five million dollars—not even if you added all two thousand days together and multiplied by three.

Then, Shay-Shaunté explained, "My birthday's coming up."

Dang! Now I knew for sure that this check and I were soon going to be parted.

I knew that Shay-Shaunté's birthday was approaching—though I doubted if too many others knew. My boss was superprivate, almost anal in her secrecy; she never shared anything with anyone about the who, what, where of her life. Articles found on the Internet estimated her age because no one ever knew her exact birth date.

But I knew because of loan papers she'd had me deliver to the bank for her about a year ago. It wasn't like I was trying to be nosy, but there on the first page right next to date of birth: 12/31/1960. I remembered thinking, dang! There was no way in the world I would've guessed ol' girl was anywhere close to fifty. Maybe because of her achievements I should've known that she had to be beyond the thirty years that she looked. But physically, no one could tell it—not from her six-foot, supermodel, size 2 physique. Not from her unblemished skin and distinct features that gave no real clue to her ethnicity. Her face was a representation of the world. With eyes slightly slanted, she could have been Asian. Below was a nose as thin and upturned as any Caucasian's. Then, there were her lips—full, heart-shaped, the pride of Africans.

It wasn't just her features that held her secret. Her golden-tinted skin suggested that some East Indian, or maybe even Hispanic, blood flowed through her veins.

But she was a sistah-girl; I knew that 'cause black people knew black people. And when Shay-Shaunté opened her mouth and got to twisting her neck and rolling her eyes—she told me what her face did not.

So, I knew the big birthday was coming up—the big five-oh! In three weeks. On New Year's Eve.

I guessed that since this was the big one, she'd decided to come from behind her private curtain and celebrate in public.

As visions of five million dollars in my bank account danced right out of my head, I wondered what kind of party Shay-Shaunté wanted for this kind of money.

"So," I began. "This check is for your birthday? For a party?"

"Yes."

I waited for her to say more; she didn't. So I said, "You want me to plan it?"

She tilted her head, as if she had to think. Then, with a smile that looked kind of sly to me, she said, "You could say that." Then, nothing else.

Okay, this was beginning to feel like some kind of game—which was strange, 'cause Shay-Shaunté didn't play. She was always about business.

After a deep breath, she explained more, "My life has been pretty hectic."

I shrugged. "Yeah," was all I said to that understatement. Of course her life was busy—how many multimillionaires didn't have full schedules?

And truth? I only called Shay-Shaunté a millionaire because that's what had been reported in the media. But I would bet all kinds of money that there was more than one black female billionaire in the country.

I didn't have a thing to substantiate it, but I guessed that Shay-Shaunté had come from humble beginnings; she'd had to grind her way to the top and never wanted to look back.

It was a guess; I didn't know for sure.

When Ms. Givens, from the employment agency, had told me about this position, I'd had three thoughts. The first: What kind of name was Shay-Shaunté? Ms. Givens had told me that was her full name and that she never allowed anyone to shorten it. Second: What was up with the funny spelling of the company name—Ferossity? And third: If Shay-Shaunté and Ferossity were so huge—Ms. Givens had said Ferossity was a twenty-year-old company with $30 million in annual sales—why hadn't I ever heard of her or the company, especially since she specialized in black hair care?

But I'd tossed away all my questions and taken the interview once Ms. Givens had told me that I'd be earning fifty thousand dollars. I'd gotten the job the next day when Shay-Shaunté had hired me on the spot.

Working for her had been a complete pleasure, so I was willing to do anything she needed me to do to make her birthday a great one.

"Okay," my boss said, "I'm gonna say this straight out." Shay-Shaunté strolled away from me, returning to her high-back chair. "I've been too busy to plan anything special."

I grabbed a notepad from her desk. "That's okay. Rachel and I are on it."

"You won't need Rachel's help."

I frowned a little. With all that was on my plate—especially standing by for holiday replenishments that any of our accounts needed—there was no way I was going to be able to handle Shay-Shaunté's party alone. It was already December 2.

Shay-Shaunté went on to say, "Don't worry; you won't need help," as if she'd read my mind. "The thing is, with the way my life is going right now, I don't have anyone special to share this birthday."

I got it—she was trying to figure out how to have a mandatory party, probably right here in her corporate building, where she could strongly suggest that all of her six hundred employees attend.

She said, "You probably don't know this, but I'm turning fifty."

I wasn't going to admit to being a snoop, so I said, "Fifty? Wow! Dang! No! I didn't know. You look . . ." When she frowned, I closed my mouth.

She said, "Well, fifty is a special birthday and I don't want this milestone to pass without some kind of celebration."

I felt a tinge of an ache in my heart for the mogul. She might have been giga-gorgeous, supersexy, and megarich, but she was alone. She was single, childless, and, as far as I could tell, without any relatives at all, since the only personal thing she'd ever shared was that her parents had passed away when she was young.

The only calls she ever got were from celebrities who wanted to thank her for one product or another. Though friendly, none seemed to be her friends.

Shay-Shaunté's life was a constant reminder to me that money wasn't everything, because no matter what Adam and I were going through, we had each other.

Shay-Shaunté said, "So, after really thinking about this . . . I want to pay you . . . for a weekend . . . my birthday weekend . . . to spend that time . . . with your husband."

Okay, clearly, I had mentally checked out for a moment. Or maybe the fact that I was still holding on to this five-million-dollar check had me delirious. I placed the back of my hand against my forehead to see if I had a fever; to see if that was why my ears weren't working.

Shay-Shaunté continued. "I know about the problems you and Adam are having. I know this money will help."

So, I *had* heard her correctly. It must've been the way I sat there, staring, that made her continue. "I don't *want* your husband, Evia. At least not permanently."

Was that supposed to make me feel better?

"I only want him for a weekend," she kept on like we were just girls, just talking. "To help me celebrate."

That was when it hit me—what she *really* meant. Now I couldn't move—I stopped blinking, stopped breathing, stopped everything!

I stared—no, I glared—at her as if she had lost her dang-blasted mind. Then I started to laugh again, and she stared back at me as if I'd lost mine.

"Girl, that was so funny." I stood up. "And today's not even

April Fool's. Whew!" I reached out to give her back the check. "Well, I've got to get back to work."

Shay-Shaunté made no move to take back the money. So I laid the check on her desk.

Her shoulders were stiff, her face solemn, her eyes small, focused, and intense, like she was stalking her prey. I'd seen that stance in so many meetings—when she'd been up against formidable opponents—when she'd always won.

"This isn't a joke, Evia. That five million dollars is yours. If you and Adam agree . . . to take this deal."

Now I was mad, because I had given her a way out. We could have treated this like a joke and neither one of us would have mentioned it again.

But, no. She had to keep it going—like she meant it. Well, I meant it, too, when I told her, "You have lost your mind!"

She settled back, crossed her legs, not at all fazed by my outburst. "I know this is unusual," she began in a tone that sounded like she was just discussing her schedule. "But there is nothing usual about my life."

I kept my anger inside because, after all, Shay-Shaunté was my boss and I needed this job. But I also needed to make my point. "Well, my life is not so unusual that my husband and I rent each other out."

"I know you need money, Evia."

That was another thing that was pissing me off at the moment . . . how did she know that? As private as Shay-Shaunté was, Adam and I were the same when it came to what we'd been going through.

Not that it mattered what she knew or how she'd found out. "We don't need money that badly." I might have kept the anger from my tone, but attitude was all over me as my head swayed and my finger pointed, like I was fourteen years old and living back in Barry Farm, where I grew up.

She tilted her head like she doubted my words.

So to make sure that she understood completely, I said, "This will never happen."

"Never say never."

No, she didn't throw that tired cliché in my face. "I can say never to this!"

I was steaming; Shay-Shaunté stayed calm. "You and Adam need that money."

Which was the only reason I didn't tell Shay-Shaunté to take that check *and* this job and shove it anywhere—up her nose, up her behind; I didn't care where.

"This could be a good solution for all of us," she had the nerve to persist.

"Look, I don't know where you got this craziness from, but we don't even need to talk about it no mo'. It ain't gonna happen." I forget every English class I'd ever taken. "If you want a man, you need to find another one."

"I want yours."

Where I grew up, those were fighting words. I saw girls get beat down so bad over boys that they had to transfer to other schools. That's what I wanted to do to Shay-Shaunté right now—beat her until she crawled out of the city.

But I was sixteen years out of high school and a long way from the place I once called home. I couldn't go back there, especially since I desperately needed this gig, which had become a sixty-five-thousand-dollar-a-year job.

So I took a deep breath, found my decorum, and smiled. "Thank you so much for the offer, Shay-Shaunté. But my husband and I will pass." Then I spun around so fast that I got dizzy. Surely, there was a trail of smoke billowing behind me as I stomped across the wide office, because I was hot!

Before I got to the door, Shay-Shaunté had the audacity to

add, "Think about it, Evia. Talk to Adam. I think after you two consider your options, you—"

I didn't hear another word once I slammed the door, totally disrespecting the woman who signed my paychecks. But Shay-Shaunté needed to be disrespected. She needed more than that, but like I said, I needed my job.

"Hey, girl, what were you doing in there so long?" Rachel asked as I stumbled by her desk.

I waved her away as I made my way into my office.

"Evia!" Rachel called after me.

Once I closed my door, I didn't have to worry about my colleague following me. She knew that whatever had gone down, I'd share the dirt with her later.

As I fell into my chair, I thought about all the days when I'd been so glad that Shay-Shaunté had given me—her most senior assistant—my own little space in her empire. This was one of those days, because I needed to be alone to figure this out. Had Shay-Shaunté really offered me five million dollars? For a weekend with Adam?

My fingers curled into fists. Glancing at the clock, I moaned—it couldn't be only two thirty. I never left the office before six, but I didn't have another minute in me today.

I grabbed my purse and down coat, then tiptoed to my door. Rachel would be waiting on the other side, so I had my lie ready.

But when I peeked out, Rachel's desk was empty. I rushed into the hall, past the elevators, straight to the stairwell. It didn't matter that I was on the twelfth floor. I would've scaled down the side of the Washington Monument if I'd had to.

Anything to get away from that crazy woman and her dang-blasted deal.

Chapter 2

PEOPLE CONFUSED MY KINDNESS FOR NAÏVETÉ. Folks thought they could walk over me, say anything to me, try to slip craziness by me. But on the real, they didn't know that Evia Early Evans Langston did not play.

Yeah, I said it. My middle name is Early, bestowed upon me by a mother with a limited imagination. She wanted her firstborn to have all *E*s as a monogram—not that she knew what a monogram was. So, instead of all the names that began with *E*—like Ebony, or Elizabeth, heck, I would've taken Edith—she'd come up with Early because, "Chile, it was early in the morning and that was the first thing that came to mind."

Even though I'd heard that story millions of times, I still had to shake my head. My mother could come up with some names! I still swore that my first name was supposed to have been Eve or Eva, but for some reason, early that Sunday morning, my mother had added an *I*.

But no matter who or where I came from, I wasn't going to be played by Shay-Shaunté.

Did that hooker really believe that she could buy me and my husband? Yeah, five million was a lot of money, and right about now, we could use five thousand, let alone five million. But this was the thing—my relationship with Adam Emory Langston was not a negotiable commodity. Please! We valued matrimony. We were solid as a rock, brought together by God, and no man—or rich woman—was ever going to come between us. Shay-Shaunté needed to take her money and go sit down. She'd never have a piece of what I had.

It wasn't until the driver behind me started blasting his horn that I even noticed where I was. I'd been rolling slowly down I-395, not paying any kind of attention because all I was trying to do was calm down. I didn't want to take all of this anger home—there were enough challenges there.

When the driver blared his horn again, I resisted the urge to grace him with the third-finger salute. It wasn't his fault that I was in a cursing-out-the-first-person-who-stepped-on-me kind of a mood.

I sped up, over the Capitol Bridge, then slowed down, made a turn onto Firth Sterling, and drove into the heart of my childhood.

In Barry Farm—what some called the cesspit of D.C.—there was no talk of million-dollar deals, not even from the best hustlers. Here, it would be easy to forget what I didn't want to remember.

Slowly, I rolled through the familiar streets and let the memories settle me. Not much had changed since I'd been an eighties child raised in the hood. Barry Farm was the oldest African American neighborhood in D.C., and it was still ninety-nine percent black and one hundred percent poor. Almost entirely made up of public housing, the neighborhood was steeped in the worst elements of poverty: violent crime, drug abuse, and the stench of defeat. The weekends were riddled with shootings, leaving on average two families weeping in the streets for their dead loved ones. Not even the mean-mugged D.C. police spent too much time here.

These streets didn't scare me, though. Just about everyone could find some solace at home—no matter where home was.

I eased the car to the curb and stopped in front of the blue slat house that had been standing on this block in the middle of the projects since the sixties. Most people would call this a shack; I'd once called it home.

Without looking, I reached to the side to press the electronic button for the window that I'd cracked open. But there wasn't a button, just a handle.

What?

Oh!

I'd forgotten—this wasn't the Lexus. I guessed it was going to take me longer than two weeks to get used to this bare-boned car.

Pausing for a moment, I debated whether or not I really wanted to get out. Yeah, the streets were familiar and some memories were good. But once I stepped into my mother's place, the craziness that I was trying to forget would be replaced by some other kind of madness.

Still, I slid out and strolled toward the house as if I wasn't fuming. At the front door, I tested the knob, and, like always, the door opened. Why did my mother keep doing this? In this neighborhood, people lived behind doors that held five, six, seven locks. But though my mother had her own security devices, fifty percent of the time she didn't use them.

I guessed she wasn't too worried. Criminals would turn right around if they came to this door. It sounded like a riot up in here with the television blasting SpongeBob and my nephews Taquan, Shuquan, and Rashaun screaming as if they were competing with the TV. The three boys ran and jumped through a maze of furniture, toys, and clothes, shrieking the whole time. It took a moment for them to notice me.

"Auntie Evia! Auntie Evia!"

"Hey, y'all." I hugged my nephews as they scrambled around my legs. "Who's watching you guys?"

Without a word, the three pointed to the couch. I hadn't even noticed my oldest nephew sitting with one of the newest electronics games between his hands.

"Hey, Apollo," I said, tossing my purse onto the sofa next to my only nephew who didn't have a rhyming name.

Even though I had greeted Apollo pleasantly, the fourteen-year-old didn't part his lips. Didn't acknowledge my presence in any kind of way. I wanted to slap him upside his head, but what good would that do? It wasn't like he had any home training.

"Evia?" My mother sauntered into the room, wiping her eyes and fluffing out the matted side of her Halle Berry–style pixie cut; I guessed I'd interrupted her nap.

"Yeah, it's me," I said, adding *"Surprise!"* to my tone.

She was surprised, all right. "What are you doing here?" she kind of growled.

Marilyn Evans was still two years away from fifty, yet she looked ten years older. Maybe it was because she had lived a rock-hard life. According to Marilyn (which is what my brother, sister, and I called her because she said she was too young to have anyone calling her Mama), her difficult days began the moment she was born in Hardtimes, Mississippi.

Yup! Hardtimes. Although she was never able to show it to us on a map, my mother actually wanted us to believe that she was born in that city Stevie Wonder sang about. (Though recently, she changed her story—now, she was born in Kosciusko because of Oprah.)

Anyway, I didn't know much about my mother's Southern roots. Only that she'd escaped (her word) when she'd had enough money to flee. (Again, her word.) She was fifteen and her savings were supposed to carry her and her lofty dreams straight to New York City, where she planned to live like her favorite TV character, Mary Tyler Moore. But naïveté and poor planning got Marilyn as far as Washington, D.C.

Undaunted, Marilyn decided to settle in the nation's capital for as long as it took to earn the rest of the money for that ticket to New York—two weeks, tops.

Two weeks, two months, two years, two decades, and more had passed. I guessed she never garnered enough to make the two-hundred-mile ride up I-95. And it didn't help that four months after she arrived in D.C., she found herself pregnant—with me.

"I came by to see you," I answered her. Leaning over to hug her, I paused when she pulled away and dipped into one of the matching winged chairs that we'd bought for her last Christmas.

"Came by to see me?" She tapped a cigarette from the packet. "Why?"

It wasn't hard to understand my mother's attitude. Even though I came to this neighborhood every Sunday for church, I hardly ever stopped by to visit. There were lots of reasons why the telephone worked best for me and Marilyn.

She said, "So, you not gonna answer my question? You just gonna sit there?"

"I'm sorry," I began, "I came by because . . . I was kinda in the neighborhood."

She raised her eyebrows, took a hard puff on her cigarette, then stared, as if she was waiting for me to take back that lie.

"Give me that!" Rashaun, the youngest, screamed as he chased his brothers. But the four-year-old was no match for the six- and eight-year-olds who tore through the living room.

I glanced at my mother, sure that at any moment she was going to shut the whole thing down. But she leaned back, her cigarette dangling from the corner of her mouth, and her eyes squinted, as if she were trying to see the cartoons on the television screen.

So, I took over. "Y'all need to settle down."

That got my mother talking, "This ain't your house, Evia; leave 'em boys alone," she scolded me. "Let those boys be boys."

There it was—my mother's brilliant child-rearing philosophy. Boys will be boys.

That's why out of the three who had come out of her womb, I was the only one with any kind of good sense, and she couldn't take credit for that. My home training came from Big Mama, her mother, who, thank God, had followed Marilyn to D.C. in time to teach me about life, love, and God.

I took a breath before I asked, "Where's Cashmere?" thinking that talking about my sister would take me and Marilyn to safer ground. "Why she got you watching her kids today?" Even though I'd tried not to say that with an attitude, my feelings were clear. I couldn't help it though, because where *was* my sister? It wasn't like Cashmere had a job or was looking for one. She'd told me plenty of times that she preferred to live off the system because the money she got was almost as much as she could make at any job that she would get without her high school diploma. If that was her philosophy, why wasn't she here?

"I'm not watching them," my mother explained. "They moved back here three weeks ago. If you would call or come by, you'd know this."

Oh, Lawd!

My mother said, "It's the same ole stuff, but this time, Lamont actually hit her."

Oh, Lawd!

"He's still accusing her of sleeping with Bubba," she explained.

Bubba. That was Rashaun's father . . . I think.

Marilyn said, "So I told her to get up on out of there and come home so that I could take care of her and the kids."

Triple oh, Lawd! How was my mother gonna take care of Cashmere and her kids when she could barely take care of herself?

I needed another change of subject! So I said, "Have you heard from Snake?"

"I wish y'all would stop calling my boy that. That is not the name I gave him."

So, to please my mother, I said, "I'm sorry. What's up with Twin?"

Marilyn smiled, as if that was better. She was serious, and she'd been serious when she'd named him, too. No, my brother was not a twin, had never been a twin—there was only one child inside her womb when Twin was born. But she'd *wanted* twins. So . . .

I shook my head again. You couldn't get more ghetto than that—except for maybe Cashmere—and her middle name: Three. Marilyn had almost named her three o' clock because . . . well, you know.

"Anyway," I said, "so, Twin's good?"

Her smile went away. "Good if you call the po-lice picking him up good."

I rolled my eyes. "He's in jail." I wasn't asking a question, just clarifying. Not that I needed clarity. Of course my brother was in jail. He couldn't seem to stay out for longer than five months at a time.

Marilyn said, "Yeah, but it wasn't his fault."

Yeah, yeah, I know. Someone planted those drugs on him.

"It was a setup," she said, pushing herself out of the chair and ambling through the maze that her grandchildren had set up with their toys. At the window, she lit a new cigarette and peeked outside. "But I told Twin I'm not getting him out this time. He needs to stop messing with those boys on the corner. They ain't nothing but bad news; always getting him in trouble."

I didn't feel the need to tell my mother that Snake was the leader of that gang who hung out at the corner. She knew that. But if she wanted to live in denial, it wasn't my place to ask her to pack up and move.

"Whose car you driving? Is it a rental or something?"

For the smallest moment, I considered telling her what the "or something" was, but if I mentioned the voluntary repossession, I'd have to explain everything else. And Adam and I had agreed to keep all of this bad news to ourselves. Not that Adam had to worry about what I would say to my mother—I would never discuss grown folks business with her.

So about the car, all I said was, "Yeah."

That was good enough for Marilyn. She turned away from the window, her scowl now gone. She smiled with a molasses sweetness, sat down, and whispered, "You think you might be able to give me my money a little early this month? I really need it."

There were lots of things that troubled me about those words, especially "my money." I guess to Marilyn, that's what it was. Adam and I were a regular supplement to her monthly disability check. My mother had been disabled for years— though I never could figure out her exact disability. The one time I asked her what was wrong with her, she told me, "It's mental. I can't get my mind to work on working."

Oh . . . kay.

Still, she was my mother, so once we were able, we did what

we could to help her. Our first plan was to move her into one of the Maryland suburbs. But she didn't want to have a thing to do with Upper Marlboro or Waldorf or any other place that wasn't Barry Farm.

"These are my people here," she'd told me and Adam when we'd taken her out to dinner, all excited about the house we'd found for her. "I don't want to be messing with those bougie folks out in PG County." She shook her head. "Hmph, those black people think they got it better than everyone else."

Well, those black folks *did* have it better than her, but I wasn't into begging anyone to take my money. Still, I couldn't leave my mother out there like that, so Adam and I started sending her a little check—five hundred dollars—on the regular.

My mother cut into my thoughts. "I only need the money 'cause y'all didn't send anything last month."

No . . . we hadn't.

"And I really need it. You think you'll be able to double up?"

I didn't say anything, but my mother didn't notice.

She kept on, "I've got to get Twin out of jail."

I frowned. "I thought you were going to leave him there?"

Her shoulders hunched as she huffed, "With some money, I can get him out before the weekend. What kind of mother would I be if I didn't do that?"

I wanted to tell her that she'd be the right kind of mother, teaching her son that there were always consequences associated with dumb-ass decisions. But I didn't say anything because I'd never be able to convince her that Twin was a casualty of her boys-will-be-boys child-rearing philosophy.

"Plus," my mother continued her case, "I've got to help out Cashmere." I'm sure her pause was meant to be dramatic, because when she spoke again there was a slight tremor in her voice. "What kind of grandmother would I be if I didn't take care of my grandkids? And with Christmas coming up and everything," she sniffed, "these boys don't have anything."

Whether it was planned or not, that got me. Not because I approved of my brother's or sister's lifestyle. Sometimes I didn't care about them because through their choices they showed me that they hardly cared about themselves.

But for better or for worse, I did care about my mother. I didn't want her worrying about anything.

"So?" she said. Her eyes were wide with expectation.

"I don't know what happened last month." I stood as I told that lie. "We'll get that money to you."

Her smile was back. "Okay. You got anything on you right now?"

I knew exactly how much I had. But still I opened my purse and gave my mother everything—eighteen dollars.

This time when I leaned in to kiss her good-bye, Marilyn held me close. "I really do appreciate you and Adam," she whispered.

I knew that was the truth. But my mother's gratitude did not make me feel any better. By the time I kissed my nephews—even Apollo—good-bye, I was feeling sufficiently worse than when I walked in thirty minutes before.

Chapter 3

I WAS HOPING THAT BY THE time the four-year-old Kia sputtered through the hills of D.C.'s gold coast, I would've found some kind of peace with what had gone down with Shay-Shaunté today. But when I pulled into our three-car garage and stepped inside our home, there was no serenity, not even in the silence.

Maybe it wasn't calm that I was seeking. I wanted normalcy—the chatter of my children. I wanted the self-absorption of my teenagers and even the broodiness of my ten-year-old. I needed my children to readjust the tempo of my day.

It was Thursday, though, their late afternoon with school activities and Ethan's golf practice. But a quick glance at my watch told me that I wouldn't have too long to wait.

I dumped my bag inside the mudroom, then trekked through the house without taking off my shoes. Even though we had a rule—no shoes to ruin the cream-colored carpet—I didn't feel like abiding by any kind of tenet today, not even one that I'd set down as the law.

There wasn't a single sound in the four-thousand-square-foot space, but still I heard my husband. That's how it was with us—I could feel his heartbeat, and I moved straight to where he was.

I stood at the archway, watching Adam for a moment. He took care of the family finances in this wide-open space lined with overstuffed bookcases, with an oversized mahogany desk in the center. Against the wall, there were a bunch of folding chairs—one for each of the children, plus me.

"I want the twins and Ethan to learn about money," Adam often said. "They're growing up very differently than we did. They'll have money, and they need to learn how to use it wisely."

So by the time the twins were ten and Ethan was just four, they would sit with Adam as he took care of our money. Even if all they did was open the envelopes, Alexa, Alana, and Ethan knew the financial side of life as a Langston. They knew about mortgages and phone bills, they knew that TV didn't come free, and heat and air-conditioning cost money, too. He even went beyond what I would've done; he told them how much their parents earned.

"There's no Santa Claus. You and I work hard to provide for them, and they need to know that."

That was the Adam Langston philosophy on child-rearing.

The girls and Ethan learned about budgeting and saving, about allowances and earnings. About setting goals and having dreams. The problem was they knew only the good; Adam hadn't brought them over to the dark side of what had been going on for the past two years.

Though he hadn't moved—Adam was still holding his head

in his hands—he knew that I was there. My heart was never whole without him, and I knew he felt the same. He didn't have to look at me to see me.

I strolled into the office and stood behind him; when I touched him, he moved. Just slightly, though—his head rocked back a bit, but his eyes were still closed. My fingers kneaded his shoulders. Gently at first. Then I applied more pressure, letting the anxiety of my day surge through my hands for his pleasure.

He released a moan that made me smile. I looked down and straight onto the paper that had been Adam's focus. It was handwritten, two neatly lined columns. One—a list of all our expenses, from the mortgage to the money that we gave to our families. The other column listed our income—only mine was there. There was a line with the word *savings,* but that was it—no number was next to it. I guess that meant there were no savings left.

My smile, now gone. My massage intensified; I needed to lose myself in his pleasure.

It worked . . . for a little while. Our thoughts for these moments were not of bills and the people who collected them. But then Adam's tension returned. Even though I still pressed his shoulders, his muscles tightened, and I knew that his eyes had opened.

"I have to tell you something," he said softly, and I pressed harder. "The bank called. They're proceeding with the foreclosure."

Had it gone that far?

My fingers still moved, but without the strength that I started with. He put his hands over mine, stopping me, then pulled me around until I faced him.

"The bank called," he repeated. He tore at my pants.

"Why didn't you tell me?" I asked, my voice filled with angry passion.

"I did. I just did." Now he ripped my slacks from my hips, and within a moment, he'd taken my panties away, too.

"You should have . . ." I straddled his lap. "Told me before!"

He pulled my naked center against his, and I was already ready. My mouth couldn't find his fast enough, but once I did, I couldn't get enough. Our tongues were at war, and so were our hands.

It was my turn to tear away his clothes, and within seconds, I lost myself in the pleasure that was his body. His steel-tight chest was as hard as his core, which was the part of him that I craved. My fingers explored him, as if I was trying to discover new places. But it was all familiar, all wonderful. All that I needed.

My husband was the best at foreplay, always wanting to please me first. But today, no preamble was necessary. When we united, my joy was instant. And so was his.

But it was not enough.

Rising from the chair, Adam carried my one-hundred-and-seventy-pound frame as if I were as light as air. Without disconnecting, he laid me on the floor, and we sought new pleasure.

I knew it was getting close to the time when our children would come home, bursting through the door and then busting in on us. But right now, I didn't care. And anyway, it wasn't as if that hadn't happened before. Our children had seen us making love so often I sometimes wondered if we'd damaged them for life.

But my thoughts left our children and I turned every bit of my attention to the man I loved. Right now, he had my mind as much as my heart, and all I could think about was the bliss that was overtaking my body. Ecstasy blanketed me, filling me with sensations that made me pray that I could stay right in this place.

I moaned.

Adam cried out.

Then the slam of the door and the shrill cry of, "Mom!"

And it was all over.

Chapter 4

WHEN ADAM YELLED OUT, "YOUR MOM and I will be right there," our children knew that was code for, "Give us a minute or you're gonna see something you may not want to see."

Two sets of footsteps dashed up the stairs as I searched for my pants on the other side of the desk. Though the zipper was broken, I still put them on. I didn't want to trudge through the hall to my bedroom butt-naked—literally.

Neither Adam nor I said a word as we dressed. We held hands as we made our way into the living room, then he waited until we were settled—Adam on the sofa and me across from him in the matching overstuffed chair—before calling out to the twins. In seconds, the two came barreling down the stairs. Alana for once moved as fast as Alexa.

Though the doctors declared that our daughters were identical, that was often hard to believe. Yes, they looked alike, walked alike, talked alike, but they had polar opposite personalities. It was not only hard to believe that they were twins;

sometimes I hardly believed that they were being raised in the same household.

Alexa was feisty. Alana was gentle. Alexa was creative. Alana was cerebral. Alexa was self-centered. Alana was a sensitive spirit who made me believe at times that she could feel down into a person's soul.

Alexa, with her confidence and her strut and her gregariousness, was most like Adam. Alana was most like me.

Right now, though, there was very little difference between the girls. Both sets of light brown eyes shined with excitement. Their long, slender legs moved from side to side, as if they were working hard to keep their words inside.

Just looking at them made me smile. Glancing at Adam, I saw that he was doing the same; our children were what we needed.

"What's got you girls all—"

Before I could finish, Alexa spoke up. "We finally got it. The first invitation to the really big sweet sixteen party!"

They giggled; Alana said, "What's so great is that it's New Year's Eve. It's Chloe Wellington's party, and that means that not only is it the first party but it's going to be our first New Year's Eve party ever!"

Alexa picked up where Alana left off. "Chloe is having a party first, with all the boys, of course."

"Of course," I said, and we all laughed when Adam growled playfully.

Alexa continued. "And after the party, some of Chloe's special friends have been invited to stay over."

"And of course, *we* were invited to stay," Alana said.

"Of course," I said again, and chuckled.

"'Cause we're special," Alexa topped it off.

My head moved back and forth from one daughter to the other. This was huge for them. For years they'd been talking about turning sixteen. That rite of passage had always been a big deal, especially in this neighborhood. But it was made even more exciting by a television show that featured rich kids having parties for their sixteenth birthday that were beyond sweet.

"Chloe's party is going to be ridiculous!" Alana said.

"But of course, ours is going to be better!"

This was proof that good times didn't last. As soon as Alexa uttered those words, my anxiety rushed back. I didn't have to look at Adam to know that the same had happened to him.

"Mom, Dad." Alexa said our names so sweetly that I knew what was coming. "Are we still going to get cars for our birthday, too?"

Our daughter had no idea that she was killing us softly; I answered, "We'll see . . ."

As if she was exhausted from her explanations and her questions, Alexa flopped down onto the couch next to Adam, while Alana settled on the arm of the chair where I sat. "Daddy, I think we should really start planning the party now," Alexa said. "I know you said that money was no object, but we should still set a good budget, right?"

Ah . . . lessons from the father.

For the first time, I looked directly at Adam. Though he tried to keep a smiley face, his slumped shoulders gave him away.

"That's a good idea, Lex," Alana said, calling her sister by the name only she used. "You and I should sit down and do the budget and then give it to Mom and Dad."

"That'll work, Lan." It was Alexa's turn to use her pet name for her sister. "Let's go and do it now."

Together they jumped up and were out of the room and up the stairs before Adam and I could blink. We sat in the quietness for a moment. Then Adam said, "I have to pick up Ethan."

"We need to talk to the girls."

He didn't reply. Just stood and walked toward the closet.

"Adam!" I followed him. "We have to tell them what's going on."

He whipped around. "No!" The man who'd just made sweet love to me now had a different look in his eyes. "No one needs to know, Shine," he said, calling me by the name that only he had for me.

"But . . ."

"No one," he hissed. "There's no need to get them upset when things are gonna get better soon. I got a callback this morning from American Express for another interview."

"For another *interview*. They didn't call you back for a job."

My words weren't meant to hurt, but when Adam flinched, I knew they had hit hard. "Baby, I'm sorry. I only meant—"

"Let me handle this, Shine." With his jacket on, he stomped through the mudroom, then closed the door behind him before I could say another word.

If there was ever a perfect love, what I shared with Adam Langston was close to that. But what kept it from being completely wonderful was not that we were going through bad times; it was that we differed on how we should handle things. I wanted him to share our challenges with me and then let our children know—at least a little—what was going on.

But Adam's pride reigned over my wishes and his good sense. He'd been that way from the beginning.

The day the Bush fallout had hit our home, Adam had said, "This is our problem and I'll figure out the solution."

I'd been totally fine with that position—eighteen months ago. But in the year and a half that had passed, Adam had interviewed for everything from becoming a flight attendant to working at Barnes & Noble, but no one wanted to hire the man who'd been the comptroller for Rapid Speed Delivery—

the biggest competitor to FedEx and one of the first major companies to move all operations overseas.

Most employers told Adam that he was overqualified. A few told him that hiring him was a risk, completely sure that after they'd trained him, he'd leave within months when he found that better job.

That better job? Where was it? My belief was that he'd already had *that* job and now it was gone. And there weren't many other $260,000 a year positions for any man, let alone a black man in this country.

The eighteen months that Adam had been out of work had felt longer than a lifetime. No household could stand losing that large an income for that long a time before the house would come tumbling down.

My husband had done an amazing job keeping our world turning. But with our savings depleted and my income covering only utilities and groceries and gas and other minor bills, the walls around us hadn't been tumbling, they'd been crashing.

There weren't many things left that could go wrong, but we needed to do right by our children. I wasn't going to allow this to go on much longer without them knowing the truth—that a party and new cars were probably not in their immediate future. If Adam wouldn't tell them, that was no problem. I would.

Chapter 5

My husband, Adam Emory Langston, was not always the MBA, Corporate America, Brooks-Brothers-suit-wearing, one-hundred-dollar-haircut-sporting man that he was today. Oh, no. Talk about humble beginnings. Our start was one and the same—the same neighborhood, the same schools, the same situations. Although we lived around the corner from each other, we didn't officially meet until we were twelve years old.

It had been one of those D.C. summer days, when the air was so hot and heavy that it didn't move. My girls—Brooklyn and Tamica—and I were just chillin' on the steps. Our plan had been to do our favorite thing—work on our dance routine. For the past three years, we'd been the champs of the summer talent contest that was held every August down at the community center. We were sure that we were gonna win this year, too, because we'd added a prop—a jump rope; we were gonna mix it up and turn it out. But that day, it was too hot to practice even though one hundred dollars was on the line.

So we sat and people-watched, which was our second-favorite thing to do 'cause there was always something poppin' in our neighborhood.

"Ooohhh, look who's coming," Brooklyn said. "Cash!" She leaned forward, jiggled her boobs, then pulled her tank top down tight so that her chest would look bigger than it already was.

I glanced at Tamica and shook my head. Our time had not yet come—we didn't have much of anything to lure boys. But our girl Brooklyn was a whole 'nother story. We may have been twelve, but Brooklyn looked bigger and better than most of the mothers and grandmothers in the neighborhood. She had huge boobs and so much booty that she could've given me and Tamica some of both and all three of us would've been stopping traffic on Martin Luther King Boulevard.

Tamica said, "Brooklyn, you need to quit."

"Quit what?" When Tamica rolled her eyes, Brooklyn added, "Don't hate me 'cause I'm beautiful."

As Cash and his boys got closer, only Brooklyn stood up, like she was some kind of greeting committee. I knew Cash and one of the other boys with him—Buddy. But I didn't know the third boy. Really, I'd just started seeing him around, and I guessed he was new to the hood.

When they stood in front of us, I couldn't take my eyes off the new boy. Not that he was all that—he was all right. What got my attention was that he was almost the same color as my favorite food in the whole world—banana pudding. Even his freckles looked like the vanilla wafers that Marilyn used when she made that dessert every holiday.

Besides that, though, he kinda looked like a nerd, wearing some big ole round glasses and a short haircut that wasn't a fade or nothin'. What was worse—he was carrying a book! A big, thick book. Now, what kind of guy was carrying a book in the middle of the summer? Nuh-uh, he was too nerdy for me. I liked boys who had a little edge to 'em.

Remember, I was twelve.

So Cash and his boys walked right up to the front of my house and stopped.

"What's up, Brook?" Cash asked my girl.

She sucked her teeth, rolled her eyes, and stuck out her chest even more. "Come correct or don't come at all. My name is Brook—Lynn!" She said all of that with major attitude, as if she was offended. Please! Brooklyn had been chasing Cash from way back—like way back in kindergarten. Every chance she got, she told me that she was going to marry him one day.

Yeah, right. That was never gonna happen because my bet was that Cash would be behind bars by the time he was sixteen. He was already running drugs for Duke, one of the biggest hustlers on these streets. Cash would never make it to being old enough to vote, let alone marry anyone.

He said, "I know what your name is," as he sucked on a toothpick like some of the older dudes did.

"So . . . what . . . y'all . . . up . . . to?" Buddy asked. He wasn't my type either. Not because he was a nerd but because he was kind of slow. Everything he did took way too much time. The way he talked—slow! The way he walked—slow! It took him an hour to finish off a twenty-cent bag of potato chips. Dang, that boy got on every single one of my nerves.

I answered Buddy's question so that he would shut up and not say another thing. "Nothin'. We're just hanging. We were gonna practice some double Dutch moves"—I held up the rope—"but it's too hot."

"Oh, yeah," the new boy said. "What you know 'bout double Dutch?"

"More than you do," I gave it right back to him. I knew Banana-Pudding-Guy wasn't trying to diss me in front of my house, in front of my girls. Obviously, he hadn't heard about my rep. I had beat boys and girls down in this neighborhood.

"Sweetheart," he said in a voice that sounded like one of those nighttime DJs on the radio, "I don't think there's a subject in the world where you know more than me."

"Oh!" Cash gave Buddy high five, and even my girls laughed.

I had to admit, I was kind of impressed. I mean, the way he said it and the way it sounded, it didn't seem like Banana-Pudding-Guy was our age. But he didn't look like he was sixteen or seventeen either. Already, he was a wonder to me.

But I couldn't let him get away with frontin' me like that.

I stood up like I was big and bad; the rope was wrapped around my hand like I was ready to use it—and I was. "You talking to me?"

He stepped closer—I guess to make sure I knew that he was. "Yeah, so what's up?"

"You got game," I said, working my neck so that he would know who he was dealing with. "Bring it."

He laughed in my face. "Ah, man, come on. I'm not into beating down no girl. I don't roll like that."

I held the rope up and stuck it in his face. "You scared or somet—?"

I don't know exactly what happened, but in two seconds flat, I was on the hard, dry ground, on my back. Banana-Pudding-Guy was straddling me, and now he was the one with the rope in his hand. He leaned forward, and his lips were so close that I thought he was gonna kiss me.

"Just for the record, sweetheart," he whispered, "there ain't nothin' in the world that scares me."

Then he jumped off me, adjusted his glasses, picked up his book, and said, "Peace," to his boys, who were standing there with my girls, laughing. Banana-Pudding-Guy strolled down the street and never looked back.

It was love at first fight.

Not that it was exactly a fight. I hadn't had a chance to do anything—not slap his face, stomp on his feet, kick him in the groin—nothing! And he hadn't really hit me. He tossed me down and then gave it to me straight—he wasn't afraid of nothing. . . .

That was our beginning. Adam's declaration that there was nothing in this world that scared him. But that wasn't exactly true. Because Adam had a very real fear—he was afraid of being Adam. He was afraid of people finding out about his life, the way it was now.

What Adam needed to accept was that being laid off from a Fortune 500 company in this economy made him common, not the exception.

But knowing that didn't make Adam's fear go away. He fought that fear, though, hid it behind his pride. And that pride had my husband tied up in a knot.

Pride.

Pride was a word that had always scared me because of what Big Mama had told me.

"Pride's a sin," she always said. Then, the part that really frightened me was when she said, "God hates pride, and He'll make you pay for it."

She even had a scripture that she used to recite that scared me straight, and I wondered if now maybe that same scripture could help Adam. I couldn't remember where to find it exactly, but I still rushed into our bedroom and opened the Bible that we kept on the nightstand next to Adam's side.

It didn't take me very long to find what I was looking for. Proverbs. The eleventh chapter.

"When pride comes, then comes disgrace."

As soon as I spoke the last word, that churning in my heart started again—just like it had this afternoon in the office when I'd held the five-million-dollar check in my hands.

I shuddered, not knowing why I felt so much uneasiness inside me. Neither Adam nor I would do anything to disgrace God, ourselves, or our family.

Never!

But then I looked down at the scripture. Read it aloud again. And the churning inside continued, this time, stronger.

Gingerly, I returned the Bible to the nightstand. I closed my eyes and hoped and wished that the pride in Adam's heart would somehow dissipate.

Because if he didn't get rid of his pride, I didn't have any idea where this road would lead us.

Chapter 6

Wᴇ ᴡᴇʀᴇ ʙᴀᴄᴋ ᴀᴛ ɪᴛ.

A few minutes after Adam brought Ethan home from his practice at the indoor driving range, he came into our first-floor master suite, where I was sitting on the edge of the bed, still praying.

My eyes were closed, but our connection to each other was so deep that I could almost see him.

He knelt in front of me, and, with the tips of his fingers, he stroked my cheek. There was no need for me to see, no need for him to speak. His apology was in his touch. I opened my eyes and silently forgave him for speaking to me the way he had before he'd left.

He leaned forward and kissed me gently, but that was where our tenderness ended. Now, it was all lips, all hands, all legs.

It was mouth to mouth. Skin to skin. Center to center. We couldn't get enough.

I adored the pieces that made him a man.

He worshipped the parts that made me a woman.

Our rite as husband and wife went on and on. Until our cries shook the walls.

Spent, we lay back, holding hands. Resting, thinking. I knew Adam's thoughts were the same as mine.

He finally spoke. "We're going to make it."

Our problems were never far from our minds, not even when we were making love.

I said, "I know, but until then, we need to tell . . ." He stiffened before I could finish, but I held his hand until he relaxed again. "Listen to what I'm saying," I pleaded. "You've prepared our children for this."

He shook his head. "Not this."

I rolled over so that I could look right into his eyes. "Yes, you have. They understand money because of you. They understand that you've worked hard all your life, and they'll understand that you were laid off."

"What they'll understand is that their unemployed father let them down."

Pride!

"We promised the girls a party and cars," he said.

I wanted to scream! Yes, we'd made a deal with our daughters: If they kept up their grades, we would give them the sweetest sixteenth birthday party and matching cars, too. Yes, they'd done their part, carrying straight As for the last two years, even while Alexa had excelled in ballet and was the editor of the school newspaper, and Alana had become freshman and then sophomore class president. But situations changed. Life happened. Our children were smart enough to get that.

"We'll explain it," I said. "And then we'll give them the best seventeenth birthday party."

He shook his head. "Don't you get it, Shine? It's not just

about a party or a pair of cars. It's about how I've always wanted their lives to be. Better than ours."

There it was—his real fear. Which was more about remembering the past than looking forward to the future.

He kept on. "Remember how it used to be? Our mothers, us, always worried about money. Coming home and the lights being off. One day, no electricity, the next day, no food." He paused and stared, as if he was reliving every single moment of those pitiful days. "How many days did you have to do homework by candlelight? Or beg a neighbor for spare food?"

"This is not the same."

"To me it is. I've worked hard so their lives would be different."

"So the plan is to say nothing? Just wait till February and hope the twins don't notice there's no party? No cars?" I shook my head. "They've already started telling their friends."

This time, his silence scared me. Because I knew what he was doing—calculating in his mind. He was really going to try to make this happen!

Finally he said, "Let me handle this."

"Maybe that's part of the problem. You've been handling this alone when I want to be in it with you. I'll always have your back."

He smiled, a little. "This I know. But you do enough; it's you and your job that's keeping us afloat."

My job. Hours had passed, but with those words, this afternoon's anger washed right through me again. My husband had no idea what had gone down today at my job. With my boss. Five million dollars. How many parts of this discussion would that check solve?

But what I'd have to do for that money made my heart stop. I would die . . . just die . . . completely die.

Adam's kiss brought me back to life. "All I want," he said,

then kissed me again, "is for you," another kiss, "to just take care of me," another one, "and our children."

I rolled over until I was straddling him and my eyes inhaled the handsomeness of my husband.

Adam's was not a face that was made for movies or magazines, though don't get me wrong—my man was good-looking. There were just many who were finer. But what brought my husband to the top of the male food chain was that he had chiseled his body to beyond the perfection that had already been bestowed upon him by our awesome God.

Adam was truly an Adonis. My Adonis. Mine. Not to be shared with anyone.

This man belonged to me, just like I was his. And with another kiss, thoughts of that five million dollars went straight out of my mind.

Chapter 7

OUR HOME HAD ALWAYS BEEN FILLED with love, but for the last few months, mounting stress had been making our house feel like a simmering volcano. So far, our children hadn't seemed to notice (though I knew they'd had to peep how often our bedroom door was closed). But the secret Adam and I held wouldn't stay hidden. It couldn't.

The children would soon catch the clues. Like the fact that Adam no longer left the house every morning to go to what they thought was work but was in fact the out-placement office that had been provided by Rapid Delivery for the last eighteen months. That had ended for Adam last week. So now he was home and our savings were gone; the children would have to notice the tension and the changes soon.

Not that I was too concerned about Alexa. She rarely saw anything beyond her personal space. But Alana—and Ethan—were sensitive children whose cares went beyond their world.

The day would come when one of them would start asking questions.

That's why, over the last few months, my concerns about home had made work so attractive. For just a few hours, I could escape into a world where money was never an issue; Shay-Shaunté had almost as much as God and Oprah.

Not that work was all escapism; I enjoyed my job. From the day I'd been hired, Shay-Shaunté had brought me into her world, exposing me, teaching me about managing a multi-million-dollar conglomerate. Although business wasn't my thing (I left that to Adam), Shay-Shaunté had a way of making it interesting. I loved watching her in meetings, making men who were sometimes a foot taller and two times wider cower to her. From suppliers to account managers all respected Shay-Shaunté for her toughness, yet fairness. I respected her because she always won.

Then there were the people I'd met because of her—celebrities who thought Shay-Shaunté was the hair god. I'd put through many calls to her from Hollywood's elite. But the best times were when her famous fans stopped by: Mary J, Vivica, Jada . . .

Thinking of Jada, why hadn't Shay-Shaunté asked to share *her* husband? Surely she found Will as attractive as she found my Adam—even if it was just because of Will's checkbook.

Maybe I needed to suggest that to her, I thought as I headed down I-395 before merging onto the George Washington Parkway. This reverse commute had always been an easy flow, but today, I didn't do my normal seventy-five miles per hour. I crawled along just below the speed limit, pissing off drivers behind me.

But I had to take this slow; I needed the time to strategize.

Last night, I'd plumped my pillow one hundred times and kicked the covers off one thousand times, wishing that I could talk to Adam about how to play today. He was an expert at office politics, but there was no way I could tell him what had gone down with Shay-Shaunté because after going off, he'd want me to quit. Since we couldn't afford that, it was best not to lay this burden onto his heart.

Figuring this out was up to me. Should I play it cool, like nothing had happened? Or should I walk in there and slam her up against the wall? Should I play it straight or straight ghetto?

As soon as the word *ghetto* entered my mind, my decision was made. I'd left the ghetto behind a long time ago.

Inside the Ferossity parking lot, I twisted the Kia down the lanes to the back, stopping in the last space against the brick wall. I was far from the front door, where I always parked.

The moment I slipped out of the car, I heard, "Hey, girl!"

"What's up, Rachel?" though one glance at her feet told me what I needed to know—sneakers. She was dressed in her normal pantsuit, but without her pumps and with her iPod plugged deep into her ears.

Rachel pulled the buds out and eyed the car. "The Lexus in the shop?" But before I could tell her a lie, she kept on, "You busted out of the office yesterday like you were making a prison break; what was up with that?"

"Nothing." I matched her stride. "I don't know what you're talking about. It's all good."

"Umm-hmm." But that was all the attention she gave me, because with her arms still swinging as she pushed to burn more calories, she puffed, "I hope all this exercise is working," as we stepped into the building.

Inside the elevator, Rachel chatted about her six-month weight-loss plan to get a man who'd already told her that he wasn't interested. "I'm telling you, James is going to be my birthday gift. When I do the big reveal, he's gonna lose his mind! And then, happy birthday to meeee!" she sang.

"Or you're gonna meet someone who will love you for you and not for what you weigh."

Rachel smiled. "See, that's why you're my girl."

"I'm just sayin'. You should have someone who knows what's really important in a person."

She shook her head. "You're talking all that perfect-man philosophy stuff. But I'll take the superficial, 'cause there aren't that many Adam Langstons out there."

I laughed. See, the whole world knew what I had. "My husband is pretty special, isn't he?"

"Ya think?"

"Well, I have faith that there's someone like him being prepared right now for you."

"You keep that faith, and I'll keep exercising!"

We laughed, but then the doors to the twelfth floor parted and the good part of my day ended.

"Good morning," Shay-Shaunté greeted Rachel and me.

"Mornin', Boss," was what Rachel said.

I didn't part my lips. I guess my plan to play this straight wasn't working.

"Evia? You okay?"

Now, why did Shay-Shaunté have to ask me that? Why did she have to talk to me at all?

"I'm fine," I said, not even looking at her. I stomped toward my office, but by the time I'd taken those few steps, I calmed down and didn't slam the door the way I'd planned to.

It killed me that I had to be there. After yesterday, anyone else would've quit, and it was the fact that I couldn't that really had me twisted. Even though I wasn't about to give Shay-Shaunté my husband, she still had control . . . over my paycheck. Which meant that she still had control over me.

I had to get out of this place, but I could only leave with money in my pocket. I paced back and forth, trying to devise a plan.

Then my phone buzzed. "Girl," Rachel whispered. "Where are you?"

"What?"

"Staff meeting."

I looked at my watch. Had I been daydreaming about making my break for that long?

I hung up without even telling Rachel that I was on my way; she knew.

When I walked into the conference room, Shay-Shaunté said, "Now we can begin," even though her six department heads were already there.

I settled into the chair right next to her—the one that was saved for me.

"So," Shay-Shaunté began. "Let's do the status reports first."

I was supposed to be taking notes, but I had a hard time focusing. I stared Shay-Shaunté down, but if she was fazed, she didn't show it.

As the discussion moved around the table, I asked myself all kinds of questions. Like was Shay-Shaunté interested in my husband? Was her offer a way to try to get him? Had she always felt this way? Did she think her money was going to be able to take him away from me?

"Evia?"

"Huh?"

"I asked about the system for the holiday reorders."

It took a moment for me to focus on Shay-Shaunté's moving lips. I'd been staring at her for so long, that her face was fuzzy.

She said, "The reorders?"

"Why are you asking about that? We've fulfilled two rounds of reorders already."

I guess my tone was sharper than my words, because around the table, the staff gasped. Even Rachel looked at me like she wondered why I was trying to get fired.

In the next nanosecond, all eyes turned to Shay-Shaunté. Like everyone was waiting for her to take me down.

"My question was"—Shay-Shaunté spoke so softly that everybody leaned in closer to hear—"is everything in place to assure the accounts that anything they need, they will have immediately."

Okay . . . so the first question I hadn't heard completely, and being taken by surprise may have been my excuse for snapping. But this time, I was aware of what I was doing.

"I've been doing this job for six years, Shay-Shaunté. Everything's in place—just like it always is."

It was a wicked, lopsided smile that she passed to me. "I know how long you've been working here, Evia." She paused and stared with a look that turned me cold. "So, are you ready to answer my question?" She paused. "Is everything in place to assure that shipping will continue without issues?"

Though she'd made me a bit nervous, I stared right back. I didn't know why I was putting myself through this—if this turned into a battle, Shay-Shaunté would win.

"Yes." That was as much of a surrender as she was going to get from me.

She didn't wait for further explanation. She'd forced me, she'd won, she moved on.

After that, it was easier to concentrate. My notes were diligent; Shay-Shaunté wasn't going to catch me not paying attention again.

She said, "Now, let's move onto marketing."

Bill Lewis said, "Obviously, it's too late for this year, but the one thing major accounts keep asking is if we can give them a campaign—especially with the combo-packs—with more of a Christmas feel."

Shay-Shaunté shook her head. "That's ridiculous. This is a hair-care company. I'm not doing anything special for the holidays beyond red packaging."

"I'm just telling you, Shay-Shaunté," Bill said, holding up his hands, to reinforce the fact that the question wasn't coming from him. "Just passing on requests. And it's coming from most of the major accounts."

Resting her arms on the table, she leaned forward and looked each of the department heads in their eyes before saying, "I will shut Ferossity down before I bring Christmas into this company."

The staff twisted like they always did when Shay-Shaunté went on one of her anti-Christmas rampages. Not that anyone could call her a scrooge—the best part of working at Ferossity was that we all received a paid vacation the week between Christmas and New Year's. Everyone loved Shay-Shaunté for that, but she was definitely nobody's Santa Claus. She was right—she never brought Christmas into the company: there were no Christmas trees, no ornaments, no change of the Muzak . . . nothing.

During my first year at the company, I asked Shay-Shaunté if she didn't celebrate Christmas because of her religion. She told me that she had no religion—I took that to mean that she was an atheist. Still, sometimes she went too far.

But it was her company. If she wanted to shut the whole thing down because an account asked for Christmas packaging, I'd say go at it. I just wanted her to wait until I found another job.

"One last thing," Shay-Shaunté said. "Evia, how are we coming with selecting an intern from Howard University?"

This time, I answered her. "Fine." But I didn't say anything more; my attitude was still showing.

Shay-Shaunté smirked a little, shook her head, then said to the team, "It's a wrap. Let's make today a great one."

I was the first to push back my chair. Even though I usually mingled with the others over the continental breakfast spread that Shay-Shaunté had at every meeting, I rushed out of the room like there was a fire behind me.

At my desk, I threw down the notepad. I was still pissed, but now I was mad at myself. Why was I acting this way?

Before I had a chance to think about it, there was a knock on my door.

"Come on in," I said, knowing Rachel wanted to get the scoop on why I was acting like I needed medication.

My plan was to just give her the great excuse—PMS.

But it wasn't Rachel.

I didn't say a word when Shay-Shaunté stepped into my space, closed the door, then slinked across the room, every curve showing in her formfitting black catsuit.

"Obviously," she began, "there's something we need to talk about."

I kinda shrugged, kinda nodded.

She went on, "You have a problem with me; what is it?"

Oh! She was gonna play it like that? Well then, I was gonna give it back the same way.

I said, "You know what my problem is."

Her half smile was back as her arms crossed. "No, I don't know. Why don't you tell me?"

"I don't like the way you came at me."

"About what?"

"About my husband."

She nodded, like she was glad I'd finally played my card; glad that I'd put the king of my heart on the table.

She said, "I was only making a business offer. You refused. It's over. So why are you upset?" She paused. Now her eyes were smiling, too. "Unless you and Adam plan to take me up on—"

"No!" I shouted, not caring who heard me.

"Then, why the attitude, Evia?"

"Because . . ." I stopped and tried to think of how to finish that sentence. "Because . . ." I didn't know what else to say, because really, I didn't have a reason for all of this—except that my feelings were hurt.

"Look," Shay-Shaunté began. "I'm a businesswoman. I make deals. I'm used to winning a lot and losing a few. I'm never offended either way; it's all about business. But I am sorry if I offended you."

Now why did she have to be all grown up and professional? I guess that's what separated billionaires from the rest of us folk—emotions never got in their way.

"We need to get this cleared up, Evia, because if we can't work it out . . ."

So much for the soft, professional touch. Not that I could be mad at her after the way I acted.

It was all good, though, because I'd said what I'd had to say. But she was right, too; the offer had been made, was declined, and was now behind us.

"It's worked out," I said. "I'm cool. I just needed you to know where I stood."

"Good. And now you know," she pushed herself up from her chair, "where I stand." She seemed to tower over me.

I watched her stroll away, all grace, all slither. At the door, she turned around and winked. It was startling, shocking. And it made me think. About wolves in sheep's clothing. Then my thoughts went deeper—to the Garden of Eden. And I asked myself, Before the fall, didn't snakes walk upright?

Chapter 8

I HAD THIS VIRGO THING GOING on; I was a stickler for time. But not even being a Virgo could help me beat my girl, Tamica. It was her flight attendant thing—she was always at least fifteen minutes early to everything. So when I walked into Rumors, I spotted Tamica, sitting at a booth, already sipping on something and flipping through some kind of brochure.

Moving closer, I saw that Tamica was wearing one of her smart suits, as we called them. For the last three months, whenever my girl wasn't thirty thousand feet in the air, she was looking the part of the corporate executive she suddenly longed to be.

"Hey, girl!" I said when I got to the table.

"What's up?"

"Just you." I gave her a hug, then slid into the booth across from her. Glancing down at what she was reading, I said, "Howard University? Really?"

"Well, I decided that it might be difficult for me to just

walk into corporate America without any experience. I was thinking maybe I should get my MBA." I nodded because I wanted to be the supportive friend. I kept my mouth shut because I didn't want to be the honest friend.

"Howard has a great program." Tamica flipped through the brochure. "And since it's right here, and I'm a D.C. resident, it should be easy to get in."

"So, Howard, huh?" That was all I was going to say. I thought about adding that even if she did follow through, and even if she did get in, did she really want to compete with all of those twenty-something-year-old bodies and brains while she was trying to find herself?

"To Howard." She raised her glass, giving herself a toast. "This is gonna be it. I can feel it this time."

The short-skirted waitress joined us and jotted down my request for an iced tea. Then she asked, "Do you want to order now or wait for the rest of your party?"

"If we had good sense," Tamica started, "we'd order now. No tellin' what time Brooklyn will show up."

The waitress stood still, frozen, trying to figure out if she should stay or walk away.

I directed, "Just bring my tea. We'll wait to order."

"So, what's new in your life?" Tamica asked. Before the question was fully out of her mouth, she had directed her attention back to the brochure. As if she already knew that whatever I had going on was boring, because out of the three of us, I was the most stable, the most dependable . . . the most boring.

But that was before I'd been offered five million dollars. I'm sure that trumped anything going on in Tamica's and Brooklyn's lives combined.

Still, my response to Tamica was, "Absolutely nothing's new."

Tamica didn't even look up. If I wanted conversation, I was going to have to turn the subject away from me. "So, how was Paris?"

She shrugged. "It's my route, it's my job, it's Paris." She sighed, as if I not only had a boring life, but I also asked boring questions. "Are you sure you want to wait for Brooklyn?" Tamica asked before she downed the rest of her wine. "Ain't no telling how long that's gonna be, 'cause you know how the first lady do. She's so important"—Tamica rolled her eyes, completely unimpressed—"that only her time matters."

"Talking 'bout me?"

Tamica and I looked up at the same time. Brooklyn was at least seven steps away, so I wasn't sure how she'd heard Tamica. But that was Brooklyn—she never missed a thing or a beat.

Her six-foot frame swept toward us like a hurricane wrapped in fur. She looked more like a Hollywood starlet, overdone in her diamonds and platinum, than a pastor's wife.

Leaning over, she sent a couple of air kisses Tamica's way, then slid into the booth next to me.

"Hey, girl!" She wrapped me inside her fur-covered arms. "Whew!" She shrugged off her snow white fox and fanned herself. "I think I'm suffering from early menopause."

Tamica said, "Or you could be hot because it's forty degrees outside and that fur coat is microwaving your behind."

Brooklyn puckered her lips as if she was blowing Tamica a kiss. "Why you hatin' 'cause I'm beautiful? You know I do what I do." Still fanning herself, she asked, "So, what's going on, my heifers?"

Tamica sucked her teeth as she looked down at her brochure. "She must be talking to you, Evia, 'cause I'm nobody's heifer." Then, she added to Brooklyn, "That's why you always having problems at church. 'Cause you don't know how to talk to nobody."

"What's got your thong in a bunch?" Brooklyn snickered.

Looking at me, Tamica said, "See what I'm sayin'? Talkin' 'bout thongs to church folks."

With a laugh, Brooklyn peered across the table at Tamica's brochure. "What's that?"

Tamica hesitated, and since I knew why, I answered for her. "Oh, Tamica got some information from Howard." I spoke in my most supportive voice. "She's thinking about going back to school."

"You're kidding, right?"

"Nope," I kinda whispered.

Brooklyn looked at Tamica. "She's kidding, right?"

"No, she's not!"

"Oh, come on." Brooklyn laughed. "Now you're going back to school? Last time we talked, you said you were going to become a missionary so that you could find yourself inside some rain forest in Africa. You can't make up your mind, can you?"

It was on now. Even though Brooklyn spoke the truth, Tamica wasn't about to let that go. So I leaned back and sipped my tea. This was pure entertainment, and the reason why, after I'd talked to Adam about our weekend plans last night, I'd called my friends to get together today.

Even though I saw Tamica and Brooklyn every Sunday in church, we hadn't had one of these get-togethers in more than three months. Tamica had tried to gather us about six weeks ago, but I'd been so busy with my life. Thank God my friends never held that against me.

Brooklyn and Tamica went on and on, back and forth, and finally Brooklyn held her palm up in Tamica's face. "Enough!" Turning to me, she said, "This is all about you. So, dish the dirt, because if you called a Saturday meeting, this has got to be big."

It was true. We hadn't gotten together in a long time, but whenever we did, because of me, we met on any day but Saturday. Saturdays were reserved for our family—the day Adam, the children, and I drove ninety minutes south to visit his mother. When Adam said last night that we'd be going on Sunday instead, I jumped right on the telephone. But I just wanted the distraction. I didn't want to talk about me. Even though we were close, they knew nothing about what was really going on in my life right now.

Our food arrived before Brooklyn could pressure me anymore, and she took my hand and Tamica's as we bowed our heads. As the first lady of Holy Deliverance All Saints Covenant Christian Center of Grace, Brooklyn always said the blessing. And her prayers over our food were always as long as the name of the ten-year-old church that she and her husband, Cash, had founded.

Yup, she'd married Cash, the man she'd loved since she was five. Not only had he stayed out of jail long enough to marry her but he'd also traded in the drug game for a new hustle. He'd gone from just being Cash, to Cash Supreme, the biggest dealer in Barry Farm, to finally ending up as the right Reverend Cash Supreme. (He saw no need to change his name.) Recently, he'd appointed himself Bishop; I guessed he could do that, since it was his church.

After her sermon-size grace, Brooklyn picked up her triple-decker hamburger. "So you wanna tell us why you called this get-together?"

Looked like she wasn't gonna let me get by with saying nothing. "Can't I just want to hang out with my girls?"

"Yeah, but . . ."

"And it's not like I can get a word in over the two of you, anyway," I joked.

Brooklyn dropped her burger on her plate, then raised her

hands. "Everybody be quiet!" She spoke so loudly that even people at the other tables stopped talking.

After a moment, she said, "Okay, Lady Evia, speak."

I could've just laughed it off. If I'd kept my mouth shut for a few seconds, Brooklyn and Tamica would have been back at it. But, no. I don't know what made me do it, but before my brain could catch up with my lips, the words spilled from my mouth. "Someone offered me five million dollars to sleep with Adam."

At first, my girls said nothing, as if my words had shocked them into silence.

"Girl, you're so funny," Tamica said, waving her fork at me.

Brooklyn laughed, too. "Yeah, that's a good one, Evia. Too bad it's not true 'cause let someone offer me five million for anything, and they got it."

"You know it!" Tamica was still laughing.

I took a bite of my garlic bread, and when I looked up, Tamica's eyes were right there. She was still chuckling. Then, small giggles. Then her eyes became slits.

"Wait a minute," Tamica said slowly. She put down her fork.

Brooklyn said, "You're *not* kidding?"

I shook my head. "Nope." Then I told them all about Shay-Shaunté's offer.

Before I could get all the way to the end, Brooklyn interrupted, "You sure she got the money?"

"Oh, yeah. This is Shay-Shaunté."

"Then do it," my friend, the pastor's wife, said.

"Are you kidding me?" Tamica glared at Brooklyn. Turning to me, she shook her head. "Don't."

Brooklyn rolled her eyes. "Spoken like a woman who's never had a man."

Ouch! I said inside for Tamica. Brooklyn didn't have to

go that hard. But the thing was—that was just B. If you were gonna be in her world, sometimes you got hit.

In her no-nonsense tone, Brooklyn asked, "Has Adam found a job yet?"

I shook my head.

Brooklyn asked, "Could you guys use the money?"

Duh? Who couldn't use five million?

"I'll take your silence as a yes," Brooklyn said to me. To Tamica, she said, "I rest my case."

Tamica may have been knocked down by Brooklyn's comment about her man-status, but she was not knocked out. "How could you tell her to do that? You wouldn't give your husband up for money."

"You's a lie!" Brooklyn said, shocking me and Tamica. "It wouldn't even have to be five million. I'd take two. And for two million, I'd give her more than my husband," she said. "For that kind of money"—Brooklyn raised her hand and began counting off points with her fingers—"she could have the good bishop, and our kids, and our cars, and the TV remote. What?" she said, sucking her teeth. "Give me a few more minutes and I'll think of a couple of other things to throw in."

"You don't have any kids," Tamica sneered.

"For two million, the bishop and I would get busy. I wouldn't mind giving up this girlish figure when you start talking about that kind of money."

Okay, I had to laugh at that. But only Brooklyn and I laughed. Tamica shook her head, and her scowl told me that she didn't find a single thing funny.

"Don't be a fool listening to her," Tamica said. "The Bible says that the marriage bed should not be defiled." She growled, but I wasn't sure who she was angrier at—me or Brooklyn. "And as the pastor's wife, you should be the one telling her that."

Brooklyn waved her hand in the air. "You don't even know what that scripture means. And even if you did know, you don't have a marriage bed. Become a wife before you start doling out marriage advice."

Tamica was not about to back down. "I may not have found the man of my dreams yet, but I found God long ago. And right now, He's the only Man we need to be concerned with."

That shut Brooklyn up for a moment.

Tamica continued, "There is no way that either of you can shape it for this to be all right with God."

"You preachin' to me?" Brooklyn asked.

"Someone needs to . . . because you're acting like you know of God, but not like you know God. Because if you really knew Him, there would be no way that you could advise Evia this way, Brooklyn."

"You don't know nothing about me."

Okay, it was time to break this up. "Ladies, go to your corners, no need to fight. I'm not even considering this deal."

"What?" Brooklyn said like she was stunned.

"There's no way Adam and I would do something like that."

"Good."

"Adam said no?" Brooklyn asked.

"No; I didn't tell him. But if I had—"

"He would've said yes." Brooklyn finished my sentence as if she knew my husband better than I did.

"He'd never go for something like this," I informed Brooklyn.

"Yeah, right!" She laughed.

That made me mad. "Look, I know my husband, and he loves me."

"And I know men," Brooklyn said, as if her knowledge on all things male trumped what I knew about Adam. "And men separate love and sex—especially if there's cash money involved."

I guessed Brooklyn thought that because she'd been with way more men than me and Tamica combined, she was the expert. But even though she'd slept her way through every quadrant in D.C., she didn't know what she was talking about when it came to *my* man.

Brooklyn added, "I'm telling you, Adam would jump on this." It must've been the look on my face that made Brooklyn soften up a little. "But only because you need the money, of course."

She couldn't even say that with a straight face.

This was exactly why I hadn't wanted to say anything, and I was so sorry that I'd opened my big mouth.

"Don't pay Brooklyn any attention," Tamica said as if our friend wasn't sitting right there. "You're right about Adam; you guys have the perfect marriage."

"If it's so perfect," Brooklyn said, "then five million won't mess up a thing. It'll just make everything five million times better."

"Ignore that woman," Tamica said, staring straight at me. "Keep your marriage pure."

"Marriage pure? Ha!" Brooklyn laughed. "This is just more evidence that single women shouldn't be allowed to speak about nothing more than which club to go to." Brooklyn shook her head. "Marriage and pure in the same sentence. Not possible."

"Can we change the subject?" I asked, while trying to figure out how to kick myself.

"Definitely," Tamica said.

"Sure." Brooklyn shrugged. "But can I say one more thing?" She didn't even wait for me to answer before she added, "When you finally tell your husband, and he breaks down the truth for you, and he gets busy with Ms. Shay-Shaunté, and you bank that big check . . . just remember to pay your tithe!"

Brooklyn leaned back and released a howl that was supposed to be a laugh. As if that was the funniest thing she'd ever heard or said.

She laughed all by herself.

Tamica rolled her eyes and I growled. Brooklyn was so lucky that she was my girl, because if she wasn't, and if she wasn't so much bigger, and if she wasn't my first lady, I would've slapped that laugh right out of her!

But all I did was look at Tamica, and both of us rolled our eyes at the first lady who was roaring with laughter.

Chapter 9

Making love to my husband was like taking a flight straight to heaven. That's exactly how I described it to Brooklyn and Tamica the first time it happened, and almost sixteen years later there were still no better words to express our connection. Our desire, our longing for each other was mutual when it began all those years ago, and it never stopped.

For me, the beginning of our love affair was when I finally pushed myself up after Adam wrestled me onto the ground. As I watched him walk away, my twelve-year-old heart knew that I had to have him.

Brooklyn, Tamica, and the guys were still laughing when I got up, but do you think that mattered to me? Nuh-huh. I was in love with that Banana-Pudding-Guy; he had me the moment I was staring up into his I'm-in-charge brown eyes. Although his hands held my wrists in a vise grip and not one part of my body could move an inch, I knew he wouldn't hurt me. He couldn't; because in those ten seconds when he was on top of me, there was this strange kind of electricity that flickered in the center of me. But it didn't stay there—it passed right through me to him. Oh, he felt it, too. I knew that because his body sent his energy right back to me. That was when I was sure he was going to kiss me.

But he didn't.

Maybe it was because we were in front of my mother's house, or maybe it was because we were in front of my friends. I don't know. But all he did was get up and walk away.

When he did that, I was like, huh? At first, I was gonna run after him, but I wasn't about to lose my cool status; not with my friends watching. So, nonchalantly, I brushed myself off as if being laid out on the ground was no big deal. Then I asked Cash, "Who's your friend?"

"Adam Langston," he told me, still kind of laughing.

"He new around here?"

"Naw, his mom stay over on Simmons. He lives there, too. Just been going to school out in Maryland somewhere. But he'll be going to Martin Luther King with us in September."

I was grinning hard, till Cash said, "Girl, he ain't interested in you. Adam likes 'em straight."

"What that mean? I'm straight."

"Naw; he likes girls who are all about school. Who like to read, study, go to the library and what-not. You know, smart girls." Cash shook his head. "He ain't into girls like y'all."

"Y'all?"

If Brooklyn hadn't jumped in, I would've broken it down to Cash myself. What did he know about me? What did he know about anything except running drugs for Duke? He needed to stay out of my business and worry about how he was gonna stay out of jail.

But I didn't have to say a thing 'cause Brooklyn's mouth was still running. She had no plans of shutting up, either. Not that I was studying Cash or Brooklyn. Every single thought I had was on Adam Langston.

I became a determined girl, but it wasn't hard to catch a boy who wanted to be caught. We bonded first over the only subject that I was good at—math. After Adam saw me in the library (which became my hangout after what Cash said about straight girls) every day for two weeks straight, we became inseparable. On our one-month anniversary, we declared our undying love for each other.

Of course, the world thought we were just young. I heard it all—y'all don't know nothin' 'bout love; it's just puppy love; it won't last; first loves never do.

Even Brooklyn, who'd been going after Cash since we were five as if *he* was a drug had the nerve to have an opinion.

"Just know that he's gonna have lots of other girls besides you, 'cause that's just the way boys are."

But no one and nothing mattered to me and Adam. No one knew what our pubescent souls knew—that before the world began God wanted us to be together (at least that's what Adam told me in a poem he wrote for me on my thirteenth birthday). From the way my heart melted at those words, I knew he had to be speaking the truth.

Strangely enough, the only person who was thrilled about our hookup was my mother. At least, at first.

"That Langston boy sure is polite," she said after the first time she met him. "He'd be a good one to keep, Evia. Think you can do that?"

But then her song changed about two years later when she came home one day and said, "That Langston boy ain't the son of Dr. Langston!"

I had no idea what my mother was rambling about, so I just stayed right at the kitchen table trying to finish my homework.

My mother had stomped into the kitchen. "Girl, don't you hear me talkin' to you?"

"Yes, Marilyn."

"So, why you tell me that he was that doctor's son?"

"Who?"

"That boy. You told me he was the doctor's son!"

"No, I didn't." I frowned. "I don't even know who that doctor is."

"Uh-hmmmm." She lit a cigarette, leaned against the counter, and glared at me as if I was a liar and a thief. She stayed quiet for a long time before she asked, "Y'all doing it?"

At first, I didn't know what she was talking about. Then she rephrased it and made her question clear.

"No!" I said, completely shocked that she would use the real *F* word with me. The one thing about my mother was that as classless as she was, she never really cursed. She'd get close, always adding a letter or two here and there. Like she'd say "fluck" or "shite." But I guess she was so mad that Adam wasn't that doctor's son that she had to use the real word. "No!" I repeated and slammed my math book shut. "We're not doing it."

"Uh-hmmmmm."

I could tell she didn't believe me, but I didn't know what I could do about it. Big Mama had talked to me about sex a little, but I'd never talked to my mother.

"Well, that little boyfriend of yours and his mother don't have nothin'. So, you better keep your legs closed."

I guess if Adam had been the son of that doctor, my mother would've been giving me sex lessons.

I'd told my mother the truth—Adam and I weren't doing a thing. Not because we were only fourteen—most of our friends were already doing the do. Our abstinence was part of our plan.

"We've got to get out of here," Adam said to me one day after we'd been hanging out at the movies with Cash and Brooklyn. Our friends hadn't seen a single scene of *The Godfather III* though. Right there, in the movie theater, Brooklyn and Cash had had sex. Not that I was shocked—they did that all the time . . . they and everyone else, but not me and Adam.

Now, Adam and I did go below the belt plenty of times. But it was just with our hands and a few, few times with our mouths. But that's where we stopped, 'cause we were gonna do this right. We had a plan and a purpose.

"Yeah, we're gonna get out of here," Adam said as we walked along Martin Luther King Boulevard. As he eyed some of Duke's boys handling their drug business in front of the liquor store, he added, "We weren't meant to be here. We're not supposed to live like this, 'cause you and me, we have a higher calling."

Many times when Adam talked, his words and thoughts went right over my head, but like all the other times, I just nodded in agreement.

"Education," he continued talking, "is our ticket. Our way out." He nodded. "Yup, that's what Ma always says. Education."

From the moment I'd met Adam, he'd talked about three things: God, his mother, and education. He had big dreams of college in New York, and studying abroad in Paris, then getting a big-time job somewhere exotic like California or Canada.

But the best part of his whole plan was that he was gonna take me with him.

"We're smart, Evia. We're going to be one of the statistics," he always told me. "We're going to be the ones who got out. The ones who were able to rise up above their circumstances. People will be reading about us one day. Shoot, one day, I might even be president!"

Oh, yeah, my boo dreamed big. I mean, the president part was a stretch. I guessed Adam forgot that he was black and there was never going to be a black president. But all I said was, "If you want to be president, baby, I'll be right there with you as your first lady."

Adam's dreams became my dreams, and that's what kept us celibate. Getting pregnant would derail every plan, so our dreams became our birth control, dreams were why we abstained, dreams helped us to hold out for three years.

Then, May of our sophomore year, the last days of school before summer. I couldn't wait—Adam had gotten both of us jobs with the parks department. We were gonna be going around the city, cleaning D.C. parks—totally unglamorous, but Adam said it was good, honest work and that's what mattered.

With only one day left, I was pulled from my last class— the history of black America—into the principal's office. There, Mr. Watson, a crinkly old man who always sounded like he had a sore throat, gave me the news that my grandmother had died. He could've just reached into my chest and yanked my heart out—it would've felt the same way.

Never had I dealt with such loss, such grief. The sorrow wasn't just in my head, it was all over me; my whole body ached. My tears just kept on coming; hour after hour, I mourned for Big Mama. Not only because I wouldn't see her again in this life, but now that she was gone, there would be no one left on earth who loved me like she did.

Every time I said that, though, I had a feeling that I was breaking Adam's heart.

"I will," Adam told me over and over when I asked him who would love me now. "It's different from Big Mama's love, but I will love you more. I'll love you always. I'll love you best."

It was because of my grief and because of his love that right after we left my grandmother in Holy Grounds cemetery, I ended up back at Adam's apartment.

While his mother worked her second job on the janitorial staff at Georgetown University, I curled up on the sofa, thought about how I'd watched my grandmother's casket be lowered into the earth, and wondered what it was going to be like to never hear her voice or feel her love again . . . and I cried. I cried so much that I could see the fear in Adam's eyes, as if he wondered if someone could die from an overdose of crying.

He held me, consoled me, kissed me. But it wasn't until his hands began to explore my body that my tears subsided. Instead of crying, I held him back. And kissed him back. And fondled him back.

This time, we didn't stop with just our hands. We kept going all the way until neither one of us could ever claim virgin status again.

I may not have been crying when I finally sat up on that couch, but I was scared enough to cry. "We didn't use anything," I whispered to Adam as I pulled down my skirt; we hadn't bothered to take off anything except for my panties. "You think we're gonna be all right?"

"Yeah." He tossed me my panties from the foot of the couch. "We're cool." Putting his arms around me, he added, "It's okay anyway, because we're gonna get married, and you're the only girl I'll ever be with . . . anyway . . . so . . ."

His words were so sweet, but I'd never heard his voice tremble until then. That was when I started praying the way Big Mama had taught me.

A couple of months later, I learned two things: that with prayer, God's answers don't always match our requests, and yes, you could get pregnant the first time.

We'd been so afraid when we'd borrowed money from five

different friends to purchase all those pregnancy tests and found out that we were going to be parents before we'd even be seniors in high school.

But although Adam wouldn't let me even consider getting an abortion, our new reality didn't kill our dreams. It was way tougher than we'd planned—school, kids, work, kids, college, kids, graduate school for Adam, kids. But just like he'd predicted, we got out—with our children and all.

Chapter 10

"YOU KNOW THE DIFFERENCE BETWEEN GOOD and evil," Bishop Cash Supreme bellowed from the pulpit. "You know the difference between right and wrong—don't try to make this all complicated. When evil comes to your door, kick it out. When you have to make a decision, choose right!" he shouted. "I said, choose right."

Brent Lamar, the musical director, hit the keyboard and Bishop Cash did his little jig, his signal that the sermon was coming to an end.

The congregation was on their feet—and that included Adam and me. I clapped with the rest of the parishioners, then the Holy Deliverance award-winning, seven-piece band did their thing and rocked the church. Church members were in the aisles, dancing, praising, all with their arms lifted.

To an outsider, we had to look some kind of crazy. But to us, the members, this was just a regular ole Sunday.

Even though Adam and I had been coming to Holy Deliverance for the almost eight years that it had been in existence, it still amazed me that Cash Supreme was the minister. I never thought Cash would leave the street game, because he was a smart-street cat who thrived as a drug entrepreneur. He rose in Duke's hierarchy to the number two position. That distinction, however, also brought him notoriety with the police—not that they were ever able to put anything on him. Cash was always way out in front of Five-O, and if it had only been the police that Cash had had to worry about, he might still have been in the game.

But it was the other hustlers, the younger, tougher guys who'd risen up as the millennium had approached, who'd driven Cash to do what no one else could.

"Man, I'm getting too old for this," Cash had told Adam one night when he'd come to our home. Though the two had remained really good friends, I hadn't liked Cash in our house, hadn't liked him or his game around our little girls.

But on that night, Cash had called—Duke had been murdered—and he'd needed to talk to Adam. I'd been scared, not sure what Duke's murder had meant for Cash. But with the way Cash had sounded, I'd known that if I hadn't said he could come to us, Adam would have gone to his friend. With me just days away from giving birth to our third child. I'd needed Adam with me. So, Cash had arrived, looking far more sad than scared.

As I'd sat next to Adam, Cash had confessed that it was time.

"There was no reason for them to take out Duke! They just wanted to drop him. They'll drop anyone in a minute over nothing." Cash had shaken his head, as if he'd still been in shock. "They don't respect their own lives, so why would they respect mine? I've gotta get out . . . now."

"Then do it." Adam had been trying to pull Cash from the streets for years. "Duke's death is a sign. Get out."

Cash had nodded, then just as quickly had shaken his head. "But what am I gonna do? All I know is hustling."

At first when I'd started moaning, Adam and Cash had thought I was just reacting to Cash's words. But then, the three of us had looked down at the water dripping down my legs. There had been no time to talk to Cash about his future—Adam had had to get me to the hospital.

The next morning, our son, Ethan, was born—and so, too, Cash's new hustle. Somewhere during the midnight hours, Cash had had an ephiphany.

"Just like Evia, I gave birth. To a new idea," was how he'd explained it to Adam.

That had been the most ridiculous thing I'd ever heard; except within a year, Cash had some kind of online divinity degree. Next, in his quest to become the right reverend, he'd married his number one ride-or-die, off-and-on chick, Brooklyn, because now that he'd been serious, he'd needed a first lady. And by the end of 2002, Holy Deliverance had been established.

When Adam said that he wanted to go to Holy Deliverance when it first opened, I'd agreed. That had shocked him; I was sure that he'd expected me to say that I wanted to stay at Solid Rock AME, where we'd been going, first with Big Mama, and after she'd passed, with Adam's mother.

But I'd had to go to Holy Deliverance—at least once. Not only was the first lady my best friend but I'd also been curious—what was a drug hustler gonna do in a pulpit?

So on the morning of the church opening, Adam and I had taken his mother and our children to Holy Deliverance. In his very first service, Cash had brought it. Seriously . . . like he had really learned something from that quickie, bootleg online class. Either he had done some real studying, or a hustler was just a hustler no matter what the game.

Though I loved his preaching, I did have to admit—he was a different kind of minister. First, unlike the pastor at Solid Rock AME, Cash never opened the Bible or really talked about scripture. His approach was more motivational, more positive, more uplifting than what I'd heard at Solid Rock. Cash preached about the goodness of God and how he wanted us to be prosperous—especially financially. How the Lord wanted blessings and not curses in our lives. And how all we had to do was claim what we wanted and with the right amount of faith, it would be ours. I left Holy Deliverance that first Sunday so hyped, more pumped up than I'd ever been at church.

The next Sunday, Adam and I became official members of the church—though his mother returned to Solid Rock, telling us that she wasn't feelin' this new kind of preaching. But Adam and I were, and now eight years later, we were founding members of one of the largest churches in Washington, D.C.

Through my thoughts, Bishop said, "Hug the person next to you and go in peace."

I hugged Adam first, then Tamica before we made our way into the aisle. It was slow moving, as usual. The church was packed with half of its forty-five hundred members. There were rumblings that Bishop was starting to look for a larger facility.

After we'd made our way through the receiving line, Brooklyn said, "So, y'all want to head over to Golden Corral?" even though it had been weeks since we'd joined them for the Sunday brunch gathering.

"Naw," I said. "We're driving down to Pearly Gates."

"Oh, that's right. You didn't go yesterday." Brooklyn gave me a hug. "Y'all tell Ma Ruby I said hello."

"Hello and good wishes from all of us," Bishop added.

As we walked away, I heard Brooklyn ask Tamica, "So, are you bringing your behind with us?"

Tamica sucked her teeth but answered, "Yeah."

I shook my head. My girls. I was glad we weren't going with them because today, all I wanted was some peace. And going to see my mother-in-law always gave me that.

Chapter 11

FOR JUST ONE AFTERNOON, I DIDN'T want to think about bills. Or finances. Or foreclosures. For a few hours, I wanted to go back to the old days when I was just Evia Langston . . . a wife and a mother without issues.

God certainly answered prayers, because right now, it felt like one of those days. The twins chatted easily in the seat behind us, their talk of simple things: school, dance lessons, student government, and the upcoming schedule of parties. Then their chatter died down to whispers, meaning the subject had shifted to boys. Our daughters were eager for their sixteenth birthdays for more than just the promised party and possible cars. Turning sixteen meant that they were eligible to date, which was going to bring along an entire new slew of issues.

But still, this was life at its most normal, and I glanced over my shoulder into the backseat, taking in this view of the wonderfully mundane.

Ethan was in the row behind his sisters, his designated seat, since he was the smallest. But the fact that he was all the way in the back never bothered him. With headphones on and an electronic game in his hands, he was oblivious to the girly whispers and giggles.

Adam's half grin let me know that through the rearview mirror, he was soaking in the same scene. He stole a quick glance at me, winked, then slipped one hand off the wheel to hold mine. I sighed, closed my eyes, and rested in the center of this calm.

Ninety minutes later, just outside of Richmond, we exited I-95. With just two more turns, Adam maneuvered the SUV through the wrought-iron entry of Pearly Gates Estates.

I didn't move, but I did open my eyes. I wanted to take in this view, which always made me feel so serene that I often wondered what it would be like to live here. I wasn't sure what it was about Pearly Gates—didn't know if it was the name or the long, winding road. Or the hundred-year-old trees whose winter-bare branches bowed to us in greeting. Maybe it was the way the sun always shined, no matter the season. Whatever it was, the founders of this sixty-four-year-old estate had named it right; I imagined the welcome gates to heaven would open to a setting such as this.

Two miles up, we pulled into the lot and parked right in front of the administration building where all visitors checked in. Adam and I held hands as we strolled behind Ethan and the twins, who'd quieted their chatter.

"Good afternoon to all the Langstons!"

Nathan, the security guard, welcomed us inside the lobby the way he did every weekend when we made this trip to Virginia.

"I didn't expect to see you on a Sunday. How you folks doing?"

"Fine," the twins answered for all of us as Alana signed our family in.

But before we stepped toward the back of the building, Nathan said, "Ah, folks, Mary Johnson left a message for you. Asked me to have you stop by her office if you came in today."

My hand was still inside Adam's, and though it was just a slight flinch, I felt my husband tense. Adam asked, "She's here today?" and the peace that had met us at the gates was gone just like that.

Nathan nodded. "I told her you never come on Sundays, but," he shrugged, "I guess she knows more than me." He laughed. "That's why she runs this place and I'm out here."

"I didn't think she'd be here today," Adam said more to himself than the guard.

Now I understood my husband's desire for a Sunday, rather than our usual Saturday visit to his mother. "You folks can go right on in," Nathan said, his tone so pleasant that one could've thought that Mary Johnson just wanted to say hello. But I knew that wasn't the case.

"Daddy, do we have to go with you?" Alexa whined.

In a softer tone, Alana suggested, "Maybe we can just go on ahead to Grandma's room?"

"Yeah," Adam nodded. "Go on." To me, he added, "You go, too."

Shaking my head, I watched as the twins dashed out the back and headed toward the two-story building across the path. Ethan followed his sisters at a much slower pace, but once he was out of my sight, I turned back to Adam.

He whispered, "Go on to Ma. I'll handle this."

I looked over my shoulder, making certain that Nathan's attention was away from us before I said, "I told you . . . I'm in this . . . with you." I took his hand.

I expected at least one more round of protests, but what

I got was a slight light in Adam's eyes. As if he was grateful. I squeezed his hand right before he knocked on the opened door.

"Ms. Johnson."

She looked up, and her greeting was a smile. She'd told me once that she was in her midfifties, but that was hard to believe. There was not one crack in her chocolate skin, which almost shined in its smoothness. And her bouncy ponytail made her look years younger rather than the two decades she had over me.

"Mr. and Mrs. Langston." She stood. "Come on in."

When she strolled around her desk to shake our hands, I noticed her denim jumpsuit was more casual than anything I'd ever seen her wear. I guessed her appearance at Pearly Gates Estates on a Sunday was definitely just because of us.

"Have a seat," she said before she went back around her desk. "I'll make this quick because I know you want to spend as much time as you can with your mother." With a breath, her smile disappeared and glasses were suddenly resting on the bridge of her nose. "Our records show," she began as she opened a manila folder, "that we haven't had a payment for your mother's room in a couple of months."

Adam twisted a bit in his seat. "Yeah, I know, but—"

She didn't let my husband finish. Still looking down at the chart in front of her, Ms. Johnson added, "Four months, to be exact." Now she looked up and into our eyes. Now she wanted to hear what Adam had to say.

"Like I told you a couple of weeks ago, I'm working on it."

Ms. Johnson nodded slightly. "I understand," she said in a tone that made her sound like she *was* in her midfifties. "These are difficult times for everyone."

"Yeah, but you're gonna get your money. We're pulling everything together."

She blew out a slight breath. "Would you consider"—she paused for a moment—"a semiprivate room? That will cut your expenses considerably."

Adam was shaking his head before Ms. Johnson could even finish. "My mother has always preferred a single."

"Well, no matter the preference, the room has to be paid for." I flinched at her words, at her tone.

Ms. Johnson continued, "And really, you're so far behind, we could have your mother released to one of the public homes."

My eyes were on Ms. Johnson, but I could feel my husband. I could feel his jaw tightening, his fingers curling. I jumped in, "We're not going to take her out of here. Let us go home, figure this out, and get back to you next week."

She shook her head slightly. "I'm afraid—"

"All right," Adam said. My eyes widened when he reached into his jacket and flipped open his checkbook. "We'll pay you for a couple of months now," he said, writing out a check, "and by the end of the month, you'll have the rest."

When he handed the woman the payment, her eyes went from me to Adam, then back to me. "Thank you. This will help me keep the board at bay."

With a nod, Adam shoved the checkbook for our empty bank account back into his jacket.

She added, "But I really need to know your intentions before the end of the month. We have to know which beds are going to be available for the beginning of the year."

"I just told you," Adam said. "My mother's bed won't be available." Then he stood, dismissing her.

"All right, then." Ms. Johnson stood with us. "Enjoy your visit, and thank you for understanding."

I didn't say a word until we were outside, crossing the lawn toward building number 12.

"I can't believe you did that, Adam."

"What?"

"You just wrote a seven-thousand-dollar check and there's less than one hundred dollars in our account."

He pressed his lips together, shoved his hands into his pocket. Said nothing.

To me, it would've been better if Adam had just told her that we didn't have the money. Even better if we moved his mother to another room.

But it was his pride that wouldn't allow Adam to tell Ms. Johnson the truth. Pride that just kept raising its head in my husband's heart. Pride that now had him doing things that were so far out of his character.

"I can't let them move Ma," he finally said. "That check is going to give me what I need—just a little time. Because by the end of the month, I'll have the job and we'll be good."

All I did was nod, because it didn't make sense to tell him the truth. My husband knew what was going to happen. When that check bounced, a semiprivate room might not even be an option. We'd probably have to find his mother a new place to stay.

That was going to break Adam's heart, so there was no need to bring him down now. Hitting the bottom was going to happen soon enough.

Chapter 12

Sacrifice.

That's what Ruby Langston was all about.

Sacrifice and survival. Before I'd even met my mother-in-law, before she'd even carried my husband inside her womb, Ruby had been surviving heartbreak and making sacrifices.

Her history was a litany of tragedies. First, as a teenager, she'd witnessed her drunken father murder her mother because he'd seen rats crawling over her. So from the age of fourteen, she'd had to provide for herself and her sisters. For the four years following her mother's death and her father's imprisonment, Ruby had done that. She'd moved herself and her sisters from relative to relative, staying in dank basements, sleeping on worn couches, living with family members who'd not been at all interested in the young girls but who'd been completely interested in the government checks that had come in the girls' names.

Even so, Ruby had trudged on. Her life had been loaded

down with school, church, and taking care of her sisters in the best manner she'd known how. She'd worked hard to instill the values that her mother had given her as the oldest—that loving Christ with all of your heart and going as far with your education as you could go were the keys to a life away from the generational poverty curse that had plagued their family.

But even with those values, even with her diligence, Ruby hadn't been able to save her sisters. By the time Ruby graduated from high school, her sisters had been lost: the one who was just a year younger had succumbed to the very nature of D.C.'s streets—drugs; the next one, at thirteen, had been put in a juvenile facility for a list of charges—including robbery and assault—that would have her behind bars until she was twenty-one; and finally, at just eleven, her youngest sister, Ruby's heart and the one for whom Ruby had had the most hope, had been gunned down in what was thought to have been a gang initiation shooting.

Yes, Ruby Langston had endured all of this, plus two failed marriages and the death of a child—Adam's younger sister, just a year after she was born. But though Ruby's heart had been broken many times, it had never hardened. Even when Adam and I brought our own wear and tear to bear on her heart, she was always there with love.

But now, six decades after she watched her mother die, Ruby's mind had decided that it was time for her to rest. According to the doctors, she'd begun her journey to the other side.

My head was filled with these thoughts as Adam and I stood at the door of the room watching Ruby with her grandchildren.

Ruby sat by the foot of her bed in a wheelchair, her hands clutching her worn Bible, but her glassy eyes lifeless, as if she saw nothing. The twins chatted away, though, as Ethan sat on the edge of the bed, his head down and his thumbs moving across the controls of his electronic game.

"So, Grandma, wouldn't it be cool if you could come to our party?" Alexa asked.

Alana added, "It would probably be too much, though. Remember you said you couldn't stand all that hip-hop music?"

Though the girls spoke as if their grandmother would answer, they knew she wouldn't. Ruby hardly said a word these days. Though in the beginning their grandmother's descent into dementia had shredded their young hearts, they now talked to her as if all was well.

One of the doctors had helped them cope by taking the time to explain the illness to them.

"The best way to understand this," the doctor had said to a then eight-year-old Ethan and thirteen-year-old Alexa and Alana, "is that your grandmother has kind of gone inside of herself."

"Why?" Ethan had asked.

The doctor had shrugged. "We don't really know. We're working on finding out, but it could be that she's done so much in her life, she's just a bit tired."

"Of us?" the twins had chorused.

"No!" Adam and I had said at the same time. Adam had added, "Your grandmother would never be tired of you. Not with the way she loves you."

Ethan and the twins may not have understood much of what had been happening to Ruby, but they'd understood one fact—their grandmother's love was the truth. Though they loved both of their grandmothers, it was hard for them to hide that Ruby was their favorite. Not that I blamed my children— Ruby Langston was my favorite, too.

The doctor had gone on to explain, "We don't know how

much your grandmother hears," he'd told the children. "Just keep on talking. Make sure that you include her in your life. I'm sure she wants to know what's going on."

So, that's what they did; that's what we all did. Once a week—almost every Saturday—we came to visit and fill Ruby in on life in the last seven days.

While the visits were a joy for the children, I could see that Adam left a little bit of himself behind every time we took the trip back home. I saw his fear with each kiss good-bye, the question in his eyes, his wonder if this would be the last time. The doctor's prognosis was that not many lived beyond seven years with this kind of dementia, and Adam couldn't be here very often. The ninety-minute drive made it a difficult weekday trip. But we'd sacrificed the time he'd be able to spend with his mother for this facility. Though we'd been used to seeing Ruby three, four times a week when she'd been well and then, of course, every day when she'd lived with us for three years, we'd traded the ability to spend time with her for these exquisite surroundings, the above-average care, and the world-renowned staff. No matter what the future held for Ruby, we were committed to ensuring that the end of her life was going to be far more comfortable, more peaceable than her beginnings.

Breaking up the children's chatter, Adam walked into the room. "Hey, Ma." He kissed her cheek.

When Ruby flinched a bit, Alana said, "See, Daddy, she heard you. She did the same thing when we kissed her."

"Oh, she hears us." Adam grinned and scooted onto the bed next to Ethan. Taking his mother's hand, he asked, "So, how's it going, Ma?"

It was the same every week—the way Adam paused and held his breath. As if the son hoped that his mother would turn herself inside out and come back to life.

But then Adam breathed and I did, too. I stayed at the

edge of the room, my heart breaking. My heart's tears were for Adam, who'd been blessed to really know a mother's love, and for our children, who deserved many more years with this incredible woman.

"Hey, I got an idea," Adam said. "Let's go get your grandmother a sundae."

Our children cheered as if this was something new, even though every week this was their ritual—to go to the ice cream sundae bar in the cafeteria.

"I'll stay here," I said, which was part of *my* ritual—this was my time alone with Ruby.

Adam kissed my cheek before he ran behind the girls and Ethan.

That scene made me sigh, once again content. Yes, Ms. Johnson and that check had interrupted my peace, but only for a little while. I was back to feeling at ease.

"How are you, Ruby?" I asked her once we were alone.

When she turned from the window and looked at me, my heart skipped. It was my turn to be hopeful. But there was not even a hint of recognition. Blankly, she stared at me before she turned her empty eyes toward the wall.

Moving to her dresser, I lifted the antique hairbrush that Adam and I had found a few years back in one of the small shops we'd explored in the market town of Stratford-upon-Avon about three hours outside of London. The moment I'd spotted the elegant set, I'd thought of Ruby. When we'd brought it home for her, her eyes had been wide with amazement.

"Oh, my goodness. This is too much," she'd exclaimed. "I'm a simple woman. I don't need extravagant things."

"Nobody needs extravagance, Ma. It's just what we do."

"You two do too much."

Adam had laughed. "Well, we're in charge now, so suck it up, Ma."

I smiled as I remembered the way Ruby had glared at her son, with one of those old-school black mama's—don't play with me, boy—looks.

But when Adam had said, "It makes us feel good to do these things for you, Ma," Ruby's eyes had filled the way they always did.

We'd done all that we could to surround Ruby with the best of everything. Even though we'd never come close to repaying all that she'd done for us, we never stopped trying.

For me, Ruby's love began on the day that I told my mother that I was pregnant. Though Adam almost wrestled me to the ground, insisting that he go with me, facing my mother was something I had to do alone . . .

"It doesn't make sense. You're not in this by yourself," Adam persisted.

"I know that. But I know Marilyn and she's less likely to go off if you're not there."

Adam frowned. "That doesn't make sense."

"My point exactly. Nothing with my mother ever makes sense, so I'm betting that if I'm by myself, she'll feel sorry for me." I paused and thought about who my mother was. "I'm hoping that she'll remember how it was for her."

So, grudgingly, Adam left me alone to face my mother.

The words "Marilyn, I'm pregnant," were barely out of my mouth before she jumped up and started wailing and flailing, talking about how I was ruining her life once again. How she'd told all her friends that I was going to be the first one in the family to graduate from high school. How now that would never happen. How I was messing it all up for her, just like I'd done when I was born.

"How could you be so dumb? How could you get pregnant? You're barely sixteen!"

I guess she'd forgotten that she'd gotten pregnant at the

same age. But then again, hadn't she just told me that being here was my fault?

That was when I wished that Adam *had* come with me, because surely his presence couldn't have made this any worse.

"Just get out of here!" my mother screamed.

"What?" I could not believe that she was actually sending me to my room.

"I can't stand to look at you. Get out of my house."

Out of her house? Her words made me do just the opposite—I froze. She couldn't be kicking me out—not when the exact same thing had happened to her.

But the longer I sat, the more irate my mother became, looking like she was about to throw her head back and howl at the moon.

So I slowly stood and made a move toward my bedroom. I wasn't sure what I was gonna do—pack a few things? Where I was gonna go—to Brooklyn's or Tamica's?

"I said . . . get out!" Marilyn screamed, letting everyone in Barry Farm know our business.

"I . . . I was just going—"

"Going where?" she interrupted. "You don't need to go nowhere but out of here."

"I was going to my room to get—"

"You don't need to get nothin'. Walk out of here with exactly what you came in here with . . . nothing!"

"But, Marilyn," I whimpered, scared out of my mind. "What am I supposed to do? Where am I supposed to go?"

"Oh, now you're asking me? You didn't ask me when you had your legs all wide open for that boy!"

I wanted to tell her that it wasn't like that. I wanted to tell her that ours was a different kind of love because God had put us on earth for each other. But I didn't say any of that because she wouldn't understand.

"Since you laid up with that boy, why don't you go to his house? Let his broke-down mama take care of you."

So that's what I did. With nothing more than the jeans and the sweater I was wearing, and the tears that were falling from my eyes, I left.

I went straight to Adam's house, and when he and his mother answered the door, Ruby pulled me into her arms without speaking a word.

She just held me until I stopped crying. When she finally spoke, she told me that while she wasn't happy about Adam's and my situation, she was going to stand by, sit by, be by our sides. Whatever, whenever, however.

When I told her that I needed a place to stay, she set me up in her bedroom with a stern demand that Adam and I were never to have sex again until we were married. We honored her wishes and lived under her roof from that day—through the rest of that summer, to our junior year in high school. I gave birth to our babies, Alexa and Alana, in February, and was back in school within two weeks.

Ruby quit her day job as a clerk in the local Safeway grocery store and stayed home with the twins while Adam and I were at school. At night, she worked while we studied and took care of our children. The summer didn't change our schedules—Adam and I went back to work for the parks, Ruby worked on the janitorial staff for Georgetown University at night.

It was a grueling, exhausting, wonderful life. In Ruby's home, I learned about family and relationships, about commitment and sacrifice.

In Ruby's home, I learned the truth about devotion and that was why, before Adam and I were even married, I considered her my mother-in-love.

Even now, sometimes I cried at the memories of those days—I cried for the joy of Ruby's love and I cried for the loss of my own mother, though on the day of the twins' birth, Marilyn had shown up to the hospital and told me that she'd forgiven me because she'd always wanted twins. But still, sometimes, the memories of how Marilyn had tossed me out so easily hurt.

Then—I felt it. The touch. I looked down to where I'd laid my hand on Ruby's shoulder; her hand was atop mine. I rushed around and hunched down in front of her.

"Ruby?"

Her eyes were on mine—still empty. I stayed there for a moment, hoping that the love that I'd felt in that touch would come once again, through her eyes, through her voice.

But there was nothing more.

"Do you know how much I love you?" I asked Ruby as I stayed crouched down in front of her.

Still nothing.

"That's all right," I said, thinking that if she did hear me, I didn't want her to feel my disappointment. "It's gonna be all right because Adam and I and the children will always be here. Even if we have to move you to another room. But having a roommate might be fun. Someone you can talk to, someone—"

"What are you doing!"

My head snapped back and I jumped up.

Adam marched toward me, his lips pressed into a thin line, his eyes squinted into thin slits.

"I was just talking to your—"

He pushed past me, dropping the already dripping sundae that he carried onto the dresser.

Behind him, our children's eyes were wide with surprise, maybe even a bit of fear, because I'm sure they couldn't remember the last time their father had raised his voice.

"Ma," Adam began, "don't listen to Evia. You're not going anywhere."

Alexa said, "Grandma's leaving—"

"No!" Adam exclaimed. He turned back to Ruby and stroked her hand. "It's gonna be all right," he kept saying, he kept stroking.

I'd been just talking, rambling, really. I would never do anything to upset Ruby, didn't Adam know that?

But I stayed quiet. Mostly because of the children, who still stood with their backs pressed against the wall, silent and tentative, their eyes moving between their father and me. The ice cream they held slowly melted in the heat of the tension, dripping into tiny puddles on the carpet.

The silence stayed for just a while longer before Adam announced that we were leaving. We gave our kisses and said our good-byes to Ruby, and headed back to our car. Back to the city. Back to our home.

Leaving all of that peace behind.

Chapter 13

IN THE TEN YEARS THAT WE'D been the five Langstons, there had never been a time when we'd driven together for more than thirty seconds in complete silence.

Until today.

There was no music piping through the speakers, no mindless chatter from our daughters. There was not even the constant electronic beep-beep-beep from Ethan's games.

Just strained silence.

Except for one question that came from our most sensitive child. "Is everything all right?" Alana asked after we'd driven the first forty-five minutes with only the rolling hum of the spinning tires filling the car.

I didn't answer right away, waiting for Adam to reassure our children, since he was the one who'd brought all this tension. But when their father said nothing, I turned around with a fake smile and reassured them myself. "Everything's fine."

The twins and Ethan lowered their eyes, as if they couldn't look at a mother who would lie so easily.

The minute we pulled up to our home, the girls and Ethan bolted from the car, into the house and upstairs to the protection of their bedrooms.

I, though, wasn't about to run from anything.

Before Adam could get away, I said, "Are you going to tell me what's bothering you?"

He didn't even look at me when he jumped out and slammed the door so hard that the windows rattled.

Now my calm was gone, too. "That's a real grown-up way to handle this," I stomped behind him. "So, you're just gonna walk away?"

Adam whipped around so fast that he startled me. "Okay, you want to talk about it?" His eyes were like red-hot flames against the frosted air. "You had no right to say that to my mother."

I held up my hands to the heavens. "What . . . did . . . I . . . say?" I asked, my voice now as loud as his.

"All that stuff about how she was gonna have to go to another room and get a new roommate. That's not gonna happen."

I shook my head, giving myself a few seconds to choose the right words. "First of all, Ruby is my mother, too, and I would never say anything to hurt her. Secondly, what I said was the truth."

"You must not be listening to me."

"No, I'm not. Because you're living in some alternate world. We don't have the money for Pearly Gates. Hell, we don't have the money to live here." I pointed to our house.

"See? This is why I didn't want to tell you anything."

A passing car's horn stopped me from saying something that I knew for sure I would've regretted. We both looked toward the slow-moving, rust-colored Volvo. From the passenger side, Lucy Miller smiled and waved; I wiggled my fingers, too. But that was it; I didn't have enough in me for a smile.

The Millers driving by reminded me and Adam that we were on the edge of our garage, in the middle of a Sunday afternoon, airing our business for every neighbor to hear.

I marched behind Adam into the mudroom.

"Look," he began once we were out of the sight and sound of the street. Calmer, he said, "I understand that you're worried, but how many times do I have to tell you that it'll all work out?"

"And how many times do I have to make *my* point?" I wanted to stomp my feet and throw a tantrum. I would have if I'd thought that would make Adam listen.

He said, "When I get this job with American Express . . ."

"*If* you get this job."

That made his head jerk back a bit. "When did we start talking about our life in terms of ifs?"

"Since you lost your job." I blew out a long breath that was meant to cool me down, but I wasn't backing down. "Since we've struggled to pay every bill. Since we've been hiding what we're going through."

"Because of that you've lost your faith?"

He had to be kidding me. Adam said I wasn't listening to him; what about him hearing me? "I haven't lost anything, including my ability to face facts. And the fact is that between our mortgage, the children's tuition, your mother's care, and my family's drama, along with everything else, we have twenty thousand dollars a month in bills and less than four thousand in income. That's the fact, and faith isn't going to change those numbers."

He lowered his head as if my words made him sad. "This is exactly why I didn't want you involved. You're emotional and I don't need that; it's distracting. Just stay out of this, Shine. Let me handle our business."

He spoke as if he was the genius and I was the fool. And because I didn't want to go off and *act* the fool, I just glared at him as I stuffed my hands into my purse and yanked out the keys. I was inside the Kia and edging out of the garage before Adam could blink twice.

If he wanted to handle it, then fine. I just wondered how he was going to answer our children when they asked him, "Daddy, how did we end up in hell?"

Chapter 14

THE SMART THING FOR ME TO do would've been to call Tamica. Because with her good sense (when it came to other people) she would've listened, then told me to get my butt back to my perfect home and work it out with my perfect husband.

But since I wasn't looking to hear anything good about Adam right now, I called Brooklyn.

"Where are you?" I asked the moment she answered the phone.

"At church."

"Still?"

"Yeah, I'm putting the final touches on the proposal for the expansion of the homeless shelter."

For all the bad press about Brooklyn and Cash being nothing but prosperity prophets and pulpit pimps, there was nothing you could say about their hearts and their commitment to the underdog, the underprivileged, and the under-represented. From the church-affiliated homeless shelter that fed and clothed many in the neighborhood, to the political meetings Bishop Cash sponsored for politicians to answer to his congregation, to setting up the church as a cooling center in the summers for those who couldn't afford air-conditioning, Cash and Brooklyn were all about the people.

"What's up?" Brooklyn asked, breaking into my thoughts.

I sighed as I rolled through the streets of D.C., heading toward the church.

"Uh-oh," Brooklyn said. Our thirty-year friendship was the reason my sigh said more to my friend than any words could. "It's not Ms. Ruby, is it?"

"No; right about now, my mother-in-love is doing one hundred times better than I am."

She was waiting for me to say more, and when I didn't, it was Brooklyn's turn to sigh. "Are you gonna tell me what's going on, or am I gonna have to beg for an hour to get it out of you?"

"Well, I'm on my way over there."

"Okay, but if you need me to start listening now, I'm ready," she said. "It's up to you."

The pressure, the stress, these fights with Adam were gurgling inside me. I was fifteen minutes from the church, but I needed to vent . . . now.

Since Brooklyn already knew about Adam's job, I started from there and told her the rest. She was pretty much silent on the other end, releasing only one "Umph" when I got to the part about all our savings being gone.

By the time my soliloquy was over, Brooklyn knew the whole truth and I was parked in front of the church. To finish up, I said, "Now, my husband, Adam Langston, the stand-up, all-American citizen, has just written a check that's gonna bounce all the way to Detroit." I stepped from the car, eager to see my friend and hear what she had to say.

Her first words were, "Oh, no. Not Detroit! Do they still have banks there?"

I froze, stopping halfway between my car and the front door of the church. I'd just laid out my heart and my life, and Brooklyn thought this was a joke? "This isn't funny," I snapped, doing an about-face and sliding right back into my car.

"I know, honey," Brooklyn said so sincerely that I felt bad for jumping on her like that. But still I stayed behind the wheel of the Kia. She said, "I was trying to lighten it up a bit, 'cause it sure got heavy." Now serious, she said, "So if Adam gets this job with American Express, none of this will be an issue, right?"

"In this economy, with the number of people looking for work, what do you think his chances are?"

"I don't know. But you have to have some hope to hold on to, right?"

"Hope doesn't pay the bills."

"Okay . . ." Then, when Brooklyn paused, I knew what was coming. I clenched my teeth and aimed the key for the ignition, because if she said it, I was out of there.

"Then I guess that just leaves Shay-Shaunté's offer."

I revved up the engine and screamed at the same time, hoping I'd busted one of her eardrums. "I already told you . . . that is not an option."

"If you're talking about hope, five million dollars can buy you a lot of that," she persisted. "I take it that you still haven't said a word to Adam."

"Why do you keep harping on this?" I took a deep breath and spoke slowly. "I'm not telling Adam, okay?"

Brooklyn was quiet, as if she was studying my words. "I'm not saying do it; I'm saying give Adam a chance to help you decide."

Okay, Brooklyn was my girl, but this chick wasn't getting it.

So, since I was tired of repeating myself, I didn't say anything; I just edged my car away from the church.

"What are you afraid of, Evia?"

"I'm not afraid of a daggone thing!" Then I wondered, why *didn't* I want to tell Adam? I mean, he would agree with me totally . . . right?

The church was in my rearview mirror when I said, "Listen, Brooklyn, I'll talk to you later."

"I thought you were on your way."

"I was."

"Evia, I know you don't want to hear—"

She was right about that, 'cause I pressed End before I could hear another word from her. But even though I hung up on my friend, I could still hear her voice.

"What are you afraid of, Evia?"

I wasn't afraid. It was just that if we weren't going to do it, why bring up Shay-Shaunté's ridiculous offer?

But inside that Kia, by myself, with the silence ringing in my ears and Brooklyn's words in my head, my heart spoke the truth. I couldn't say a word to Adam because what would I do if Adam said yes? What would I say if my husband agreed to sleep with another woman?

Because that's how I saw this—Shay-Shaunté's offer was only about sex . . . it didn't have a daggone thing to do with money.

At the red light, I stopped and sighed. No, Adam would never agree to this. Not the man who'd loved me since I was twelve, who'd married me just a week after our high school graduation and spoken words that day that not even the best Hallmark cards could match . . .

The room designated for civil marriages in the Superior Court was small and stuffy, but we all piled in. It was Friday— we had the three o'clock appointment and the clerk had just called us for our turn.

Adam and I entered the room ahead of everyone else, and a man who was as wide as he was tall, motioned for us to hurry forward.

"Evia Evans and Adam Langston?" He said our names as if he was asking a question. "You two are pretty young, aren't you?"

"Yes," Adam spoke for us. "But we have our parents' permission."

Both of us turned to acknowledge our families. Our mothers stood side-by-side for the first time ever, each holding one of the twins. Behind them were Cashmere and Twin. Even though my fourteen-year-old sister and twelve-year-old brother had to be dragged here, I was happy that Marilyn had forced them. Today, we were becoming one, and I wanted everyone here with me to make it complete.

"Well, let's get this started," the man said wearily, as if he'd been marrying folks all day and he was just plain tired of it. He jumped right in, "We have come together today, in a community of love, to support the union of Evia Evans and Adam Langston."

I had to admit, this was nothing like the wedding I'd imagined when I was a little girl and Tamica and I used to dream. (Brooklyn never played the wedding day game with us because she said all men were dogs.)

But even though I was wearing a yellow shift and not a flowing white gown, and there were only six guests (if I counted the twins) and not the two hundred people I'd planned to invite—I was still the happiest girl on earth.

"We celebrate this occasion which is both solemn and joyful—"

"Wait!" Adam said.

I became statue-still.

Oh, my God! He had changed his mind. He didn't love me.

Or maybe he couldn't stand the thought of being related to Marilyn, Cashmere, and Twin.

Behind me, my mother grumbled, but I didn't care what she had to say. I just started begging God.

Adam said, "Do we have to do those same old tired words that you say for everybody?"

The man looked stumped. "Well . . . I guess not . . . this is a civil ceremony . . . and there are no rules . . ."

"Well, this is what I want to do," Adam said, taking charge. "I have something I want to say to Evia, then we can just put the rings on our fingers and get on up out of here."

"Oh . . . kay," the man said, shutting the worn book he held.

"With a nod," Adam turned to me. "Evia, this is not the way we planned this, but it is still part of our plan. Our plan to be together, forever. I loved you when we were twelve and I will love you when we're one hundred and twelve."

Behind us, my brother cracked up, like Adam was telling jokes. But if Adam heard him, he didn't show it; he just kept on going.

He took my hand. "In front of God, my mother, your mother, your sister and brother, and," he paused before he said, "our beautiful daughters, I promise that I will love you and only you, forever. And, I mean that in every way. You are and will always be the only woman I will love physically, mentally, spiritually. I will go to my grave with you being the only woman I've ever loved or made love to. The only woman who will always have my heart."

I melted.

He kept on, "The best way I know to honor God is to love and cherish you, Evia Langston."

The court clerk coughed. "Um . . . she's not Evia *Langston* yet."

Everyone laughed, except for me.

I couldn't laugh—I could barely stand. From the time Adam started talking, I was done. I was seventeen and already knew what it was like to be loved completely . . .

It was on our wedding night that Adam had called me Shine for the first time, because he'd said his life had a whole new light.

No, the man who'd spoken those words on that day would not want anything to do with Shay-Shaunté's deal.

That was my truth and that's what I told myself, all the way home.

Chapter 15

Before I had a chance to step all the way inside my house, my mini-me was at the door.

"Mom!" Alana hugged me as if she was relieved to see me. "Where've you been?"

"Whoa," I said, wrapping my arms around her. "I was just gone for a little while. I had to do something with your aunt Brooklyn."

"Oh. 'Cause Daddy wants to hold a family meeting." She lowered her voice. "We thought the meeting was gonna be about you."

I laughed. Okay, I saw what was going on. After we'd come home, my girls had probably gone up to their rooms, sat, wondered, discussed, and then figured out—or thought they'd figured out—what had gone down with me and Adam. With Alexa's drama-filled mind and Alana's sensitive one, the twins had taken anything they'd heard much too seriously—which I understood, because our children rarely saw us fight. So, they'd conjured up something like me leaving home and moving to Mexico.

"Well, if your dad wants to have a meeting, it's not about me."

I knew Adam was behind me before he even spoke. "No, it's not about you." When I faced him, he added, "This is a meeting about all of us."

One side of Adam's mouth twisted upward—half a smile, a full apology. He said, "It's time we talk to the children."

"Mom! You're home!" Alexa bounced down the stairs, her tone filled with the same surprise as Alana's.

Adam directed the girls into the living room, then called for Ethan. We all settled into our regular places—Alana resting on the edge of my chair, Alexa sitting at Adam's feet, and Ethan stretched out in the middle of the floor halfway between me and Adam.

Alexa spoke first. "Is this about our party?"

Now that I was home, all of Alexa's concerns had turned back to where they always were—to Alexa.

Adam's eyes met mine, and with a smile and a nod, I told him that I was with him.

He said, "Well, something about the party, but not the party alone." He took a breath. "You know, I've always talked to you guys about what's going on in our family because being a member comes with responsibilities."

The twins sat, their eyes on their dad, but the way Ethan was lying so still, I wondered if he'd fallen asleep.

"Well, some things have happened. . . . Now, I don't want you to worry . . . but the company I worked for moved its operations to Japan."

Ethan sat up with wide eyes and a huge grin. "We're moving to Japan," he cheered.

Adam said, "The company moved to Japan, but they didn't take the people with them . . . at least not most of the people."

"So they closed the whole company?" Alana whispered. I could see that she was already studying, figuring out what this meant. The children had visited their father's office many times, always impressed by the seven-story building teeming with fifteen hundred employees.

Adam nodded. "They shut the whole company down."

Ethan said, "I think we should go to Japan."

Alexa glared at her brother, then turned to Adam. The terror was on her face before the words came out. "Please, Daddy, no! Don't make us!"

"We're not moving," Adam said, holding up his hands.

Alexa fell out, spread-eagle on the floor, pretending to faint with relief.

Alana asked, "If the company's gone, what are they going to do with you?"

"Well, they let me go."

"As in fired?" Alexa popped straight up. "They fired you? Can they do that?"

"Yeah, babygirl. They can do that, though I wasn't technically fired—just let me go."

"It's the same thing, right?" Alexa asked.

"Yes." He nodded. "So for right now, I don't have a job."

"Wow!" The word came out in a three-part chorus, though our children sang different tunes. The girls sounded shocked; Ethan sounded impressed.

"What are you gonna do?" Alexa asked.

"I'm gonna find a new job. I've had some interviews, and I have a promising opportunity with American Express."

"Oh!" Alexa waved her hand as if it was a done deal. "So, you're just gonna start working somewhere else."

"Yeah."

"So, our house is not gonna go into foreclosure, right?" Alexa asked, surprising me. I guessed I was wrong—she did pay a little attention to the world beyond her bedroom door.

Adam glanced at me before he shook his head.

Alexa's inquisition continued. "And we're still gonna have our party, right?"

He looked away when he answered that question. "Well, that part . . . we're not sure. But we're still gonna try."

I think it was the horrified look on Alexa's face that made Adam's shoulders slump.

Alexa asked, "So, that means we won't get cars either?"

"We're working this all out," I said, watching Adam shrink right in front of me. "We just wanted to give you guys a heads-up."

"So what are we supposed to tell everybody?" Alexa asked.

"Nothing . . . yet," Adam said.

The twins looked at each other, then Alana said, "That's okay, Daddy. We'll be okay even if we don't have a party."

After a couple of quiet seconds, Adam cleared his throat of sadness and asked, "Do you guys have any more questions?"

The twins shook their heads, but Ethan piped in, "Can I still play golf?"

"Yeah," Adam said. "Definitely."

Ethan nodded. "I wasn't sure, because I know the lessons are expensive."

"They are," Adam said. "But we're gonna work it out. I only told you because you might see me home a little bit more, and we might . . . have to cut back on a few things. But your mom and I"—he paused for a second, as if he wanted to make sure I heard that he was including me—"are gonna make sure everything's okay."

When the children glanced at each other and said nothing more, Adam added, "In a couple of weeks or even maybe a few days, we're gonna have another meeting, this time with nothing but good news. And we'll start planning your party then." He looked at the twins. "Okay?"

Alana nodded right away. She jumped up, sprinted across the room, and wrapped her arms around Adam. "It's okay, Daddy."

Alexa stayed at Adam's feet, her face stiff. I wanted to shake my daughter. Couldn't she see how hurt her father was? But I inhaled to dilute my anger and just kept saying, *Teenager, teenager, teenager* in my mind.

Then, Alexa did the right thing and followed her sister's lead. She hugged Adam, though unlike her sister, she had no reassuring words for him. Just a hug and a kiss—which was more than enough.

And even though Ethan had told Adam a week ago that he was too old for hugs, our ten-year-old knew that tonight was not the time for handshakes; he embraced his father.

I didn't move until our children were upstairs and I heard the last bedroom door close. Then I stood and gave Adam my own hug.

Chapter 16

HAVING THAT TALK YESTERDAY HAD TAKEN a lot out of my husband, and my thoughts were still on Adam even as I tried to ply through these sales reports.

"That was hard," Adam had said to me after the children had left us alone.

"Hard, but good. Now they know what's going on and they'll be prepared for . . . whatever we can do."

But my assurances had not been enough.

When I'd followed him into our bedroom minutes later, he'd already tucked himself into our bed with his head snuggled deep into the pillow. This had been a first. In the sixteen years that we'd been married, our bed had served three purposes—sex, sleep, or rest . . . but it had never been a retreat from reality.

I'd wanted to shake him, pull him up, not let him slip into the deep abyss of depression. But all I'd done was ask if he'd wanted something to eat, then kissed his forehead when he'd told me that he wasn't hungry, that all he'd wanted was a little time alone.

After dinner with the kids, I'd retreated to the bedroom, too. While Adam had slept, I'd sat up in the bed, though I'd never got past the second page of the novel I was reading. It had been hard to concentrate when my husband had been snoring beside me and it hadn't even been nine o'clock.

Then this morning, Adam had stayed in bed—yet another first—while I'd prepped the kids and finally left the house myself.

Now I couldn't stop wondering if I'd done the right thing in pushing him to have that talk. I remembered the way Adam had slumped and slouched as he'd faced our children. The way he'd worn what he saw as his failure like a cloak.

A quick knock on the door cut through my concerns, and Rachel popped her head inside.

"Shay-Shaunté wants to know if you're done with the sales analysis."

I shook my head. "Give me a few."

Rachel pushed her whole body through the door. "What's up with you? You usually have these done like that." She snapped her fingers.

"Cover for me. I'll have them in thirty minutes."

She left me alone and I forced my eyes to focus, but I had no control over my wandering thoughts.

Another knock made me snap, "I said give me thirty, Rachel."

The door opened and my frown faded fast when Adam stepped in, smiling. Forget about being dressed to the nines— he looked like the perfect ten. His designer suit peeked from beneath his unbuttoned cashmere overcoat, and his shoes were spit-shined.

"What are you doing here?" I jumped up. This was clearly

not the man I'd left at home. Did he come bearing great news about a job?

He closed the door behind him and hugged me. "I didn't get a chance to kiss you good-bye and tell you to have a good day."

"Oh," I said, melting like I did whenever Adam made me feel like I was the heroine of a romance novel. "You came all the way down here to tell me that?"

"And to give you this."

I hadn't noticed how Adam was keeping one hand behind his back, holding a flower. It was a rose all by itself, but its perfume was potent, filling my office with its aroma, filling me with happiness. For the moment, I forgot all about foreclosures and bills that couldn't be paid and parties that would never happen. All that was on my mind was what was most important—and he was right in front of me.

"I love you, Adam."

"I love you more, Shine."

"I love you most."

"And I love you best."

His lips were on mine for only a second before there was another knock.

I moaned. "Rachel! I told you—"

The door opened, and Adam backed away from me.

"I'm sorry," Shay-Shaunté said, though she was already halfway inside my office. "I was checking on those reports."

"I'll have them to you in half an hour."

Shay-Shaunté nodded, then turned to Adam. "How're you?"

I frowned at the way Shay-Shaunté's eyes scanned my husband. As if she was surveying every inch of him. Had she always looked at him that way?

"I'm good, Shay-Shaunté," Adam nodded with a smile. "What about you?"

With her signature lopsided grin, she said, "Very well."

Shay-Shaunté needed to back up, and Adam needed to stop playing nice with the enemy, but then, he didn't know that Shay-Shaunté was the enemy, did he?

With her eyes still on my husband, Shay-Shaunté said, "I'm sorry if you were as offended with my offer as Evia."

Oh, no! I never expected her to say anything! Why was she even bringing it up when we'd agreed that it was not gonna happen, so therefore, over and behind us? "Ah . . . Shay-Shaunté . . ." I said, shaking my head. It was supposed to be a hint—from one sistah-girl to another.

Whether she got it or not, she kept on, "No, I really want to apologize to both of you." Turning back to Adam, she said, "As I explained to Evia—"

"Ah . . . Shay-Shaunté . . ." This time I was gonna have to say more, because for some reason, this high-powered, educated, rich chick wasn't catching my clue. "There's no need to apologize again." I waved my hand and walked toward the door. "Like we agreed, it's behind us."

"It's behind you and me." Shay-Shaunté hadn't taken one step away from my husband. "But I want to make sure that Adam has no bad feelings either."

"About what?" My husband's forehead was creased with confusion.

"My offer." Shay-Shaunté frowned, as if she was stumped. "When I asked Evia about you and me . . . you know, the five million dollars?"

Now I watched my high-powered, educated, but not-so-rich husband look like he couldn't put together two sentences.

"Oh!" Shay-Shaunté held her hand over her heart as if she was surprised. Looking between me and Adam and finally resting her eyes on him, she said, "I'm sorry. I thought you knew."

"No," I said, finally getting a word in, although it was too late. "I didn't tell him. Because like I told you, it was never going to happen."

Adam held up his hands. "Would somebody tell me what's going on?"

Before I could say a word, Shay-Shaunté slid down in the chair in front of Adam and crossed her legs as Adam and I both watched the hem of her already too-short Tadashi sheath ease up her thigh.

"Well, Adam," she began like she was going to be the one to tell him the story.

As if I would let that happen!

I stepped right in front of her, blocking her view of my husband. I had to or I was gonna slap her, and I didn't think that would work out too well for me.

"Shay-Shaunté." I said her name so slowly that it came out in ten syllables. "I will handle this."

She nodded. "Are you going to tell him?"

I could not believe this trick was sitting here questioning me about my husband.

And she kept on! "I mean, it seems like Adam"—she leaned to the side so that she could see around me— " . . . it seems like he wants to know."

I need this job. I need this job. I need this job.

"Shay-Shaunté . . ." This time her name had twenty syllables. "I will handle my business."

That mask of concern that she wore faded from her face. "Okay," she said. She stood and looked over my shoulder so that she could see Adam. With her triumphant smile, she said, "It was so good to see you."

"You, too."

I kept my eyes on Shay-Shaunté, making sure that she was gonna really leave this time.

She moved with her signature stroll . . . that soft, slow sway of her hips. I was all woman, but the way she walked almost hypnotized me; I couldn't imagine what she did to men, especially the one standing behind me.

With a final glance over her shoulder, she sauntered out the door, and I breathed again. I had to take another deep breath, though, before I faced Adam.

With his arms folded, he asked, "You wanna tell me what's going on?"

No! Not even with Shay-Shaunté outing me like this—I still didn't want to do it.

"Shine?" Now it was my name that sounded like it had multiple syllables.

"Yeah. We need to talk." I grabbed my coat and his hand. "Let's get out of here."

Chapter 17

THERE WAS NO WAY I WAS going to sit inside Shay-Shaunté's office—that space that she owned—and tell Adam about how Shay-Shaunté wanted to own him and me. Once we were downstairs, I saw our SUV parked right in front, and I headed for it.

We hopped inside and Adam revved up the engine, turned the heat to high, then sat back and waited for me to speak.

But he wasn't patient, because the moment he could part his lips without quivering from the cold, he said, "So, what's going on?"

I took the deepest breath I could, since I didn't know when I was gonna get a chance to breathe again, then I started at the beginning. "Shay-Shaunté called me into her office last week and gave me a check for five million dollars." I told him every detail of that conversation and the one after, in which I'd put her on notice that there was no amount of money that could buy us like that. "So," I began wrapping it up, "I don't know why she brought it up today. As far as I was concerned, as far as she was concerned, it was over."

Then . . . nothing but silence.

I said, "Are you going to say anything?"

He didn't speak; just reached for the heater and turned it off. As if being offered five million dollars for his body made him hot.

I shuddered. The heat of my anger was no longer enough to keep me warm. Were all of my thoughts, all of my doubts coming true? I asked, "You're not thinking . . ."

I couldn't even bear to finish that thought.

Adam hesitated a bit too long for me. But then he spewed out nothing but righteousness. "Nah, nah. Of course not. No. Are you kidding me? Never!" He almost sounded indignant. "I can't believe she even came at you like that." Then, with his little rant over, he asked, "Why didn't you tell me?"

"Because you had enough on your mind. Why waste a conversation about something that was never going to happen?"

He nodded, like he agreed. But his eyes . . . he squinted, as if he was contemplating something deep. He said, "I still wish you'd told me."

"Telling you wasn't going to change anything. Whether I told you or not, the answer was going to be the same." I paused. "Right?"

"Of course, Shine. We don't need money like that." Again, he reached for the button to the heater. Pushed it until it was back on high. He exhaled before he asked, "After that . . . do you think you can keep working for her?" His eyes were on the building where I spent my days with Shay-Shaunté.

I shrugged. "Do I have a choice?"

At first, he frowned, as if he didn't understand my words. But then he remembered our predicament, realized my dilemma.

"I'm gonna get this job," he said, his voice now strong, now steady. "As soon as I do, you can quit the next day."

"Okay."

"I don't even want you giving her two weeks' notice. I want you out of there!"

"Okay."

He reached for my hand and gave me a squeeze that was meant to be reassuring. But it was hard to feel comforted when I felt his sweaty palms. He said, "I'm sorry you have to keep working here, but it won't be for much longer."

"I'm cool. I can handle Shay-Shaunté."

"I know you can." He hugged me and we were back to being Adam and Evia.

"I have to get back in there," I said.

Adam twisted in his seat and kissed me, but not his ordinary send-me-back-to-work peck on the lips. This was a full-on assault—a kiss that was filled with tongue and passion. A kiss with something to prove.

I pulled back, breathless. Waited for him to give me an explanation. He said nothing.

"What are you thinking?" I asked.

His cell phone rang and freed him from responding. "Hello."

The excitement in his eyes, now in his voice, nudged aside the tension that had joined us in the car.

"Yes, yes, Mr. Yearwood," Adam said. "Yes. Definitely, just tell me when." A pause. "Thank you. Thank you." He ended the call. "I told you this was gonna work out." He laughed like a kid. "That was American Express. They want me to come in next Monday—for the third and final interview."

"That's great, baby!"

The call and that news eased the tightness that had taken over my body. Still, I wondered—what was Adam thinking before he took that call?

But right there I decided that some questions were best left without answers.

Chapter 18

IT WAS THE BEST OF NIGHTS, and now it was the best of mornings. At least for me and Adam. Alexa still moped around as if her father had lost his job just to make her life miserable, and even though Alana and Ethan wore happy faces, their smiles were strained beneath their new burdens.

Except for the sizzle of the frying turkey bacon and the scraping of forks against their plates, a somber silence hung over the kitchen. But I smiled, and hoped that the children could feel my newfound joy.

I wanted to tell them so badly about their father's upcoming job interview. But Adam and I had decided that there would be no more family talks, not until we could give our children more than hope.

The front door slammed, and after a few seconds, Adam strutted into the kitchen. "Good morning, everyone!" he said, full of cheer, as if this morning was an occasion to be celebrated.

"Morning, Daddy," Alana and Ethan said at the same time. Alexa's greeting was simply a grunt.

I rolled my eyes at my daughter.

"How is everybody this morning?" Adam shrugged off his jacket, then laid the dry cleaning that he'd just picked up across one of the barstools.

"Fine." Again, just two of our children spoke.

Adam didn't seem to notice, though. With two giant steps, he was behind me with his arms wrapped around my waist. He swayed as if he heard music and guided my hips to his rhythm.

Leaning back into his embrace, I multitasked—did the little hip salsa with my husband and flipped over the bacon at the same time. He held me as if he wanted me to remember last night—our lovemaking, filled with more pleasure than urgency this time. We were close to the end of our tunnel, and we could make love freely now, just because we were in love and nothing else.

When Adam nuzzled his lips against my neck, I said, "You'd better let me take care of this breakfast or else you're gonna have some seriously burnt bacon."

"And if you burn it," he whispered seductively, "what are you going to do to make it up to me?"

I grinned. Years and years of marriage and the magic was still there, always there, forever there.

"Hmmm," I hummed and glanced at the clock. Would I have enough time between getting the children off and having to leave myself?

And then . . .

"Mom!"

Alexa's scream was so startling that I dropped the fork to the floor. Shifting the pan to the other side of the stove, I swung around quickly, as Alana and Ethan began shouting, too.

With wide eyes, they yelled and pointed toward the window. I didn't understand a word they were screaming, but Adam must have, because with just a few steps, he pounced from the kitchen, through the foyer, and out the front door. I rushed behind him, and our children trailed me.

"Hey!" Adam yelled to the two men who were hitching the bumper of the SUV to their tow truck. "What are you doing?"

"Sorry, dawg," the black guy said. "We're just doing our job."

"But, but . . ."

I couldn't hear more of Adam's words because behind me gibberish filled the air. A few words came through the wails: "Mom!" "Why?" "What?"

With shaky hands, I pushed the children back into the house so that they wouldn't be traumatized by the sight that was shocking enough to me.

"Go back into the kitchen," I demanded. "Finish your breakfast."

Not that I really thought they would listen. They half obeyed, moving from the door to the window, where they pressed their faces against the glass.

As I stepped outside, I folded my arms across my chest to fight the biting wind. If I'd had any sense or any time, I would've grabbed my coat, but by that time, our Escalade might be gone.

Standing behind Adam, all I heard now were his pleas. "Please," he kept saying. "I can make a payment."

The two men stopped and hunched their shoulders in unison. "We can't take your money. Take it up with the bank." They returned to their business.

Looking down our driveway, I noticed the sudden traffic jam. It was only three cars, but there were only six homes on this cul-de-sac. The cars rolled by slowly—first the Jaguar, then the BMW, and finally the Mercedes. I could feel my neighbors' curious eyes, their wonder about the bright red tow truck with bold, yellow block letters: Quik-Repo.

There was no need for us to watch them take our car away, though that seemed to be Adam's plan until I took his hand. His fingers were as stiff with cold as mine were, and we rushed back inside. There we had a new confrontation.

"Why did they take our car?" Ethan asked.

"Because they were repo guys," Alexa said as if she knew everything. "I saw it on television. There's this show and they take cars and boats and planes from people who don't pay when they're supposed to."

If this wasn't happening to my family, I would've asked Alexa more about that show. Really? They didn't have anything better to do with thirty minutes than to video people in the middle of their misery?

"There's nothing for you to worry about," Adam said, his strong voice back.

"We have to be worried," Alexa cried. "Our car was just taken away from us!"

The veins behind my eyes throbbed; my headache came quick, came hard.

"What's happening to our lives?" Alexa sobbed more, increasing the pain in my head. Dramatically, she threw her hand up to her forehead.

I swear, if she fell out on the floor, I was going to tell everyone to leave her right there.

Adam said, "We're gonna get the car back."

"But when?" Still Alexa. Still drama.

"In a few days. Maybe a week."

Why was he lying like that? He was going to have to tell them another lie next week.

"But how do you know they'll give it back?" asked Alana.

She questioned Adam hesitantly, as if she wanted to be careful with her father and his feelings.

"They will. And if they don't, we'll get a new one."

"But we don't have any money," Ethan said sadly.

I wanted to scoop all my children—well, at least two of them—into my arms and cover their eyes and ears until all of this was over. But I stood next to Adam, supporting him as he consoled them.

"We have money, Ethan," Adam said. Then he took a long breath as if he needed a lot of air to say the next words. "And what's better is . . . I got that job."

Those words surprised our children. Those words stunned me.

"You did?" the three sang together.

I stepped away, not wanting to stand beside him anymore. I leaned against the wall and crossed my arms. No one believed in positive thinking more than me, and truthfully, I really believed that Adam would get this job.

But was I ready to dance a jig? No. Was I ready to write some checks? No. Was I ready to tell the children? No! Because until Adam had the offer letter, he didn't have a job. And if he didn't have a job, what he was saying now was a straight-up lie.

"You have . . . like a real job?" Alexa asked, her sobs, her tears, miraculously gone.

"Why didn't you tell us?" This time, it was Alana who had the question.

"Because your mother and I . . . we wanted to wait . . . until we could have a celebration."

"That's wonderful, Daddy!" Alana said, and she and Alexa hugged Adam together. A couple of seconds later, they made room for Ethan—a group hug that didn't include me.

"Isn't this great, Mom?" Alana asked, as if she was measuring my reaction.

"Yeah, it is," I said with a smile on my face, but not in my voice. "Okay, guys." I really wanted to rush them along now. "Get your stuff. You gotta catch the van."

The three scattered, gathering their bags and lunches while I stayed where I was. As if he knew that I wasn't pleased, Adam helped the children, and within minutes, there were hugs and good-bye kisses, and they were out the door.

Now alone, Adam had to face me.

He held up his hands, stopping me before I even began. "I know what you're thinking. I didn't want them to go to school worried."

"So, lying was better?"

"At least they don't have to sit in school all day and think about what they saw."

That made sense, but still.

Adam said, "It's not going to be an issue, because it's really not a lie. Mr. Yearwood said this last interview is a formality." He paused and took me into his arms. "Don't worry," he said.

I nodded as he kissed my forehead. "Well, I guess you'll have to take me to work," I said.

"Not a problem."

"Okay, let me shower and get dressed. I'll be ready in thirty."

He swatted my butt as I passed him. His kiss, his touch were meant to be reassuring. But the peace I'd felt since yesterday was gone. Maybe it was the lie he'd told. Maybe it was the stress of the repossession. Whatever it was, every good feeling I'd had had been replaced by one heck of a headache.

Chapter 19

THE SPREADSHEET THAT I'D TAKEN FROM Adam's desk this morning was laid out in front of me. He'd always shared the reality of our finances with me, just like he had with the children. And from the very beginning, that reality had filled me with fears.

"We're spending too much," I'd said when we'd moved straight from an apartment to a home that came with a four-thousand-dollar monthly mortgage.

"We deserve this," had been Adam's reply. "We work too hard."

My concerns had continued to be overlooked when we'd purchased top-of-the-line cars or clothes that could've been bought in discount outlets.

"We're not in that place anymore, Shine," Adam would say when I would tell him that we didn't always have to shop in the most expensive stores.

He'd been right. We weren't in Barry Farm anymore, and

neither one of us had wanted to backslide into the chasm of poverty where dinner was the same bowl of cereal as breakfast, where utilities were considered a luxury, and hopelessness and defeat hovered over the entire community.

But those memories of our shared history had had totally different effects on us.

Adam wanted to put space between his past and his present by acquiring all the things we'd never had so that he wouldn't remember.

My plan was to save, save, save because I could never forget.

But Adam was the one who worked hardest for the money. He was the head of our household, and I deferred to him.

Truthfully, there were many expenses that were difficult for me to challenge. When Adam decided that our children would attend the Ritz-Koster Academy, one of the most expensive schools in D.C., I didn't say a word. I didn't want to skimp on their schooling, and I also knew that any objection I had would go unheeded by Adam, whose top priority for our children was education.

Then when he announced that Ruby would have a room at Pearly Gates Estates, I certainly couldn't speak up. How could I complain about my mother-in-love having the best of care?

But our commitment to upward mobility had cost us bigtime. Even with our income, after the huge fixed expenses we were left with a bit over two thousand a month to take care of school loans, and car insurance, and utilities, and telephones, and cable and groceries and . . . and . . . and. Not to mention anything that the children needed—or, if they went to their father, anything the children wanted. In truth, it was amazing that we actually did have some savings, though that meager stash had only lasted three months after Adam's six-month severance had ended.

My heart and my head were pounding. "We cannot ever be

back in this place," I made a soft vow. "No matter what we had to do."

A knock interrupted my thoughts, but before I could tell Rachel to come in, the door opened and Shay-Shaunté peeked inside.

"Got a moment?" she asked.

"Sure," I said with a frown. Okay, so this was the third time in as many work days that Shay-Shaunté was in my office. Three times more than she'd been in here in the last three years. What was up with that? Why was she all up in my space?

She strolled toward me doing that one-long-leg-crossed-in-front-of-the-other strut and finally wiggled into the chair. "Sorry about yesterday," she said.

I didn't blink, I didn't nod, I didn't give her a thing. What did she want me to say, anyway? She'd known what she'd been doing; she'd set me up. But since I couldn't prove it, and since I wasn't going to play whatever game she was serving up, I just sat there and tried to make the silence so uncomfortable that she would change the subject or leave.

She said, "So, have you made a decision?"

My jaw fell. Audacity! That's all I could call it. Did she honestly think that because she'd sashayed into my office and ambushed Adam, something had changed?

I glared at her. "I told you already," I said, though my lips barely moved. "That's not going to happen."

She frowned and rubbed her forefinger against her chin. "But we agreed. I want to support Howard University with their internship program and you'd be the perfect person to mentor one of their students. Why're you changing your mind about this now?"

Dang! The internship program. That's what she was talking about. I said, "I'm sorry. Yes. The intern. Yes. You're talking about the intern."

She cocked her head a bit. "What did you think I was talking about?" The words oozed from her lips.

I ignored her question. "I got a couple of résumés right here." Thumbing through the pile of papers stacked high on my desk, I found the résumés and offered them to her.

She left me holding the papers as she stood. "That's okay. I want you to make the decision."

Then why did you come in here? I wanted to ask.

She took a couple of steps toward the door, then glanced back over her shoulder. "Are you sure you're okay, Evia? You seem a little . . . uptight."

"I'm fine," I said. "I'm more than fine. I'm better than I've been in a long, long time."

"Really."

I looked her up and down and gave her my own lopsided smile. "Really," I said. "Everything's cool. Better than cool."

She raised an unbelieving eyebrow, then said, "Great" in a tone that emphasized her doubt. Like a dancer, she twirled, grabbed the doorknob, and glided out. But before she was completely out of my sight, she added, "Just to let you know, if you need me, I'm here."

It was the way she said it and the way she looked at me that left a scowl on my face.

The only thing I wanted from Shay-Shaunté was out—of Ferossity! And thank God, that was gonna happen soon.

Chapter 20

THE WEEK BETWEEN THE CALL ADAM had received from Mr. Yearwood and the actual interview crawled by at a sickly snail's pace. It wasn't just our anxiety that slowed the passing of time. Our life was crumbling; every day brought new adversity, dragging us closer to the brink.

It had started, of course, on Tuesday, with the repossession of our SUV. But then on Wednesday, despair made another visit.

"Mom!" Alexa exclaimed the moment I came home from work. "Our cell phones are off!" She sobbed so deeply that I thought she was going to faint—yet again. "And so is the regular phone, and the cable. And even the Internet! How are we going to do our homework?"

I inhaled a long breath, then did my best not to release a deep sigh. We'd done one of those cable bundles that had been meant to save money. But it hadn't saved us enough to keep the services on.

"Mom!" Alexa cried again when I didn't answer right away. "What are we gonna do?"

I don't know, I cried back on the inside. On the outside, I played the strong mother role and told Alexa that all would be well.

My mini-me backed me up. "Mom's right, Lexa," Alana assured her sister softly. "Remember, Daddy got a new job." She looked at me before she added, "Right?"

I nodded, because I didn't want to lie aloud.

"Well, if Daddy has a job, why did this happen?"

"You know it takes a couple of days before he can be paid." Then I asked, "Your father's not home?" I was eager to pass these questions over to Adam, since this was his lie.

"No," the girls spoke in unison.

"Well, let's wait to talk to him," I said, knowing that he couldn't have gone far without a car. "He'll be home soon."

That wasn't good enough for Alexa. "I just don't know," a long breath, "how we're supposed to live!"

I couldn't hold it back anymore—that deep sigh eased on out of me. Yes, life had changed, but Alexa didn't know how good she still had it.

The privilege that Adam and I had worked so hard to give to Alexa, Alana, and Ethan was supposed to be an asset. We gave them the best we had to give so that they would return the favor—by doing the very best they could in school and in their lives.

But now those positives had shifted. Our daughters—especially Alexa—didn't know that most of what they had were privileges, not rights.

So how were they going to handle what was to come if Adam didn't get this job? Would they be able to handle living in a smaller home, or even an apartment? What about sharing a bedroom or having only one television in the entire house? Or a life without cell phones, and cable, and Internet services?

It wouldn't be as bad, but would they be able to even imagine the way I'd been raised?

"This is all too much," Alexa cried before she dashed up the stairs and into her amenity-packed bedroom.

It was over-the-top, unnecessary drama, but the fact was, Alexa's words were the truth. Because by Thursday, it *was* becoming too much.

With our cell phones turned off and our home phone not being reconnected until that afternoon, the call came into me at the office.

"Evia? This is Ms. Johnson, from Pearly Gates."

I started praying right then, already knowing the purpose of the call. But I needed to stall to get my thoughts together.

So with a level of drama that I'd learned from my daughter, I said, "Oh, my goodness! Is my mother-in-law all right?"

"Yes, yes," she rushed to assure me. "She's fine. I'm calling about a totally different matter."

As if I didn't know.

She said, "I'm calling about the check that you gave me on Sunday."

"Oh, that. Yes, we were supposed to give you more by the end of the week, right?" It was a move meant to buy time, but I didn't know what I needed more time for. I knew how this conversation was going to end no matter how much I tried to postpone the inevitable.

"The thing is, Evia, the check you gave me bounced."

I wanted to tell her that I hadn't given her a thing, but I wasn't about to throw Adam under like that. I waited for the gauntlet to come with her next words.

And it did.

"We're making plans to move your mother-in-law into a

double occupancy room, but if we don't have the full payment by the end of the month, she'll have to be moved to another facility altogether."

"Okay," was all I said.

My simple agreement seemed to baffle Ms. Johnson. "Oh . . . okay."

What did she expect? A fight? For what?

I assured her that she would have all the money, plus some, by the thirty-first, and then I hung up and wondered if things could get any worse.

While life was crumbling at home, life at work was steady, but so different. One of the advantages of my job was that from day one, Shay-Shaunté had let me work autonomously. There had often been weeks when I'd only seen Shay-Shaunté once or twice.

But in the last week, I'd seen Shay-Shaunté more than I'd seen her in my six years at Ferossity! Almost every morning, Shay-Shaunté came into my office (instead of calling me into hers) for a quick meeting to review the day's agenda. That part, though different, I could handle. It was the little extra meetings that began to creep me out.

Like when she showed up when I was in the bathroom— even though she had a private one in her office. Or the lunchroom—even though she always had her food delivered.

But the freakiest thing was the number of times I saw her in the elevator. Not that she took the steps, no. It was just that she never went to any of the other floors. Whenever she held a meeting, it was in her space. If she needed to see someone, she summoned them to her. So, why, all of a sudden, was she in the elevator every time I got on?

Then there were the times when I'd be in the hallway, turn around, and Shay-Shaunté would be behind me. Or in the copy room. Even the mail room.

She almost felt like . . . a stalker.

Scary!

But I pushed those thoughts away for two reasons. First, because what I was thinking was ridiculous. And second, even if it wasn't ridiculous, it would be over soon.

I just had to make it through this weekend, and then on Monday, Adam and I would be able to celebrate nothing but good news.

Chapter 21

THERE WAS NO NEED FOR US to hide out anymore—the jig was up. So on Saturday, our regular visiting day, we piled into the Kia and trekked ninety miles down the interstate to Pearly Gates Estates.

This trip was so different from the dozens we'd taken before. The weight of all that we carried—not only Adam and I, but the children as well—filled the air. It didn't help that Alexa, Alana, and Ethan were stuffed into a backseat that was less than half the space of the Escalade's. The twins' long legs were pushed so far back that their knees were almost in their laps. And poor Ethan was squeezed so tightly between his sisters that he had no room to play his games.

Life only got worse when we arrived at Pearly Gates and found Ruby's new room. I wasn't sure which broke my heart more—the look of utter failure in my husband's expression or what we faced with his mother.

In the facility where the single rooms were housed, where

Ruby had been living, the walls were pristine white, a perfect backdrop for the expensive art that had been bestowed by benefactors of the estate. With new furniture and live plants, Pearly Gates always felt like some kind of oasis rather than an extended-care home for the elderly.

But the serenity that was part of Pearly Gates did not extend to where they'd moved Ruby. This building felt more like an old dormitory, a building that might have been better suited for the staff. Maybe.

It seemed like these double rooms were smaller than the singles. The walls were gray, not from paint but from the dinge and the dirt. The furniture was aged, and where there had been laughter and cheer in the halls of the other building, silence reigned in this one.

When we entered Ruby's room, the first bed was occupied by a petite woman completely covered by a sheet. Although we couldn't see her, soft moans told us someone was there for sure.

A nurse was by the bedside, adjusting a machine so nonchalantly that I assumed that whoever was under the sheet was all right.

"Hello," Adam nodded to the attending nurse. "We're here to see Ruby Langston."

The young woman smiled at Adam's greeting, then directed us to pass to the other side, where Ruby's bed was jammed against the wall.

The children gasped as we stepped closer. Ruby's eyes were stretched wide, as if she was trying to see everything, or as if she was scared. She'd curled herself into a tight ball, her arms wrapped around her legs, her chin tucked into her neck.

"She's all right," the nurse rushed to tell us. "Her vitals are good and she's been sleeping through the night; she still takes naps during the day, which is good, too." Then her voice became deeper, softer, as if now, bad news was coming. "But she's been this way"—the nurse pointed to Ruby, who was now trembling—"for the last two days. Since she was moved in here on Thursday."

"She hates it here," Adam whispered.

I squeezed his hand before I asked the attendant, "Has she eaten anything?"

The nurse nodded slowly, sadly. "A little, but if we can't get her to eat more, the doctor will have to put her on an IV."

"I thought you said we weren't moving Grandma," Alana said as her eyes slowly scanned the room.

Adam was ready with an answer. "We thought she'd be better with company."

"Well," Alexa began, crossing her arms, "it doesn't look like she's better." She glared at the nurse as if this was her fault. "You need to move Grandma right on back to her own room," Alexa demanded.

The way the nurse tossed attitude right back at Alexa, I knew there was a teenager somewhere in her life. After she stared my daughter down, the nurse shook her head, then left us alone.

For long, long minutes, the five of us stood awkwardly around Ruby's bed, as if we were holding some type of vigil. There was no chatter, no sharing of the week's events. There was no dashing off to the cafeteria for ice cream sundaes and no private moments for me.

Today, our anxiety was palpable, and we bided our time. Before today, we hated to leave; today, we couldn't wait.

We didn't last a whole thirty minutes before we kissed Ruby good-bye with promises to be back next weekend, then we stuffed ourselves into the Kia for the silent ride home. There wasn't much that awaited us there, but it was better than watching Ruby, crammed into that room, trembling with fright.

By the time Adam turned the car onto our cul-de-sac, my thoughts were on leftovers, and anything else I could do to make the rest of Saturday night easier for my children.

But then any plans I had came to an end when I saw the rusty, battered black pickup truck parked in our driveway.

"Oh, no," the children moaned together. Then I realized they hadn't sung that chorus alone—Adam and I had groaned, too.

"Hey!" My mother was out of the truck and waving her hands wildly before Adam even turned off the ignition. She traipsed across the lawn, her stiletto boots digging up the dirt until she was standing right by our car.

"How're my grandbabies doing?" my mother asked as she hugged Alana, then Ethan, then Alexa.

By the time Adam and I crawled from the Kia, Cashmere's brood was doing what they did best—bouncing and jumping and running.

"What's up with the rental car?" Cashmere asked.

"Yeah," Apollo chimed in. "I wanna go for a ride in that big ole Escalade. That's what's up."

"Let's go into the house," I said, guiding my mother gently with my hand. I figured if she went first, Cashmere and her children would follow.

I peered over both shoulders, wondering if any neighbors saw us, hoping that none remembered the last time my family had visited; then, my nephews had bumped their bicycles across lawns, and busted a couple of front windows, but no one had called the police.

Behind closed doors, Cashmere's boys really set it off—running to the left, dashing to the right, zigzagging their way through the living room, all the while releasing piercing screams that could shatter glass.

My children stood, frozen in amazement. Sure, they'd seen

their cousins in action before, but I knew that each time they were as shocked as I was.

I glared at Cashmere, then Marilyn. Wasn't someone going to say something?

But my sister and mother did nothing—just acted like crazy was normal. I guessed in their world it was, but not in mine.

"Y'all hold it down now. And stop all of that running," I shouted.

Cashmere barked back at me, "Why you always got to be on my kids like that?" She sucked her teeth and rolled her eyes before she plopped onto the couch. She shrugged off her winter-white coat and left it right where it fell on the floor. "Dang, Evia. You always acting like my kids don't have any home training!" She yelled because that was the only way I was going to hear her above her home-trained children.

Finally, my nephews dashed up the stairs, and my children took off right behind them. Alexa, Alana, and Ethan had been through a few tough things this last week, but nothing was going to be as tough as keeping their cousins in check. I felt sorriest for Ethan. By the time those boys whirled through his room, there was no telling what would be left. I prayed that my son came out unharmed.

"So, Marilyn," I began when it was just the adults, "what brings you guys around?"

"What!" she said, "I can't come and see my grandbabies?"

"Of course," though inside I thought totally different words.

"Yes, ma'am! I came to see my grandbabies."

"Can I get you guys something to drink?" Adam asked after he hung up our coats. He eyed Cashmere's coat on the floor but didn't make any moves toward her. My mom still had hers on, like she didn't plan to stay long.

Cashmere grabbed the television remote. "Nah, 'cause you

ain't tryin' to give me what I need to drink right about now." She pressed buttons, trying to get the screen to change from its permanent state of black. "What's up with y'all's TV?"

"Nothing." I grabbed the remote from her and turned the TV off.

Cashmere stood and folded her arms across her chest, like we owed her an explanation. For the first time I really noticed my sister—and the two yards (okay, maybe it was ten yards) of spandex that she had wrapped around her body and fastened with safety pins. Really . . . huge . . . safety pins. And this fashion statement was completed by short ankle boots that left her legs bare—no stockings, no socks, totally bare—when it was twenty-five degrees outside. Dang, wasn't she cold?

I shook my head. I guessed hoochies carried their own heat.

"First y'all driving a rental, now your TV's out. Something's going on."

You think? My sister, the genius.

My mother held her cigarette away from her lips long enough to ask, "Is that why you haven't sent me my money?"

I glanced at Adam. It was time for him to take over before I said something they were going to regret.

Stepping up, Adam said, "We're handling some things right now. I had to change jobs—"

My mother held up her hand. "Wait, you don't have your big-time job no more?"

He shook his head.

The expression on my mother's face explained where Alexa inherited her drama gene. The look of horror that had been on my daughter's face was now on my mother's.

I guessed Adam could see my mother's heart attack coming, because he quickly added, "But I got another job."

Marilyn breathed. "Are they paying you the same money you were making?"

"Marilyn!" I jumped in. "That's none of your business."

"I'm just askin' 'cause I need my money."

I sighed.

"We'll send you something in a few weeks," Adam said.

I could see by the way my mother glanced at Cashmere that something was up. Of course this was the reason for their visit, but what did they need money for? Food? Naw, they had their food stamps. It wasn't anything the boys needed for school because Adam and I had taken care of uniforms and school supplies back in September. It was probably some garish outfit one of them wanted from one of those cheap shops around the way.

My mother grabbed Cashmere's coat from the floor and tossed it to her before she started tying the belt on her own. "Well, I guess I'll have to wait."

Adam frowned. "Is something going on, Marilyn?" he asked, always the family man.

"Well, Cashmere and I wanted to hang out a little tonight and we needed some money to pay for a babysitter." She paused and grinned at Cashmere, then me. "Unless—"

"No!" Cashmere and I said at the same time.

My sister added, "I'm not leaving my kids with her."

I smiled; I'd always known there was a God.

When my mother's plan didn't work, she asked Adam, "So when you getting your first check?"

I wanted to yell at her again, but then I thought, why waste a good scream?

"I'm not sure, but I always take care of you, right?"

She smiled at my husband like she loved him something lovely. "Yeah, you do." She paused. "But, look here. Can you break me off a little somethin'? 'Cause you know, you guys haven't sent me anything in a while and."

She stopped right there as if she didn't need to finish the sentence.

Adam actually reached into his jacket, pulled out his wallet, and pissed me off. What about the money we needed for our house, and for Ruby, and the fact that we had one car?

But there was nothing to say, because Adam believed in family—no matter how bad you really wanted to deny that you even knew them.

Adam handed a single bill to my mother. She studied the money, grunted, then shrugged as if she understood that was all she was gonna get.

To Cashmere, she said, "Get your brats and let's get going."

"Ain't nothin' but a word. No TV, nothing to eat or drink around here." She paused at the foot of the steps. "Apollo! Y'all come on down here! And don't make me wait 'cause I'll leave your behinds right here with Evia for two weeks."

I started to climb the stairs and get those boys myself, but the four came barreling down. I guessed the threat was as scary to them as it was to me.

The twins and Ethan followed, looking worn out.

My mother's good-byes weren't as warm as her greetings; now that she'd gotten at least a little of what she'd come for, there was no need to pretend anymore that she loved anyone in this house.

Even though the cold air rushed inside, we stood at the open door, all five of us, watching my mom, Cashmere, and my nephews scramble into their truck. We stayed until the rusted metal was out of the driveway, then out of sight.

With a collective sigh, we staggered into the living room. My mother, sister, and nephews had blown through and put an exclamation point on an already horrible week.

"Anybody hungry?" I asked, though I didn't make any kind of move toward the kitchen.

The no's, were as weak as I felt.

Alexa yawned and was the first to stir from where she

lay stretched out on the floor. "I'm going upstairs," she said. But then, as if a thought just hit her, she jumped up. "Mom! Daddy!" Her eyes were wide, her energy was back. "I know how we can get our cell phones back on. And even our cable and TV!" Alexa turned so that she could see her father and me at the same time. "Apollo said that all we have to do is call the telephone company and put the phone in my name or Lan's name."

"How are we supposed to do that?" Adam asked. "You don't have a job."

"Ah-ha!" Alexa exclaimed, pointing her finger in the air as if she was about to make an excellent point. "You don't *need* a job. All you need is an address—I got that. And a Social Security number—I got that. And good credit—I got that, too. Apollo said they don't ask your age or nothin'. Just like that," she snapped her fingers, "they'll give you a phone or anything else you want."

Ethan rolled over. "I have a Social Security number. Can I get something?"

"Well, first, I think we should all get new cell phones," Alexa said as if she was in charge. "I want that Droid—"

"Hey, hey, hey," Adam shouted. "Hold up!" He took a deep breath. "Apollo told you that you could do that?"

"Yes," the twins said together. Alexa was grinning like she thought her cousin's idea was brilliant. Alana wore a frown, as if she wasn't so sure.

Adam glanced at me with a look that said it was my fault that we were related to those people.

"Well," Adam said, "we're not—"

Alexa interrupted him. "It's okay to do it. Apollo said that Aunt Cashmere does it all the time."

"Yeah," Alana piped in. "He said that all of them have all kinds of things in their names."

Alexa picked up, "Apollo has the lights in his name and Rashaun has the cable in his name and Shuquan has the . . ."

I groaned and lowered my head. I'd been married to Adam for all these years and we'd been through so much together. We had no secrets, told no lies. He knew everything about me, and I knew all about him.

But right now, forget about crawling under a rock. I almost wanted to move to another country.

Adam told our children, "That's not the way we do things around here."

"What's wrong with what they're doing?" Alexa asked.

"Well, let me see . . . does Apollo have a job?"

"No, but . . ."

"Do you think the cable company and the telephone company and all the rest of those companies know that your cousins are kids when Cashmere calls up and does that?"

"No, but . . ."

"So, how can you say it's a good idea?"

"Because, Daddy, they *have* cell phones and they *have* cable. Whatever they're doing over there is better than what we're doing over here."

I couldn't imagine how much those words hit and hurt Adam, because they sure stung me.

Softly, he said, "Well, we're not going to do it that way. In our home, we do things decently and in order. Understand?"

Adam looked from Alexa to Alana and they both nodded. When he turned to Ethan, our son said, "What did I do?"

"Nothing. None of you did anything. I want to make sure you understand how we roll in the Langston home. We're clear and cool?"

"Yes," they sang together.

The mood was back to the way it'd been all week—tight and heavy. The children sulked toward the staircase before

Alexa turned around and asked, "Daddy, are we going to have everything turned back on soon?"

"Yes," he said, his voice full of surety and authority.

They nodded as if they believed him, but then glanced at each other as if they did not.

When the last bedroom door closed, Adam laughed. "Be glad I rescued you from those people, woman!" he kidded.

But I didn't laugh. Cashmere and my mom were turning my nephews into criminals before they even reached middle school. And now their antics had reached into our home.

"Oh, come on, Shine," Adam said, hugging me. "Don't take this so seriously." He hugged me.

It was hard not to be at least a little serious, and a little sad. Our children were already trying to find ways to provide what we couldn't give them, and it had only been a few days. What would happen if the days turned into weeks or months? What would happen if Adam didn't . . .

I shook my head and held my husband tighter. I refused to have those thoughts. Adam was going to get that job; all I had to do, like Bishop Cash always told us, was believe.

*C*hapter 22

JUST ONE MORE DAY. JUST ONE more day. Just one more day.

That was the mantra I sang as the praise and worship team belted out "The Center of My Joy." Not that I wasn't getting my own praise on, because that song was the truth—Jesus was the reason I was still standing, I was still smiling.

I had lots of joy; nothing but joy.

But still, all I could think about was that we had only one more day before Adam's final interview.

My mouth stretched wide in a yawn, and I pushed my hand against my lips, trying to stifle the sound. I was downright exhausted; I hadn't had more than two hours' sleep last night even though I'd gone to bed tired. But sleep hadn't come easy. I'd lain staring up at the ceiling, as if signs of our future had been hidden in the crevices of the stucco. I'd kept wondering what was going to happen to us.

It hadn't been until the break of dawn when I'd finally allowed the mantra—just one more day—to lull me to sleep.

But those two hours of sleep hadn't been enough; right now, I felt like laying my head on Adam's lap the way I used to do with Big Mama when I was little and got sleepy at Solid Rock AME.

"Let the church say Amen," Bishop Cash sang when the choir sat down. The congregation complied, but once was not enough, because Cash added, "Say Amen again." The church once more did as we were told.

"All right now."

Cash hadn't said more than ten words, and already he was patting the edges of his forehead with his handkerchief. Although the domed sanctuary was air-conditioned, I was sure that glass ceiling always heated Cash up a bit. The sun beamed through, shining bright, giving the Bishop the appearance of being the only one in the room who was in the light. Cash had planned it that way, no doubt.

The Bishop said, "Now that we've all paid our tithes and offerings"—he paused for the church to add more Amens—"let's get to what y'all paid for. Who in here wants to hear a good message?"

"I do," and chuckles rang through the sanctuary.

I wiggled my butt far back into the oversized pillows on the pew and wondered how I could close my eyes for just a couple of minutes without anyone seeing me. This was one of those times when I wished Cash would have us open our Bibles. Then I could put it on my lap and pretend that I was reading. But even without the prop, I tucked my neck and closed my eyes. I just needed a minute or two or four. Maybe fifteen—that would be enough.

"This morning, church," Bishop said, "as we get closer to the new year, I want to talk about expectations and the plans that God has for you in 2011."

Amens rang out.

"You see," Bishop continued, "it's time for us to leave all that negativity behind, right here in 2010."

My eyes were still closed, though there was no way I was going to get a nap in. Not with the way people around me were shouting, "Amen" and "Hallelujah!"

Cash said, "Here's the thing that many people just don't know, and this is my message for today. . . ."

Five chords rang out from the keyboard.

Then, silence.

Then, Bishop said, "God blesses the positive."

Then the congregation went wild, stomping their feet, raising their hands, shouting out praises.

My head was still bowed, and I moved my lips as if I was praying, as if I was giving my own praises to the Lord.

Cash waited until the parishioners settled down before he went straight into his message. "If you want something from God in your life, you have to be positive about it. And once you're positive, you can step to God. All you have to do is ask and you shall receive."

"Thank you, Jesus!"

"Just believe, Saints," Bishop said. "You need that new job . . . just believe."

My eyes sprang open.

Cash wiped his brow before he continued, "If you need money for that mortgage . . . just believe."

Was he talking about us? Had Brooklyn told him everything? I was going to kill her if she had, right after Adam killed me.

I inhaled and glanced at Adam. But my husband showed no signs of concern. Instead, he was on the edge of his seat, leaning forward, as if he was trying to get closer to the message. And nodding his head the whole time. I exhaled.

"If you need money for anything, I say all you have to do is believe. But here's the thing—God knows if your belief is real. God knows if you're just saying it or faking it."

"That's right!"

"But when He feels that real faith, that mustard-seed faith, that moving-mountain faith, He rewards that. Because that's the business that God's in—the faith-blessing business. And His desire for you is that you prosper. His desire is that if you want to get out of Barry Farm, you prosper. His desire is that if you want a better job, you prosper. His desire is that in everything that your heart has ever wanted, you prosper."

"Amen," the parishoners cried out.

And I mean they were crying for real. The women around me were sobbing like someone had died. Tears flowed from the men, too, and they dabbed their eyes with handkerchiefs.

"Prosperity," someone shouted.

"That's right!" Bishop Cash answered. "Prosperity. You can have that," the Bishop declared as he pounded the podium. "Just name it and claim it."

He had to wait for five minutes to say another word through the holy celebration that unfolded in front of him. "You can design what you want 2011 to look like—you can prophesize your own future," he shouted.

"Thank you, Jesus."

"Understand and remember . . . God blesses the positive. Ask and you shall receive, church!" He danced his little jig before he closed with, "Amen and Amen."

I had to be the only one in Holy Deliverance still sitting, so I rose, too. Just minutes before, I'd been exhausted, but now I was nowhere near tired. That's how it always was for me with Bishop Cash. He gave me hope, he ignited my faith, he had me believing!

Adam was going to get this job—all we needed was mustard-seed, moving-mountain faith. And I had that.

Next to me, Adam's eyes were closed and his hands were raised in praise. The sight of my husband worshipping like that gave me so much joy. I could see the peace on his face, and I could feel his faith.

His thoughts were the same as mine.

That job was his. Tomorrow. Just one more day.

That was when I closed my eyes and raised my hands in complete and total praise, too.

We heard the phone ringing the moment Adam eased the car into the garage. Once he turned off the Kia, Ethan jumped over Alexa, then out the door.

"Don't worry," I called behind my son once the phone stopped. "Whoever it is will call back."

"Yeah," Alexa said. "They should've known that we were in church anyway."

But that didn't deter Ethan, our self-appointed Langston family telephone answerer; he zipped into the house—gloves off, coat off, boots off—and in less than a minute, he was at the telephone, picking up, because like I predicted, the caller had phoned again.

"Yeah, she's here," he said. Then, "Mom!"

"Who is it?" I asked, kicking over my boots.

He shrugged. "I don't know. But his voice sounds funny. Like he's a boy and a girl."

The receiver was only inches from Ethan's mouth when he yelled that out. I wondered which one of our friends he'd insulted before I grabbed the phone from him.

"Hello, Evia."

"Shay-Shaunté?" All kinds of thoughts went through my mind, since my boss never called me at home.

"I'm sorry to disturb you."

"We're just getting home from church," I felt the need to say.

She coughed. "Well . . . I needed to know if you'd chosen the intern yet."

This was the reason she was calling me? Why couldn't this have waited until tomorrow?

"Yes, I was going to give you her résumé in the morning and then arrange an interview with you."

"Great!" she said, all enthused. "Like I said, you're in charge of this; so I don't even need to interview her."

"Then why are you calling me at home on a Sunday asking about this?" The words came out before I could think.

"I wanted to make sure that this was getting done."

I wondered if she heard how contradictory her words were. But Shay-Shaunté was a smart woman—she knew what she was doing, even if I couldn't figure her out.

Then when she said, "I hope things are getting better for you and Adam," I sensed this was the real reason for her call.

I waited, because if she said one more word to me about Adam and her five million dollars. . . .

She coughed. Then she coughed again. "I want you to know that I've been," another cough, "praying . . . for you and Adam."

A chill that felt like it came straight through the telephone surged through me. If anyone else had said those words, I would've thanked them. But inside, my heart twisted and I heard Big Mama's warning words: *You don't want everyone praying for you.*

All I said was, "Well . . ." and hoped that single word was enough to let Shay-Shaunté know that this conversation was over.

"Well . . . ," she answered back.

What did this witch want? After a couple more seconds of silence, I said, "I'll see you tomorrow."

"Definitely!"

I hung up without saying good-bye. Even though I was standing in the living room of my heated house, still wearing my full-length coat, I shuddered.

"Just one more day," I whispered. "All I have to do is believe. Just one more day." And with another shudder, I rejoined my family.

Chapter 23

It was five o'clock exactly when the phone on my desk rang.

"I'm close by. Can you meet me downstairs in ten?"

Before I replied, I replayed my husband's words in my head—his words, his tone, his cadence. There was nothing for me to read. So I just said, "Yes."

My hand shook as I lowered the phone back into the cradle. In my head, I turned over the ten words that Adam had spoken. But there was nothing to glean except that I should meet him in ten. I sighed; how could I possibly wait that long?

I watched every single second tick by on the clock and counted along with the moving hand: sixty seconds . . . one hundred seconds . . . four hundred and twenty seconds . . . five hundred and ninety-nine seconds!

I jumped up, grabbed my coat and purse, then glanced at my briefcase. I hadn't taken that home since my life had changed at work. If Adam had the news that I'd been praying for, that briefcase would never go home with me again.

I opened my door slowly, then peeked into the hall. There in front of me was the first sign that blessings were on their way—Rachel wasn't at her desk. I tiptoed through the vestibule, then dashed to the stairwell. This was quickly becoming my regular means of escape. The stairs were best if I totally wanted to avoid Shay-Shaunté.

On the first floor, I slowed my roll, safe now. Shay-Shaunté wouldn't be anywhere near the lobby for another couple of hours, since she never left the building before nine.

"Please, God, please, God, please, God," I whispered my prayer-mantra.

The moment I turned toward the triple-glass entry doors, I saw the Kia, parked illegally, in one of the handicapped spaces right in front. Even though the December chill had thawed a bit, it was still cold—too cold for Adam to be outside the car. But there he was—with a little bit of a gangsta lean—against the hood. Arms folded, lips set in a straight line, eyes shielded by his sunglasses. There was not a clue of what was coming.

"Please, God, please, God, please, God!"

I pushed the front door, and though I was still many feet away, I couldn't hold it in. "Did you get the job?"

Adam took off his glasses, and there was my first glimpse of a smile. "I think so."

His words made him grin, but they did nothing for me. "Think?" I needed more than that.

He nodded. "Mr. Yearwood and I met with the CEO, and afterwards when he walked me to the elevator, he welcomed me to the team."

"So, it's official?"

"Yeah, well, no. I mean, not completely official. Mr. Yearwood has to go back to see if the big boss agrees, but"—he slid his hands down the lapel collar of his overcoat—"you know how I do."

Adam had never been overconfident. Self-assured, yes, but always grounded in the truth. So, if he thought he had the job, he probably did. Right?

"I got the job, Shine," he said as if he heard me reasoning with myself. Lifting me off my feet, Adam swung me around.

"I'm so proud of you, baby," I said, grabbing hold of him.

Gently, he let my feet touch the ground, then he led me around to the passenger side of the car. "First thing tomorrow," he began, already planning, "I'm gonna start setting things straight. I'm gonna call the mortgage company and Pearly Gates and the kids' school and . . ." I was waiting for more words, but suddenly, Adam pushed me against the car and kissed me deeply. For a moment, I wondered if I really wanted to be making out in the parking lot of my place of employment.

But then, I thought, what place of employment? By next week, I was going to be nothing more than a memory to these people.

I wrapped my arms around my husband and returned his kiss. But the moment I opened my eyes, I stepped back, startled.

"What?" Adam asked, then followed my gaze.

"Oh, I'm sorry," Shay-Shaunté said as she batted her eyes. "I came out of the building . . . for something and the two of you . . . were just there." She smiled. "It was so sweet, so lovely."

Her words were innocent enough, but inside the tenor of her tone there was so much more. Like her comment was not the casual observation of a friend. Like Shay-Shaunté was suddenly everywhere—as if she was always watching, always waiting.

Like she was a stalker.

But like I thought before, that was ridiculous, right? And a boss couldn't be a stalker—not really, not truly.

Still, I grabbed the door handle and jumped into our car like I was being chased. Adam followed my lead and trotted to his side, never glancing up or back at Shay-Shaunté. He cranked up the engine, then sped away.

Through the side-view mirror, I could see Shay-Shaunté on the edge of the curb, still watching, still waiting.

Scary!

I didn't take my eyes off her until we were out of the lot. Then I turned to Adam and saw that his frown was as deep as mine.

"That was weird, wasn't it?" I asked.

He shook his head slowly and said nothing for many moments. Finally, "Let's just say I'm glad this job came through."

My heart beat like a war drum as I thought about what Adam meant by that.

But since Adam got the job, there was no need to go there. All I needed to do was be happy that the job had come through.

Chapter 24

THIS WAS WHAT PEACE FELT LIKE. I'd almost forgotten, and Adam and I chatted easily on our way home.

But the moment we turned into the driveway, the front door of our home swung open and the twins busted out.

"Mom!"

If it had been Alexa alone, I would've taken my time stepping out of the car, knowing that her emergency was nothing more than a hangnail or a button missing from a top. But with Alana right by her side, wearing the same expression of distress, I knew that something was wrong.

Adam stopped the car halfway up the driveway, not even pulling into the garage, and we both jumped out of the Kia.

Now the twins were yelling, "Dad," but that was all I could understand. They shouted at the same time, over each other, not even sounding like they were speaking English. Adam snatched the paper that Alexa was waving, and as he read, I tried to calm the twins down.

"Whatever it is, we'll take care of it," I assured them. "Let's go inside." Whatever this was, I wanted it handled behind closed doors.

"But, Mom!" Alexa planted herself in front of me. "You said everything was going to be all right." With arms flailing, she turned to Adam. "You said you had a job. And now they're taking away our house."

With a quick glance, Adam handed me the paper.

"I do have a job," he said, leading the twins back inside.

My steps were slow as I followed, scanning the fore-closure notice. Masking tape was still affixed to the top of the paper, which helped me piece together the puzzle—the girls had come home and found this notice taped to the door.

"It was embarrassing, Mom," Alana cried. "Chloe was with us because we were going to study. But then when she saw this, she got scared and went home."

"And she's going to tell *everyone* in school," Alexa sobbed, "that we don't have any more money."

"And she knows that we don't have our cell phones any-more either," Alana added to the story.

"This is completely humiliating!" It was Alexa's turn.

"Okay, calm down," Adam told them as we stepped inside.

There, Ethan waited at the foot of the staircase, with wide, scared eyes. "Are they coming to take our house like they took our car?" he asked in the softest voice.

"No!" Adam declared strongly. "I told you guys, we're fine now. This is going to be taken care of."

"But if we're all right, why did the bank put this up here?" Alexa asked. "For the whole world to see."

"Because I haven't had time to contact them and let them know that everything is fine."

A long look passed between our daughters—one that said

they'd never believe that their responsible and efficient father would not take care of something like this.

"Look, I don't want you guys to worry about anything," Adam said, lowering his voice in a way that was meant to be calming. "It's gonna take me a couple of days, maybe a few weeks to get everything back on track, but none of this is an issue anymore."

They were quiet, but not too many seconds passed. Then, "Daddy, do you *really* have a job?"

I would've expected this from Alexa, but it was Alana who'd put the question right out there.

Before Adam could answer her, the telephone rang, and he used that moment to step away. But Ethan ran ahead, as if answering the telephone was his chance to escape the confusion.

"Hello!" Then, "Okay." A pause. "Dad, it's for you."

"Who is it?" Adam and I asked together.

Ethan shrugged. "I think it's the same guy from yesterday."

From yesterday? Shay-Shaunté! She was calling again? This time, asking for Adam?

In two giant steps, I passed by my husband and snatched the phone from Ethan.

"What do you want?" I was ready for a fight.

"Uh . . . is this the Langston residence?"

I frowned. It really was a man's voice. "Yes."

"May I speak with Adam Langston? This is Browning Yearwood from American Express."

Oh, my God!

"Oh, Mr. Yearwood. Yes. Please. I'm sorry. Yes. Please. Please." When I finally stopped jabbering, I prayed that not having a coherent wife wasn't going to cost Adam this job.

My hand was shaking when I handed the phone to Adam and stepped away. "Please, God; please, God; please, God!" I whispered.

"Yes, Mr. Yearwood," Adam's voice came through my prayers. Silence, then, "Yes, yes, yes. Oh, thank you, sir. Thank you so much. No, I understand. I don't need any time. I'll be there first thing in the morning."

He hung up and threw a fist pump into the air. "I got the job, Shine. I got it, for real." His hug was so tight that I was sure he'd punctured my lung. But with the way I felt, that was okay . . . I had another one.

Adam got the job! This wasn't conjecture. This wasn't hope. This was real.

Finally.

"Daddy, I thought you said you already had a job." Alexa stood in front of us with suspicious eyes and crossed arms.

"I knew this job was coming—we were just waiting for the official word," Adam explained. "And that was the call."

"So, you really have a job now?" Alana asked.

"Yes." He nodded.

"And you really are going to take care of the bank?" Alexa asked.

"Yes," Adam replied, patient with the inquisition. "And the greatest sweet sixteen birthday party ever is about to go down in the Langston house!"

"That's what I'm talking about," Alexa said as she gave her sister high five. She grabbed the cordless phone, then dashed up the steps. They had a few calls to make, I guessed. Ethan followed his sisters, though I didn't think he had anyone he wanted to call.

"Hey," Adam yelled out after them. "Doesn't anyone want to celebrate?"

"We are," Alexa yelled down, right before her room's door slammed.

Adam's laugh startled me. Yes, it was loud. Yes, it was hearty. But my surprise came from the fact that *he'd laughed.*

A real laugh. When was the last time that had happened? His laughter filled our house with a joyfulness that had been missing. His laughter was the period on these last two years.

No, not a period—it was triple exclamation points. And tomorrow, I'd be able to put my own ending to my situation. Tomorrow I'd walk in *and* out of Ferossity for the very last time.

I reached for my husband and held him as tightly as I could.

Then I laughed, too.

Chapter 25

HOURS LATER, I WAS STILL LAUGHING. Well, laughing wasn't quite the word. For the last few hours I'd been moaning and groaning, basking in complete ecstasy.

This was our celebration.

Now, Adam and I lay side by side, skin to skin, sated with pleasure. We held hands in the quiet, engulfed in complete peace.

"In a way," Adam began, breaking through our tranquillity, "I think this made us better, Shine. We made it through the worst, now we can live in the best."

I smiled. Then I giggled. Then I laughed.

"What's so funny?"

"Nothing," I said, leaning over him. "I'm just happy."

He joined me in laughter because he understood.

Then gently, he pulled me to him. Our lips met—a soft, lingering kiss.

When we eased away, I rested my head on his chest and

he embraced me. He held me close; not even air could pass between us.

I sighed.

Silence returned long enough for my eyelids to begin to feel the weight of my exhaustion. Right before my eyes closed completely, Adam said, "We came so close."

His words, his tone, put a crack in my peace.

Adam continued, "Between our house, and Ma"—his voice quivered when he mentioned his mother—"and especially our children and even your family . . . I didn't want to let anyone down."

"I understand." I held him tighter. "You never have."

"I felt as if I had. I'm the man. I'm supposed to take care of my own."

"You always have."

I could feel him shake his head. "We were never supposed to be in this situation."

I wasn't going to repeat all that I'd been saying and everything that he already knew. This had to be the male ego talking. Pride. And other emotions that he had to let out so that he could let go.

"But I can tell you this, Shine; I wasn't going to let us go down. It was never going to come to us walking away from this house. I was never going to let Ma stay in that room . . . and the kids, especially the twins . . ." He shook his head. "I would have done anything."

Poof! Just like that the crack turned into a chasm—all of my peace was gone. I was completely awake now, and trouble was brewing slowly inside me.

He repeated, "I would have done anything," and I sat right up. It was dark; all I could see was the outline of his face. But I didn't need the light; I'd be able to read every little expression—even in the dark. "Adam?"

He didn't say a word at first. All he did was stare at me and I knew.

Then he told me the truth. "I thought a lot about it. I thought about the promise I'd made to you when we got married. And then I thought about our family today. And God help me, but I would've done it, Shine," he whispered. "I would have had to."

I eased away from the arms where I'd always felt safe . . . and loved . . . and adored.

He said, "It would've meant nothing to me except saving my family. As a man, I would've done what I had to do."

"That's the part that scares me." My voice trembled, and I was pissed at myself for showing how much his words hurt me. "You're a man . . ."

"Who would've done it only to save his family." I guess it was because I was so quiet that he felt the need to explain more. "We were on our last leg, Shine. For two years, I'd done everything that I could, interviewed for every job. What else would have been left for me to do? But," he exhaled a long breath, "thank God for American Express. Because now I have a job and I can keep my vows."

I rested my head back on his chest and let the quiet peace settle in. But I twisted, then I turned. No matter what, I couldn't find that place I'd been a few minutes before.

It was like that place of peace wasn't here anymore.

Chapter 26

THE SMELL OF FRYING BACON WOKE me up.

This had to be a dream. We'd let our housekeeper/cook go long ago, and there was no one left in this house besides me who ever did any kind of cooking. That meant if someone *was* cooking, then this wasn't a dream . . . it was a nightmare.

I glanced at the clock and shot straight up in bed. Eight ten? That was almost two hours later than I normally awakened. What had happened to the alarm? And why hadn't Adam gotten me up?

Grabbing my bathrobe, I dashed into the kitchen, where Alexa and Alana sat chattering, their plates still half-filled with food. Ethan was on the other side of the table, swirling his bacon in syrup that had dripped from his pancakes.

Bacon and pancakes?

This was a nightmare for real.

But on second look, the food appeared edible. My children

were still alive and even seemed to be enjoying the morning meal.

Adam, wrapped in his bathrobe, stood at the dishwasher, dumping plates and pans inside. "Morning, Shine!" he said like his getting up and cooking breakfast was a regular occurrence.

The kids looked up. "Morning, Mom," they chorused.

I kissed Adam before I did the same to our children. "The alarm didn't go off."

"I didn't turn it on last night."

"Why didn't you wake me?"

"I wanted you to sleep."

"I have to go to work."

"Well, about that . . ." He closed the dishwasher, then, with a tug of my hand, pulled me away from the children. "I was thinking that maybe you could take the day off," he whispered, "and we could celebrate."

I grinned. "We celebrated last night."

"And now we can celebrate all day, right after I get back from signing the contract at Amex. I'll only be gone for an hour or two."

"I really wanted to go in," I said, eager to put Shay-Shaunté and Ferossity behind me.

"Give her your notice tomorrow."

"I'm not giving notice, remember? I'm gonna quit and leave."

"So then, what's one more day?"

It was the way he kissed me that changed my mind. "I'll be here waiting when you get home."

He grinned. "That's what I'm talking about, woman!"

I gave him a peck on his lips, though I wanted much more. But we had all day now. Picking up the last strips of bacon, I joined the children at the table.

"Are you going to work today, Daddy?" Alexa asked. I had a feeling that after yesterday, our children would be asking that question for many days to come—just checking.

"Yup," Adam said. "I'm going to get dressed now!" He kissed the twins, then backed away from Ethan and bumped fists.

Ethan grinned, as if he was officially part of the grown-folks club now.

"I'll see you guys tonight!" Adam said. "Love you all to pieces!"

I spent the next minutes getting the children out of the kitchen, checking to make sure they had their books, enough money, everything they needed to make it a great day. When I returned to our bedroom thirty minutes later, Adam was dressed, decked out in his blue pinstriped.

Umph. Umph. Umph.

That was the thing about my man. He looked as good with his clothes on as he did with them off.

My eyes were locked on his buns of steel when I asked, "So, you're only gonna be gone an hour?"

"Or two." He glanced back at me through the mirror where he stood adjusting his tie. "But I'm gonna make it as quick as I can." Adam leaned over and planted a soft kiss on my lips. "You don't even need to get dressed." Another kiss. "I'll call when I'm on my way home." This time, his kiss lasted longer; I wanted to grab his tie and pull him down on top of me.

"I love you, Shine."

"I love you more."

"I love you best," he said before he walked out of the bedroom.

When I heard the two beeps of the alarm, then the door close, I stretched out on the bed. My plan was to rest my eyes for just a few minutes, since it was too early to call Brooklyn or Tamica and share this great news. But then, in what felt like a few seconds, I was awakened by the shrill ring of the telephone. I grabbed the receiver before checking the ID.

"Hello," I said through a voice filled with sleep.

"Ms. Langston? This is Ms. Talbott, from Ritz-Koster Academy."

Oh! I groaned into my pillow. Didn't take a genius to figure out what this call was about.

"How're you, Ms. Talbott?"

"Just fine," she said in a tone that was meant to dismiss the niceties. "I was calling about the notices we've sent to your home."

"Yes," I said, although I didn't know anything about that. But Adam did—I was sure.

"Well, we haven't heard from you." She paused like she wanted me to say something. I didn't, so she continued, "You are behind—"

Now it was time for me to talk. "Ms. Talbott, before you go further, we're handling this."

"You're behind several months—"

"Yes, but my husband just . . ." I stopped; no need to go into our business. I continued with, "We'll be bringing our accounts current . . . before the end of this week." I wasn't sure when Adam would actually receive his signing bonus, but whenever it was going to be, we could postdate a check and make my promise to her the truth.

"So by Friday we'll have your check?" she asked, sounding like she didn't believe me.

"By Monday," I said, just to be sure.

Her sigh told me that she didn't like how I'd changed my promise that quickly. But she settled for what I'd said and once again pressed upon me the importance of the school receiving that money.

"The next semester begins in a few weeks, and if it's better for Alexa, Alana, and Ethan to change schools now—"

"Ms. Talbott, you'll have your money. Thank you for calling." I didn't mean to be rude when I dismissed her by hanging up, but I wasn't going to listen to anything about my children transferring.

Thank God this was all coming to an end.

I glanced at the clock, and for the second time in a few hours, I shot up straight in bed. It was almost noon.

Adam had said he'd be gone for only an hour or two, but like I'd suspected, it was taking much longer. New hire paperwork always did, especially at his level. I probably had time to do one more thing to make this morning complete—before Adam came home.

Inside our bathroom, I turned on the stereo system, then sat on the edge of the Jacuzzi tub and turned the faucet to full blast, hot water only. The oversized basin filled slowly, but when the water reached the top's edge, I slipped out of my robe and waded in.

It was so hot that my skin screamed. But I eased down deep into the tub, letting the water rise until it hovered at my chin.

Leaning back, I closed my eyes. My thoughts were empty for a moment, but then the black space filled with memories of Shay-Shaunté and our first meeting.

Impressed was not a strong enough word to describe how I felt from the moment I walked into Shay-Shaunté office. She explained who she was and why I hadn't been able to find any information about her.

"I'm extremely private," she told me, just ten minutes into the interview. "And the person I hire would have to respect that."

I told her she'd have no problems from me. I'd stay out of her business—unless, of course, it had something to do with Ferossity.

She laughed at the way I said the name of the company. She kidded me a little, said that I sounded like a snake when I said it. She explained that the spelling was an homage to her own name—the two *S*s.

I didn't know what she wanted me to say to that, so I responded with an, "Oh," and she hired me on the spot.

"You're exactly who I've been looking for," she told me.

I asked, "How long have you been interviewing candidates?"

"You're the first."

She wanted me without seeing anyone else. That definitely made me feel good, but before I accepted, I had one more question for her.

"What happened to your last assistant?"

"No, really . . . I just told you . . . you're the first. The first assistant I've ever had."

Huh? She'd built a multimillion-dollar empire over the last twenty years and hadn't had an assistant?

That seemed so weird to me, but the money she was offering made me forget all about it—especially when she decided to give me a five-thousand-dollar bonus if I accepted the job right then.

From that day forward, Shay-Shaunté had me mingling with celebrities, arranging appointments with businessmen, politicians, and athletes. She led a whirlwind life and allowed me to come into her world.

It had been more than a pleasure to work for one of the best and brightest that black America—or America, for that matter—had to offer.

But it was time to go—for real. I'd find another gig. My job search would be different from Adam's. Everyone needed a great assistant, and with a recommendation from Shay-Shaunté, who would deny me?

My eyes popped open. Would Shay-Shaunté even give me a recommendation, though? Not if I quit without giving her notice.

Dang! I was gonna have to stay—at least for another two weeks. Well, I could do that—it was all about doing what you had to do.

Just as I settled back in the water, I heard the two beeps to the alarm—Adam was home! Eager to see him, I pushed my hands against the tub, ready to jump out, but in the next second, I eased back down. I'd wait for my husband right here.

Adam's footsteps were hidden in the deep pile of the carpet, but I counted the seconds, knowing just how much time it would take for him to enter the house, take off his shoes, walk through the mudroom then into the hall, drop off his keys by the front door, then come into our bedroom.

By my count, he was just ten seconds away.

One, two, three, four.

I was eager to hear the details. What would he be doing specifically? Would he be reporting directly to Mr. Yearwood?

Five, six, seven, eight.

When would he get his signing bonus?

Nine.

I couldn't wait to see him.

Ten!

I opened my eyes, and Adam was there.

But the joy on my face didn't match the pain I saw on his. Barely an instant passed, and I knew. I didn't know the details, but I knew enough.

My eyes stayed on him as he took slow steps toward me. I trembled when he sat on the edge of the tub, the moisture on the porcelain seeping through the Italian wool of his suit. He didn't speak a word before he leaned over and kissed me. My face was already moist from tears.

He tried to kiss away the emotional water that trickled from my eyes, but then, my cries began coming too fast.

What happened? I sobbed inside.

But I didn't ask that question aloud. I just held him, with water-soaked hands, and I pulled him closer.

It was as if my sobs released our urgency, and his kisses were no longer gentle. His lips pressed hard against mine—there would be bruises for both of us, I was sure. And when our tongues met, one tried to swallow the other.

Without releasing me, Adam pushed me against the back of the tub, then slowly, he lowered himself into the water—right leg first, then his left. I took myself away, for just a moment . . . wondered if Adam had even taken off his shoes. But really, what did that matter? All I knew was that I wanted more of him, wanted all of him.

The water sloshed around us, cascading over the side—a musical milieu to our moans. I yanked his silk tie to pull him closer. Then, when he was as close as he could get, I tore his tie away. Next, his jacket.

His clothes were heavy from the weight of the water, but I tugged and pulled—jacket, shirt, pants—working to free him.

All the while, he stroked my body—his fingers first on my shoulders, then dancing to my chest, where they lingered on the most sensitive parts of me. Then his fingers crawled down, down, down, settling in the land that made me a woman. I wrapped my legs around him, wanting to get from him as much as I could take.

When he was finally as naked as I was, we wasted no time. He shifted his legs, lifted mine to meet him. And under the chill of the water, we became one. Our heat, my bliss was instant, but my groans came from the deepest parts of my hurt. We rode together, in rhythm with the water, thrusting harder, faster. It was a race—we had to keep our pleasure ahead of our pain.

I needed to feel every inch of my husband, the length of his fingers, the strength of his chest, the shape of his legs. I needed to reach deep inside of him, and I wanted to give him every bit of me.

I have no idea how long we lasted; it could have been minutes, hours, days. All I know is that I finally reached the top.

But afterward, when our heartbeats returned to some semblance of normal, it was clear that making love had not been enough. Because I was still here—in our home. In our bedroom. With my husband.

Who didn't get the job.

That was when the pain surged ahead and won the race. There was no pleasure at all. We sat in the almost icy water, holding each other. I leaned my head into Adam's chest and I cried until there were no more tears inside of me.

Chapter 27

THE SUN SHINED THROUGH OUR BEDROOM windows, rising slowly, marking the passage of time and filling the master suite with its winter heat. Still, I shivered. Even though we lay beneath the down comforter, I couldn't stop trembling.

We lay side to side, facing each other, saying nothing.

Then the sun inched a bit higher, and soon the children would be home. That was the only reason why I asked.

"What happened?"

Adam's eyes closed slowly, then opened. He did that again, as if he had to blink to remember something he wanted to forget. He said, "I've never seen anything like this. I was in the HR office filling out forms, and while I was there, the order came down. For a freeze. An immediate hiring freeze."

"Weren't you already hired?"

"I thought so. But when Mr. Yearwood explained it, he said that my paperwork hadn't been completed and not even the most imperative positions were being filled." He shook his head. "Shine, I couldn't even leave. I sat outside that building, hoping, praying that the job would come back just as fast as it had been taken away. But . . ."

My eyes stayed on Adam's, and his were fixed on mine. Not another word was spoken, but still I knew that we were thinking on the same things: our families and our home. Without the job with American Express, what would be next?

I told him, "The children's school called this morning."

That was enough—Adam knew the conversation.

Time passed and I waited for Adam to speak the words that had to come. The words that he'd spoken last night.

But then I realized that he didn't want to be the first to say it.

So I would do it.

As I opened my mouth, that spiritual alarm inside me blasted away. But I ignored it and spoke above the sound in my heart. I had to, for the sake of my family.

"I think we can do it." I took a breath and inhaled more courage to say the next words. "It'll be hard, but we have to do it."

A long moment passed, but finally Adam nodded and my heart broke.

He reached for me and his hand fell against my chest. His palm pressed against the place where my heart had stopped. "A long time ago, I made that promise to only be with you, but the greater vow is taking care of you and my children."

I swallowed my fear and my pain. I nodded.

"I'm doing this for us."

"I know."

It won't mean a thing to me, Shine."

"I know," I cried.

"But before we agree . . . there's only one way that I'll do this." He paused as if considering carefully his next words. "I never want to talk about it. Not one word, Shine." He said it as if that was a warning. "I don't ever want to have a discussion about . . . it."

I would never object to that. "No discussion. I would never want to talk about it anyway."

"Are you sure?"

"Yes."

He pushed, "That has to be the deal, because whatever happens . . . during that time . . . I don't want to bring it into our home. I don't ever want it to be close to you or a part of who we are."

In the middle of all this sorrow, I wasn't sure why those words pleased me. "I wouldn't want it any other way."

A moment of silence, then, "For the sake of our family." He said aloud what I'd been saying inside.

"For the sake of our family." My repetition of those words were the seal on this deal. It was our Amen.

His fingertips traced the lines of my face. "I love you, Shine."

"I love you more," I sobbed.

"I love you best." And then he tried to kiss my pain away.

Chapter 28

I BECAME A ROBOT.

That was the only way I would survive getting out of the bed to meet the children as they came home.

Ethan arrived first, dashing through the door, dumping his coat and shoes in the mudroom, then racing up the staircase.

"Hi, Mom! Bye, Mom!" he said as if it was all one syllable. He huffed, "I gotta check something on the computer that Dougie just told me about on the van."

About midway up, though, he slowed down, then paused, then turned around. He looked down at me and said, "Oh, I forgot. We don't have enough money to have Internet." That memory and realization made him sulk to his room.

"This is why," I whispered. "This is why we're doing it."

I was still talking to myself when Adam came out of our bedroom.

At the foot of the stairs, he asked me, "Was that Ethan?"

"Yes." I turned away from him.

Next came the twins, strolling in. But their eyes were filled with suspicion when they walked into the kitchen and saw both Adam and me.

"Did you go to work today, Mom?" Alana asked me as she dumped her messenger bag onto the floor.

"What happened to hello?" I asked.

"Hi. Did you go to work today?" my mini-me asked again.

"No," I said, pulling a package of chicken wings from the freezer.

"Are you sick?"

I wanted to tell her that I wasn't before but that I was beyond sick now. "No. I just hadn't had a vacation day in a while."

Her look was fifty-fifty. Like half of her believed me and half of her didn't.

Alexa's voice was tight when the inquisition was turned over to her. "Did you, Daddy? Go to work?"

"Yes," he said, shifting his glance toward me.

Our eyes met, but I couldn't keep looking at him—three seconds, tops.

That was the story of our night. I moved through the hours doing what was expected—feeding the children, helping with homework, getting all ready for bed. Then I took to my own bed, because I was nauseous from all the hours that my heart had cried.

Although it was early, not quite ten, Adam joined me, in our bedroom, in our bed. But when he reached for me, I did something that I'd never done; I cringed. And eased to the edge of my side of the bed.

"Shine, do you want to talk about this some more?"

"What else is there to say?"

"We don't have to do this if you don't want to."

"Don't put this all on me, Adam." My voice was sharper

than I wanted it to be. But then I wondered why. Hadn't we made this decision together?

But Adam must've understood, because his voice stayed soft. "I'm just saying, if you don't think you'll be able to handle it . . ."

"I'll handle it," I whispered, my eyes wet with tears. "It's just that now . . . I need . . . just tonight."

"Shine . . ."

"I'll be okay tomorrow. I just need tonight to . . . get used to this."

A beat, then a soft, "Okay." He rolled to his side of the king-size bed, miles away from me.

I wanted to hold him. I needed him to hold me. But I stayed right where I was—on the edge.

I wept silently through the night. But still, I rose at six fifteen and did what I had to do as a mother, as a wife, like a robot.

By the time I got the children off to school and I was dressed for work, my head was on the verge of exploding.

"Do you want me to go with you?" Adam asked.

"To work?"

"To talk to Shay-Shaunté."

"No!" I exclaimed. "I can handle this."

"I really want to be there with you. I don't want either one of us to do any of this alone."

He would be doing his part without me. So this part I wanted to do by myself. "I'll be fine."

He squinted, and I knew he wasn't sure, but I had no doubts. I could handle Shay-Shaunté, trust that. Plus I didn't want Adam anywhere near her. Didn't want her to have the pleasure of his company for any longer than we agreed.

A weekend.

A weekend!

A weekend?

Could I really give my husband up for that much time to another woman? A weekend. Three days. Seventy. Two. Hours.

Adam embraced me, and it was all that I could do to hold back my sobs. "We're going to get through this. Together," he promised.

I nodded.

I dashed to the car, and when I put the key in the ignition, Adam was at the door, watching me. Grief was etched on his face; he looked like a man sending his wife off to war.

I reversed the car and never glanced back. Never said good-bye to my husband.

Like everything I'd done in the past hours, I drove to work like I was some kind of mechanical woman. My eyes were straight ahead, my mind was blank except for this one thought: I was about to make that deal with Shay-Shaunté. That's all I could think about. It was as if my brain wasn't big enough to handle anything else.

When I finally turned into the Ferossity lot, I drove the car right to the front of the building. Embarrassment had kept me from doing that for weeks—the shame of having to explain how we'd returned my Lexus or how the Escalade had been repossessed. But what was there to be embarrassed about now? Nothing would ever match the humiliation of what I was about to do.

I had to take slow steps to the elevator; my heart knocked against my chest as if it was trying to escape. But by the time I got to the twelfth floor, I couldn't feel my heart at all.

Inside my office, I was convinced the muscle that was supposed to keep me alive had given up. Now, I had to fight for every breath.

But I wasn't going to let my body trick me out of doing what I had to do. With or without a heart, I was going in there.

For the greater good.

For the sake of my family.

As if this was just an ordinary day, I hung up my coat, tucked my purse into my desk, checked myself in the mirror, and straightened the jacket of my pantsuit.

Then I headed to Shay-Shaunté's office.

Chapter 29

A QUICK KNOCK AND THEN I peeked inside.

"Got a minute?" I asked Shay-Shaunté as if I didn't hate her.

Not that I hated her. Not really. We'd been cool—till two weeks ago.

Shay-Shaunté's lips spread into a smile that could only be described as sly. She leaned into that huge-back scaly chair of hers and beckoned me in. "I have all the time in the world for you," she said.

I closed the door behind me and wished now that Adam was with me. Or maybe not Adam. Maybe Brooklyn. Or even Alexa. Yeah, Alexa! Because my daughter did not play and she would've ripped Shay-Shaunté knowing what this woman was about to do to our family.

But since I didn't share my daughter's teenage naïveté, and Adam and I had to live in reality, I was here alone.

"Sit down," Shay-Shaunté said.

I sat and inhaled a deep breath. Then took another one, deeper this time, to get a double dosage of bravado. "We're going to do it."

"Good," she said simply, though through her smug tone, I heard more. Something like: I knew you would.

"This is strictly business," I said, laying down the beginning of my rules. This was her deal, but it was gonna go down my way.

She shrugged. "Of course. I already told you that." Her face was blank, without emotion at first. But then her lips slipped into that lopsided smirk and she added, "Just business . . . what else would it be?"

If there was any way that I could've slapped her and still gotten the five million dollars, I would've done it. But like I'd just told her, this was business—no room for my hurt feelings.

"And . . . ," I said, suddenly thinking of something, "we want a contract." I wasn't really sure why I said that. Really had no idea what having a contract would do. But at least she understood my mind-set—business. Asking for the contract made me feel like I was in control of something.

"A contract?" she said, seemingly surprised. "Is this Adam's idea?"

Now, why did she have to bring Adam into this? I mean, yeah, he was part of it—the major part—but not until I said so. Plus, I did not like the way she said my husband's name. Like she knew him, really *knew* him, biblically knew him— already.

"No, the contract is my idea."

Her eyes sparkled. "Impressive," she said as if she never thought I would've come up with such a thing. "What would you like to have in the contract?"

I hadn't thought about that. I mean, it was just an idea I had a minute ago. But I wasn't going to let her know. So, I began with the basics. "You're going to pay us five million, and . . ." I couldn't think of anything else.

I must've done all right, because Shay-Shaunté still smiled. And really, the only thing that was important was the money—right?

Now I was the one who leaned back in my chair. Until Shay-Shaunté reached into her desk and placed two legal-size pages in front of me: Legal Agreement between Shay-Shaunté and Adam and Evia Langston.

Huh?

I glanced through the two pages quickly, not taking in much, just shocked that she already had a contract. Was this a case of great minds thinking alike, or was Shay-Shaunté some kind of . . . what? Psychic? Was she clairvoyant?

I scanned the agreement, slower now. Everything was here in writing—that Adam would be with her from 9:00 p.m. on Friday, December 31 until 9:00 p.m. Sunday, January 2.

Well, at least this first part was good—if there was anything good about this deal. She wouldn't have him for seventy-two hours; it would only be for forty-eight.

I could do that, right?

Then there was some legalese about Adam's services—that the sole purpose of the weekend would be for Adam to escort her to various social events over the weekend.

That made me look up. Was that all Shay-Shaunté wanted?

As if she knew the part that I was reading, she said, "That is to protect all of us. We want this to be a legal contract. Can't have it looking like prostitution, can we?"

I had to work hard to keep my groan inside. Looking down again, I finally got to the reason for all of this—that we would be paid five million dollars. Legalese followed those words: about breach of contract, and other things that I didn't quite understand.

On the second page, my eyes stretched so wide, that they hurt. "What is this?" I asked her.

I turned the paper around and pointed, but Shay-Shaunté didn't even look down.

"Evia, you're a valued employee."

"And?"

"Maybe I should've said that you're invaluable and it's going to be hard to replace you."

"Not in this economy."

"Specifically, it's going to be hard to replace your skill set."

"I don't think so. You'll probably be able to find someone much better than me," I said, still trying to argue her down. I had to get her to take this part out.

"Even so," she said, shaking her head. "You have to stay with me, with Ferossity, for six months after the deal is done. I can't afford to have your position empty and—"

"What about Rachel?" I interrupted. "She's been here almost as long as I have, and not only can she take my place, she can train anyone who—"

She held up her hand. "This contract is the contract," she said in a tone that I'd heard many times in meetings with men who were bigger and smarter than me. "Without your agreement to any part, it becomes null and void."

I could not believe this! After she spent a weekend with my husband, I was supposed to spend six months with her? How was I supposed to look at her every day after that?

No! Definitely not! I couldn't do it.

But without that agreement, there would be no deal. And without a deal, there would be no five million dollars. And without five million dollars, we would have no house, our children, no school, Ruby, no safe haven . . .

"Will I still be paid for my work *if* I stay?"

"*When* you stay—yes."

So, that took the deal to a little more than five million. As if that made this any better.

"I need to look this over with Adam," I said.

"Of course you do. He's your husband. You should share everything, and he has to sign the contract as well."

I stood, needing to get away. These ten minutes had already been more than I could take. "We'll talk about it tonight and let you know tomorrow."

She leaned back in her chair, folded her hands across her lap. "That's fine, no rush," she said. "My birthday is still almost two weeks away."

I was halfway to my escape when she called out to me.

"I know this is difficult," Shay-Shaunté said. She sat regally, in that huge-back chair, as if she was the queen of something. "Why don't you take the rest of the day off?"

What happened to me being so invaluable?

But I wasn't about to look a gift-snake in the mouth. I marched to my office, grabbed my coat and bag, and dashed to the staircase. I didn't want to chance running into Rachel coming into the office.

I'd make my getaway and take myself right on home.

Chapter 30

FOR THE FIRST TIME IN A really long time, I started to pray. Not that I didn't believe in prayer—Big Mama taught me that oftentimes a conversation with God was all that you needed. And in the beginning of our marriage, that's what Adam and I used to do. Before we ate a morsel of food, we prayed. Before anyone shut their eyes at night, we prayed. Before anyone left the house, we prayed. We prayed for grace and traveling mercies. We prayed for God's best. We prayed just to send up praises.

But then we had those sermons from Cash. Not that he didn't believe in prayer. It was just that he taught us that the way to prosperity was beyond prayer. You couldn't just keep asking God for what you wanted—you had to change you. It was about *your* true thoughts and *your* true desire to succeed. So Adam and I focused more on our positive affirmations than on prayer. And it worked.

Right now, though, this thing with Shay-Shaunté seemed more like a prayer moment. That's why I kept asking, "God, should we do this?" all the way home.

But that alarm that blasted yesterday was silent now. Could silence be God's answer?

Now I was more confused than before.

When I left home this morning, the decision was made. But now . . . after that meeting . . . after that contract . . . with Adam spending forty-eight hours with her and me spending six months . . . could we do this?

I couldn't imagine what the six months would be like. Seeing her during the day. Wondering what she'd done with my husband. Being with Adam, at night. Wondering what he'd done to Shay-Shaunté. The images, the torture would be relentless.

Slowly, I curved the car into our driveway, but I didn't make a move. What I wanted to do was march into our home, tell my husband how the meeting had gone down, and then have him stand up and say, "That's enough! That's it! We'll find some other way!"

But that wasn't going to happen. Adam had already turned everything over in his mind. He had studied this, dissected this, pondered this, and solved this. He couldn't tell me that we'd find some other way because there was none.

"God, what should we do?"

I tried to snuggle into the seat the way I used to in my other car. But the cloth in the Kia didn't give the way the leather in the Lexus did. Still, I closed my eyes and searched for some semblance of peace: There had to be serenity inside five million dollars.

This really was a no-brainer.

"So, is that what you're telling me, Lord?"

I tried to imagine our lives on the other side. Without the five million dollars, we were on the verge of total collapse. That couldn't be what God wanted for us.

But if we really took this deal, then Adam would lay with another woman—no matter our vows—for forty-eight hours. All that time, he'd be with a gorgeous woman. Who looked better than me. Who was smarter than me. Who had more money now than I would have in ten lifetimes.

None of that would matter, though. Not to Adam. Not to the man who loved, honored, and cherished me.

But.

When I closed my eyes, I could see him with Shay-Shaunté. Lying with her, enjoying her, wanting more of her. I could see them making love for forty-eight hours straight—Adam never wanting to stop because he'd never been with a woman like her.

I groaned.

"Shine! Shine!"

I blinked my eyes open and saw Adam standing at the door. I sat there, watching him as he waved for me to come in.

"Shine," he called again. "What are you doing out there?"

It wasn't until he began walking toward me that I moved. I pressed the brake, started the engine, then shot off before Adam could get near the car.

"Shine!" he called after me.

But I didn't look back.

I had no idea where I was going, but I knew where I couldn't be—and that was anywhere near Adam. At least not right now. Not until I could get rid of the images. Of him and Shay-Shaunté. For forty-eight hours.

Chapter 31

"So, you're really going to do it?" Brooklyn whispered, even though there was little chance of anyone overhearing us above the din in the Martini Bar. "Wow!" It might've been a Wednesday evening, ten days before Christmas, but the intimate and popular club was packed with professional men and women. These were D.C.'s best by day, but at night the journalists, the lobbyists, the political assistants stripped away their work ethics and turned into pickup artists—men who were looking for a good-time, onetime hookup. And women who wanted so much more.

Brooklyn, Tamica, and I fit in pretty well with the thirty-something crowd, except for the wedding bands that graced Brooklyn's and my fingers.

I wasn't big on drinking. It wasn't a Christian thing for me; I just didn't like the way alcohol tasted. It was the ambience that turned me on here. I was intrigued by this crowd of folks, meeting and greeting, navigating through a social world I'd never been part of. Not that I wanted to—I wouldn't trade my life with Adam for anything, especially since most here were striving to get to where Adam and I were.

So, this is where I ended up after I left home. At first I had some hors d'oeuvres and too many iced teas. But the more I sat, the more I thought. It was all of that thinking that made me decide, today and in this place, I'd have my first martini—a peppermint one to start.

After I ordered my second drink, I called Brooklyn, because I knew she'd eat and drink with me and I'd be able to keep this table. She called Tamica and they joined me for Happy Hour—though there wasn't much to be happy about, since I told my friends my whole story.

"Wow!" Brooklyn said again. "I just cannot believe you're going to do it."

Tamica and I both stared at Brooklyn with wide eyes.

"You're the one who told her to do it," Tamica snapped, saying to Brooklyn exactly what I was thinking.

"Yeah," I took another sip of my drink. "You said you'd do it all day long."

"There's a difference between theory and reality. And anyway, you said you'd *never* do it."

Another sip before I said, "There's a difference between theory and reality." I giggled; it was so funny that her words were appropriate for both of us even though they had opposite meanings. I glanced down into my glass and turned somber. "Our reality is pretty tough right now."

"I kinda figured that things were getting bad," Tamica said, "when you stopped calling."

"She couldn't call 'cause her cell was off." Brooklyn sipped her chocolate martini.

Tamica shook her head. "I wish there was something I

could do." She lifted her hand, motioned to the waiter, and ordered her second peach martini.

"I know something you could do." I licked the edge of my empty glass. "Order me another one of these."

Both Tamica and Brooklyn frowned.

"How many of those have you had?" Tamica asked.

I shrugged. "Not too many. Maybe two . . . or five."

She shook her head. "Just bring her some water," she told the waiter.

It was my turn to frown. "What's up with that?"

"You don't even drink," Tamica said.

"Yeah, well, Adam doesn't sleep with other women."

Brooklyn and Tamica exchanged a glance, then their faces drooped, their sorrow for me even more apparent.

"So you're really gonna give your husband away for a weekend with that woman?" Tamica asked.

Hearing the words from someone else's lips made me cringe. "Sixty percent sure. Naw, why am I lying? I'm ninety-nine percent sure. I mean, I still have to go over the contract with Adam tonight."

"Dang, y'all getting down like that?" Brooklyn said, sounding a little impressed. "A contract?"

"Yeah, it was my idea." I left out the part about it being Shay-Shaunté's idea, too.

"Wow!" my girls said together.

Brooklyn reached over and placed her hand over mine. "You know what? If I was in your place, I would do it, too."

"Would you make up your mind?" Tamica demanded. "I thought you just said you wouldn't."

Brooklyn shook her head. "I didn't say that. I was just surprised that you"—she turned back to me—"were going through with it, and I said it's a different thing when you're talking about the real deal rather than just making jokes.

"But jokes aside and the truth . . . in your situation . . . with your problems . . . if this deal had come to me and Cash . . . I'd do it." Then she waved her hand at the waiter and ordered *her* second martini—as if she needed another drink after what she'd just confessed.

Tamica shook her head. "You are so wrong, you know that, right?" she said to Brooklyn.

"What? I'm telling her the truth. You tell her your truth and I'll tell her mine."

"You're her first lady and this is the advice you're giving her?"

"Please, I'm her friend first. I was giving her the truth as her friend, not as the pastor's wife."

"The only truth she needs to hear," Tamica said as if I wasn't sitting right there, "is the truth of God's word."

"Oh, lawd!" Brooklyn poked out her lips, and I felt another fight coming on.

But before she could say anything, I piped in with, "I have been praying."

"About this?" Brooklyn and Tamica asked together.

I nodded. "I know God doesn't want us to be financially ruined."

"No, but He doesn't want you doing this either!" Tamica said.

I shrugged. "I don't know that. He hasn't told me not to do it."

"Oh, lawd!" This time, that came from Tamica. "You're waiting for God to tell you not to do this?"

"Yeah." I frowned.

Tamica shook her head. "You know, when we were growing up, I thought you were so grounded in God. Especially because of your grandmother. But I guess you don't really know God at all."

"Dang, Tamica." Brooklyn sucked her teeth. "Why you gotta come at her like that? After what she's going through?" She added, "That's why you don't have a man, 'cause you ain't got no compassion."

I was kinda feeling the same way as Brooklyn. I always hated when I heard someone judge another person's relationship with God. As if God had given them permission to do that.

"My relationship with God is just fine," I said. "You act like you're on some higher level or something just because you don't have problems."

She shook her head strongly. "That's not what I'm saying. But I am gonna call you out because that's what—as your sister in Christ—I'm supposed to do." She rolled her eyes at Brooklyn. "I'm gonna call you out and tell you that praying and asking God whether you should do this or not is a major fail."

I frowned.

Tamica was on a roll. "Come on, now. That's like asking God if you should sleep with that guy over there." She pointed to a blue-suited MBA-looking dude standing at the bar. "Or asking God if you should rob a bank or cheat on your taxes." She shook her head. "God's not gonna answer that mess. You already know the answer."

"So tell me what I'm supposed to do?" I asked, really pissed at how Tamica was coming at me. "We're in a bad, bad place."

She leaned forward, then spoke to me as if I was a child. "Those are just circumstances."

"Just circumstances? Well then, because of my 'just circumstances,'" I began with total attitude, "can my husband, our three children, and I move in with you? And oh, by the way, his mother is coming, too, because we don't have any money to continue her care. And then, can you take off from flying for a few years to homeschool my children? And oh, by the way, my ghetto family just might drop by sometimes . . ."

She held up her hand, knowing that if she didn't stop me, I was gonna go on and on. "I don't care how mad you get at me," she said. "I'm just sayin' don't play with God."

I motioned for the waiter, asked for the check. He handed it to me and I passed it to Tamica. "Since you're going to be handling my 'just circumstances,' you can start by paying my bill."

Brooklyn cracked up as Tamica's mouth flew wide open. But she didn't get a chance to say a doggone thing, because I grabbed my coat and walked away before either of my friends could say a word.

I pressed through the thick crowd, but outside, the cold air was like a knockout punch and I sobered up quick. Well, not totally—because as I made my way over the uneven sidewalk, I staggered a bit.

Dang! There was no way I could drive—not that I was all that drunk, but I wasn't about to get behind a wheel to find out how drunk I was. And since we only had one car, I couldn't just take a cab and have Adam come back tomorrow.

I slipped into my car and lowered my head onto the steering wheel. I just wanted to cry.

"God, how am I supposed to get home now?"

I heard a knock on my window, and for a moment, I wondered if it was God. But then, in the window, I saw Tamica's judgmental face.

I growled.

Tamica waved her hand at me like she was shooing me away. "Go to the other side, I'm driving you home."

I wanted to tell her no. Wanted to tell her that our long-term friendship had just come to a screeching end. But I crawled over the console while Tamica slid into the driver's seat.

"I'll let you take me home," I said, "but I don't want to talk to you."

She shrugged. "Ain't nothin' but a word. I told you, I don't really care about your feelings, since all I was trying to do was save your life."

"Even though they're pretty big, I don't think my problems are gonna kill me."

"I'm not talking about physical death."

There was no way I was gonna listen to one of Tamica's lectures, so I changed the subject. "How you gonna get home?"

"For someone who's not talking to me, your lips are doing an awful lot of moving." She peeked at me from the corner of her eye and grinned. "Brooklyn drove. She's gonna follow us and then take me home."

I considered jumping out of my own car and going to ride in Brooklyn's Bentley. That would serve Tamica right—making her drive in the Kia alone.

But I wasn't that rude.

Still, I didn't want to talk to her, because she had hurt my feelings. I mean, I wasn't playing with God, but what else were Adam and I supposed to do? We were on the edge of total disaster after we'd done everything right. God couldn't possibly want that for us.

There was nothing left to do—except take the deal.

When Tamica finally pulled my car into the driveway, she said, "You know, E, I wasn't trying to hurt you."

Looking down at my hands, I told her, "I know."

Outside the car, Tamica hugged me. "Whatever you and Adam decide, you know I got you, right?"

I nodded.

"And that goes double for me," Brooklyn said as she came over and wrapped her arms around me. "If I had a million dollars, I'd give it to you. And you wouldn't even have to give me Adam." We all laughed. "Hell," Brooklyn continued, "I'd give you another million if *you'd* take the Bishop. What! For a weekend? Please! That would be like heaven for me."

I laughed, but I knew what Brooklyn was saying was the truth. She and Tamica would help if they could, but they couldn't.

As I watched them drive away, I came to accept the sad truth . . . that no one could help Adam and me . . . except for Shay-Shaunté.

Chapter 32

I FELT A LITTLE BAD COMING in after eight. Not that it was late or anything; there were plenty of times when I worked much later than this. But Adam knew that I hadn't been at work. I'd left him stranded at home, without any explanation of what was going on or where I'd gone. With his having no way to reach out to me, I knew I owed my husband a big-time apology.

But Adam met me at the door with a hug and a kiss. "I was worried."

"I'm sorry. I needed a little time."

He stepped back; he was so focused on me that I was sure it was obvious that I'd been drinking. But all he said was, "I understand."

"Are the kids home?" I asked, moving away from him.

He nodded. "All three present and accounted for."

I asked, "Are they all upstairs?"

"Yeah; we should talk in our bedroom." He stepped ahead of me, moving anxiously, as if he couldn't wait.

Inside the master suite, he perched on the edge of the bed, but there was no way I could sit and tell this news. So I paced the width of our bedroom and told him the story.

"I told her we would do it."

Adam stayed silent; there was nothing for him to say to that bit of old news.

"She's happy, of course." I paused to see if he was happy, too. But Adam gave me nothing more than a straight face and a blank stare.

That was good enough, for now.

I nodded and continued, "There are two things, though."

"What?" His nerves were in his voice, as if he was afraid that I was going to do something to blow this deal.

I told him about how I'd asked for a contract. "I thought it was a good idea, but then she already had one ready." Moving to my purse, I pulled out the papers.

Adam glanced over the first page. As his eyes scanned, I wondered if he thought it was as strange as I did that she'd had a contract prepared when we'd given her no signs that we would ever agree to this.

Reading my thoughts, he said, "This doesn't surprise me. Shay-Shaunté's a businesswoman."

"And this is a business deal, right?"

He nodded. "A business deal."

I guessed if we both kept saying that, one day soon we'd believe it.

I said, "Well, I don't know much about contracts, it all looked fine to me except"—Adam glanced up when I said that—"she wants me to continue to work for her after . . ."

I let *after* hang in the air like that on purpose. After. After. I closed my eyes and tried to imagine the after.

Oh, God!

"For how long?" Adam interrupted my descent into despair.

"Six months. She said that's how long it'll take her to find someone and have me train them."

Adam studied the last clause, which tied me to this indecent ménage à trois for far longer than the "after" was supposed to be. The way he looked up, then down, then repeated the action made me think that this—those six months—was too much, even for him. This would be the straw that would break the deal.

But Adam broke my hope instead when he said, "Okay." Then added, "Tell her you'll stay for six months *or* until you find her a new assistant, whichever comes first."

I nodded.

Adam gave a little bit of my hope back when he added, "Then we'll work like crazy to find someone for that job. How hard can it be? In this economy?"

"That's what I said!"

"We'll get you out of there, Shine, I promise."

Okay, well at least Adam got it; at least he understood that it was going to kill me to keep working with the woman he'd . . . slept with.

"So," Adam began as he reached for me. Taking my hand, he gently pulled me down onto the bed next to him. "Are you still okay with this?"

"Yeah." I gave a little shake of my head. "I have to be. I mean, what else can we do?"

He shrugged.

"Trust me, though," I added, "this is going to be hard. Really hard."

"I know."

"I feel like we're giving up a lot."

"I know. If we had any other choice, Shine, I'd be right on it. But this is it."

There it was. Adam's decision had been made. It was over.

"One thing I want you to know," Adam said, kneeling in front of me, "is that this will never affect us. The reason our intimacy is so special is because it's way beyond the physical. You're in my head, in my heart, in my soul. Shay-Shaunté will never have that. She'll never be close to any part of me."

I wanted to correct him on that last part, because there was going to be a part of him that she would be very close to. But I didn't want to talk about this anymore. I needed to stop trying to delay and deny the inevitable.

"Shine . . . are you *really*—"

"Don't ask me that again, Adam," I snapped. "Don't put whether or not we do this all on me."

He nodded.

I said, "Maybe I should be asking you . . . are *you* sure?"

It didn't even take him a moment to say, "There's no other way."

"Well, it's decided, isn't it?" I pulled away from him. "I'm going to check on the twins and Ethan."

As I climbed the stairs, I realized this was really going to happen. I might not have had an answer from God, but I had one from Adam.

The deal was done.

Chapter 33

IT WAS THE FIGHTER IN ME that had to give it just one more try. The fighter in me that really wanted to blow this deal up.

I'd devised this plan during the middle of the night. Once again, I'd lain awake through most of the midnight hours, tossing in our bed as I'd turned this idea over in my mind.

Now, as I sat in front of Shay-Shaunté, I was waiting for the right moment. The toe of my stiletto boot bounced as my leg trembled with a bit of fear and excitement—fear that this wouldn't work, but excitement that it just might.

I tried to keep myself straight and steady as I watched Shay-Shaunté read over the addendum that Adam had prepared—that said that I wasn't going to be here six months after . . . not if Adam and I could help it. The addendum made it clear that if we found someone to replace me before the six months were up, I would walk out of Ferossity that day.

Finally, Shay-Shaunté looked up. From her throne, she said, "This was Adam's idea, wasn't it?"

It seemed like she was just looking for reasons to say his name.

"No," I said. "It was mine."

"Really?" She tossed the addendum onto her desk and shook her head. "Why didn't you ask for this yesterday?"

"I didn't think about it until last night."

"I see," she smirked. "Well"—she checked the page for our signatures—"I'm fine with this. So, all that's left is for me to sign and—"

Before she could move, I leaned over and pressed my hand onto the paper, blocking her from signing anything. "There's one more thing. Something else that I thought about last night."

She looked down at my hand, then back up at me. Raised one eyebrow and pursed her lips.

I didn't care about her attitude. From this point on, I was running this show, and if she was salty now, wait until she heard what I had to say. "We want half the money up front."

It took her a second to respond. "'We'?"

"You're right. Not we, me. I want half the money."

"So, you want me to give you two point five million?"

I didn't respond. She knew that's what I wanted.

My blood pumped faster as I watched her expression. Excitement had kicked in full-throttle. What I'd been conjuring up all night was going to work!

Her eyes became thin slits, her brows furrowed together. "But suppose you and Adam change your minds?" She sucked in her lips as if she was in deep thought. "We're still two weeks away, and that's a lot of time. So much can happen."

"True," I said nonchalantly, wanting to encourage those doubts.

"If you change your minds, it'll be hard to get that money back. Two point five"—she shook her head—"that's a lot of money to lose. Even for me."

I needed to protest, just a little. So that she wouldn't see that she was slinking right into my plan—which was to get *her* to call this deal off. "We'd never keep the money if we changed our minds."

"Never?" Shay-Shaunté smirked. "A couple of weeks ago, you said you'd never do this. And now, here you sit."

Okay, now see, she was trying to turn this into a fight.

She said, "That's why I told you before, that's why I'll tell you again; never say never."

I had no idea why Shay-Shaunté was doing all of this talking. Why didn't she just tell me, 'No, it isn't going to happen,' and then I could tear up the contract, go home, and tell Adam that she'd reneged.

"Whatever, Shay-Shaunté, we're not going to do this unless we get two point five million." Then boldly, I added, "Now, today," just to push her over the edge.

It was my turn to smirk even though her wide eyes and open mouth made me want to laugh. Finally! I had the upper hand.

I wanted to jump up, go old-school and do the cabbage-patch or even get down with the running man; but before I could get my dance on, Shay-Shaunté pushed back her royal chair. Slowly, she slipped open the same drawer she'd pulled the contract from yesterday, then, just as slowly, slid a rectangular piece of paper across her glasstop desk. As the paper inched toward me, I leaned forward to see it more clearly.

My mouth flew open.

A certified check. In my complete name: Evia *Early* Langston. For two . . . point . . . five . . . million. I blinked twice, then three times. The check was still there, the numbers were still the same.

What the . . .

I looked up and, for a moment, stared into eyes that were so piercing, so full of fire and fury—and hate—that I was pushed back in my chair. But then, in the next moment, it was all gone and Shay-Shaunté's eyes were now filled with concern.

"Are you all right, Evia?"

I swallowed. I nodded. I couldn't speak; I could barely breathe.

She smiled. "Okay. Then I guess we have a deal." She signed and handed me the now fully executed contract. "I'm assuming that you don't want Rachel to make a copy of this."

I shook my head, still without words.

She continued, "Then you make the copy and bring the original back to me."

Taking the papers from her, I stood and moved to do what I was told. Before I got to the door, Shay-Shaunté said, "Evia, you forgot something." When I turned, she said, "This is yours."

I'm sure I was moving like a zombie when I went back for the check. My mind was still swirling, twirling.

Outside Shay-Shaunté's office, Rachel greeted me. "Hey, girl, what's up?" Then, with a closer look, Rachel added, "Girl, what's wrong? You look like you've seen a ghost."

There was too much going on inside my head to speak. No, I hadn't just seen a ghost. Shay-Shaunté was alive and I remembered that look in her eyes. Made me want to grab a pair of Nikes and run straight out of that building. But surely, I hadn't seen what I thought.

This deal was taking over my mind, playing tricks. I needed to get it together.

When I glanced down at the check, though, I wasn't so sure that the problem was with me. Staring at all of the numerals, I just had to wonder, who in the hell was Shay-Shaunté?

Chapter 34

IT HAD TAKEN ONLY HOURS, but in that time, our lives had completely changed. As I stood at the door, watching Adam put the Kia in reverse, I thought back to all that had happened since this morning. . . .

I was still functioning like a zombie when I came home from work just an hour after Shay-Shaunté gave me that check.

"What's wrong, Shine?" Adam asked the moment I lugged through the door.

"Shay-Shaunté sent me home." The cadence of my words, the tenor of my tone made me sound like a robot.

My husband's face filled with fear. His assumption: My coming home was a sign of bad news.

I explained, "She gave me this and told me to take the rest of the day off."

I handed the check to Adam and watched him do exactly what I'd done. Big eyes, open mouth, hyperventilation came next.

"What the . . ." He stopped before he actually cursed, just like I'd done. "Shine," he began again slowly, "what is this?"

"It's a check. Half. For . . . you know."

He staggered backward to the couch, and then, when his legs were too weak to hold him upright any longer, he lost his balance and plopped down.

But he held on to the check. With both hands.

I gave him another minute to digest this truth, and then I sat next to him. Together, we stared.

"What do you think we should do?" I asked.

Slowly, Adam lifted his eyes, as if he was coming out of a trance. He focused on me and gave me one of those looks that he sometimes gave to our children when he thought their questions weren't too smart.

"What should we do? We should go to the bank!" he said, then he jumped up. "We need to get to the bank . . . now!"

I swear, not even a minute passed before we were inside the car and swerving out of the driveway. I'd expected Adam to push the pedal to the metal, but instead he drove conservatively, staying right on the speed limit. No policeman, no speeding ticket was going to slow us down.

Still, we were at the bank in less than ten minutes. I would've expected a little more of a challenge depositing so much money. But I guessed that because we already had a personal banker with the Bank of DC, and because we'd moved lots of money through our accounts over the years (though most of our accounts were busted before we walked in with this check), it only took about thirty minutes before Darren Grey, our banker, had our funds deposited and cleared. It helped that the check Shay-Shaunté had given me was written on a Bank of DC account, though I didn't notice that until we got to the bank. Really, that surprised me. It was a Ferossity check, and I handled all of the company's banking. Never before had we used Bank of DC.

By the time Adam and I were back in our car with the money deposited and a few hundred dollars in Adam's pocket, I'd forgotten all about the check and where the funds had been drawn from. It didn't matter—all of that money now belonged to Adam and Evia Langston.

For the rest of the afternoon, it was Christmas two weeks early . . . at least for Adam. We'd come so close to going over the cliff that I didn't want to spend any more than the cost of two chai tea lattes from Starbucks. But Adam assured me that we were only going to spend a little.

"Imagine how the girls will feel when they come home and we have their cell phones waiting."

That was not my idea of the first thing we should do with the money. I was thinking that we needed to go home and plan, but when the girls arrived home, I had to admit that Adam was right.

We were waiting in the living room, and the suspicion in the twins' eyes crushed my heart. They were dealing with adult issues, the same way Adam and I had had to when we were growing up. For all of our planning, our children were in the same exact place we'd been.

"Did you go to work?" Alexa was the one who asked today.

Though the question was directed to both of us, I left it to Adam to answer. But he didn't say a word. Just handed the twins matching boxes.

When Alexa and Alana realized that they were holding the Droids they'd been talking about, they looked as stupefied as Adam and I had when we'd first seen that check. Their mouths were open, but not a word came out—which was a feat for Alexa.

"OMG!" Alexa finally exclaimed. I guessed it no longer mattered if Adam or I had gone to work.

A hug-fest broke out in that living room. Alexa hugged her sister, then her father, then me before she began the round of hugs all over again. "If I don't get another thing, it will be all right," Alexa cried. "It will still be the best Christmas ever!"

It was a little sad that this single gift was enough. But I guessed something good had come out of the last few weeks. Now the girls were filled with gratitude instead of entitlement.

It did my heart good to see glee instead of gloom on their faces, and by the time the two dashed up the stairs to turn on their phones, call all their friends, and get on the Internet (since the cable was back on), I was smiling, too.

But the moment they were out of our sight, I said, "Adam, I don't want to blow this money."

"That would be impossible. I mean, we're talking millions here."

"But if we don't sit down and plan this . . ."

"Okay." He glanced at his watch. I still have a little over an hour before I have to pick up Ethan."

We walked into our home office, where the first thing I wanted to talk about was the house.

"What's the payoff? Let's buy it outright."

"I don't think we should do that, Shine. I'm going to find another job; trust that. We're going to need the write-off."

It felt like a lifetime ago, but just three days had passed since our children had come home to find that foreclosure notice taped to the door. The looks on their faces, the combination of fear and confusion and helplessness—I never wanted to see that again. I told Adam that.

"I guess we can do it," he said, giving in. "But with all of the foreclosure costs and legal fees, we're probably talking the original price for this house, plus some, since the little bit of equity we had is long gone."

"That's okay. Even if we have to pay eight hundred thousand, I don't care."

"It may be closer to nine."

"I don't care," I repeated.

He shook his head. He'd given in, but he hadn't given up. "Buying this outright isn't the smartest thing to do financially."

"It is when we have this kind of money. Let's do this, please? Everything else . . . I'll leave up to you."

He gave in for real this time. "All right."

It was because I wanted Adam to remember the upside that I said, "It'll be okay, because we still have the other two and a half million coming to us after . . ."

With those words, I sucked all the joy from the air. For the last hours we hadn't really thought about what this money meant. We'd both pretended that this was some kind of wonderful, benevolent gift.

With the pleasure now gone, Adam and I got down to the business of planning. After we made the decision to definitely pay off the house, we decided to pay the children's tuition through next June, and pay for Ruby's care for the next year.

We were done with the planning in time for Adam to pick up Ethan from golf practice. He hugged me as we stood. The check I'd received no more than nine hours ago had relieved the pressure that had become the frighteningly normal state of our lives. But heaviness hung between us with the thought of the true cost of this money and what we had to do. . . .

As I watched Adam pull away in the Kia, I pushed thoughts of what was to come from my mind. We had fourteen days before we had to face that; I didn't want to waste the little bit of good feelings I had right now.

Adam tapped the horn lightly and waved. As the Kia disappeared down the block, I wondered how much longer that car would last. By the end of the weekend, we'd probably have at least one new car—paid for in cash, if I had anything to do with it. No one here would ever witness a car repo again—at least not from in front of this house.

When laughter drifted down the staircase, I leaned against the front door, reveling in the sound. There was a high cost to what we had to do, but if it made my children happy and if it brought security to Ruby and if it gave my husband peace, then we were doing what we were supposed to do.

For the greater good.

Chapter 35

THE COUNTDOWN BEGAN.

Two weeks stood between me and the day when I'd have to turn over my husband. But the fact that the thirty-first of December was quickly approaching seemed to be a concern of mine alone.

Adam showed no signs of having thoughts of Shay-Shaunté, New Year's Eve, or any part of our deal. From the moment we deposited that money, his focus was only on his family—and re-creating the life that we'd once known.

He started when he returned home with Ethan . . . and a Christmas tree. Our son dashed up the stairs to drag his sisters down to the living room for the surprise. My three children *oooh*ed and *aaah*ed as Adam hauled in the Virginia pine and steadied the eight-foot tree in the stand. The girls grabbed the decorations from the basement, and the rest of the night was filled with holiday cheer—carols streamed through the surround-sound speakers, glasses filled with eggnog, and the children chattered on about the grand Christmas that was to come.

I was present with my family in body only; my thoughts were far away, on the fifteenth day from now.

That night, though, Adam and I made love with a gentleness, an easiness, a loveliness that reminded me of our beginning. Through his kisses, Adam told me that I was his shine, the one who made his day bright. Through his touches, he told me that he loved me most, and that he would always love me best. And when we united, he told me that no one, nothing, could ever touch us or separate us. We would be one, forever.

The next morning, I awakened satisfied and at peace. Then at seven, the telephone rang.

"Girl!" Rachel blasted through the phone. "Don't even think about getting up and leaving your house. The office is closed."

"What?"

"Yeah, girl. Right after you left yesterday, Shay-Shaunté called a meeting with all the executives, and shut . . . the . . . place . . . down."

"Why?"

"All she said was that she was ecstatic about a deal she'd just made and she wanted to go home to celebrate."

Oh, my God! She was talking about me and Adam.

Rachel continued. "She said that she'd been working on a project for a long time, for a couple of years, actually, and she'd been told that she was about to be paid."

I hadn't even realized that I'd been holding my breath until I exhaled. Shay-Shaunté *hadn't* been talking about me and Adam—not if this was about something she'd been working on for so long and certainly not if she was about to get paid. We weren't paying her—at least not monetarily.

Rachel said, "So anyway, girl, that's the deal."

"Are we still off next week?"

"Oh, yeah. She announced that we could pick up checks next Friday. HR will be open, if you don't have direct deposit. But Shay-Shaunté won't be there. She was going around telling everybody that she had big plans for her birthday."

If she wasn't talking about us before, she was now. Big plans? For her birthday? If I had time or tears, I'd have just sat down and cried.

"Did . . . did . . . did she say what her plans were?" I whispered.

"Nah, girl. You know how private she is. But I know you know something."

"Why'd you say that?"

"Please! All those closed-door meetings—just the two of you. What's up? What you know about her birthday?"

Even though Rachel couldn't see me, I shook my head. "I don't know anything . . . you know . . . about her birthday . . . you know . . . or about . . . her plans." I could hardly get the words out straight.

"Dang, girl." Rachel laughed. "Why you stuttering? If it's a secret, I'm cool. Whatever she's gonna do, I just hope she parties the night away. I hope she finds somebody and hooks up, 'cause sometimes, I think all she needs is a good lay." Rachel laughed. "Yeah, I hope she gets it good. Just like I hope to get it with James on New Year's."

The best thing that ever happened was Rachel turning the conversation to herself, because I couldn't have taken another "Shay-Shaunté needs to get laid" comment. For a few minutes, I listened to Rachel talk without interruption, about her continuing plans to snag the longtime unrequited love of her life.

But though I said, "Oh," and "Yeah," in all the right places, after what Rachel just told me, the only thing I could think about was the fact that there were just fourteen days until I had to pay.

That's how I began to measure time . . . not by the ticking of the clock, not by when the sun rose and set. For me, time was measured in how many days until I handed my husband over to Shay-Shaunté.

After Rachel's call, Adam and I spent the rest of the day at Pearly Gates, meeting with Ms. Johnson, paying the past due amount, and then writing a check that would cover Adam's mother for the rest of the year. Once Ms. Johnson checked to see if the funds were good, we insisted that Ruby be moved back to her room; then we stayed for four hours more, until it was done.

The weekend—days thirteen and twelve—moved at space shuttle speed. We spent more money as Adam gave the twins one thousand dollars each for Christmas shopping and then took all of us to buy a new car.

"I'm so glad we're getting another Escalade," Alana said.

"I'm so glad you got a new job!" Alexa exclaimed.

My husband had worn an everlasting smile from the moment he'd realized that two-point-five-million-dollar check was good. But Alexa's words took a bit of the light from his face. I guessed Adam didn't see what he was about to do as a job, though that was the only way for me to look at it.

Then on Sunday, we joined Bishop Cash, Brooklyn, Tamica, and a host of other Holy Deliverance members for our first after-service brunch in months.

"Did it go down already?" Brooklyn whispered to me as we strolled in front of the others into Georgia Brown's.

"No, not until next week. You know, on Shay-Shaunté's birthday."

"That's right. New Year's Eve. So, y'all still gonna do it?"

I shrugged. And lied, "I'm not sure."

"Uh-huh." All kinds of doubt was in Brooklyn's tone. "Well, something's up with y'all."

When Alexa ran over and asked if she and Alana could sit at a table by themselves, I was so grateful for my self-centered child's interruption, since I really didn't want to talk to Brooklyn about this.

On days eleven and ten, the twins had their own activities, meeting with friends to go shopping, to the movies, to lunch and dinner, while Ethan's best friend, Dougie, and his dad took our son to a couple of indoor driving ranges.

Adam and I spent those days behind his desk doing more planning. It took us hours to negotiate a deal with the bank; I thought paying off a large mortgage would be easy. Not! Next, we spoke to the administrator of the children's school to arrange for payment for the rest of the year, and I even talked Adam into paying some of our smaller bills, like our cells, and cable, and the utilities, and the phone and Internet, several months in advance.

"I know you're going to find another job," I told Adam every time he said the best way to use this money was to put it away and let it work for us. "But this way we'll never have any concerns again."

"We won't have concerns anyway, Shine. Not with all of this money in the bank."

"I know, but remember this is only half. Let's do it this way with this part of the money. The other half, we'll save when we get it after . . ."

After.

I'd done it again. Taken the sun out of our day with that single word.

On day nine, Adam and I went to see my mother, bringing Christmas to her three days early.

When Adam counted out all the one-hundred-dollar bills

(we couldn't give her a check because no one who lived in that apartment—my mother, Cashmere, or Twin—owned a bank account) my mother fell back on her dingy sofa and gaped at the pile of money in her hand. It was five thousand dollars, but more money than my mother had ever seen at one time.

"This is all for me," she gasped.

"Yes," Adam replied, while I stood next to him with my arms folded.

I wasn't the happiest camper in the park. When Adam had told me he planned to do this, I'd asked him if he'd lost his mind. He knew my mother. Giving her that much money was like giving it to a child. She'd have nada before the weekend was out.

Adam acted like he had total faith in the woman who'd raised me. But he knew that I was speaking the truth.

"Now, Marilyn," Adam began in a tone that sounded like he was speaking to one of the twins. "I haven't found a job yet, so this is gonna have to last you a couple of months."

Yeah, right was the look my mother and I both gave him.

He continued, "You're not going to be able to keep running back to us—"

"I hear you, I hear you," my mother said, trying to stuff all of those bills into her bra. "I won't be asking for anything more." Then she asked, "Can you break off a little something there for Cashmere and Twin?"

So much for not asking for anything else.

On day eight, I slept. Well, most of the day. With the twins and Ethan out of the house again all day with friends, Adam and I stayed in bed, talking through new plans for our future.

"I've been thinking about starting my own business," Adam said. "Why should I sit around and wait for someone to give me a job?"

"That's a good idea." I really thought it was; I just had no idea what kind of business Adam would be looking for, since being an entrepreneur had never been his dream.

"I'm gonna do some research on the Internet and go to some seminars."

I nodded. "There's an entrepreneurial conference coming up in a couple of weeks. I just saw the ad on TV."

"I'll definitely go to that."

For the whole day, we dreamed in bed (and did other things) and imagined the wonderful state of our future—though for me, wonderful couldn't begin until after the deal was done.

Day seven—Christmas Eve—was all about faith, family, and friends. First, we went to the noon service that Holy Deliverance held every year, then the five of us battled traffic and made it down to Pearly Gates.

The children were relieved to see their grandmother back in her old room. While Ruby sat, staring out the window, Alexa, Alana, and Ethan chatted about their hopes for their gifts tomorrow. The best part was when they each gave Ruby something they'd picked out for her. They had to unwrap the gifts, of course, but now Ruby's dresser held a candle encased in a shell-covered glass from Alexa, a picture frame engraved with *Grandma's Lovelies* with a picture of the twins from Alana, and a journal with a silver pen from Ethan. To them, Ruby's Christmas was now complete.

Finally, we ended the late night with dessert at Brooklyn and the Bishop's mini-mansion in Vienna, Virginia, along with other friends, many of whom we'd known back in the day. We sang carols, told old tales, and wished each other Merry Christmas after Cash read the story of Jesus' birth from each of the four gospels.

Day six was a Christmas to remember. The children

received so many gifts—most from Adam but many others as well, including even a few from my mother. Then, once we all finished unwrapping presents, Adam put his hands over my eyes and led me as I stumbled to the front door. He swung it open, and there in the driveway was a Lexus coupe wrapped in a gigantic red bow—just like in those commercials.

Even though I was trying to be responsible, I couldn't say that I wasn't thrilled; I just hoped Adam had paid cash.

As the girls drooled over my car, Adam said, "Get ready; you guys are next."

The girls had been so thrilled, with their father's words, that I'd reconsidered my position on Range Rovers being too expensive for sixteen-year-olds. Maybe if Adam got a good deal on used ones, I would come around before their birthday.

Then Christmas passed. I had to start counting down to the lowest numbers. On day five, I spent the afternoon in the bathroom with diarrhea. Then on day four, my emotions were released from the other end—I spent the day hugging the toilet. On day three, I decided to stop eating altogether. There was no need; I couldn't keep anything down anyway. And on day two, I discovered that I didn't have to eat—the white wine that Adam kept in our bar filled me up something lovely.

But though the wine kept me from eating, it didn't keep me from thinking. My head was filled with all kinds of questions—the same questions I'd always had. But with the wine, the questions kept replaying . . . like, how would Adam feel . . . after? After being with an older woman. After being with a worldly woman. After being with a rich woman.

Would Adam be able to come home, truly come back? Would he be able to get Shay-Shaunté out of his mind . . . after?

I wasn't trying to be a masochist; it was the wine that made me keep asking stupid questions.

I kept telling myself—and the wine—that the deal was done, the money was spent. Questions. Answers. None of that mattered.

The time had come. It was time for us to pay Shay-Shaunté.

Chapter 36

IT DIDN'T SEEM TO HIT ADAM until the day before. That was the first time he initiated any kind of conversation that had anything to do with the deal.

The morning before he was set to leave, he rolled over and wrapped his arm around my waist. I was barely conscious when the heat of his morning breath tickled my ear and he whispered, "What time are the girls leaving for their party tomorrow?"

Tomorrow. The day. No more countdown.

"Early, I think. About five."

There was a pause before he asked, "What about Ethan?"

Adam couldn't see my frown. My plan had been to have Ethan here with me. We'd watch the ball in Times Square together and maybe toast the new year with some sparkling cider.

But really, I hadn't thought that all the way through. Did I really want Ethan to see his father walk out the door to be with another woman? I mean, we could have told him a couple of lies—we'd become good at that. But watching Adam leave was going to be traumatic enough for me. I didn't want Ethan to witness that.

Adam said, "I want us to spend New Year's together."

I rolled away from him, swung my legs over the edge of the bed, then twisted to face him. "You must've forgotten. You have a date."

"Don't say it like that, Shine. It's not like this is something I wanted to do. We both agreed."

I held up my hand. "I know. I'm sorry." I ran my hand along the side of my hair, pushing the edges back into my ponytail. I wasn't really trying to fix my hair, I just needed time. Then I started over. "What were you talking about? Us spending New Year's together?"

"I know I have to . . . leave at nine. But we can have a few hours just to ourselves before then."

I shook my head. That's not what I wanted to do. Really, I wanted to wallow in my misery. This would be the first New Year's since I was fifteen that I would spend without Adam— my plan was to cry all night.

He said, "Please, Shine. I won't be able to do this, to go through with this if I can't . . . first . . . be with you."

There it was again. Those special words that made me melt. And made me return to our bed.

I leaned over him. "We'll celebrate together. Tomorrow. Before . . ."

Our kiss ended our conversation.

Chapter 37

God was full of mercy for me on New Year's Eve, because I had no time to think about the hour that was closing in.

The day was all about the twins, and getting them ready for what they called their first real grown-up party. I rushed to the store for last-minute accessories, packed for the slumber party, and listened to all the chatter and the giggles about who was going to be there.

Now the bags were packed, the girls were downstairs, and we were just waiting for their ride.

Until Alexa yelled out, "OMG!" startling all of us. "I don't have my PINK pajama bottoms. What was I thinking?" she yelled, dashing up the staircase. "I would just die if I didn't have them."

My eyes were on Alexa, my drama queen, until I turned back to Alana. Her eyebrows were bunched together—a unibrow frown.

"What's wrong, honey?"

"Are you all right?" She directed the question to me but glanced at Adam at the same time.

It took me just a moment to get myself together enough to lie to the sensitive one. "Of course. I'm just fine."

Then Adam piped in with, "Your mom's just a little sad."

Now my eyebrows were as burrowed as Alana's.

"Why?" our daughter asked.

I asked the same thing, but only I kept my words inside. Was he really going to bring our children into our mess? He couldn't be thinking that—it would be too much for them. Hell, it was too much for me.

"Well, tomorrow," Adam began, "I have to go on a business trip." His lie was so fluid, so smooth. "I'll be back on Sunday, so it won't be long. But it's not the best way to start the new year. So, your mom's sad about that. And I am, too."

"Oh," Alana said, grabbing me. "But you won't be going till tomorrow, right?"

Both of us lied with our nods.

"So, you'll have a great New Year's together, and then I'll take care of Mom while you're away, Daddy."

"Take care of Mom for what?" Alexa said, rushing into the living room.

Outside, a car horn blared three long beeps, and Alana peeked out the window. "They're here!" she exclaimed. To her sister, she said, "I'll fill you in on Mom and Dad in the car."

Two weeks ago, Alexa would have stopped right then and asked me and her father if we still had jobs. But now that her life had returned to normal, it didn't matter whether her parents were employed or not.

Each girl grabbed her suitcase, gave us hugs and kisses with extra wishes for a happy new year, then trotted out the door. We watched as they jumped into Sara Templeton's SUV and waved until the car disappeared.

Facing Adam, I said, "This next one we're going to have to handle together."

Ethan was in his room, stretched out on his bed with his headphones on. But when Adam and I walked in, he shot straight up, leaned against the headboard, crossed his arms and legs, and glared at us.

"I'm not going!" He made sure we heard every bit of his anger and determination.

If I was in my son's place, I would've been saying the same thing. But what was I to do? Dougie, Ethan's best friend, had left for vacation with his family. And Sylvester, his next closest friend, was in bed with the flu. I couldn't call Tamica or Brooklyn, the next logical choices, because then they'd want to stay with me, and I needed to do tonight alone.

So the only person left to take care of my son was my mother. Since Cashmere and her kids lived there, Ethan would have to spend the night with his criminals-in-training cousins, too.

"Ethan . . ." Adam began, but he didn't get further than our son's name.

"I'm not going," he said to his father. Then to me, he pleaded, "Please, please, Mom. Don't make me go."

"If I had any other choice," I began. Then I started thinking—why *did* Ethan have to leave? Why should he be punished because of what Adam and I were about to do?

But Adam must've known that I was beginning to crack, because he said, "Son, it's just for one night. Do this for me, please."

"I can stay here by myself. You and Mom can go out and I won't do anything. I'll stay in my room, I promise."

"It's going to be fine, son. Just one night. You guys will watch the ball in Times Square and then go to bed. By the time you wake up in the morning, your mother will be there to bring you home." Adam paused and went for the bribe. "I have to go away . . . on a business trip . . . tomorrow. But when I get back, we'll do something special . . . together . . . okay?"

Our son didn't budge.

I grabbed Ethan's bag. "Come on," I said, in the gentlest and kindest voice I could. "We have to leave now."

Ethan snatched his PlayStation, stomped by his father, refused to say good-bye, and jumped into my Lexus as if he was being driven to death row.

The look on Adam's face told me that he was feeling exactly the way I was, but we needed these last few hours together, alone. This time was going to be as important for our children as it was for us.

But I was hit hard by the realization that what we were about to do was already affecting our children. I'd never thought that the deal we'd made was just about me and Adam; everyone would benefit from the money. I just hadn't realized that anyone else would be adversely affected by our actions, too.

Just forty-eight hours, I thought as I drove Ethan to my mother's house. *Just forty-eight hours.*

Chapter 38

IT TOOK ME A MOMENT TO turn off the ignition after I maneuvered the car back into the driveway. In just a couple of hours, I would be saying my second difficult good-bye of the day.

The huge tears that had been in Ethan's eyes when I'd stopped in front of my mother's home had almost made me call off this whole thing. But I'd sucked it up and had begged Ethan to do the same thing.

He'd tried, but when my mother had opened the door and Ethan had stepped inside, his sadness had been palpable. Though he'd needed me, there was no way I could have stayed. Not even for a little while, because if I'd stayed, I'd have taken him with me when I'd left.

So, all I'd done was kiss Ethan good-bye with a promise to be there before he even woke up in the morning. He'd blinked back his tears and glared at me as if by morning, he might not love me anymore.

That was when I'd left—I'd left my son so that I could go home and watch my husband leave me.

Now I was back home. I didn't want to go inside because as soon as I did, it would be the beginning of our good-bye. But like I'd asked Ethan to do, I inhaled courage and made the trek to our front door.

I stepped inside. And stopped. And took a deep breath as I stared at the garment bag at the base of the staircase. Adam's bag, already packed—the first sign that this was really happening.

I blinked back emotions—no need to get upset or angry or even to be sad. All I needed to do was to pray for time to move forward so that this could be behind us.

It was just a weekend.

It was just forty-eight hours.

Still, it was hard to take my eyes from the suitcase. Not even when I heard our bedroom door open. Not even when I felt Adam come to my side.

"You packed," I stated.

"I didn't want you to waste time on that."

The thing was, though, I wanted to be the one to pack his bag. Not only because that's what I always did, but now I had to wonder what he was taking. What kinds of clothes did he think were appropriate for Shay-Shaunté? Was he taking his best? What about nighttime—did he pack pajamas, or did he plan to sleep the way he did with me—in the nude?

I trembled, but Adam was right there to steady me.

"Are you all right?"

"I will be."

He paused, waiting a moment for me to get myself together. When it looked like I would make it on my own two feet, Adam said, "I fixed you a little something. A light dinner. Something special. In here." He led me toward our bedroom, and when I stepped inside, thoughts of what was about to go down were tossed aside by memories of 1993.

I giggled with surprise at the tray tables at the foot of our bed, covered with the best feast—a platter of steamed shrimp and a plate piled high with grilled cheese sandwiches.

"Oh, my God." I pointed to the clear plastic pitcher. "Don't tell me that's Kool-Aid?"

He nodded, full of excitement. "Do you remember?"

"How can I forget? Our first New Year's Eve."

It was 1993 and the first time Adam and I were going to celebrate New Year's together. I didn't have any money—I was only fifteen—but I still wanted the night to be special. I'd asked Adam earlier in the day what his favorite foods were. He told me shrimp and grilled cheese sandwiches.

So since this was going to be the first meal I would ever make for my man, I wanted to serve all of his favorites. That's what I did: shrimp, grilled cheese sandwiches, and a bottomless pitcher of red Kool-Aid packed with sugar.

"This is wonderful," I said as I kissed him.

The kiss was meant to be a thank-you, because of course we were going to share in this feast first. But the moment our lips touched, a current surged through every part of us and the sparks were ignited.

Adam tore my clothes away as if he was desperate to get to my body. In just a few rips, I was naked before him, and he lifted me, but passed by the bed. Instead, he laid me on my back in front of the fireplace.

He stared down at my nakedness, but I was impatient. I reached for him, but he shook his head. "I just want to take in you. All of you."

Long, agonizing moments went by before he gifted me with his presence and lowered himself next to me. "You are so beautiful," he whispered right before his tongue danced behind my ear.

It was my turn to return the favor and I split his shirt in two before I ripped his jeans from his waist.

The chiseled perfection that was his chest was hot to my touch. His heat revealed his desire, and that only made me want him more. For a millisecond, an image of Shay-Shaunté with her own perfection floated through my mind.

But then the tip of Adam's tongue found my chest, and I fell back into the pleasure, losing control of my mind and every thought inside. The tips of his fingers followed his tongue and I moaned—one deep, continual groan of pleasure.

Adam took his time, as if we would be together all night. He tasted every inch of me, this cool tongue setting my skin on fire. It was all that I could do to hold back the volcano that was bubbling inside.

Every part of my body ached for him, craved him, wanted him so badly.

"Please," I whispered.

He shook his head. "Tonight," his voice was as low as mine, "it's all about you."

His tongue trailed a path to my center, and by the time he got to that place that held every bit of my glory, I swore that smoke was seeping from my pores.

"Please," I begged him again.

But he was not done until a complete rush of bliss consumed me. Only then did he give himself to me.

At the end, there was no way that I could move. Really, I wondered if I'd ever be able to move again. But then Adam took my hand and lifted me from the floor. Snatching the comforter from our bed, he wrapped both of us inside before we sat in front of the feast that was our dinner.

With only the hum of Northwest D.C. surrounding us, we fed each other shrimp, took bites of the perfectly grilled cheese sandwiches, and sipped Kool-Aid out of mason jars that were just like the ones our mothers had had when we were growing up.

Satisfied in every physical way, we stretched out in the silence and leaned against the edge of the bed and each other.

Behind us, the clock pushed the minutes forward even as we tried to ignore that our time was coming to an end.

It was Adam who broke our quiet, our peace. "There's one last thing that I want you to do with me."

I nodded, though I didn't like his use of the word *"last."* Arm in arm, we walked to the shower, and there we washed each other; not sexually, only sensually.

Gently, we touched all of our secret places, all of the parts that till now no one else had ever seen, touched, or explored.

But after the next forty-eight hours, we'd never be able to say that again.

As the water drenched us, I sobbed inside, and Adam held me as if he could hear my cries. I was the first to step away, leaving Adam alone to make his final preparations.

Inside our bedroom, I wrapped myself in my robe. In the long minutes that lingered, every regret made its way through my mind. But I kept telling myself two things—that it was too late, that it would be all right.

It was five minutes to nine when Adam stepped out of the bathroom in black wool pants and a white shirt. Casual, yet professional. Dressy enough to go out to dinner, relaxed enough to have fun.

It was Adam. It was perfection.

The tears inside battled to come forward, but I held them behind my eyes.

Adam leaned over to kiss me, but before his lips could touch mine, a light beamed from the street through our window, casting a long shadow across our bed. Then the gentle purr of a car's engine made us take our eyes from each other and turn toward the sound.

Shay-Shaunté had come.

Though I'd been fighting hard, I lost the battle. A single tear crept out and crawled down the path from my eye to my chin. With his lips, Adam wiped that tear away, then he took my hand and helped me stand.

"Come with me," he whispered.

I didn't want to, but I walked with him, as if this was an ordinary day, as if we were parting for ordinary reasons. My mind screamed not to let him go. But though my conscience spoke, my mouth didn't. How could I say anything, anyway? Because of me and my grand plan, we already had half the money; we couldn't turn back now.

Adam hoisted his garment bag onto his shoulder. When he looked into my eyes, for a moment I thought he was going to ask again if I could handle this because if I couldn't, he wouldn't leave.

Then I would beg him to stay.

But he only said, "I'll call you."

And I only nodded.

He walked to the door, opened it, and turned back. He was a shadow in the dark, with only Shay-Shaunté's car lights illuminating a beam behind him.

"I love you, Shine."

"I love you more," I squeaked.

He let a long moment go by before he said, "And I will forever love you best."

Then my husband closed the door to the home that we now completely owned. My husband left to spend forty-eight hours with another woman.

Chapter 39

I HAD TO BE OUT OF my everlasting mind.

I was a grown woman, but I couldn't figure out how to move. Couldn't figure out how to lift myself from the place where I'd fallen the moment Adam had closed the door, leaving me all alone.

How long ago was that? It was hard to judge minutes when seconds consumed me. Every second that ticked by was filled with images of Shay-Shaunté. Sometimes Adam was with her—that surprised me. I was sure my thoughts would be totally on my husband, but it was Shay-Shaunté who had captured my mind.

Inside my head, she mocked me, laughed at me, and finally bid me farewell as she took my husband away. The pictorial torture played like a movie reel, from beginning to end. Then stopped and started over. Again and again—the mocking, laughing, farewell!

I pressed the heels of my hands against my temples and

tried to knead away those images. But Shay-Shaunté's presence was stronger than my fight.

Maybe if I took myself away from the last place I saw Adam, I'd be able to get away from this agony. But there was no life in my arms, no strength in my legs.

So I rocked forward, pushed myself onto my hands and knees, and crawled. Until I was too tired to go any farther.

I was only about fifty feet away from where I started, but at least I was in the living room. In front of the fireplace. In front of the mantel. The streetlamp outside cast a blue hue onto the wall, and from where I rested, I could see our wedding picture. But only half of the photo was visible; I was there, Adam was blacked out.

I rocked back, sat and pondered that image—me without Adam.

This time I didn't have to hide them—my tears flowed. As I cried, time passed. Passing time meant that I was getting closer to when Adam would come home.

I needed to know when that would be, so I crawled to the sofa and pushed myself up enough to see the mantel clock.

I shrieked! It was only nine twenty. Nine twenty! Only twenty minutes since Shay-Shaunté had taken my husband away.

Oh, God!

If this was the pain of the first twenty minutes, I would never survive forty-eight hours. By the time Sunday night arrived, I would have already succumbed to insanity.

A joyful sound floated through the windows, startling me. It was faint laughter from the house next door. Our neighbors, the Donaldsons, were having a party to celebrate the arrival of 2011. Last week, they'd invited us and we'd politely declined. Now I wished that I'd accepted the invitation just so I would've had someplace to go. Just so I wouldn't have been so alone. Just so I wouldn't have felt so empty.

I wondered if the Donaldsons would mind if I just showed up. We'd been neighbors for years; surely they had enough food and holiday liquid cheer—they wouldn't turn me away.

Except that it might look crazy when I arrived at their home on my hands and knees, dressed in my bathrobe. And I wouldn't want to explain where my husband was.

Where *was* my husband?

Why hadn't he called? I knew it had only been twenty minutes, but surely he would have reached out to me by now. To let me know where he and Shay-Shaunté were going.

I hadn't thought this part of our deal through. I should have demanded to know where Shay-Shaunté was taking my husband. Were they going to her home, or was she taking him somewhere else? Were they even going to be in the D.C.-Maryland-Virginia area? Or had she taken my husband outside of the country?

Oh, God!

Those questions gave me strength, though. The strength I needed to get answers. I pushed myself up, but then I had to wait for the dizziness to pass before I took slow steps toward the telephone. *Breathe in, breathe out,* I reminded myself as I pressed the numbers for Adam's cell. His phone rang. Once. Twice. Then, before it went to the third ring, it hit his voice mail.

I stared at the phone for a moment. Two rings? That meant that he had pushed Ignore. He'd done something we'd told our children never to do. But here, right now, Adam was ignoring me!

I dialed again, pressing each number harder this time, as if that was a way for him to feel my . . . what? Anger? Desperation? Despair?

This time the call went straight to his voice mail. In the seconds it'd taken me to dial again, he—or someone—had turned off his cell.

I dropped the phone back into the receiver and glanced at the clock—nine twenty-five.

Just five more minutes had passed.

It was a fact—I was never going to make it. I wasn't even going to survive the hours between now and 2011.

Maybe bed was the best option. Unconsciousness would stop all thoughts and get me closer to tomorrow.

But when I got to our bedroom, I couldn't even cross the threshold. In front of me were all the signs of the man I loved—leftover shrimp, and grilled cheese sandwiches, and a pitcher half filled with red Kool-Aid. My eyes wandered to the fireplace—where we'd made love before he'd left to go make love again.

I slammed the bedroom door shut, then staggered into the family room. Behind the bar, I grabbed a bottle of Riesling that Adam said went with everything from appetizers to desserts; I wondered if it went well with agony and despair.

Turning to the staircase, I used the banister to pull myself up. I was already groggy and I hadn't had a single drink. I was groggy from grief.

Now I had this decision to make and I took my time, staring at the bedroom doors. Finally, I chose door number one.

Inside Alexa's bedroom, I stepped through the pink netting that fell over her canopy bed, then pulled back the duvet before I slipped onto the sheets. I hadn't thought about bringing a glass upstairs with me, so I just sipped wine from the bottle, as daintily as I could. I sipped until my skin became warm. I sipped until my toes were tingly.

Finally, I sighed, not happily, but with relief. Here, inside the bedroom of my oldest, I was close to all of my children. Here, I could imagine that Adam was with Shay-Shaunté only because he loved me and Alexa and Alana and Ethan.

Here, inside this pink haven, is where I finally escaped from the empty feelings that threatened to kill me. I fell asleep.

Chapter 40

The ringing. The ringing. The ringing.

I couldn't stop the ringing. No matter how many times I turned over. No matter how many times I tried to dive back into that place of deep slumber, the ringing just kept on.

My mind crawled through the tunnel that led toward consciousness, and my first thoughts were of my husband.

Adam!

The ringing.

My hand grasped air as I reached toward the telephone. But it wasn't there. I forced my eyes to flutter open; focus. But I wasn't in my bedroom.

Where was I?

I saw pink. All around. Alexa's room.

Why was I in here?

Then, the ringing. The ringing. The ringing.

The telephone.

Adam!

I shot up from the bed, though my mind moved faster than my body. The air was like water and I waded through, pushing against the current. In the hallway, I called out Adam's name.

"Please, don't hang up," I begged, as if he could hear me.

By the time I stumbled down the steps, the phone had stopped. I grabbed the receiver to call Adam back, but there was already someone on the line.

"Adam!" I shouted.

"Mom!"

"Ethan?"

"Mom!" my son cried.

"Ethan!"

"I've been calling you over and over. You were supposed to come get me."

"Where are you?"

"At Grandma's. You left me here. Please come and get me," he cried again.

Clear memories of last night rushed back to me. Adam. Shay-Shaunté. And how I promised to pick up my son first thing this morning.

Squinting, I focused on the clock in the living room.

Get out! Was it already past noon?

"Mom, you promised to get me this morning."

"I know. I'm sorry. I'm coming now."

"Hurry up," he pleaded.

I hung up because I couldn't bear to hear his voice anymore. I didn't want to hear another cry, didn't want to think about how I'd let him down. I was desperate to call Adam, but Ethan needed me now.

Feeling more hungover than groggy, I staggered toward my bedroom. At least I wasn't on my knees; that felt like progress to me.

But then I hit my bedroom door. The shrimp, the grilled cheese, the memories—were all still there.

I couldn't go in. But then Ethan's cries rumbled through my ears like thunder, and I pressed forward, mother-love propelling me. I had to get my son, and I couldn't do that wearing my bathrobe.

I jumped into the first pieces of clothing that I could find—gray sweatpants and a red-and-white ESPN Memorial T-shirt. I topped it off with a green sweatshirt; I didn't even bother with my coat. Inside of five minutes, I was in my car.

As I pulled out of the driveway, I dialed Adam's cell. No ring—straight to voice mail. I trembled. Last night I felt empty; now, I felt scared.

The ride to my mother's gave me too much space to think. I counted—it'd been fifteen hours since Adam had left with Shay-Shaunté. A lot of time for a lot to happen.

Screech! I put a brake on those thoughts. *Don't go there,* I told myself. I couldn't wonder about what had happened over the last hours. I wouldn't make it if I did. My focus needed to be forward. So, I counted ahead. Thirty-three hours were left.

Thirty-three hours?

That was more than double the time that had passed. If so much could've happened in fifteen hours, how much more could happen in thirty-three? How many times could Adam and Shay-Shaunté make love in that amount of time?

As fast as it came, I crushed that thought. Whatever Adam was doing with Shay-Shaunté, it wasn't love. It wasn't anything close to what we shared.

My fingers ached; I had a death grip on the steering wheel. I breathed deeply to relax and waited until I was at a red light to close my eyes and breathe even deeper.

If I was going to make it, I had to take my thoughts away

from Adam and Shay-Shaunté—even if it was just for a few moments.

As I passed the Nationals' stadium, I began to think of Ethan. I sped up as I crossed the Capitol Bridge, and two minutes later, I eased my car in front of my mother's.

The wind whipped across the Anacostia River, assaulting these streets that sat on the water's edge, and dropping the temperature from cold to arctic. Folding my hands across my chest, I rushed to the door and tested the knob. Just like I knew it would, the door opened.

I was ready to scream, to tell my mother that as long as one of my children was in her house, she needed to keep her doors locked. Then I stepped into chaos and saw my son.

"Mom!" Ethan sprang from the couch, almost knocking me over. His spindly arms wrapped around me like he never planned to let me go.

Around us, it was bedlam. My nephews ran over toys and jumped over furniture and screamed at no one and nothing. The television blasted, and through it all, Apollo and my mother did what they always did—just sat back and watched.

"Hey, sweetheart, what's wrong?" I had to tug at Ethan's arms to get him to release me. That's when I saw it. My son had a black eye. A black eye! "What happened?" I screamed.

"Ain't nothin' happen to that boy," my mother said from where she rested in her lounger.

"How can you say that?" I dragged Ethan over to her. Maybe she hadn't seen what had happened in her house. "Look at his eye!"

Marilyn sucked her teeth. "Please. He just got a little scratch, that's all."

"This is not a scratch." Since I needed to get the details

from someone who had some sense, I turned to my son. "What happened?"

"It was Taquan and his friends."

"See what I'm sayin'," my mother said. "How can an eight-year-old hurt a thirteen-year-old?"

"Ethan is ten," I said before I sent him to get dressed and get his bag.

When he dashed away, my mother said, "However old he is," and pointed her finger at me. "He's soft. You and Adam done babied that boy so much, he can't take up for himself."

"He shouldn't have to defend himself at his grandmother's house," I said.

"Don't get an attitude with me. I'm still your mother. They were just horsing around, you know, boys will be boys. Ain't nothin' for you to make a big deal out of."

"Hey, girl!" Cashmere sauntered into the living room before I could say another word to Marilyn. Wearing a sheer black nightie that made me want to cover my eyes, Cashmere said, "What's up?" Then she had the nerve to look me up and down as if what I had on was ridiculous. "Happy New Year."

"Yeah," I groaned and wondered what was taking Ethan so long.

"What's wrong with you?" Cashmere asked.

My mother answered, "She's mad about Ethan's eye."

Cashmere waved her hand in the air like it was nothing. "Oh, that little thing."

If another person said another word about my baby's black eye being a little thing, I was going to act out every bit of the frustration I had about Shay-Shaunté and Adam right in the middle of my mother's house. And that meant it wasn't gonna go down pretty.

"Please," Cashmere continued. "He'll be all right. Where's Adam?"

"At work."

She raised her eyebrows. "Who has to work on New Year's Day?"

"Adam," I said with attitude.

"Uh-huh," my mother and sister sang together. As if they knew something.

My mother said, "Well, I, for one, don't give a fluck where Adam is, as long as he keeps bringing in the money." Then she had the nerve to give my sister a high five.

"Mom, can you not curse?" I asked. "You shouldn't be saying stuff like that in front of your grandchildren."

"First of all, I didn't curse. It's because of my grandbabies that I add an extra letter here and there. And second of all, don't be coming up in my house telling me what to do, you hear me?"

My answer to her was, "Ethan! Come on!" Whether he was dressed or naked, whether he had his bag or not, we were getting up out of this place.

My son came running, looking a mess, kinda discombobulated and mismatched, like me. But he was ready to go.

"Thanks for watching him, Marilyn," I said without a bit of gratitude in my voice. I guessed I should've been thankful, though; my son was still alive.

As we walked toward the door, stepping over all kinds of clothes and toys, my mother called out, "You're not gonna give me a hug?"

Ethan looked at me first; I could tell he didn't want to do it. But with a little nudge from me, he leapt, in a single bound, to his grandmother. She gave him a little air-hug, then pushed him away.

"So, you just gonna leave like that, Evia?"

"Huh?"

"Don't huh me. You're not even gonna break me off something for taking care of your brat?"

"Brat? He's not a—"

"Oh, don't get your panties all twisted. That's just a term . . . of endearment."

Wow! If I wasn't so mad, I would've been impressed. A ten-letter word—where had my mother learned about endearment?

"I mean," she said, "I didn't even go out last night watching your kid."

I was gonna say something about the other kids who lived in the house with her, but I wanted to make a quick getaway.

I took out every bill in my wallet—a twenty, a ten, three ones . . . I paused.

Thirty-three dollars.

Thirty-three hours.

My hand shook as I handed my mother the money.

"What's wrong with you, girl?" She reached for the bills and counted. "There's only thirty-three dollars here. You acting like you giving me a million dollars or something."

"I'm giving you all that I have."

That's what I'd given to Shay-Shaunté.

"It'll do." My mother stuffed the money down her bra. She had what she wanted, so she dismissed me and Ethan with a "See y'all."

Ethan said good-bye to his aunt and cousins only because I made him. Then the two of us flew through the door.

Inside the car, I apologized to Ethan.

"It's okay, Mom," he said, full of grace.

I figured that I should take him somewhere—to McDonald's or somewhere—to make up for the torture he'd endured, but I'd given my last thirty-three dollars to my mother.

Thirty-three dollars.

Thirty-three hours.

I trembled again.

"I'm gonna tell Dad what happened and Taquan is gonna be in trouble."

I glanced sideways at my son's black eye and my heart twisted. If Adam had been home . . . if we hadn't made the deal . . . if Shay-Shaunté hadn't made the offer . . . if Adam hadn't lost his job . . .

"When is Dad coming back?" Ethan asked.

His eye shined as he looked at me, and all I could think about was how our choices, our decisions, our sins had now come upon our son.

"Soon," I said. I added more life to my voice when I said, "Tomorrow." In thirty-three hours.

"I can't wait to see him," Ethan sighed.

And I sighed, too.

Chapter 41

I HADN'T HEARD FROM ADAM. NOT a call, an email, or a text. Even though my BlackBerry had become an appendage at the end of my right hand, even though I knew it was working because I'd ignored countless calls from Brooklyn and Tamica, even though I was so sure that I would get that call that I needed, nothing came from my husband.

I was scared.

We were approaching the halfway point—twenty-four hours had passed, twenty-four hours to go. In all the years that I'd known Adam, since we were twelve, no more than seven hours went by without us communicating—and that only happened when we were asleep.

How could he not have time to call me? Was he so enamored of Shay-Shaunté that he'd already forgotten his family? Forgotten about me?

What was going on? Were they talking a lot? Were they

eating together? Were they going out or staying in—wherever they were? And if they were staying in, what were they doing?

The tension surged from my mind, sent the shock to my body, exploded in my hands.

I heard the shatter of the glass before I felt the pain.

"Mom!" my children screamed at the same time.

The stem of the glass was still in my hand.

"What happened?" the twins asked as they jumped up from the table and rushed to me.

I looked down at the shattered pieces of glass in the sink. "I guess it slipped from my hand," I said, though I knew that's not what happened.

"You're bleeding," Alexa said.

"Does it hurt?" Alana asked as she reached for the first-aid kit under the sink.

"I'm okay," I told both of them. "You guys go on back—finish eating. I'll be all right."

Neither obeyed as they stood by my side and watched me run cold water over the cut between my thumb and forefinger. Then I applied pressure to my flesh while Alexa gathered the slivers of glass from the sink and Alana handed me a Band-Aid. They stayed by my side, as if they weren't sure they should leave me alone.

"Would you guys go on and finish eating," I said.

I hated that I had taken some of the joy out of their day. Until that moment, all three of my children had been totally elated with our family celebration of the arrival of 2011.

Though Ethan's new year hadn't started strong, it had made a powerful comeback. Because of my guilt.

I'd showered my son with food, snacks, and gifts all day. He'd started with a supersized meal at McDonald's and then added three sugar cookies to the order once he'd realized that

I'd been so guilt-ridden that he could have had anything. Then I'd taken him to the Golf Center, where I'd purchased that driver that he'd been talking about. Yesterday, I hadn't seen any way to spend eight hundred dollars on a single golf club for a ten-year-old. Today, I was convinced that Ethan had earned it.

By the time Ethan and I had come home, the twins had met us at the door, bursting with their wondrous stories about their fabulous night.

"Mom, it was stupid," Alexa had said.

I'd guessed that had been stupid in a good way.

"And you should've seen the Range Rover that Chloe got," Alexa added.

"Yeah," Alana said. "It was cool; now I'm kinda getting excited about our party."

"And I'm getting excited about our cars," Alexa said. "Are we getting Range Rovers?"

Alana answered for me, "That would cost too much."

"I know, but wouldn't that be ridiculous? A pink one for me and a purple one for you."

"I don't think they come in those colors," Alana said.

I'd let the girls chatter on about parties and cars until Alexa had said, "I can't wait till Dad gets home tomorrow so we can start planning this whole thing."

The emptiness, the fear, the questions were never far away, but when Alexa had mentioned her father, those emotions had overwhelmed me. When his sisters had finally noticed Ethan's black eye, my shame had overflowed.

So I'd called Takeout Taxi and told the kids to order whatever they'd wanted from The Cheesecake Factory.

"Whatever?" the three had asked together.

When I'd nodded, they'd looked at me with wary eyes, but then, under the leadership of Alexa, they'd ordered—whatever—as fast as they could.

We'd been sitting around the table for hours, devouring a hodgepodge menu: barbecue pizza, roadside sliders, fried macaroni and cheese, four-cheese pasta, and then the sides: mashed potatoes *and* French fries. It hadn't even bothered me that the bill, with all the charges, had come to almost two hundred dollars. How could I have cared when I'd scarcely been able to breathe?

Once the girls had started talking about their father, I'd gotten up from the table with my plate and my glass. That was when I'd stood at the sink and started thinking about Adam and Shay-Shaunté and my emptiness and my fear. That was when my flesh had started bleeding as much as my heart.

When the girls finally left me alone, they returned to the table and their chatter, their focus still on their father.

"What time is Daddy going to call?" Alana asked me.

I looked down at where the Band-Aid covered my broken skin and wondered if my hand stopped bleeding would my heart do the same?

"Mom," Alana called before she repeated her question.

It was a normal question: Anytime Adam left on a business trip, he called every day, usually right before the children went to bed. He could never sleep without speaking to the loves of his life—those were his words.

But this time, there'd been no calls. Did that mean that we were no longer his loves? No longer a part of his life?

I didn't want my children to be suspicious, so I lied. "He called me . . . on my cell . . . this afternoon . . . before I got home . . ."

Ethan frowned. "Why didn't you let me talk to him, 'cause I can't wait to tell him what Taquan did."

My mini-me peered right through me. "Why would he call right after he left this morning? Why wouldn't he wait until he could talk to us tonight?"

See, that was the problem with lying to smart children.

I shrugged. "I'm sure he'll call tonight."

Alexa said, "Great, 'cause I can't wait to tell him about the party."

"I think I want a birthday party this year, too," Ethan piped in.

"You had a big one last year," Alexa said. "For your tenth. No one cares that you're turning eleven; it is so not a special year."

"Uh-huh. Yes, it is."

I glanced down at my cell—8:59. I slipped out of the kitchen, leaving my feuding children behind. Inside the foyer, I sat on the bottom step, exactly where I'd been twenty-four hours ago. When the digits on my cell turned to 9:00, I closed my eyes and begged God to bring my husband home.

Chapter 42

SHAY-SHAUNTÉ: WAS IT HER MONEY OR her looks?

That was the five-million-dollar question I'd asked myself all night as I'd lain awake waiting, waiting, waiting. For the call, email, text.

Nothing had come.

Adam had forgotten all about me.

Was it her money or her looks?

Rolling over to the empty side of the bed—Adam's side—I inhaled his lingering scent. I wrapped my arms around his pillow and imagined that it was him.

But there was no way I could keep lying there, thinking about Adam deserting me. Sitting up, I glanced at the clock. It was twenty to nine, but if I hurried, I could make it to church. I could be ready and out of the house in twelve minutes. I wouldn't be on time, but I wouldn't be too late.

Last night, I'd told the children that we'd sleep in this morning; that had been my plan. I didn't want to go to church without Adam. Didn't want to explain to anyone that Adam was working. That may have gone over with our children, but the lie wouldn't pass the sensibility test for most adults.

Now that morning had come, I needed to be in church. Just felt like I really had to be there to glean some of the hope that Bishop Cash always gave me.

Decision made, I was in and out of the shower in three minutes, and four minutes after that, I was totally dressed—in a black, sleeveless tank dress that was far more appropriate for spring. But how could I be expected to make any intelligent decisions, including wardrobe choices, when I was dealing with the probable loss of my husband.

The loss of my husband! Did I really believe that? My groan was so deep, so long that I had to lean against the dresser to keep standing. I moaned, not because I was so sure that Adam was gone but because I wasn't sure that he was coming back.

I piled my purse, coat, and hat onto the settee by the door, then tiptoed upstairs and into Alana's bedroom, which was exactly like Alexa's, only overflowing with purple instead of pink.

Shaking her gently, I whispered, "Alana."

Her eyelids quivered, then slowly opened. "Mom." Her voice was full of sleep.

"Listen, I'm going to church."

She pushed herself up. "Okay," she squeaked. "I'll get up . . ."

"No, no. I'm going. You go back to sleep. Just make sure that when you get up, you help Ethan with breakfast, okay?"

"'Kay." She stretched, released a drawn-out moan. "Is Daddy going with you?"

Her mention of her father doubled the size of the lump in my throat. I didn't have to answer her, though; her head was back on her pillow, her eyes were closed, she was once again asleep.

Another two minutes and I was inside the car. Twelve minutes, just like I thought.

I'd always been good at estimating time. Always had complete control over the minutes and hours of my day. But not this weekend. Not only did time control me but time had slowed down, giving Shay-Shaunté more time with Adam. Time was nothing but torture.

Why hadn't I seen this before? Why hadn't I known that this was going to happen? Now that I was living through the consequences of our decision, it seemed so clear. There was not a woman on earth who would've ever agreed to this.

"So, why did I?" I whispered.

I had plenty of answers: I'd done it for the children, for Ruby, even for my broke-down family. But wasn't I, wasn't Adam smart enough to count the cost? Shouldn't we have measured our decision?

But that's not what we'd done. All we'd seen was the money. Now we were locked in—in a deal with the devil.

Inside the church parking lot, I pulled into a faraway space at the other end of the lot, then stuffed my uncombed hair under my hat. Lifting my coat collar as high as it would go, I got out of the car. With my head down, I marched forward.

The choir already had the sanctuary rockin'. The usher recognized me and, with a smile, directed me toward the front, where I normally sat with my family.

I shook my head, then ducked into the far end of the very last row. I didn't want to see anyone today—I was just here for the hope.

The service proceeded quickly, through another song by the praise team, the offering, and the welcoming of visitors, though I didn't greet a soul.

Finally, Bishop Cash rose, wearing his special-occasion burgundy-and-gold robe. "Happy new year, church!"

The congregation greeted him the same way.

"Welcome to two-k-eleven; isn't that how the young people say it?" He laughed, and many joined him. "I pray that everyone within the sound of my voice and those outside of these walls had the best New Year's ever."

I groaned. I didn't mean to do it so loudly; didn't know that I had, until the lady next to me glanced my way with a frown.

Bishop said, "Well, on this first Sunday of the new year, I've got something for y'all; is that all right with you?"

"Preach!"

Bishop Cash laughed. "That's what I plan to do. But before I begin, I want you to know that anything I say today, I'm not talking about you." He pointed to the congregation, and the sanctuary filled with laughter. "'Cause I don't want to get no emails, no snail mail, no hate mail, nothin'! You hear me? 'Cause this is not 'bout you; it's all about me." He pounded his fist against his chest. "And my life. And how I've had plenty of days . . . and plenty of nights . . . where I found myself . . . dancing with the devil!"

The musical director hit the keyboard with one of those *da-da-da-daaaaaaaaa*s—like something dark was about to happen.

I sat up straight in that pew.

Cash said, "I admit it." He swiped a handkerchief across his brow once more. "I've danced with the devil. But at least I'm not 'shamed to tell the truth."

"Amen, now!"

"Oh, somebody, help me now, because you see, there are plenty of times when we do things and we blame it on the devil. And I got a secret for ya . . . sometimes, it ain't the devil's fault. Sometimes, all that trouble came from you."

Most of the congregation laughed; I trembled.

"Come on, somebody. Sometimes, trouble comes because

you did something you weren't supposed to do or you didn't do something that you were supposed to do. Amen!"

The congregation chanted the same behind the Bishop.

"But I'm here to tell you that the most dangerous times, I say, the most dangerous times, are when it is the devil . . . listen to me now." He paused. ". . . it *is* the devil"—his voice was real low—"and you don't even know it!"

Brent went to work on the keyboard again, and now many people were on their feet. I would've stood too,—if I'd been able. But the Bishop's words had me frozen.

"Yes, I tell you," the Bishop kept on, "there are times when the devil has knocked at our door, sat at our table, played with our kids—and we don't even recognize him. Because we're Christians: Nobody can touch us. And then we find ourselves all up with the devil. Can I get an Amen?"

The bishop got a lot of "Hallelujahs" and as many "Preach its" to go along with the "Amen!" But not a word came from me, though the tears had already begun to pool in the corners of my eyes.

"Once we start dancing," Bishop Cash continued, "it's hard to stop. We're caught up now 'cause the dance looks good, feels good, and we think it's gonna do us good. But it's counterfeit, Saints. Because the dance is just a distraction to take your focus away. 'Cause when you're distracted, the enemy can get all up and involved in your life. Yeah, just a way to keep you dancing over here while he's taking away everything from you over there."

I closed my eyes and the tears began to fall—this was happening to me and Adam. We'd made a deal, and now we were dancing with the devil.

"Oh, yeah, Saints, I'm telling you, it's happened to me. The devil has slithered right up to my door, and it wasn't until we'd had a couple of drinks and started dancing and then the devil stepped on my feet that I recognized. I had to jump back and say, 'Oops, there it is! That ain't nothin' but the devil.'"

The congregation roared like they were at some kind of comedy show.

And I cried.

"But here's the thing," Cash said, slowing down. His voice was lower now. "We've had a good time laughing about this, but you know what? This isn't even funny when it's happening to you."

I would've cried out "Amen" if I'd been able.

He said, "The thing is, Saints, let's not get so caught up in our problems that we don't recognize our enemies. You may not want to admit it, but there are people who hate you. People who have come into your lives to destroy you. People who have come to steal from you and even"—he lowered his head—"come to kill you."

There was nothing but silence, and I had to fight hard to keep my sobs inside.

"I'm not trying to scare you, Saints. This is not a fire-and-brimstone church. I don't believe in that. You know I believe in the prosperity that God has for you. But if you want to be prosperous, you have to prepare sometimes to do battle. And you can't fight . . . and dance at the same time. You can't be friends with your enemies."

It was only because of the host of praises that filled the sanctuary that no one could hear my cries.

"I will close with this: Dance with the devil if you want to, but don't expect to get out without at least getting burnt!"

Everyone around me was on their feet, but I didn't have the strength to stand. Bishop Cash had been talking about me. About me and Adam. About Shay-Shaunté.

But this message had come too late for us. We'd made the

deal, we were doing the dance. All that was left was to find out how hot our burns were going to be.

My head hung so low that it was almost in my lap. While everyone around me stood in praise, I bowed in reverence, praying that even though we'd done wrong, God's mercy would somehow protect us from the fervent flames of Hell's fire.

Chapter 43

THE CHILDREN LEFT ME ALONE; I guess they thought I needed some quiet space.

That was a problem, though—because with each of them behind their own closed doors, the house was so still, so silent that it was suffocating.

I'd been terrified all day—ever since I'd heard Bishop's message. I couldn't stop wondering if, when Adam came home, he would bring Hell's fire with him.

That's what I'd been pondering for the last seven hours, torturing myself as I watched the second hand of the clock tick slowly toward the forty-seventh hour.

I tore my eyes away from the clock for just a few seconds, and I saw my reflection in the antique-silver leaning mirror. Did I really look like that? So sick, so tired, so empty? I was horrified.

I crawled to the bottom of the bed, rolled off, then crept toward the mirror. The linen dress I'd worn all day was crinkled with wrinkles, but it wasn't my clothing that made me look like a disaster zone. My eyes were dark with dread. My skin was dry and dead. My lips turned downward, as if my soul knew that I'd never smile again. My hair was matted against my head, evidence that I hadn't enlisted the help of a comb since Adam had left.

Adam had just spent forty-eight hours with Shay-Shaunté. He couldn't find me this way.

That realization gave me life and I hopped into the shower for the second time that day. Not because I felt dirty but because I wanted to feel clean. I took my time making decisions: lotioned my body with the Japanese cherry blossom fragrance that Adam loved, chose the low-rider designer jeans that he'd given me for Christmas and paired them with a classic, tailored white shirt. Before I put on my makeup, I moisturized my face, then applied my foundation—not too heavy—mascara, and clear lip gloss. There wasn't much that I could do with my hair in the time that I had. But blessedly, Adam's favorite style was off my face, pulled all the way back. So with gel, I twisted my hair into a simple bun, to look pleasing to my husband.

I didn't rush on purpose, trying to use up the minutes, hoping that as much time as possible would've passed when I stepped back into my bedroom.

It was ten minutes to nine and I looked like the wife Adam loved.

For the first time in more than forty-eight hours, I smiled. I sat on the edge of my bed. And waited.

Chapter 44

It was ten minutes after nine.

Not a call, not a text, not an email.

Not a sign of Adam.

I couldn't breathe sitting down, so I paced in my bare feet.

It was funny the way time passed now, moving quickly. The seconds ticked by . . . from ten after nine, to nine thirty, to nine forty-five.

I never sat down. I walked with the time, kept pace with the seconds so that I could keep thinking, keep breathing, keep living.

Now it was ten o'clock.

He'd spent forty-nine hours with Shay-Shaunté.

I wondered: Was she going to pay me for overtime? That thought made me giggle. I pressed my fingertips against my mouth, pushing my laugh back inside. But it exploded past my lips anyway. I closed my bedroom door so that my children wouldn't hear me. I didn't want them to see me losing my mind. Because I had no doubt that's what was happening. Insanity—a patient vulture—had been hovering all weekend. Now it had swooped down and taken its prize; I was going crazy for sure.

Why was I laughing? Was it because I didn't want to cry? I couldn't answer that—all I knew was that I couldn't stop. I laughed like a hyena, sounding almost diabolical, but I had no control.

So I just kept laughing. And laughing. And laughing.

As the clock ticked to ten thirty, I climbed, fully dressed, under the covers. Then time sped toward eleven. Between my giggles, I tried to calculate how much more Shay-Shaunté was going to owe me. And what would she give me if Adam never returned?

Never returned?

Those two words stopped the laughter. Now my tears were fast and furious, destroying the perfect palette on my face. But what did it matter? Adam wasn't going to see my face, or any part of me.

He wasn't coming home.

My greatest fear was coming true. Was it her looks? Or her money?

But then, in the darkest hours of the night, car lights beamed into my bedroom. I sprang up. The lights remained, shining, and I waited. Then I heard a car door slam.

I scooted to the edge of the bed. Counted . . . one, two, three, four, five, six, seven. Then two beeps of the alarm, the signal that a door had been unlocked and opened.

I closed my eyes.

Footsteps that I couldn't hear, but movement that I could feel. I took one thousand breaths, and then I opened my eyes.

Adam stood in the doorway to our bedroom, his garment bag hanging low off his shoulder.

I rushed to him but stopped two steps away. He hadn't moved toward me. Just stood. With dark eyes and a sad face.

Was his sorrow because of me? Because he'd had to come home?

I gulped back fear. Let a "Hi," squeak through my lips.

He nodded and let his bag drop, but said nothing.

I searched for words, though I couldn't find anything profound to say to the man whom I'd loved since forever, who was coming home from spending a couple of nights with another woman. Because it was all different now. I'd never been with another man, but now, he'd been with another woman.

So what was I supposed to say? The only thing that came to mind was, "How are you?"

He shrugged and still stayed quiet.

Not knowing what to do, I took another step forward, then stopped again. I wanted to get closer but couldn't. I wanted to touch him but didn't. Because there was a shield around him. A block that prevented me from moving forward. It was like a force field, an aura that was stopping me. Shay-Shaunté's aura?

But finally, he moved. Came to me and wrapped his arms around me. Held me as if he hadn't forgotten the love of his life.

I closed my eyes and breathed normally. For the first time in fifty hours, I breathed like I was going to live. It didn't matter that he was late—all that mattered was that he was home.

Adam pulled away, though, much too soon, because I wanted to hold him forever. But he took two giant steps back. "I need . . . to take a shower."

Those were his first words to me? A shower? Why? Had he just . . .

I pressed my lips together so that my question wouldn't come out. All I did was nod.

My eyes stayed on him as he moved toward our bathroom, then stopped. Turning back, he came to me but stood an arm's length away. "I almost forgot," he said. "This is the money."

Adam had almost forgotten—but in the minutes that had passed between him walking into our home and now, I had totally forgotten. Because this wasn't about the money anymore. The last fifty hours had made me see that five million dollars was hardly worth anything.

But still, I took the envelope. Because we'd earned it. We'd done what we'd had to do, and now we could deposit it and leave this weekend behind.

I looked up at Adam and waited for him to take my hand and invite me to bathe with him—just like he'd done before he'd left. Just like he'd done a thousand days before that. But with a small smile, he turned away, walked into the bathroom, and closed the door.

That's okay, I thought and released a long breath.

Falling back onto the bed, I was filled with gratitude. My husband was home. That was all that mattered.

Looking down at the envelope, my head jerked back a bit. Evia *Early* Evans was scrawled in the center. Again, I wondered how she knew my middle name. But that's how she'd written the first check. The shocker to me now was the two words that followed my name: Thank you!

What?

Thank you!

Thank you? Was she kidding me?

What was I supposed to say? You're welcome?

I dug through the nightstand drawer, found a pen, then with what felt like five million strokes, I scratched out Shay-Shaunté's gratitude. I scratched until those words could not be seen, could not be felt. Then I placed the envelope on the edge of my nightstand and scooted back against the headboard.

Now, I would wait for Adam.

Chapter 45

EVEN THOUGH ADAM WAS BACK, IT didn't feel like he was home.

As I reached into the pantry to pull out boxes of cereal for the children, I thought about last night and how I'd waited and waited for Adam to come out of the bathroom . . .

The shower had stopped long ago, but there was no sign of my husband. For a moment, I wondered if he'd somehow fallen asleep in there. But just when I was going to check, he opened the door and looked right into my eyes.

He jumped back, as if he was startled. As if he never expected that I'd still be awake.

While he was startled, I was shocked that he'd come out fully dressed. I mean, covered from head to toe. Not in street clothes, of course, but in pajamas—a bottom *and* a top.

Now, that might have been normal for most people, but that was not the way Adam and I rolled. Most nights, ninety-nine percent of the time, we slept in the nude. The other times, Adam wore bottoms, *never* anything on top.

The black silk pair wasn't even anything that I'd ever seen. In fact, they looked brand-new. I was frozen, not believing what I was seeing. No way—would Adam actually do this? Would he wear something that he'd received from Shay-Shaunté?

I didn't blink as he lumbered across the bedroom with slumped shoulders and heavy feet.

When he got to his side of the bed, I couldn't hold back any longer. "Where did you get those pajamas?" I did my best to keep the accusatory tone out of my voice, but I wasn't successful.

Adam looked down. "These?" Then, with a frown, he made eye contact again. "These are from your mother. For Christmas. Remember?"

I gulped in air. I did remember—a little. Not that I paid attention to anything my mother ever gave to anyone in my family. For years, she'd given my children clothes that had been too small and toys that had been too juvenile, so when she'd given us boxes on Christmas, I hadn't even opened mine. And I'd never asked Adam about his.

Now I wished I had, because he said, "Where did you think I got these?" Then he held up his hand as if he didn't want me to answer. "Never mind," he said, shaking his head.

I guessed he didn't want to hear what I had to say. Didn't want to get into any discussion about how I thought he'd bring a gift from Shay-Shaunté into our bedroom.

But here's the thing—he shouldn't have been mad at me, because clearly the game had changed. We were playing under a new system; from the moment Adam walked in that door, nothing was the same. He didn't greet with the cheer and the love that he had every day of our lives. And now he was coming to bed fully dressed. He'd only been home for a bit more than an hour, but it felt like a lifetime of changes had occurred. I couldn't be blamed for not knowing, not understanding.

Adam tossed back the duvet, then climbed in. Even though I was sitting up, still dressed, obviously waiting, he turned and rested with his back to me. He teetered on the edge, like he was going to fall off the bed at any second and didn't care.

No, it wasn't going to go down like this. He had just come home, and this was all that I was going to get?

I said, "Adam . . . I want to—"

He didn't let me finish. "I'm really tired. I can't talk."

That was it. Nothing more. No other explanation. Not a kiss or another hug.

I sucked in my hurt and told myself that this was normal, though I didn't have any other situation to compare this to. But it had to be normal. If Adam's weekend was half as traumatic as mine had been, he needed time. Isn't that what they told spouses whose partners returned from war?

So without getting undressed, I settled into my side of the bed and stayed awake for the rest of the dark hours, wondering what I was supposed to do now.

As dawn approached, I convinced myself that once the sun rose, and my husband did, too, the Adam that I'd loved would greet me and love me like he always had . . .

But the sun had been up for almost an hour and Adam was still tucked in bed.

"Is Daddy home?" Ethan asked as he darted into the kitchen.

Behind him were the twins with the same question.

"Everybody sit down," I said, motioning toward the breakfast nook. "Your dad's home, but he's still asleep."

"Really?" Alexa said. I was waiting for her suspicion; waiting for her to ask me twenty questions about whether Adam was going to work. But she didn't say a word about that.

She did say, "I tried to wait up for him, but it was such a long, wonderful weekend. I was too tired."

I agreed with the long part, the tired part.

Alexa continued, "I fell asleep before ten."

Alana said, "Well, I didn't fall asleep till eleven, and I didn't hear him."

"Are you guys talking about me?"

"Daddy!" My three children jumped up and into the arms of their father.

It was the lovely greeting that he always gave to Alexa, Alana, and Ethan. It was the same greeting that I'd expected last night.

"Happy new year, Daddy," Alana said, as she kissed him over and over on one cheek.

"We really missed you," Alexa said, doing the same on the other side of his face. "Wait till you hear about the party!"

"Daddy, do you know what Taquan did?" Ethan asked. "He gave me a black eye."

"Whoa!"

That took the smile off Adam's face as he backed up and inspected his son. Ethan filled him in on all the details, and as I listened, I felt guilty all over again.

"What are you gonna do, Dad?" Ethan said with a tinge of excitement in his voice. As if he hoped that his father would go over to his grandmother's house and beat up his cousin.

With his hands tenderly inspecting Ethan, Adam said, "I'm gonna handle it."

Ethan sulked back to the table; clearly Adam's words weren't threatening enough.

"Daddy," Alexa said, making Adam look at her. "Do you want to talk about the party now?"

"No, sweetheart," he said, grabbing a banana from the counter. "You've got to get to school and . . ." He paused, as if he was thinking about something. "I've got to get out of here, too."

I frowned for more than one reason. First, Adam had yet

to say good morning to me. And second, where was he going? I needed to talk to him . . . about the thank-you note from Shay-Shaunté . . . and other things before I had to face her in the office.

"Are you going to be home early?" Alexa asked. "Because we have a lot to discuss."

"I'll be waiting when you get home from school." That's when he turned to me. Finally. "Good morning," he said. He tried to smile. His effort wasn't enough.

Things were really bad, because I didn't even know what to say to his good morning. So, I tried to smile back. My effort didn't work either.

He said, "I gotta make a run."

I lowered my voice and said, "I wanted . . . needed to talk to you before I . . . went in to work today, and." I left it right there. He knew what I meant.

He stood as if he was trying to figure out what he should do. Kind of nodding, kind of shaking his head, he said, "I'll talk to you later. When you get home."

That'll be too late! Of course I only screamed that inside because the children were right there.

So, I gave him a nod—this time, without the effort of a smile—and sent him on his way. He kissed the twins and Ethan before he left; he had nothing for me. And the hole in my heart widened.

Now, I had a new emotion to mix in with all the turmoil already inside of me. Now, I was heartbroken, anxious, fearful—and suspicious.

This was a deadly combination, I was sure, because I had one thousand new questions. Where was he going this early in the morning? What did he have to do that was more important than talking to me? He had to make a run—wasn't that the language of drug dealers and adulterers?

I couldn't believe how much our lives had changed since Friday. Now I didn't trust my husband.

After sending the children off, I returned to our bedroom and the envelope that waited for me. Even though I could no longer see Shay-Shaunté's thank-you, I could feel it. I wanted to tear this envelope and what was inside into a million little pieces, but good sense prevailed. There was no need to be mad at the money. After what we'd been through, we needed this.

"Five million dollars will buy a lot of therapy."

It was supposed to be a joke from me to myself. But since it wasn't funny, and I didn't laugh, I just tossed the envelope into my purse and went into the bathroom. I had to prepare to see the lady who'd had my husband. It was gonna be tough, but I'd handle it. Hadn't I made it through the weekend?

I was Evia Langston from Barry Farm. I could handle Shay-Shaunté; I could handle anything.

At least, that's what I kept telling myself.

Chapter 46

I WAS ALREADY COUNTING DOWN.

Half a year. Six months. One hundred and eighty two days. It was a good thing that the shortest month of the year fell on my side of this deal.

No matter how I counted, though, staying at Ferossity was not going to be easy. The only reason I was gonna make it was because of this check in my purse and the chance to get out of there sooner if I found another assistant for Shay-Shaunté.

As I turned my car into the parking lot of Bank of DC, I kept my thoughts on the money. This half of the five million was all about saving and investing. If Adam and I had been back to normal, we would've talked this morning about meeting with our personal banker and setting up our financial plan.

I released a big ole sigh, then told myself that once I made it through today and got home tonight, we'd talk like husband and wife and get back to the business of being the Langstons—

the lovely family who was financially set now because of the sacrifice we'd made.

I strolled into the bank with my head high—I guess depositing several millions into your bank account could do that to you, but it wasn't just the money. I strutted like a peacock because I was rich *and* I looked good. For the first time in days, I felt like that five million dollars we'd earned.

I had to bring it when I walked into Ferossity this morning, I knew that. When I faced Shay-Shaunté, I had to be elegant and eloquent. No matter what had gone down between her and Adam, she was gonna see that my husband had come home to me for a reason. She was gonna know that Adam was with the woman he loved and wanted.

So, I'd done what I'd had to do—hit the best pieces in my closet: my black fitted St. John's tank knit dress that tricked the eye and made my size 12 figure look like a 10. Then, the black Ferragamo heels that were an inch taller than what I was used to, but which I handled because of the way they made my legs look longer. I'd even decided to change up my coat—left my down jacket at home and traded it in for my ankle-length cashmere with the fox collar.

Inside the bank, there was already a line. It was the first month, the first Monday, the first business day after the holiday, and I had expected the crowd. But the line at the teller didn't affect me, because I had this check in my purse.

Mr. Grey greeted me. "You're back, Ms. Langston."

Adam and I hadn't bothered to tell the banker that we'd be back with another two point five million dollars. "I have a deposit."

He offered me the chair on the other side of his desk. "And I take it that since you're not going to the tellers . . ." He pointed across toward the line of other customers.

With a smile, I nodded. "Yes, it's another large deposit. The same as last time."

All that gave away his surprise was the slight rise of his left eyebrow. I guess he was trained to deal with these kinds of deposits.

As I took the check from my purse, I said, "Right now, we're just going to deposit this, but Adam and I want to come back and talk to you about the best way to handle this money."

I glanced at the front, then endorsed the back. "Maybe we can see you later this week," I said as I handed the banker the money.

"My schedule is open on Thursday and Friday right now. Call and we'll set something up." He glanced at the check. "You want to deposit this into your joint account?"

"Yes, just like before." Then I thought, "Unless you think I should do something else. I mean, we were writing checks against the other deposit, but this one, we want to invest. Would it be smart to put this two million into our personal savings for now, or should I open something else today?"

He was frowning before I finished. "Two million? Ms. Langston, this check is for two hundred and fifty thousand."

"What?" It wasn't rudeness that made me snatch it out of his hand; it was shock. I studied the check this time. Just like before, I saw the two and the five, but I hadn't counted the zeros. I hadn't paid attention to the commas. I hadn't even read the line where it clearly said "Two Hundred and Fifty Thousand."

"Dang! This is a mistake."

Mr. Grey looked at me as if he wondered what I expected him to do about that.

"Okay, look," I said with a sigh. "Somebody must've prepared the check for her . . . she'll just write me another one. I'll deposit this." He nodded, and then I added, "Would you mind making me a copy before you deposit it?"

"No problem."

The tip of my shoe tapped the desk as I waited. I couldn't believe Shay-Shaunté had made this kind of mistake. It was ridiculous—especially since she'd also kept Adam for two hours longer than she was supposed to.

Mr. Grey returned with a copy of the check and my deposit slip. "I look forward to hearing from you later this week."

Even though I was annoyed, once I left the bank I left my thoughts about the money there, too. Although I wasn't crazy about Shay-Shaunté, I knew who she was. Her word was her bond. She did business fairly, never cheated anyone. She wouldn't cheat me.

So, money wasn't the problem. My problem was all about Shay-Shaunté *and* Adam. And their weekend. And how the two had shared time that I knew nothing about.

I had to decide how I was going to play this. A good part of how the day went down depended on Shay-Shaunté—and how she came at me. I didn't know if she was gonna be professional or if she was gonna try to come strong.

Whichever, whatever, I was ready for her.

Chapter 47

"Girl!" Rachel sang. "Where you going?"

Rachel's desk was right in front of the elevator banks, so as soon as I stepped off, she'd jumped up from her chair.

Her hands were resting on her ample hips when she shook her head and grunted, "Umph. Umph. Umph. You look good."

"Thank you," I said, then added, "happy new year."

"Forget about a happy new year for me, it must've been a beast for you."

My smile dimmed at that, but I wasn't about to tell Rachel anything. So, all I did was lower my voice and say, "Let me get to my office before she—"

"Oh, you don't have to worry about Shay-Shaunté," Rachel said, all loud. "She's not even here."

I slowed my steps. "She's not in yet?"

"Nope."

Okay, something was up. In the six years that I'd worked here, Shay-Shaunté had always been the first one in and the last one out. The joke was that she slept here. So, why was today different? Why, after a weekend with Adam, was she late getting into work?

"Has she called?"

"Yeah, but she didn't give me anything to gossip about," Rachel said. "Just said that she had to make a run."

My stomach did a somersault. Make a run? Like Adam!

Oh, my God!

"Evia, you okay?"

I didn't even realize that I'd closed my eyes. I opened them and waited until the fuzzy lines around Rachel faded before I said anything. "Yeah, I'm fine."

"It looked like I lost you." Then she asked, "So, what do you think Ms. Shay-Shaunté is up to?"

I didn't even want to know.

Rachel said, "Maybe it had something to do with her birthday weekend."

Oh, God!

"Maybe her birthday weekend isn't over," Rachel giggled, "and she's having a hard time getting out of bed. *Hard* time. Get it?"

"Rachel!"

"What?"

"Do we have to do this?"

"What? Talk about Shay-Shaunté? We do it all the time."

"Well, I don't want to do it this morning."

"Happy new year, ladies."

Slowly, I turned and looked right at Shay-Shaunté. I didn't know how she'd sneaked up on us like that; I hadn't even heard the elevator doors open.

"Happy new year," Rachel said in a tone that didn't sound like she'd just been talking about the woman. "I hope it was a good one. And your birthday, too."

I knew Rachel was fishing, but the only good thing about Shay-Shaunté was that she would never tell anything.

She gave Rachel more than I expected when she said, "I had a great New Year's and an even better birthday." She spoke to Rachel, but her eyes were on me. "I hope you ladies had a good vacation, too."

"Oh, yes, definitely," Rachel said.

I nodded because I wasn't yet ready to speak. This morning was already off-track. I was supposed to have had a little time to myself. Go into my office, take off my coat, check my makeup before I had to face my boss.

"Great," Shay-Shaunté said. "Then a good holiday was had by all. But," she swayed toward her office, "it's time to get back to work. Evia, would you mind joining me?"

"Uh . . ." That wasn't the way I wanted to start our conversation, but that's all that came out. "Uh . . . let me hang up my coat."

"No, you can keep on your coat or hang it up in here; I need to talk to you now."

I followed her, though I wasn't sure how I was able to put one three-inch heel in front of the other. I was adding the equation: Adam's mood last night, his silence, then a run this morning, plus Shay-Shaunté's absence from the office because of a run this morning equaled what?

Shay-Shaunté paused at her office and stepped aside for me to walk in first. After she closed the door behind us, she took her time, sashaying across the room, her hips, like always, hypnotic.

I wondered if Adam had watched her this way. Had she swayed her body for him like this? Had she done it with her clothes on or off?

This was pure unadulterated torture. How was I supposed

to survive six months with Shay-Shaunté in front of my face? Every day!

"Evia?"

It wasn't until she called my name that I realized that I hadn't moved. "Evia? Are you all right?"

"Yes."

"Well, why are you all the way over there?"

"I'm fine here."

The lines on her face deepened. "So, you're just going to stay there?"

"Yes."

"Wearing your coat?"

"Yes."

Shay-Shaunté paused, taking in all of my words. I hit the Replay button in my mind, and I wanted to slap myself. So much for being eloquent and elegant. I was acting like a fool. This was not the way to show her that I was totally unaffected by this weekend.

I wobbled across the room (in those doggone heels that were already hurting my feet) and took a seat.

"You can take off your coat," she said.

I did.

Shay-Shaunté leaned back on her throne. Looked down on me and said, "Before we get into business, how's Adam?"

My mouth opened wide, but not to speak. It was just my shock showing. She'd never asked me about Adam before, and now she was asking like this was going to be an everyday occurrence. As if she had to care about his well-being. As if the two of us now shared one man.

Oh, no—it wasn't going to be that way. We should've put an extra clause in the contract, something that said that after she slept with my husband, she could never mention his name again.

I said, "Adam? My husband."

"Yes, your husband."

"I didn't say that for clarification. I was making a point—that Adam is my husband."

Her eyes brightened and light lines appeared around her eyes. "You don't have to remind me who he is," she said, her face sparkling with her amusement. "I know him." She stopped talking, but with her eyes, she added, *"I know him well."* She waited a beat before repeating, "So, how's Adam?"

She was pushing me. To go there. But I couldn't. Because if I did, I just might bring Barry Farm with me. So to save her life, I changed the subject.

"There was a problem with the check," I said as I reached into my bag for the copy.

"Really?"

My strategy worked, because her smile was gone—she was back to all business.

I handed her the paper, and she studied the copy of the check. "What's the problem?"

I couldn't say that she was stupid, because I hadn't noticed it until the banker had pointed it out to me. "There's a zero missing. You had the bank issue a check for two hundred and fifty thousand instead of two million, five hundred thousand."

She shook her head. "No, the check is fine."

My mouth opened wide. What kind of game was this chick playing? "What?"

"I said," she spoke louder, as if I was hearing impaired, "the check is fine."

The fact that she actually had the audacity to repeat it let me know that she was really going to try to play me and Adam. Did she forget that we had a contract? Trust and believe, I was gonna sue her behind, take this whole thing public if she didn't come correct.

I said, "The deal was for five million," reminding her of what she already knew.

"Yes," she nodded, "that's exactly what I gave you. Five million minus the taxes."

The shock of her words was a force, shoving me back in the chair. "Taxes?"

"Yes," she said in a tone that sounded like she thought I was stupid. "With the federal, D.C., Social Security taxes, and everything else, your take-home from the five million was two million seven hundred and fifty thousand." She pushed the paper back toward me. "That's exactly what I gave you."

I had to wait until I could breathe. "You didn't say anything about taxes." I wondered if she could hear me, because I could hardly hear myself.

"I didn't think I had to." She frowned as if what she'd done was so obvious.

I said, "I thought this was a fee for services."

"Yes."

"Like a gift."

"A gift?" It started out as a smile, then a giggle came through her lips before she leaned her head back and laughed. Laughed so hard that it scared me. Laughed so hard that it sounded diabolical. Exactly the way I'd sounded last night.

All I could do was wait. She wiped her eyes from the tears that spilled from the corners.

"Oh, my," she said, giggles still escaping. "A gift." She looked at me, her glee—at my expense—still all over her. "Please tell me that you were kidding?"

I wasn't sure how I should play this, so I just sat there, glared at her. Hoped my look would intimidate her into doing what she was supposed to do.

But the only thing that happened was that she glared back. "You were aware that taxes had to be paid on that money, right?"

I didn't say a word because I didn't know; I hadn't thought about it, and obviously, neither had Adam.

Shay-Shaunté continued, "Well, Uncle Sam is always gonna get his. If I had given it to you as a gift, then I would've been the one responsible for the taxes . . . and Evia, that wasn't going to happen."

"You set us up. You set this whole thing up so that we would assume it was a gift."

"No, I didn't. The contract was written on company letterhead, and then the checks were only made out to you, not Adam, because you're my employee. And both checks were company checks. Payment from Ferossity to an employee."

I sat there, taking in the truth of her words. Then I thought about the truth of mine—this witch *had* set us up!

My heart was pounding wildly when I said, "I would've never done this for only two million."

Her eyebrows shot up. "Two million seven hundred and fifty thousand."

"No." I shook my head.

"Oh, please." Shay-Shaunté waved her hand. "Look at how you've already deposited this check." She pointed to the copy on her desk.

How did she know that?

Maybe she had some kind of alert on her phone. Still, I pushed my shoulders back. "I cannot believe—"

She held up her hand, stopping me. "Before you start, think about what you did." She paused. "You . . . sold . . . your . . . husband. And the truth of it, Evia"—she lifted her hips and leaned so far across the glass that I thought she was going to climb across the desk to get at me—"is that you would have done this for whatever I offered."

I sat still as a stone.

She kept on, "Two million, three million . . ." Finally she sat back down. Added, "I was just being generous when I offered you five million."

Generous! It was my turn to pop out of my chair. It was my turn to lean across her desk. And I went straight hood. The only thing that was missing was the switchblade that I carried back in the day. In my best poltergeist voice, I said, "Witch, you better give me my money!"

She sat back, folded her hands in her lap. "Or what?"

There were so many ways to answer that . . . like, I will cut you, I will beat you until not even your mother will recognize you, I will bury you where bodies are never found—and I know guys who would do that for me for just twenty bucks . . . I wanted to say all kinds of things like that.

But I knew enough to know that those words, that threat in today's times would land me right in jail. This was all about the money. I needed to keep my focus there.

So I said, "If you don't give me the money . . ." I paused. What would I do? In a softer voice, I said, "If you don't give me the money, I'm outta here."

She shook her head as if my comeback was pathetic. But as I looked into her face, I began to think that maybe this wasn't such a bad thing. We wouldn't have the money we'd thought we'd have, but now I could walk out of here and not have to deal with Shay-Shaunté anymore.

"Yeah, I'm outta here!" I repeated.

"I wouldn't do that."

I smirked.

She added, "What would Adam think?"

I wanted to cut her for real. My jaw was tight when I said, "It doesn't matter what Adam thinks, this is about you and me. But you know what? Adam is *my husband*. He'll support me."

Her silent smile said much more than words could. Like she knew things about my husband that I didn't know. But I knew it was all a game to make me feel insecure. So I just asked, "Are you going to pay me?"

"I already did."

"Then I'm out." I whipped around and marched, grateful that I *had* deposited that check this morning.

Before I got to the door, Shay-Shaunté said, "Evia, quitting is not a good idea." I kept moving until her next words stopped me cold. "If you leave, I will sue you, and then where will you and your children and your mother-in-law and your mother . . . and even Adam . . . be?

It wasn't her threat that got me. It was what she knew about my family. Had Adam, my private husband, shared our personal life with her?

"Look," Shay-Shaunté began, "just make this easy on yourself. We have a legal deal. I've paid all the money, and not only did you agree verbally, you signed a contract and cashed the checks—both of them."

I inhaled.

"So," she stood and walked toward me.

I didn't know why I felt the need to back up, but I did. Until I hit the wall and had nowhere else to go.

Just inches separated us when she said, "Let's just keep it the way we decided. Six months. Or . . . you can work hard and find someone else for me and get out of here before then." She spoke in a tone that sounded like we were two friends who'd had a little disagreement.

"Okay?" She smiled.

I didn't move a muscle.

"I'll take that as a yes," she said. "Because face it. You can't go anywhere."

I stared at her for a moment longer before I grabbed the door handle and stomped out. As I passed Rachel's desk, she whispered, "Did she tell you anything about her birthday?"

I didn't say a word. All I had to do was hold on until I got into my own little space.

Inside my office, I closed the door quickly. Held in my emotions until I got to my desk. Then I leaned over, held my head, and cried.

Chapter 48

THE CLOCK STRUCK MIDNIGHT.

Okay, that was a slight exaggeration—it was only five, but it felt like midnight. Really, my first day back at Ferossity felt like a month of midnights.

There was too much contact, that was the problem. I should've put yet another addendum in the contract—that after the deal, after the dance, there would be no direct contact with the devil.

But this was just another point that I hadn't thought through, so now I had to face Shay-Shaunté every minute of the day, it seemed. It was bad enough that I had to work with the woman who was cheating me; now I had to look into her eyes and know that she'd cheated with my husband.

I knew it wasn't exactly cheating. I mean, how could it be cheating when I knew about it and had approved? But it felt like cheating all day long. Every time I looked at Shay-Shaunté, I thought about Adam.

It had started this morning, as I'd sat in my office, still stunned at the revelation that Shay-Shaunté was shorting us two million dollars. I'd called Adam over and over, left message after message. But my calls had gone straight to his voice mail, and he'd never called back. Making me still wonder what kind of run he'd had to do this morning.

While I'd sat wondering, Shay-Shaunté had sauntered into my office as if life was grand.

"Do you have the résumé of the intern we selected? I want to send out a newsletter."

I'd sat staring, mesmerized by her ruby-colored lips, wondering why I hadn't paid more attention to them before. Their perfect shape, perfect size, plump on the bottom, full on top.

"Evia?"

She'd interrupted my scrutiny by repeating her question. But it had been hard to hear Shay-Shaunté when all I'd been able to do was think about how many times those lips had touched my husband.

I'd coughed to make sure that my voice came out strong. "I have the résumé right here." I'd passed her a manila folder, then studied her soft, flawless hands. The hands of a model in a lotion or anti-aging commercial. And I'd wondered what those long, slender fingers had done with my husband.

She'd strutted away, swayed, all slither, all sex, her sensuality almost spellbinding. All I'd been able to think about were Adam's eyes on her body; I hadn't had the guts to think about what other parts of him had touched her.

Today, I died a thousand times; every time Shay-Shaunté came into my office, or I passed her in the hallway, or I heard her talking to Rachel with a new joy, I passed away again. But then the clock struck quitting time and I was set free.

With my coat on my arm, my purse on my shoulder, and my shoes in my hands, I raced to the stairwell. I cringed as I thought about going down twelve flights in my stocking feet, but what else was I supposed to do? The moment I was furloughed, I had to get away from Shay-Shaunté—aching feet and all.

Which made the thought of returning tomorrow beyond intolerable. How could I come here another day just to die another death?

Adam was going to have to figure this out for me. Whatever he had to do, he had to get me out of here. After all, after what he'd done this weekend, he owed me that much.

There were so many things to talk to Adam about—how Shay-Shaunté was cheating us out of millions, how she'd tortured me throughout the day, how I just didn't see how I'd be able to continue working. But the anxiety I'd had all day, along with the jam-packed, rush-hour ride home, added up to one sistah with a serious attitude. Then, combined with the fact that when I walked through the door Adam didn't make a single move to greet me, my boiling blood took me to new levels of pissitivity.

So in that moment I didn't go through the agenda; I didn't think about what would be the best issue to bring to Adam first.

Instead, when I saw my husband sitting in the living room, reading the newspaper, with his cell phone next to him (the cell that I'd been calling all day), all I could say was, "Where did you go this morning?"

Not a hello, how're you doing, nothing. I just gave it to him straight, no chaser, with total attitude.

Adam looked up, and the tracks on his forehead told me that he had no idea what I was talking about. But that wasn't going to stop me—I wanted answers. I wanted to know if our deal had turned into their affair.

"Hey!" he said softly, smoothly, as if he was trying to defuse the explosion he felt looming. His eyes roamed over me, inch by inch, and I knew that my outfit surprised him. He said, "You look nice."

I wasn't going to let him distract me. Isn't that what cheaters always did? I didn't know for sure because Adam had never cheated before.

"Where did you go this morning?" I repeated, letting him know that we were going to deal with this, now.

"What?" Adam asked, putting down the newspaper.

How many times did he want me to repeat what I'd asked? So I tried it a different way. Rephrased the question and slowed it down like I was talking to a two-year-old. "When you left us this morning, while the kids were having breakfast, where did you go?"

His eyes blinked, as if he was still confused. But I knew the real deal—he was stalling, trying to come up with a good lie.

He said, "This morning?" Looked down, then back up at me. Said, "I went to Marilyn's."

I frowned. "My mother?"

"Yes. I wanted to talk to Cashmere . . . and Marilyn about what happened to Ethan."

"You went there this morning." It wasn't really a question; this was an interrogation, so I stated what he wanted me to believe as fact.

"Yeah. Where did you think I went?"

My lips pressed together. I was not going to say her name. But he did. "Shay-Shaunté. Is that what you thought?"

My answer was my folded arms and silence.

He shook his head, but he didn't get a chance to say anything more because the twins busted through the door.

"Daddy!" The two pushed past me as if I was not chopped, but chewed-up, liver.

But then my mini-me hit reverse, and she came back across the room and made me feel not so invisible. "Hi, Mom." She hugged me.

The girls were wearing giant smiles. A good day at school.

That's what they told Adam when he asked about their day. Then he told them to get their homework done so that we could talk about their party.

"No homework today, Daddy," Alana said.

Alexa explained, "The teachers always give us a break the first day, as if they know our bodies are back on Monday but our brains won't join us till Tuesday."

Three people in the room laughed.

Adam asked, "So, you guys wanna start some of it now?"

"Yeah," the girls cheered and led him up the stairs.

I studied Adam as he followed the twins. Studied his movements, thought about his explanation.

So, he'd been with my mother. It made sense—I guessed. Except—it didn't make sense. Why would he go over there without me? And if he had, why hadn't he just told me where he was going this morning?

Naw, he was lying. And I wasn't going to be one of those wives who believed anything. Adam was going to tell me the truth!

Then I remembered something that Brooklyn once told me—that M-A-N stood for Men Admit Nothing. So I didn't go upstairs and drag Adam back down, demanding that he tell me everything. No, I was gonna have to find out the truth my own way.

I already had my plan, but I waited until Ethan came home, since I didn't want to be interrupted. Then I checked on Adam and the girls, upstairs inside that shroud of pink.

"Mom, you should stay," Alana encouraged.

"I'll be part of the planning, don't worry," I said, glancing at Adam, who was sprawled out on the floor with his back against the bed. Good—he looked like he would be there for a while. "But right now, I'm gonna get dinner started."

"Okay," the girls chorused.

I waited for Adam to say something, and when he didn't, I just walked out. That was okay; I didn't have anything to say to him either. Not until I handed his lie right back to him.

In sixteen years of marriage, I couldn't remember another day when I'd carried anger—and so much of it—for more than a couple of hours. That was what, I believed, made our marriage so special.

But that was then.

Downstairs, I grabbed my cell from my purse, then slipped into our bedroom. I almost wanted to have a glass of wine or something before I dialed this number. But I didn't need a drink; fury drove me to do what I had to do.

"Hey, Marilyn," I said as soon as my mother answered.

"Oh, Lawd, what you want?"

I shook my head, not believing that those five words were the way my mother chose to greet me.

Before I could tell her why I'd dialed her number, she said, "Don't tell me you're callin' to go off, too."

I frowned. "What?"

"I still cannot believe the way Adam came at me this morning. Messed up my whole day. Didn't Ruby teach him any kind of manners?"

If this call was about anything else, I wouldn't have let her talk about my mother-in-love that way. "So Adam was over there? This morning?"

"Don't act like you don't know. Hmph, coming over here,

waking me up, talkin' like he owns me just 'cause you guys give me a little bit of change every blue moon."

I needed this to be clear. "So, Adam came over there, this morning?"

"Ain't that what I just said? You know, I'm tired of y'all disrespecting me like this. I am still the mother. You are still the child."

I rolled my eyes. Now that I had what I'd called for, I didn't need to listen to Marilyn's rampage.

But she went on. "So, if you can't treat me the way I'm supposed to be treated, then just keep your bougie behinds over there and leave me alone."

She slammed down the phone so hard that I had to pull my cell away from my ear. But at least she'd given me what I needed to know.

I pressed End. "So, Adam wasn't lying," I whispered.

"Did you *really* think that I was?"

I didn't even want to turn around. How had this happened? I hadn't felt him, like I always had. Hadn't known he'd been anywhere near me, like I always had.

Now I was the one stalling, trying to come up with a good lie. But since I didn't know how much he'd heard, I had to go with the truth.

Facing him, I could see there was nothing but hurt on his face, and I wished that I could take back my doubt.

He took a step forward, then stopped as if he didn't want to get too close. "How could you go behind me like that?"

"I just . . . I needed to know."

"I told you what you needed to know."

I shook my head. "But it was just so weird, the way you and Shay-Shaunté used the same words today. She said she had to make a run. And that's what you said, too."

He frowned. "So, two people can't make a run?"

"It was more than that. It's everything—like the way I called you all day and you never answered."

"My phone is dead and I can't find my charger. I was waiting for you to come home so that I could use yours." He held up his hand, and for the first time, I noticed that he was holding his cell. "That's why I came downstairs. To get your charger."

I grabbed my purse, digging inside for the charger and giving myself time to find better words. When I handed the cord to him, I said, "Baby, I'm sorry. It's just that since you came home . . . you're so mysterious."

He frowned, as if he had no idea what I was talking about. "I guess everything is mysterious when you're suspicious."

"I don't mean to be, but you've got to know that things aren't the same between us."

"But things aren't so different that I would lie to you." He looked down when he said, "I can't believe you did that, Evia."

I swallowed a mouthful of air. It was a simple word, a simple name. My name. But it was like a punch to my gut. Evia. I couldn't remember the last time he'd spoken my name.

From the day we were married, I'd always been Shine. His Shine. His sunshine! What happened to that?

I would've asked him, but he turned around and, with the charger in his hand, walked out of the room.

Chapter 49

I DIDN'T RECOGNIZE ANY PART OF my life. I wasn't the same woman, Adam wasn't the same man, and this definitely wasn't the same marriage.

After Adam left me alone to think about what I'd done, he didn't speak another word to me. He didn't even sit down to dinner with us, telling the children, in a voice loud enough for me to hear, that he had to make a run.

It was all that I could do not to ask him where he was going. And for the time that he was away, it was all that I could do not to wonder if he was with Shay-Shaunté.

I was relieved when he returned in less than ninety minutes with two huge bags from Staples. Not much of an affair could be carried on in an office supply store in that small bit of time.

I knew these doubts were ridiculous, and really, I tried to talk myself out of them. But once Adam came home and marched straight into his office, there was nothing I could do to turn off the suspicion, the new fears that stirred inside me.

Even after the twins and Ethan were in their rooms, Adam stayed behind closed doors in the office. I went to the door, knowing that I had to reach out, knowing that Adam and I had so much to talk about. But I couldn't bring myself to knock, and I couldn't open the door. All of our wonderful years of marriage had come to this. After one weekend, my tongue was as tied up as my heart.

Why couldn't he feel me there, and rush out, and hold me, and tell me that our world was coming back to normal? After long minutes of silence, I gave up my post outside the office.

I dragged myself back into our bedroom, undressed, and slipped into bed, waiting for my husband, my real husband, to join me.

But my husband never came. I stared at the ticking clock, watched minutes pass into the new day, and now it was after two in the morning. There was nothing good that he could be doing in his office even if this wasn't about Shay-Shaunté. Even if this was only about me not trusting him, it wasn't good for Adam to be away from our bed like this.

I got up, covered my nakedness, then traipsed down the hall. I knocked on the door, then stepped inside, not waiting for him to answer.

I'd expected Adam to be sitting behind his desk, reading or sulking. But the light was out, and even though I couldn't see him, I felt him. Stepping further inside, I found the pallet that he'd made, and I shook my head.

Kneeling beside him, I watched his chest rise and fall, then I tucked myself next to him. In his sleep, he stirred. I backed it up, my back to his front. Wiggled my butt, and he wrapped his arm around me. Pulled me closer and held me the way he used to.

My real husband.

I sighed.

This floor was hard and cold, but not unfamiliar to us. How many times had we made love in here? Just like every other room in the house—save the children's spaces—we had christened it with our love.

Those memories made me want to stay inside Adam's arms, on the floor, saying nothing. But I could feel him, and I knew that he was awake. That meant we had to talk.

"There's so much to tell you," I whispered into the dark.

There was a pause before, "I don't want to fight."

Rolling over, I faced him. There was only the pin light from the smoke detector above, but it was enough because I could feel his eyes without seeing them completely.

"I'm sorry. I never should have doubted you. I should have believed you."

I felt his relief and he pulled me close, held me tighter.

And I sighed again.

But there was more to say. I had to forget about our love for just a moment. I had to take this back to business. So, with my head resting on his chest, I told him, "The check Shay-Shaunté gave you yesterday, it was only for a quarter of a million dollars."

"What happened to the rest?"

"She took out taxes."

He stiffened and I braced myself, ready for his rampage. He said, "She didn't say anything about taxes."

"I said the same thing."

I felt his head nod. I heard his sigh. Then I sensed his resignation before he said, "I guess there's nothing we can do."

That's not what I wanted to hear, but I was going to stay in this place of peace. Raising myself up, I looked down at him. "I told her that she had to give us all the money or I would quit. Just walk out and not wait for the six months to pass."

He shook his head. "You can't; we have to finish the deal."

I rose even further. Sat straight up and scooted away from him a little bit. "It's finished if she's going to cheat us out of two million."

His voice was stronger now. "She's not cheating us . . . not really. Someone has to pay the taxes."

Every part of me got tight. "Are you taking up for her?"

Adam rolled over and pushed himself up. Said nothing as he walked away from me, toward his desk, and clicked on the lamp.

In the light, he looked straight into my face. "You've gotta stop thinking that there's something going on between me and Shay-Shaunté."

"What am I supposed to think? You should be as upset about this as I am."

"I am," he said. "But there's nothing you or I can do."

"I can stop working. If she wants to play games, I can quit tomorrow."

He shook his head. "You do that and she'll sue us."

"She said she would, but I don't believe her."

His eyes widened just a bit, as if he was surprised. As if he was only talking in theory. "Well then," his words came out in a sigh, "you have your answer."

"She won't do it."

"We can't take that chance."

I shook my head.

He said, "We have to play it out. For six months. I did my part, now you have to do yours."

Adam stood as if he had no plans to fight. But Adam Langston was a warrior—he'd been about winning his whole life. So, what was different now? Why was he giving in? Why had the weekend changed him so much?

"Adam, what happened this—"

I didn't even get the words out. "We're not going to talk about it."

"We have to," I said, sitting firm. "Because you're different. And because Shay-Shaunté said some things."

He stuffed his hands into the pockets of his jeans. "What things?"

I saw the way his body stiffened, but I kept the conversation going. "She talked about our children, and our mothers. She talked as if she knew us." I took a breath and added, "She talked to me as if you'd talked to her."

He stayed still and stared blankly, as if he was waiting for the question.

"Did you . . . talk to her?"

"I was there . . . with her . . . for the weekend," his words stumbled out. "We talked . . . of course . . . we talked."

From the pit of my stomach, the lump rose slowly until it rested in my throat. "About us?" I could hardly speak. "About our family."

"No, never about our family. Nothing about us."

I breathed. Okay. Well, he'd answered one question, but I needed to know so much more. "Where did you go? What did you do? Did you—" The questions tumbled out, but before I finished asking the first one, Adam was already shaking his head.

"We agreed never to talk about this."

It was only because I wanted to keep the peace that I waved my white flag and said, "Okay," even though it wasn't okay with me. But then I added, "I can't work with her, though. Not if I don't know what happened."

"What does that have to do with anything?"

"It's hard for me to look at her and . . . not see you. It's like the two of you share a secret now."

"There's no secret, Evia," he said, punching me again with my name. His eyes bore into mine when he said, "You know what happened."

Well, I'd asked for it. And now it was a fact. Yes, it was dumb, but until Adam actually said it, a small, small part of me could believe that nothing really happened. That I was still his and he was still mine.

But that wasn't true anymore.

Pushing myself up, I said, "We should go to bed."

His eyes were glassy. As if he wanted to cry because of the hurt his words had caused. But he had only spoken the truth.

He clicked off the light, then, side by side, we walked to our bedroom. Together we disrobed and then, together, we slipped into bed.

But he stayed on his side and I held on to my edge. And tonight the distance between us didn't even bother me.

Chapter 50

The world had fallen off its axle.

For real, because that was the only way to explain why Adam and I were so disconnected. We were miles apart in our bed, in our conversations, in our thoughts. And that explained why for a third time in two days Adam left the house while the children were eating to make a run.

At Ferossity, the madness continued.

The once aloof boss was now walking among us, talking among us, and constantly in my face. All morning, I was accidentally bumping into her, though in my soul, I knew all the accidental meetings were set up by her.

It started first thing this morning. I was minding my business; I had just parked my car and was trying to get out of the wind whipping across the lot. I was rushing toward the building, head down, fighting to get inside fast. I reached for the door, but someone's hand grabbed the handle before I did.

"Hey, Evia," Shay-Shaunté said when I looked up.

Frankly, I was stunned to see her. It was clear that she was just getting in—she had that fresh look of the morning all over her. But why was she just arriving at nine? What happened to her believing that she needed to be the first person in the office?

"This is going to be a wonderful day," she continued talking with way too much cheer for me. Continued talking as if I cared. "I am loving 2011!"

I glanced at the staircase and thought walking up the twelve flights might be easier than riding in the elevator with Shay-Shaunté. But since I didn't have that kind of energy, I just grinned and beared it, and prayed that in the elevator, God's grace would help me keep my hands off her neck.

Then, less than thirty minutes later, she showed up in the bathroom.

"Hey, Evia!" she said, like she was so happy to see me.

But the killer was when I thought I'd found a surefire way to get away from Shay-Shaunté, even for just a few minutes. I bounced into the break room, ready to hide out and relax, and who was in there?

She was chatting it up with Rachel. I turned around, hoping to sneak out, but Rachel caught me.

"Hey, girl! You decided to get some coffee?"

I pivoted and pasted a plastic smile onto my face. "Yeah, I needed a break," I said to Rachel and acted like Shay-Shaunté wasn't there. I grabbed the coffeepot.

"Well, Shay-Shaunté and I," Rachel said as I began pouring, "were just talking about her birthday."

"Ouch!" I yelled out as the steaming liquid overflowed from the cup onto my hand.

"Girl," Rachel said, coming to my rescue and pulling the pot away from me. "What you trying to do?"

I blew on the red-hot spot on my hand. Right in between

my thumb and forefinger—the same place where I'd cut myself three nights before.

"You need to be more careful," Shay-Shaunté said.

I rolled my eyes.

As I blotted up the coffee on the counter, Rachel continued, "So, like I said, I was just asking Shay-Shaunté about her big day."

I took a small sip and worked to keep my eyes on Rachel.

"Yes," Shay-Shaunté began. "Rachel seems very interested in how I spent my birthday."

"Well, I wasn't trying to be nosy or anything."

"I didn't think you were," Shay-Shaunté said, as if she hadn't once been the most private person on earth. "You're just interested, right?"

"Yeah." Rachel nodded, not having a clue that she was being used. "So, how was it?"

Shay-Shaunté leaned against the counter, casually, like she was one of us. "Well, I don't believe in kissing and telling . . ."

Oh, God!

"But let's just say I had more than just a lovely birthday. I had an amazing weekend."

"Really!" Rachel giggled.

I wanted to slap her for laughing.

Rachel asked, "So, is this Mr.-Kiss-But-Don't-Tell someone special?"

I'd tortured myself enough. "I'm going back to my office," I said.

Shay-Shaunté said, "Wait, don't you want to hear about it?"

I didn't know where this test was coming from—if it was from God or the devil. Or maybe it was just Shay-Shaunté. Maybe she was *trying* to get me to quit. Maybe she *wanted* to see me in court.

But I wasn't going to give her any kind of satisfaction. Not by quitting and not by standing there listening. "No, I don't want to hear about your birthday," I said. I tried to put enough bass into my tone so she would hear my warning. So she would realize that I was not one to play with.

But she just leaned her head back and laughed. Rachel laughed, too, though she had no idea that she was doing so at my expense.

I marched, with hard steps, back to my office. I tried to hold my head high, but by the time I reached my destination, my chin was resting on my chest. Behind my closed door, I collapsed into my chair.

Why hadn't Adam and I considered every aspect of this deal? Was this pain, this embarrassment, this heartache worth the money?

Only a little more than thirty-six hours had passed since Adam had been home and I already knew that we'd paid too high a price for the five million, which had turned into two million less.

But then I inhaled a deep breath and retrieved happy thoughts from my memory. So much good *had* come out of this—our children were smiling again, Ruby was safe, we now owned our home.

There was so much good, even as I was living in torment.

For the greater good.

Isn't that why I'd signed on the dotted line?

All I had to do now was pray that the greater good didn't bring my entire family down.

Chapter 51

ADAM'S VOICE CAME THROUGH CRISP AND clear.

"Please leave a message," his cell phone told me again. I'd called so many times that I half expected his voice mail to address me personally.

I clicked off, leaving no message.

Just like yesterday, I'd called him, not getting any kind of answer, not getting any return call—and this time, I knew his phone was charged. Now his car was missing from our garage. Where was he?

Never before had Adam's whereabouts concerned me. I'd always known he loved me; I'd always known he was coming home. But the doubts from this weekend had spilled over into the week. And since Adam wouldn't talk to me, there was nothing I could do to get rid of my suspicion.

I tried his cell one more time. No answer.

My heart dipped way below where it was supposed to be.

In just forty-eight hours, my world had been rocked.

I wasn't imagining this. This wasn't paranoia. This was agony, inflicted on me deliberately by Shay-Shaunté. That's why I'd been calling Adam all day. I needed to talk to him. I needed him to know what she was doing—how she was trying to twist my belief in my husband.

The break room incident had been bad enough. But Shay-Shaunté didn't stop there. Every time I was near, she had something to say about the beauty of her birthday.

But it was the last thing that was the last straw. I tried my best to stay away from her, hanging out in the HR department as long as I could. But when I returned to the twelfth floor, the picture in front of me took my breath away.

Shay-Shaunté was perched on the corner of Rachel's desk surrounded by at least a dozen women—mostly clerical employees whom I was sure Shay-Shaunté couldn't call by name. But there they all stood, with the boss holding court.

Shay-Shaunté's head was back, her eyes were closed, her mouth was open, as if she was in the middle of a laugh. Whatever she said, it must've been funny, because the floor rocked with laughter, the women sounding as silly as my teenagers.

I paused; surely, I was in a parallel universe. Shay-Shaunté chatting and laughing? This was so out of character. It was as if after this weekend, she was a different woman. Just like Adam was a different man.

I took slow steps around the crowd, not wanting to draw any kind of attention to myself. But then Shay-Shaunté's head tilted, her eyes opened, and she saw me.

"Yes, you could say he's my new man."

Her words made me freeze, but only for a moment. I ran and locked myself inside my office, as if that could really keep her away. Behind my door, I paced and dreamed of one hundred and one ways to kill her.

I thought about waiting until she was alone, then marching into her office and demanding that she start behaving like an adult. But I chose the coward's way. It didn't matter to me that it wasn't even one o'clock. I grabbed my coat and bag and walked right back out into the crowd.

Only Shay-Shaunté noticed. "Leaving, Evia?"

I didn't even turn around.

Once again, the elevator wasn't an option. I would've had to stand there, listening to more chatter, more laughter, and only God knows what else Shay-Shaunté would've said to tear at my heart. So I made my escape down the stairs.

More than an hour had passed since I'd had to endure that scene. But in that time, I had relived it five million times.

"I have to speak to Adam," I cried out to the walls in my home.

My voice bounced around, then died. There was nothing more that I could do. I had to just sit and wait in the emptiness of our home for my husband to return from wherever he was.

Chapter 52

I RESTED. IN THE MIDDLE OF the day. In the middle of my bed. Not because I was tired but because I didn't have the energy to do anything else. I didn't feel like cooking, I certainly couldn't eat. And so I lay in the bed and waited for sleep to come.

But just like it did night after night, sleep eluded me; ran from me as if it hated me. So I fell back on my new hobby—watching the clock.

Outside, I heard car after car, door slam after door slam. But none of those sounds were for me. There was still nothing from Adam.

Then I heard the two beeps of the alarm. But I didn't move because it was my children's voices that floated into my bedroom. I was surprised, though—I heard the twins and Ethan. It was unusual for the two vans to drop them off at the same time.

Their voices still sounded a bit far away—like they were in the mudroom—and I wondered why they'd come in through the garage.

I pushed myself up; I needed to greet them, hug them, kiss them, and then tell them to order a pizza.

Then I heard Adam's voice and I bounced off the bed. I rushed into the living room just as the four of them came traipsing in from the other side, all filled with glee.

"Hi, Mom!" Alexa said first. With a hug she added, "Daddy came to pick us up."

"Me, too!" Ethan cheered.

"And then we stopped at Maggiano's," Alana explained. "We picked up dinner."

"Yeah," Alexa continued the story. "Dad let us order all our favorites."

"Mine, too!" Ethan piped in.

Adam held up the shopping bag and grinned like he expected a medal. "And then we stopped by Grace's and got your favorite—banana pudding," he said.

If I didn't have such an attitude, I would've noticed that he was the old Adam.

He said, "I didn't want you to cook tonight."

Was it the way I folded my arms or was it the way I glared at Adam that stopped them all cold?

Alana was the only one who stepped closer. "Are you all right, Mom?" She kept her voice low, as if she was afraid that even a decibel louder might set me off.

I nodded, but my stare stayed on Adam. "I need to talk to your father."

Not another word was spoken as the children's eyes darted from Adam to me.

"Can you girls take the food into the kitchen?"

Alana grabbed the shopping bag and the twins dashed away. Ethan bolted up the stairs, putting distance between himself and trouble.

I glared at Adam some more before I turned and stomped into our bedroom.

"What's wrong?" he asked after he followed me and shut the door behind us.

"Where were you?"

At first, he stared. And then he sighed. It was all over him—how he was already tired of hearing that question from me. As if he had no intention of answering, he walked by me, loosening his tie as he passed. That was when I noticed for the first time how he was dressed. In one of his suits. A designer suit. A serious one.

I was not going to be denied, though; I still needed an answer. After all, men in suits had affairs all the time. But I did soften my voice. "I . . . I just really needed to talk to you earlier today," I said. "I called. And I couldn't find you. And I called. And then, I called back. And you didn't return my calls. And . . . and . . . and." I don't know what happened after that. My lips trembled, my shoulders shuddered, tears crept from my eyes. I could not believe that I was crying.

I was not one of those women who cried to foster sympathy from a man. But my tears flowed, and just like any other man would, Adam came right back to me.

"I'm sorry," he said. "I was at the Entrepreneur's Expo at the Convention Center. I didn't know that you'd called. See, here." He grabbed his phone from the holster on his hip. "It's on silent. When I got out, I thought about the kids, and so I went to get them. I'm sorry," he apologized again.

I bowed my head. "I didn't know you were going. . . ."

"Yeah," he said, easing me down onto the edge of the bed. "Remember, we talked about it a few weeks ago. You were the one who suggested it."

I covered my face with my hands.

"Evia." Even though he whispered my name softly, my heart yearned for Shine to come back. He said, "I don't know why you're doing this. I don't know why all of a sudden you don't trust me."

"Because you won't talk to me," I cried.

"About this weekend?"

"Yes!"

He stood. "I'm not gonna do that."

"Don't you see that not talking about it is worse? Because now I have to imagine what went on."

"Don't think about it," he said, as if it was that simple.

"Even if everything was normal, it wouldn't be that easy. But now it's impossible not to think about it because of Shay-Shaunté."

He shook his head. "I keep telling you; there's nothing going on—"

"No, I don't mean that." I recounted my day for him. Told him how she used every opportunity to get inside my head, to trudge all over my heart. When I told him that she'd called him her man, he dropped back down onto the bed next to me. Leaned forward a bit, rested his elbows on his legs. "I don't know why she's doing this."

"I can come up with a million reasons—and they'll all lead back to her just wanting to get to me. But that's why I have to quit."

"You can't do that, you can't let her win."

"But she is winning because every time I see her or hear her, I wonder. I know my imagination is worse than reality. . . ."

I waited for him to agree with me, but he didn't.

I said, "That's why I need to know. I've heard it from her, and now I have to hear something from you."

His lips became a solid line, pressed together like he planned to never speak another word ever again.

I pushed on, "I need us to be how we used to be."

"Talking about this weekend won't take us back there. Because if we talk about it, everything is going to change."

"We're already changed!" Just like I'd never been a crier, I wasn't a whiner. But nothing was the same anymore. "Can't you see it? We're already a lifetime away from where we were before you left on Friday."

In the quiet that followed, we both thought about the truth of what I'd said.

"You're right," Adam said softly. "But we've got to find another way back to each other. Because trust me . . . you don't want to talk about this weekend."

The only thing that stopped me from screaming was that after he said those words, Adam leaned over and hugged me.

I held him, too, and kept my mouth shut, even though his words played again and again in my mind.

Trust me . . . you don't want to talk about this weekend.

Why not? What happened?

But I stayed silent—at least on the outside.

Chapter 53

THIS WAS WAR!

And like any good military woman or gang associate, I decided to plan. So, I spent the night strategizing, plotting how I was going to win this war with Shay-Shaunté. Adam was right—I couldn't let her win. I was Evia Langston, and up to this point, I'd always won. Why should this be any different?

So when I walked into Ferossity, I was convinced that today would be my day of triumph. The first day that—no matter what—Shay-Shaunté was not going to get to me.

The first good sign was that I walked into the building without a glimpse of Shay-Shaunté. I didn't really care if she was already inside, or if she had not yet made it in. All that mattered was that she wasn't in my face.

When the elevator doors parted, there was another good sign. The space was empty. No one was congregating around Rachel's desk, surrounding Shay-Shaunté like they were the members of her royal court.

This was going to be a very good day.

My steps took me closer to Shay-Shaunté's office. I heard her voice—that was surprising, because she never talked on the telephone, never had a meeting with her door opened. It was that privacy thing that she cherished—or at least, she used to.

The plan was to just keep it movin' until I heard, "I always wanted a baby."

My first thought was that she had better be talking about adoption. I stopped. When I didn't hear another sound, I held my breath, and slowly, slowly, slowly leaned forward. I didn't want to take the chance of Shay-Shaunté seeing me when I peeked in.

She was sitting, facing the window, her back to me; she was on the telephone, listening.

Then she spoke. "Well, that was my hope. To be pregnant."

I tried, but I couldn't hold my cry inside. I rushed to my office—wrong direction, because I already felt the bile rising up in me. I was only two steps inside before I grabbed the wastebasket, knelt down, and paid homage to the container. It was only emotions that spilled from me, since I'd ingested so little food in the past days. But even when there was nothing left inside, I was too spent to move.

So I just sat there, with my coat still on, resting on the floor and letting her words replay.

"*I always wanted a baby.*"

No! No way! She'd only been with Adam for two days and just three days had passed since then. How would she even know if she was pregnant?

"*That was my hope. To be pregnant.*"

Was this her plan all along? I trembled at that thought. But somehow I knew in my soul that this was a trick—by a trick, for a trick. She was fifty, for God's sake! She was not pregnant.

Her words played some more in my mind, and each time,

I actually became stronger. I pushed myself from the floor and grabbed the bucket.

I couldn't fight if I gave up. This heifer was playing some sort of game, and up to this point I'd let her. I'd stayed on the sidelines, like a spectator, for the last three days.

Well, her free pass was up; I was gonna get in the game. Shay-Shaunté just didn't know. For me, this wasn't about playing. I never showed up just to play; I only showed up to win.

God! That was the only way to explain why I didn't call up Brooklyn and have her bring me one of her switchblades. I guess it was another one of those lessons that Big Mama had taught me—revenge belonged to the Lord. So I'd let Him handle the getting-back-at-a-skank part. But I still had business to handle.

After I washed out my mouth and dusted myself off, I marched right into Shay-Shaunté's office. She was still facing the window, her back to me. If I was low-down, I would've attacked her and she would've never known who'd knocked her upside her head with that paperweight that rested on her desk. But all I did was close the door. Really, I more like slammed it, hoping to shake her up a bit.

But she didn't flinch. Just said, "Hey, Evia," without even turning around.

Okay, this wench was scary. How did she know it was me? What was up with this clairvoyant crap?

But I didn't let her spook me. I strode straight to her desk and got straight to the point. "Are you pregnant?"

Slowly, that throne of hers rotated until she faced me. It was almost as if she was laughing, the way her eyes danced and her cheeks were high, the way her lips were spread into a smile that filled her face. But still she said, "What?"

I folded my arms, leaned slightly to the left, one leg just inches in front of the other. A fighting stance. And I was ready for a fight when I said, "You heard me."

"What would give you that idea?"

"I heard you." There! Now what?

She leaned back on her throne. "You were listening to my private conversation?" Putting her hand across her chest, she asked, "Were you eavesdropping?"

"Whatever you want to call it, I'm askin'. Are you pregnant?"

She paused, too long for me. But just when I was about to reach across the desk and snatch her, she said, "No, I'm not pregnant. I think that time has passed for me."

"You said your hope was to be pregnant," I said, pushing her, because she needed to explain this whole thing to me.

"I was talking about years gone by."

Then, in the flash of a second, I saw something in Shay-Shaunté's eyes. What was it? Sadness? No, it was deeper than that. Sorrow? Yeah, sorrow mixed with regret. Maybe even some grief thrown in.

Just as quickly those emotions disappeared.

"So," I began, wanting to make this clear, "you are not pregnant . . . by my husband."

She leaned forward. "I got a lot of things from your husband this weekend, but a child wasn't one of them."

She was pushing it, but I told myself to let it slide.

"I wasn't trying to get pregnant," she added.

That was when I should've left. I should've just turned around and walked right out of her office. But I didn't.

"But though I may not have gotten pregnant by Adam, he definitely gave me my five million dollars' worth all . . . weekend . . . long." She paused, so that I could take in those words, I guess. But she didn't give me a standing ten-count, didn't give me a chance to breathe before she added, "And I gave it all right back to him." Now, she laughed. Tossed her head back and roared, really.

I felt like two cents.

The knife was already in . . . and the twist came when she said, "It was so good between Adam and me that I think I'm going to go back for seconds."

She was unbelievable, and if I didn't hate her so much, I would admire her. Because she came to the battle prepared. She had her own switchblade—her words, which were deadlier than any weapon I could carry.

I staggered toward the door.

"Oh, yes," she said, her words following me. "I think I'll give Adam a call," she taunted.

I was halfway to my office when she shouted, "If you quit, I will sue you."

I moved like I'd already planned my exit strategy. Maybe somewhere inside, I had. Maybe I already knew that today was going to be the day that it was over. Maybe leaving was as close to victory as I could get.

Inside my office, I swung my coat over my shoulders, then snatched my purse. I glanced at the picture frames that covered my desk and the plants that I'd nurtured. But I didn't have any time to pack. I had to get out now because if I saw Shay-Shaunté again, I was either going to cry or kill her, and neither would work out well for me.

With a farewell glance around my office, I opened my door. Shay-Shaunté was standing right there.

Today, I'd come into Ferossity determined to be victorious. But it was Shay-Shaunté who wore triumph and delight all over her face.

And rightfully so. Because after what she'd said to me, what she'd done today and yesterday and Monday—I had to give it to her. Shay-Shaunté was on a whole 'nother level. The only way for me to survive was to get totally out of this game.

She smiled. And warned, "I will sue you."

"Do what you have to do." I aimed for her shoulder and bumped her on purpose as I pushed past. I know—it was a dastard's way out, but what else could I do? It was the only way to get in just one blow.

But after I made contact, I had to work hard to keep my scream inside. Dang! I stopped and rubbed my arm for a second. The woman didn't look that solid, but I felt like I'd hit a concrete block.

I didn't spend too much time on my aching arm, though. Without looking back, I headed toward the staircase. For the last time.

I was getting the hell out of Ferossity.

Chapter 54

ALL I HAD TO DO WAS tell him what she said about being pregnant, about him giving her five million dollars' worth, and about her going back for seconds. Once I told him all of that, Adam would understand.

I didn't know how we would fight Shay-Shaunté in court, but truth? I was sure that mud duck was lying. She wasn't going to sue us; the threat was all part of her game. After all, would she want the world to know that she, Shay-Shaunté, the billionaire beauty mogul had to pay for sex? Naw! She was too smart, too private for that.

One thing was certain—she was smarter than me and Adam. I could not believe that we had fallen for this. All we'd been able to see was the money. Neither one of us—with all our degrees—had looked past our problems to see the consequences of this choice. Because it had been far more than a decision—it was a choice that we'd made, and it had brought crazy into our lives.

So now we had to deal. And we would deal. Shay-Shaunté could trust that.

I worked this all out in my head as I drove toward home. An extra bit of relief flowed through me when I saw Adam's car in the garage.

As I slammed my car door, I wondered if Adam had heard the garage open. If he had, he already knew that there was a problem. Why else would I be home before noon?

Stepping inside, I heard his voice right away. It sounded as if he was on a call, a business call maybe.

He said, "Yes." He paused, and I shrugged off my coat. He said, "Yes." He paused, and I kicked off my shoes. He said, "Yes, Shay-Shaunté," and my heart stopped beating. But when he said, "I'll talk to you soon," I barreled into the living room, arms flailing like a windmill, eyes on fire with fury.

I snatched the telephone before Adam could take two breaths. "You're talking to her?" I didn't even recognize my own scream. I hurled the phone, smashing it against the wall. With a thud, it splattered into a thousand little pieces.

"Evia!" Adam jumped up from the couch. "Calm down."

"You were talking to her?"

"Because she called here!" His hands cut through the air, moving as if he was trying to get me to lower my voice.

"So, you *are* still involved with her?" I cried.

"No! She wanted to talk to you. She said you'd quit and she wanted to remind you that she was going to sue us if you didn't come back."

"I'm not going back there," I screamed. "Do you know what she said to me?"

"Calm down," he said.

"She said that she was pregnant. And she insinuated that you were the father of her baby!"

"Mom!"

The breath I inhaled at that moment almost choked me. With wide eyes, I turned and stared into Alana's terrified face.

"Sweetheart!" I called to her, but I didn't move right away. First I had to cover the tears that drenched my face. I had to hide my hysteria. I had to make myself look presentable before I could go anywhere near my horrified daughter.

"What are you doing home?" I asked, as if that was the most important point of this moment.

Her face was still frozen with shock when she said, "Daddy came to school and got me." Her voice sounded robotic. "I was really sick and I threw up and the nurse sent me home."

Since he was far more composed than I was, I let him speak. "Go back upstairs, sweetheart. Everything is all right."

I could've done better than that. Apparently, Alana thought so, too, because she turned from her father and spoke directly to me. "Are you all right?"

I nodded because I wasn't sure if my voice could be trusted.

"See, sweetheart," Adam said. His calm in the middle of this turbulence was so soothing, and I wondered who it was meant for—Alana or me. He said, "I want you to rest."

She nodded, though the way her eyes shifted back and forth let me know that she was unsure. "Okay." Then, "Mom, can you come upstairs with me?"

I didn't have to look at Adam. Feeling him, I knew that he wasn't crazy about me being alone with our daughter. Frankly, I agreed.

He asked, "Alana, do you want me to—"

"No!" She didn't let him finish. "I want Mom to come with me."

The discussion was closed when our fifteen-year-old pivoted, then marched up the steps. As if she was the parent and I was the child, I followed her.

The seconds that it took for us to climb the stairs gave me the time I needed for my blood pressure to drop and my heart to start beating again.

Inside her bedroom, she faced me with arms folded, leaning slightly to the left, one leg just inches in front of the other.

A fighting stance.

I said, "I really want you to get some rest," as if she hadn't just witnessed her mother playing the part of a madwoman.

"What's going on with you and Dad?"

Okay, her moment for behaving like the parent was over. I shook my head as I pulled back her comforter.

The child returned. "Mom!" she whined. "Something's going on. Something bad. And I want to know."

I took a breath before I motioned for her to get in the bed. "There's nothing that I need to discuss with you." Once she was under the covers, I added, "This is between me and your father. And like he said, we'll be fine."

"Is he having an affair?"

I stiffened but said, "No," without further explanation.

"You said that he'd gotten someone pregnant."

Oh, God. "I said that someone was accusing him of getting her pregnant," giving too much of an explanation.

"If someone can accuse him, that means he's having an affair," she cried.

How was I supposed to stay the composed mother when all I wanted to do right now was crumble? "Look, it's complicated, but I don't want you to worry." The tears in my daughter's eyes told me that the hurt that Shay-Shaunté had brought to me had been passed to my child. Sitting on the edge of the bed, I stroked the side of her face. "Really, Alana, you know your father and me. You know we have a wonderful marriage, don't you?"

She paused, as if she had to think about that. "You used to, but . . . ever since Dad left on New Year's, everything's been different."

I'd worked hard to keep all of this away from my children, but though I could block what they heard, I couldn't block what they felt.

I said, "Have you ever been upset with Alexa?"

She peered at me through puzzled, squinted eyes as if she wondered if the crazy woman that she'd seen in the living room had returned. Because obviously, my question had nothing to do with what was going on now. But since she'd been raised right, she answered, "Yes."

"Even when you were upset, you still loved your sister, right?"

"Yes."

"Your anger was just for a moment."

She nodded.

"And then, when you weren't angry anymore, it kinda made your relationship as sisters a little better, right?"

"Yes."

"Well, that's what's going on with your dad and me. It's not a big deal. We had a little disagreement, but I promise you in a few days, we'll be back, even better than before."

She nodded again, now understanding the analogy. "But the other lady."

"There is no other lady!" My tone closed the door—there would be no further discussion.

Her eyes tested me; she stared as if she was trying to see if there was an opportunity to ask just one more question. But seeing no opening, she just sighed. Said, "I never thought that you and Daddy really ever got mad at each other."

"We're human, sweetheart." I kissed her cheek. "I'll be right downstairs if you need me."

"'Kay."

In the hallway, just as I was about to close her door, Alana yelled out, "I love you," as if she knew that those were the exact words that I needed to hear.

Thank God for the sensitive one.

Slowly, softly, I stepped down the stairs. But still, Adam felt me. He was waiting at the entrance of the living room when I got to the bottom landing.

"Is she all right?" he asked.

I nodded but didn't give him anything else. Before he could ask for more, I said, "We have to talk."

His glance wandered above me. Moved to the second floor, as if he could see through walls. "Not here."

I agreed; I wanted to keep my anger in check, but there were no guarantees. I didn't recognize myself, my life anymore. I had no idea what would happen next.

So I walked past him, through the living room, headed to the garage. When I opened the door to the passenger side of the SUV, he was right there beside me; he helped me step in.

From his driver's side, he pressed the remote, and when he shifted the car into reverse and backed out, I said, "We can't leave. Alana."

"I know." He stopped at the end of our driveway and peered through the windshield, again his gaze on the second floor of our home, as if he could now see through brick.

With a shake of his head, he twisted the steering wheel, then eased to the curb and parked in front of our home.

When he turned off the ignition, I said, "I'm sorry she heard me." My eyes were still looking for signs of our daughter watching.

"I tried to get you to calm down."

Even though I was the one who'd lost control, I was critical of him. "You should've told me that she was upstairs."

"It happened too fast." He shook his head. "Everything is happening too fast."

I understood what he meant. The deal had begun five days ago. Five days were more powerful than our sixteen years. "We have to fix this," I said.

He nodded. "I know."

Then he angled his body so that he faced me; I did the same.

He took my hand and drew a deep breath. "I know it's going to be hard, but you have to go back to Ferossity."

This was where he wanted to start the conversation? Even after I told him about her claiming to be pregnant?

I shook my head. "It's not going to happen." I kept holding on to his hands, though, when I added, "I just don't have enough in me."

He nodded, as if he understood, but he didn't have a clue. If he did, he'd be on my side.

So I told him everything that she'd said. Started with the five million dollars and how she was going back to him for seconds.

He released a long whistle, as if he couldn't believe it.

"But as awful as that was," I said, "as awful as everything has been this week, the worst thing, Adam, is that she said she was pregnant." I left out the part about how she'd changed her story. I wanted Adam to be focused on just how miserable it had been for me.

He asked, "She actually said that she was pregnant?"

"Well, she didn't tell me directly. At least, not at first. But we talked about it."

He shook his head. "I don't know why she's doing this."

"There is no rationalization for the devil." I paused, hoping that now he could see what I saw. "So, you understand, right? You see that I can't go back there. Not with everything: the taxes, her threatening to come after you—"

He squeezed my hand. "You don't have to worry about that. That will never happen."

I wanted to believe him, but I didn't recognize my life anymore. Anything could happen.

"And I really can't go back with that talk about her being pregnant."

"You don't have to worry about that either; she's not."

He spoke with the same conviction that I had about that; just like me, he knew for sure that she wasn't pregnant and my load was lightened. "I didn't believe her. She's too old," I said, taking some satisfaction in the one advantage I had over her. "Plus, I knew you'd use . . ." I hated to say the next words because it was such an acknowledgment of the deal. "I knew you'd use a condom."

I don't know which came first—the way his eyes shifted or the way I gasped.

"Oh, my God. You *didn't* use a condom."

He still held on, but he didn't look at me. "No."

I jerked away from his grasp and punched his arm. "Are you crazy?"

He flinched, just a little, though I was sure it wasn't my punch that hurt him. "She didn't want me to use a condom," he whispered.

"Who cares what she wanted? Why didn't you insist?"

His eyes were back on mine. "She was paying us five million dollars. I had to do everything her way."

I couldn't even keep my head up. This situation was like a weed, growing wildly, getting worse every moment.

"Then, she could be—"

"No."

"If you went at her bareback, how do you know?" He let so much silent time pass that I wanted to scream. "You can't stop talking now, Adam! You owe me this."

"I never wanted to bring the weekend to you . . . into our home."

"It's already here; it's already ruining us."

"I know," he said softly.

That may have been the most hurtful thing that I'd heard today. I didn't want Adam to so readily agree that our marriage was in trouble.

"What happened?" I whispered. "How did she take you away from me?"

He reached for me again, and though I wanted to pull back, I didn't. "She hasn't taken me away. She can't." His fingers curled around mine. "I'm still here."

"It feels like you're not," I said. "It feels like you're still there . . . with her."

He shook his head. "That's not it at all. It's just hard for me to talk . . . to you through all of the guilt."

"Guilt about sleeping with her?"

With a little shrug, he said, "Some of that, because now I will never be the man that I'd promised you that I'd be." He paused. "But mostly I feel guilty about being with her."

That made no sense to me, but Adam explained.

"In the beginning, when I first left, it was the sex that got to me."

You know that cliché about being careful what you ask for? Well, I was living it—I'd been begging Adam to talk, but now I didn't know if I had the courage to listen.

Adam kept on, "I had to keep reminding myself that I was there for my family."

I nodded. For the greater good.

"But then, it wasn't about the sex anymore. In fact, after Friday night, we didn't have sex much at all."

Whoa!

"I mean," he began, "we didn't have it as much as I thought we would—for five million dollars."

I wondered if he'd counted, and if he had, would he tell me the number of times. Maybe then I'd feel better. But then, maybe not.

"After a while," he said, "it became about just the two of us, hanging out, being together, talking and sharing." He swallowed. "That's why I know she's not pregnant. We talked about it."

I laughed, but not because I thought anything was funny. I laughed because this was all so sad. "You talked about her . . . wanting to be pregnant . . . by you?"

"No, she wasn't even thinking about a child. This wasn't about that for her. It was about being with someone. Being part of a couple. Shay-Shaunté just wanted to make a connection."

I squinted, shook my head, and shrugged—all at the same time.

Adam continued, "We talked a lot, and one of the things she told me was that she could never have children."

I sat in horror as he told me the story of how she'd been brutally raped as a teenager, with so much damage to her body that she'd never be able to conceive. He said, "The shame of what she went through made her pour herself into school, into work, never wanting a relationship, knowing that she'd never be able to give her partner children."

I would've felt sorry for Shay-Shaunté if I'd cared. Not that she needed any concern from me; the tone of Adam's voice let me know that he felt sorry enough for both of us.

"Why did she tell you this? Why was she talking about that when she paid so much . . . to be with you?" I folded my arms and wondered. Shay-Shaunté didn't have to pay anyone just to talk—at least not that much money. There had to be more to this. I said, "Five million dollars is a lot for just talking."

He shrugged. "When you have the kind of money that she has, you buy what you want. And that's what she wanted. Someone to be with. Someone to talk to. She told me that the things she shared with me, she'd never told anyone else. She told me about her lost hopes and new dreams . . ."

My head pounded as Adam went on and on about the beauty of Shay-Shaunté. That wasn't the word he used; the adoration was in his tone.

"Before we began talking," he said, "it was hard being there with her. But once we connected on a different level, I stopped thinking about my reasons for being there; there came a point when I was just there." He paused. "And that's what I've been feeling so bad about. That's why I didn't want to talk about it. Because part of the time with Shay-Shaunté, it stopped being about you and the kids, and my mom, and your mom. At some point, it became just about her . . . and me."

There were no tears left in my eyes, but there were plenty on my heart. I cried so hard inside that my chest hurt.

"Have you . . . are you . . . in love with her?" I asked.

"No," he said gently, too gently for me. Where was his indignation at my question? "No," he repeated. "I'm not in love with her. It's just that something happens when people talk, and they're in your arms—"

"You held her? Like that?"

He nodded. "That's what she wanted. Someone to hold her while she talked. Someone to hug her when she got to the parts of her life that hurt. Someone to say to her, 'I love you.'"

"You *did* that?"

He couldn't even look at me when he answered. "That's what she wanted."

"Oh, my God. This isn't even about what I thought this

weekend would be. This is worse. I thought I was going to lose you in her bed, but I lost you on her couch or at her dining room table, or wherever it was that you held her and told her you loved her."

"She knows I don't love her. She knows it was part of the fantasy; just part of this weekend."

"Then why are you acting like you love her?"

"I'm not. And again, I don't. I just need some time—to decompress. Get those days out of my mind."

"Because she's still with you."

"Not in the way you think. But I do feel sorry for her. And now I understand her." His eyes were back on mine when he said, "That's why you have to go back."

"What?" I screamed, not believing him. "After what I just told you and what you told me?"

"She's only lashing out at you because she's wounded," he rationalized.

"Well, whatever her problem is, she is not about to work it out on me. I am not going to sit anywhere and let anyone beat me down for six months . . . not even for you."

"But now that you know where that comes from . . ."

I twisted so that I faced him, because I wanted him to not only hear me but to read my lips, too. "You're right. Now I *really* know where this comes from. And it's not because she's wounded or hurt. It's because she wants to destroy me to get to you."

"It will never be that way," he said strongly. "I am with you, Evia. We're going to make it through this. But we have to get past this lawsuit, which will happen if you don't go back."

"You're not hearing me."

"And clearly, you're not hearing me. Because this is the deal we made. I gave up a lot and did my part, now you have to do yours."

I let some time go by so that nothing would interfere with the words Adam was about to hear from me. Because I vowed that I would not say this again. "I'm not going back," I said slowly.

"Not even if it will ruin us financially—and even our marriage?"

I stared him down. "Is that a threat?"

"No, it's a question."

"Well, I've given you my answer. That's what I'm going to do, and now you do whatever you have to do." I jumped out of the car, slammed the door, then stomped across the lawn.

That was when I felt the pull; I looked up. To the second floor, the center window, the one to Alana's room.

Alana's face was pressed against the pane. Even from where I stood, I could feel her despair—from the tears in her eyes to the way her bottom lip trembled. My sensitive child looked as if she feared that something horrible was happening.

That made me sad . . . because this time, it wasn't just some teenage machination. This time, whatever was going on in my child's mind was probably very close to the truth.

Chapter 55

THE GREAT DIVIDE THAT WAS BETWEEN us was no longer physical.

Yes, Adam still hugged his side of the bed and I hugged mine. But the miles that separated us in the king-size bed were no longer about our flesh alone. The chasm was mental, emotional, even spiritual now that I knew that Adam truly had been unfaithful. He'd cheated on me and connected with Shay-Shaunté on levels that were far more dangerous than sex.

It was that new pain that had kept me awake all night and made me ecstatic to see the first light of the new day as it peeked through our window.

I was so close to the nightstand that all I had to do was reach out and touch the alarm before it even did its thing. Obviously, I didn't need to be awakened, and Adam . . . well, these days I preferred my husband asleep. That way I could make believe that we were living in the time before the New Year's weekend, before the five million dollars, before Shay-

Shaunté. But the moment I turned and lay on my back, Adam rolled over to me.

Two things surprised me: one was that he was even awake, since Adam never climbed out of bed before seven. And the second was that he'd slid so far across the bed that his body was touching mine. He actually wrapped his arm around my waist.

I rested in this feeling that was once so familiar and now felt so foreign. We'd only held each other once since he'd been home, and we'd yet to connect as husband and wife.

Remembering that made me realize that Adam was probably still asleep. His body was just doing what it was used to doing; his mind was not aware.

Then he whispered, "Good morning," in his predawn voice, the tone deep and filled with sleep.

The way he spoke, the way he held me, made me wonder if I'd just imagined yesterday. Maybe all those things Adam had said about him and Shay-Shaunté were just a dream.

But when he asked, "Did you think about it? Are you going back to work?" I slipped away from Adam's embrace, realizing that this was nothing but the same old nightmare.

As I shrugged my bathrobe onto my shoulders, Adam sat up. "Evia, we have to—"

I held up my hand. "I don't want to talk about it anymore, Adam."

"So now you don't want to talk?" he said, his voice rising. "When I told you that I didn't want to talk, you insisted."

"Well, I don't want to talk because my answer is the same." Before he could start singing that song about how Shay-Shaunté was going to come after us, I belted out my own tune. "She's not gonna do anything."

He shook his head, silently telling me I was so wrong.

"Well, if you're concerned," I said, "go talk to her. Don't you two have a special connection now?"

I didn't give him a chance to protest the fact that I'd twisted his words a little; I just marched out of the room. I was sorry about one thing, though—why in the world had I told Adam to go see Shay-Shaunté? I didn't want him anywhere near that woman; didn't want the chance of more damage being done to our marriage.

But these days, I didn't recognize my words, didn't recognize my actions.

In the kitchen, I set the coffeemaker, then climbed the stairs to wake the children. I knocked on Alexa's door first, but when I peeked inside, my child, who was always the hardest to awaken, was already up, already in the shower.

Alana was up, too, laying out her clothes on her bed, waiting for her turn in the Jack-and-Jill bathroom she shared with her sister.

"What's going on?" I asked as I gave my daughter a hug. "You and Alexa are up already?"

Alana's voice did not match the fake cheer that I'd put into mine. She said, "Yeah, we were up almost all night—we couldn't sleep."

I didn't want to ask—really, I didn't need to. My girls had probably had one of their let's-figure-this-out sessions after Alana had filled Alexa in on the madness she'd witnessed yesterday.

"Are you okay, Mom?"

"I should be asking you that," I said, knowing she was still stuck on yesterday. But I wasn't about to let her go there. "How are you feeling?" I asked, as if I could deter my smart, sensitive fifteen-year-old.

"Physically, I'm fine." She sounded as if she had some type of medical degree. "But I'm really worried about you and dad and that other woman—"

I held up my hand. "Alana, I told you. I'm not discussing

this with you." She sighed, as if the weight of all that ailed this family rested on her. I asked, "Are you sure you're feeling up to going to school?"

"Yes."

"Well then, I'm going to get breakfast ready. You want some toast and fruit?"

"I'm too upset, Mom. I don't think that I can really eat."

I guessed she was trying to bait me with guilt, but my only response was a slight smile and a warning not to tarry too long.

But though it was relatively easy to subdue Alana, it wasn't the same with my oldest. I was sure that Alana had passed on my message of no discussion to her sister, but twenty minutes later, Alexa bolted down the steps, busted into the kitchen, and posed in front of me as if she was the commando-in-chief.

"Mom! Are you and Daddy getting a divorce?"

Goodness! The girls' discussion had gone really deep, though I should have expected this from the dramatic one.

"Good morning," I said, greeting her and ignoring her at the same time.

Neither my words nor my stern stare did anything to dissuade her from her mission.

"Mom!" Alexa spoke as if that was a demand.

Because of her never-ending drama, there were few times when Alexa could move me. But in this moment, with her eyes filled with fear, sadness, and doubt, I was affected—softened and sickened at the same time.

"No, Alexa," I said, cushioning my words with a gentler tone. "Your father and I are not getting a divorce."

"Who's getting a divorce?" Ethan asked as he came into the kitchen.

Alana followed him, though she was silent.

"Listen," I said to all three of my children. "Whatever's going on between me and your father has nothing to do with you. This is grown folks business and you three just need to focus on the things that matter to you."

"Huh?" Ethan grunted, evidence that my son was oblivious to the craziness that Adam and I had brought into our home.

But the twins were not going to let it go.

"Mom," Alana began in a gentle voice that was supposed to coax me into giving in. "Everything that happens with you and Dad matters to us."

I shook my head. "We matter, but not our business."

"Daddy said," Alexa jumped in, "that we're a family and that means we have responsibilities to each other. So what's going on does matter to us."

This would've been much easier if I had been one of those old-school mothers who told their children to sit down and shut up before she smacked them upside the head. That's what Marilyn would've done.

But since I was never going to be anything like my mother, I swallowed the "sit down and shut up" urge and said, "I'm not going to discuss this any further. Now, I'm going to put some bagels in the toaster, and what else do you guys want?"

"Cereal!" Ethan yelped.

But the twins were defiant. They sat with their arms folded, glaring at me, as if they could stare or scare me into telling them what they wanted to know.

After a few seconds, Alexa said to Alana, "You know what this means, right? They're getting a divorce."

There was only one way to explain what happened next: Adam, Shay-Shaunté, forty-eight hours, taxes, her man, her pregnancy, Adam's confession that he'd told her he loved her, him wanting me to go back to work . . . now Alexa was pressing, pressing, pressing me . . .

I snapped!

In just three steps, I was in Alexa's face. Grabbing her by

the white collar of her school uniform, with one hand, I lifted her from the chair.

"Mom!" Alana and Ethan screamed, though Alexa—whom I still held by the throat—was silent from her shock.

I growled, "Didn't I tell you that this was none of your business?" Grasping her collar even tighter, I pushed her against the wall. "But you're hardheaded. You couldn't leave it alone. You couldn't just do what I told you to do, could you?"

Alexa was in my grasp, but all three of my children whimpered.

I still had Alexa pinned against the wall when I heard "Evia!"

We all turned at Adam's voice and slowly I relaxed my fingers—one by one—until I released Alexa.

Now trust me, though I was pissed, I had not hurt my daughter. I'd definitely scared her, but she was not injured in any way.

Still, when I let go of her, she crumpled to the ground. No one made a move to her, though. Maybe they all knew what I knew—that her collapse was nothing but drama. Or maybe it was because I'd scared them all and no one wanted to make any sudden moves.

"You all right?" Adam asked me.

"We're fine," I said, as each one of my children shivered behind me. Glancing over to the counter, I added, "I was just fixing breakfast."

He nodded. "Okay, I can finish if you want me to." His eyes were steady on me, without even a blink.

I was pretty sure that no one in my family would have an appetite for a couple of hours. But still, whatever our children wanted or needed right now would be best handled by their father.

So, without looking back, I marched past Adam. But in just a few moments, I wanted to run back and hug them all.

Pressure and misery had made me snap, but I could never let that happen again. Adam and I needed to fix this. And fast . . . before this horrible sin that we'd committed became a price that our children had to pay.

Chapter 56

ONE AND A HALF MILLION DOLLARS.

I could almost hear the angels singing! The ones who were protecting us even in the midst of this madness. Because according to Adam's records on the computer, even though we'd paid off our house, bought new cars, paid past due bills, and even made payments into the future, we still had $1,575,860.04 left. Even after Shay-Shaunté played us, we were still in the millionaire game.

Not that I was overly confident—I knew this money wouldn't last long, not in today's times, and not with all the obligations that we had to our extended family. But this was still a major blessing. Adam and I would have new jobs soon—and with this money, we were free.

I surveyed those beautiful numbers on the spreadsheet once again. This had been our goal: to get our finances back in line . . . to make sure that our children wouldn't have any kind of change in their lifestyles. We'd achieved that objective, and we deserved a high grade for that.

But we'd failed overall because we hadn't counted the high cost. We'd paid a price that was now burdening our children.

My heart ached as I thought about what I'd done to Alexa this morning. Adam and I prided ourselves on never having raised our hands to our children. That child-rearing philosophy had been passed down from Ruby. But though it was the path that Adam's mother had taken, my mother had had a different journey. Marilyn had beaten me so many times, often for no reason other than she'd had a bad day.

I'd vowed that I'd never be like her.

But this morning, I'd turned into my mother.

I'd grabbed Alexa in my frustration, my sadness . . . my anger.

Of course, there were plenty of reasons to explain why I'd jumped over the edge—Shay-Shaunté's taunting, Adam's confession. But neither should have driven me to put my hands on Alexa.

Really, all I wanted to do right now was go down to Alexa's school, pull her out of class, hold her, and apologize, though I was sure that if she saw me coming, she'd run the other way. I'd have to wait until she got home. Not only Alexa, but Alana and Ethan, too—all of my children needed an apology, a hug, and a promise that they'd never see me go off like that again.

But though I was truly sorry and couldn't wait to be with my children, I couldn't dwell. It would just be another hour or so before they'd be home, and I'd already wasted too much time today, wallowing, sipping wine, and wishing for the old days.

I clicked from the spreadsheet to the web browser, not really sure where to begin. Should I browse the Internet or go through an employment agency? Either way, it wouldn't take me long to find a job. Not only was I confident of my abilities as a top-notch assistant but I'd also worked for Shay-Shaunté.

The thought of her made my confidence wane just a little. My position at Ferossity was a major asset, but how was I going to explain not having a recommendation from my boss?

I sighed. Adam was going to have to help me figure that out.

Adam.

This was only the millionth time that I'd thought about my husband since I'd stomped past him after almost choking one of his children. He'd stared at me with such utter amazement and disappointment that I'd truly expected him to follow me into the bedroom and demand to know what I'd done with his wife because surely what he'd witnessed had not been the woman he loved. I'd been ready to tell him that his wife had disappeared with my husband and that I wanted that other guy back, too.

But after he'd helped the children off to school, Adam had left without a "what's wrong with you" or a "good-bye." And now, eight hours later, I still hadn't heard a word from him.

I leaned back in the desk chair, closed my eyes, and channeled better times. Looking back, our marriage had been so easy—overflowing with the vows we'd taken . . . to love, honor, and cherish. Sixteen years of bliss—and then we'd hit a wall. But even with all of our financial problems, I'd felt loved, and adored, and safe with Adam.

Until the money. What was supposed to have saved us was destroying us!

My eyes popped open at that revelation, and right over me stood my husband.

"Dang!" I said, so startled that I almost toppled the chair. "You scared me."

"I'm sorry. I thought you heard me come in."

No, I hadn't heard him, hadn't felt him. It was like every bond between us had been severed.

He said, "You looked like you were asleep."

"I wasn't; I was just thinking about something—I wanted to talk to you."

"I wanted to talk to you, too."

I'd expected him to let me speak first, like he always did, but just like everything else in our lives, that had changed. He said, "What happened this morning?"

My mind had been on another track; I'd wanted to forget the pain of the past week and make a pact with my husband to move to the future. But before I could talk to Adam about my new thoughts, I had to handle this old deed.

"I don't know," I said. "I was upset with Alexa, but I should've never let it get out of control like that. I'm going to apologize when she gets home."

He sighed. "You know it's the pressure that's getting to both of us, right."

"I know." I stood up. "That's what I wanted to talk to you about."

He kept on. "And if we think this pressure is bad," he paced in front of me, moving fast, like he was nervous, "it's going to be ten times worse if we end up in court."

We were back to that? I didn't want to talk about Shay-Shaunté suing us, and I told Adam that. "There're so many other things to talk about. No need to waste energy on something that's not going to happen."

"But what if it does?" He didn't give me a chance to answer. "You have to go back to work, and I think I've figured out a way."

I folded my arms and poked out my lip. Why wasn't this man listening to me?

He said, "I'll talk to her, we can talk to her together. I'll tell her to stop playing games."

He paused, as if he expected me to cheer, but I kept my lips pressed hard together, determined not to repeat what he already knew.

"I'll tell her that she has no chance with me . . . that that wasn't the deal."

I gave him more silence.

"And even if she doesn't stop, you know that whatever she says isn't true."

Now he gave me something to work with. "I don't know that, Adam. And I don't want to be running home to you every night asking if this happened or if that happened based on how Shay-Shaunté decides to torment me that day. I'm not putting myself through that, and I'm not putting that strain on our marriage."

"The strain is already there, Evia," he said, his voice shaky.

"But it doesn't have to be." I stayed calm for the both of us. "Even with the trick that Shay-Shaunté pulled, we still have over a million dollars left. Why can't we just take that and move forward?"

"Because if she sues us we're not going to have that money. And it's too much to lose because your feelings were hurt."

"Is that what you think?" I asked, tightening every part of my body. When I balled my hands into fists, I wanted to hurt more than just his feelings. "You think this is just a little temper tantrum because my feelings were hurt?"

"I don't know what you'd call it, but whatever it is, it's putting everything, especially our children, at risk."

"I would never do anything to hurt our children."

His eyebrows rose, like he wondered if I remembered this morning. I needed a different approach.

"Look, Adam, I'm telling you, it would be more dangerous

for me to go back there. Every day that I'd be around Shay-Shaunté would mean that's a day that she's around our family. And with what she's pulled, and the things she's said, I don't trust her. I think there's more to her agenda."

"There's nothing she can do to us if we fulfill our part of the contract. You have to just handle her because it's too much to ask the twins and Ethan and my mother—"

"Your mother?" I couldn't believe he went there. "Don't throw her in my face."

"Why not? If I don't come to you, where do I place the blame if this deal blows up? You're the one who's backing out, wanting to take the easy way, not caring how it will affect everyone, even your ghetto family."

I couldn't count the times that I'd called my family ghetto. But hearing those words from Adam hurt.

"Is that what you think about my family?"

He shrugged. "You got another name for them?"

For a moment, I just stood still. This was not the man I'd married. I stomped across the room and jumped right into his face. "You must've forgotten where you grew up. You and I are from the same block, the same blood, the same hood. If I'm ghetto, you are, too."

His nostrils flared with an anger I'd never before seen in my husband. "You need to back off me, Evia," he warned.

"Or what?" I screamed. "What are you going to do, Adam? Hit me because I won't do what you tell me to do?"

"Mom!"

I froze. My first thought—this couldn't be happening again. But then, I heard "Dad," and the whimper of our son.

When I turned around, I saw that today was far worse than yesterday. Because next to our son stood his best friend, Dougie, looking as traumatized as Ethan.

Today, I let Adam handle our child. With quick steps, he

approached the boys, and with a smile, he welcomed Dougie into our happy home.

But Dougie said, "Mr. Langston, can you take me home now?"

Five seconds in our house and Ethan's friend wanted to get out. I bet Ethan did, too.

"Sure," Adam said as if it was normal for his friend to want to leave so soon. To Ethan, he asked, "Wanna ride with me?"

Our son couldn't nod his head fast enough. He wasn't about to be left in the house with his mad mama.

The boys charged out of the room, and Adam turned to me. We stared at each other, for just a moment, the same disbelief in his eyes that was in mine. Again, one of our children—and now one of their friends—had seen us at our worst. Because of Shay-Shaunté.

With only a slight nod, Adam left, putting our fight on pause. But it was still inside of me, brewing, and I knew it was the same for Adam.

This was just a cease-fire; the combat had stopped for a moment. But there would be no peace until Adam came to my side. That was the only way to end this war.

Chapter 57

THINGS HAD CERTAINLY CHANGED IN MY world.

Today when I walked into Rumors to meet my girls, Tamica was there, as expected. But when I saw Brooklyn already sitting at the table, too, I knew I was in an alternate universe. I was right on time and Brooklyn was here before me?

I paused for a moment, staying steps away from the two of them, just watching. Their battles were always pure Calgon moments that took me away—just for a little while—from every problem I'd ever had.

But as I studied my girls, I could already tell that today wasn't going to be one of those parties. Tamica and Brooklyn were in serious mode—leaning so close together that their foreheads almost touched. I knew their whispers were about me and my sudden phone call this morning asking them to meet me this afternoon.

Every incident of the past week rushed through my mind, and for a second, I wanted to turn around and go home.

But for what? Nothing was waiting there for me.

So I strolled toward the table as if my life wasn't falling apart.

"What's up?" I slipped into the booth next to Tamica, hugged her, then blew Brooklyn a kiss.

"The question is," Brooklyn said, "what's up with you?"

I shrugged off my coat. "Nothing much."

"Uh-huh." Brooklyn twisted her lips. "That's why I haven't spoken to you since 2011 began."

"Sorry about that," I said. "Oh, and happy new year. You, too, Tamica." I grinned as if this was a regular get-together.

The waiter must've been following me, because he was right there at our table asking if we had made our lunch selections.

I said, "I wanna get a drink first."

He pointed to the glass in front of me. "They already did that for you."

I hadn't even noticed the iced tea, and I pushed the glass away. "Let me have a glass of white wine."

He nodded. "Do you want to order your entrees now?"

I shrugged and, with a glance, passed that ball to Brooklyn. It wasn't like I was going to eat much.

Brooklyn and Tamica ordered their usual—a three-mile-high burger for Brooklyn and the seafood lasagna for Tamica.

"I just want a side salad," I said, keeping my eyes on the waiter. I could feel Brooklyn's and Tamica's stares, but I wasn't about to order food that I wasn't going to eat.

"That's all you're having?" Tamica asked.

I turned back to the waiter. "Okay, make it a side Caesar."

When the waiter walked away, Brooklyn said, "So, now you're only drinking and not eating?"

"These days, I'm surviving on a diet of coffee, wine, and nightmares."

Brooklyn exchanged a long glance with Tamica before she

said, "I guess things didn't quite turn out right . . . with the money, the deal."

I shook my head.

"Why haven't you called me back?" Brooklyn asked.

"I'm sorry, but I've kinda been busy with trying to save my life. But now that I'm not working, I'll have plenty of time."

It was perfect timing—the waiter brought my wine just as I was getting ready to confess all to my friends. I took a single sip, then told them the whole story—everything since they'd last seen me on Christmas.

Tamica held my hand as I told them about the pain of the fifty hours when Adam had been away; then they leaned forward with anticipation as I told them about Adam coming home. When I got to every antic Shay-Shaunté had pulled, their mouths opened wide.

"Taxes!" Brooklyn exclaimed. "Oh, you should've called me. I would've cut that witch; if she wasn't going to pay with dollars, she would've paid with her blood."

"I thought about calling you." I laughed, hoping that would take a little edge off this conversation. But my little chuckle did nothing—my girls were still on the edge, riveted and waiting to hear the rest.

At the part about Shay-Shaunté saying she was pregnant, Tamica gasped, but Brooklyn shouted, "The devil is a lie!"

"Turns out, you're right. She's not." Did I feel bad as I told my girls all of Shay-Shaunté's business about not being able to conceive and how that had happened? Not. At. All.

Finally, I closed out the story with what I'd come to call Adam's confession.

This time, both of my friends gasped.

"Did Adam say he's in love with her?" Tamica whispered just when the waiter came with our lunch.

"Adam said he doesn't love her." But then I shrugged, my body saying what my mouth wouldn't.

"He's not!" Tamica said strongly, as if the force of her words were greater than all of my doubts.

"Well, let's bless this food," Brooklyn said. She bowed her head and said, "Thank you, Lord."

My and Tamica's heads were still lowered and our eyes were still closed, waiting on Brooklyn to continue her usual sermon-size grace. But when she said, "Would you come on and tell us the rest," I realized that I'd just witnessed the shortest blessing in Brooklyn's history.

Pushing my salad aside, I said, "There's nothing more to tell. Besides the fact Adam and I hardly speak to each other and my children have all seen the worst in me."

"Wow!" Tamica and Brooklyn said through stuffed mouths.

They ate, and I took another sip of my wine.

Tamica shook her head. "This is what I was talking about. I hate to say I told you so. I knew this wasn't a good idea."

"Dang, Tamica! Do you have to come down on E like that right now?" Brooklyn glared.

"I'm not talking to her. I'm talking to you!" Tamica pointed at Brooklyn. "You were the one who told her to do this."

"No," I touched Tamica's shoulder trying to pull her back from the brink of a battle with Brooklyn. "She didn't do this; I'm a grown woman."

"Naw, she's right in a way," Brooklyn said, surprising both of us. "I mean, I did kinda tell you to do it."

"Not kinda," Tamica smirked.

"All right." Brooklyn rolled her eyes. "I guess I was just looking at the money part. I mean, you were my friend, you were in trouble, you needed money . . . how much damage could be done to a good marriage over a weekend?"

"Obviously, a lot!" Tamica answered for me.

Brooklyn ignored her. "I just thought you and Adam were so solid that nothing could affect you."

"Nothing but the devil," Tamica said, continuing as my spokesperson.

Brooklyn held the palm of her hand up in Tamica's face while she spoke to me. "I never looked beyond the money, sweetie, and I'm really sorry for that."

"You should be sorry," Tamica said. "As friends we have to hold each other up. We can't be leading each other down the road to hell."

Brooklyn pushed back against the booth. "Okay! How many times should I say I'm sorry?"

"You don't have to apologize." I jumped in before Tamica could say something like seventy times seven. "Like I said, this was all me and Adam, and really, as bad as it's been, I think we're gonna be okay. We were too solid before to fall apart now."

"You're right about that," Tamica said.

Brooklyn's mouth was full, but she held up her fork to show her agreement with me.

"So can we now change the subject?" I asked, feeling bad enough. "How was the new year for you guys?"

"It was quiet. We were just in church. How's Ms. Ruby? You guys decided not to go see her today?"

Brooklyn had no idea, but she'd just taken the conversation right back to where I didn't want to be. "No, Adam and the children went." I sipped the last of my wine as my girls stared first at me and then at each other.

I knew what they were thinking—for me not going to see the woman that I loved so much things had to be bad!

I stared into the bottom of my empty glass, still having a hard time believing that I hadn't gone with Adam and the kids. But this morning, when Adam had met me in the kitchen with only the mutter of a "Good morning" and then told me that we'd be leaving for Pearly Gates around noon, I knew I didn't want to go. Not that I didn't want to see Ruby. My mother-in-love, even in her incapacitated state, was the only thing that was steady in my life. I could've used my special time alone with Ruby, could've used the love that I still felt from her.

But I didn't want the trade-off; for that short time with Ruby, I didn't want to spend the hours riding down, then back, choking in tension. And I didn't want to subject Alexa, Alana, and Ethan to that as well.

So I'd bowed out with a simple, "I'm not going."

Adam had barely responded. Just given me a little nod like he hadn't cared.

That was when I'd called my girls.

Tamica wrapped her arms around me and Brooklyn reached across the table, touching my hand.

"God's got you," Tamica said.

"And we do, too," Brooklyn added.

I nodded. There was never a doubt in my mind that God and these two women would always be there for me.

The question was, With all that we were up against now, was it too little, too late?

Chapter 58

A WEEK PASSED. THEN ANOTHER. AND a third. The calendar was getting ready to change to February, and we'd heard nothing from Shay-Shaunté.

Not that her silence—or the lack of any kind of lawsuit—had made things normal at home. I'd apologized to all of my children, collectively and individually, and they'd all accepted my apologies, but they still tiptoed around as if an extra word or sound might detonate my wrath. I'd turned Alexa, Alana, and Ethan into the Stepford children—I swear, I'd never heard so many "Yes, ma'am's," and "No, ma'am's," in my life.

Even though the twins' birthday party was fast approaching, they stayed subdued—at least in front of me. I heard them, though, sometimes in their bedrooms, or in the office talking to Adam, the air charged with their excitement as they planned the party, which was going to be held at The Waterfront, an upscale restaurant in Southwest. Their sweet-sixteen bash (for teenagers only) would take place in the private area—the Red Room—downstairs.

Snagging that room at such a late date had been a major coup and cost big bucks, but it was what the girls wanted, and Adam was determined to bring joy into their lives. The twins and Adam had already laid out the party room for the restaurant manager—with a dance floor, a stage for the live band, and even a bar that would serve nothing but soda and fruit punch.

I smiled whenever I heard the twins, though it all seemed to be happening without me. I'd asked on many occasions what I could do to help. But according to my girls, Adam had done everything that was wanted; I wasn't needed.

As a consolation prize, the twins asked me to help them address their invitations. I gladly jumped in, though even that process with my girls was strained. As we sat at the dining room table, Alexa and Alana kept their voices low and their chatter short. The thrill I heard in their voices whenever they were with Adam was not there for me.

Still, I helped them address the ninety envelopes, then the three of us carted the invitations to the post office.

It was then that my sensitive child conjured up the nerve to say something to me besides "good morning," "thank-you," or "please."

As we stood in the post office line, Alana asked, "Mom, have you stopped working?"

It was a strange time to ask that normal question, but then it occurred to me that my daughter thought she was safer in public.

Keeping my voice as gentle, as soft, as normal as I could, I told the truth. "Yes and no. I've stopped working at Ferossity, but I'm looking for a new job."

I was sure the twins had plenty of questions about that, but they didn't dare ask any more. They'd gotten away with that one—they were satisfied.

Alexa and Alana weren't the only ones who stayed far away. Poor Ethan only said hello and good-bye. And although Adam kept me informed about the party and the matching Toyota sport coupes (instead of Range Rovers) that he'd ordered for the girls, he didn't speak to me about much more.

There were times when I felt like I'd been cast off on an island. But I vowed to make it through this storm—didn't everybody go through at least one in their life?

In the meantime, I did have enough to keep me busy. In the three weeks since I'd left Ferossity, I'd had four interviews. Everyone had been impressed with me; two of the companies were places where I could see myself building a career. I'd already returned for a second interview for the position I wanted most—the assistant to a literary agent.

Ellen Cohen had been an executive editor with one of the big New York publishing houses and had retired early to return to the place of her birth and open her agency away from the hustle of that big city. She was looking for someone to help with the start-up and was impressed with my credentials.

"Although, I have to admit, I've never heard of Ferossity," she said as she stared at my résumé. "What an unusual spelling."

"Yes," I said. "It's not a typo, it's just unusual."

"Why did you leave?"

I had anticipated this question; my desire had been to discuss it with Adam and come up with a great response. But since our communication was just about nonexistent, I'd worked this out by myself.

I inhaled a deep breath, then started my lie. "My intent was to take off a year because my daughters are getting ready to enter their last year of high school and I wanted to make sure that I had time to devote to helping them with college entrance exams and applications. And my husband and I wanted to take them on a college tour—all of the good things that come with preparing for this important part of their lives."

"That's exciting. So, what made you jump right back into the workforce?"

Part two of the lie: "Well, my husband just started his own business, working from home, and to be honest"—I lowered my voice—"we didn't anticipate the . . . interesting issues that arise from us working in the same space. We realized pretty quickly that it wasn't necessary for both of us to be home."

Ellen laughed. "If this doesn't work out with you and me, definitely apply for a job as a diplomat. What a wonderful, politically correct way to put it," she said. "Trust me, I understand. My husband and I tried to work side by side when we first got married, and were almost divorced before our second anniversary."

I just smiled. After a little more chatter, she thanked me for coming in and said she would get back to me within two weeks.

I had no doubt that she would. I had what a person needing to get a business off the ground needed.

Still, I kept looking, treating my job search like employment. I woke up early to get the children off to school, then I hit the office and the computer, searching until noon, when I would turn the office over to Adam—since he was still looking for work, too. Back in the day, we would've worked this job-hunting thing together, but it was safer these days to turn over the downstairs computer to him while I continued my search in one of the twins' rooms.

As the days passed without an outburst from me or a letter from Shay-Shaunté, the frost that filled our home thawed. The children's laughter returned—even in front of me. And Adam and I began to talk—not the normal, unabridged conversations that had always been a part of our marriage, but we spoke, cordially, carefully, ten words at a time.

Until last night, in the middle of the darkness, I'd rolled over and touched Adam by accident. I'd awakened right away when I'd felt the electrical current that surged through my body when my fingertips had grazed Adam's bare thigh.

I'd scooted away fast, back to my side of the bed, as if I'd seen a mouse. But the feelings had stayed with me, and for the rest of the night, I hadn't been able to sleep. All I'd wanted was that moment again; I'd wanted to touch him again, even if it had just been for a second.

But as I'd lain awake, and thought, and wished, I'd decided I wanted much more than a touch. I wanted my husband back.

When Ethan had announced over his breakfast that this was the last day of January, I'd paused. One month ago, we'd been preparing for Adam to leave to be with Shay-Shaunté. And in truth, Adam Langston had never come home.

I'd decided then that tonight, I'd welcome Adam back, make him remember who he was, who we were.

Once the children were off, I went into the office as usual, but I didn't sit behind the computer. Today, I paced, with thoughts and plans swirling through my mind.

In the past, it had been easy to go to Adam and tell him that our disagreement had to end. But that had been when we'd argue for thirty minutes. Never had we argued for thirty days.

Maybe I was doing too much planning. Maybe all I needed to do was walk up to him and start talking, letting the words come from my heart. So I took a deep breath and headed toward the door. Right before I got to the threshold, Adam came in.

"Adam!"

"Evia!"

We spoke at the same time. Then chuckled a little, hesitantly, together.

Then when we said, "I wanted to talk to you" at the same time again, we laughed outright—together.

Adam held up his hands. "Okay, we've got to do this decently and in order. You first."

That was a good sign. I said, "I don't want this to keep—"

I didn't get the chance to finish. Adam's lips were on mine before I had a chance to close my eyes. But once I did, I fell right into the familiar feeling.

A kiss had never done so much for me, and when we finally separated—minutes or an hour later, I didn't know—neither one of us could hardly breathe.

"What were you saying?" he had the nerve to ask me.

As if I could remember. As if I cared.

This time, I leaned into him, wanting more. I couldn't remember the words I'd planned, but I definitely remembered what I wanted to say with my lips. As I pressed my body into his, I told him that I was sorry, that I wanted him, needed him. My tongue told him that we had so much more of a life to live together. And my hands—my hands were totally out of control and revealed to Adam just how much I'd missed him.

Then it was my turn to pull back and ask him if he had something to say.

He spoke as if his words were already there, right on the tip of his tongue. "Through it all," he started, "I have loved you and missed you and wanted you." Like in the old days, I melted.

"What happened to us?" I asked.

"Does it matter?"

"I guess not. It's just that—"

He pressed his fingers to my lips. "Let's just think about where we go from here."

I nodded, and he pulled me into his arms again. "I think," he said as he kissed my neck, "that we need to have a special night," another kiss, "so that you can make all of this up to me . . ."

"Up to you?" I laughed. "Gladly."

"Oh, don't worry, I have some things I want to make up to you, too."

I jumped into his arms and he lifted me, my legs wrapped around his waist. Forget about tonight; I was ready to get this party started.

"What about the celebration?" he asked. "Tonight."

As he held me up, I shook my head, letting my tongue explore his skin, the terrain that I'd missed so much. "The celebration, tonight can wait, but I can't."

He laughed, but just before our lips met again, the telephone rang. Now me, I was willing to let the voice mail pick up that bad boy, because I had work to do.

But Adam's sensibility took over. "It could be about a job. For either of us."

My first thought was that they would call back, but I knew Adam was right—in today's times, you couldn't give an employer any reason to move on to the next candidate.

Adam grabbed the phone, since I couldn't. It wouldn't have been a good idea for anyone to hear me panting this way.

"Yes," I heard Adam say. "Yes," he repeated, this time with much more enthusiasm. "Mr. Yearwood, thank you. Thank you so much!" He hung up the phone and grabbed me by my waist.

"Was that . . . American Express?" I asked, remembering the name of the man who'd interviewed him before.

"Yes. They've lifted the hiring freeze for a few high-level positions and he wants me to come in now and get those papers signed."

My eyes were wide. "This means . . ."

"Yup! I'm hired . . . again." He lifted me and swung me around. Though I was beyond excited, I couldn't stop my first thought—that if we had just waited . . . just waited one month . . .

My feet touched the ground as Adam set me down. "We are back! You hear me." He turned away from me, paced the length of the room. His smile was so wide that the ends of his mouth were just about touching his ears.

Just one month.

I needed to shake away that thought, because what did it matter? Adam had the job, we had over a million dollars in the bank, and Shay-Shaunté had gone away.

"I'm going to run down to Amex right now." He kissed me. "But when I get back . . . oh, girl, you better be ready."

I laughed at the way he pimp-strutted out of the office and down the hall, and within fifteen minutes, he met me in the living room—dressed and ready.

He planted a final kiss on me that made me moan and want him now, but I waved when he backed away and jumped into his SUV.

Back inside the house, I'd expected to feel Adam's exhilaration; I wanted all of his excitement. But it wouldn't come.

Instead my thoughts were on the fact that we could've waited . . . we should've waited.

Although the door was firmly closed, I swear I felt a breeze blow right through the wood, making me shudder and making me wonder.

Chapter 59

THIS WAS THE DAY I'D BEEN waiting for: For days that had turned into weeks, weeks that had almost turned into a month, I'd prayed that the moment would come when Adam and I would move beyond a truce to the end of the war. And the end had come—rather quickly, with this extra piece of good news.

I was still standing by the door, minutes after Adam had left; my mind was filled with wonder.

The ringing telephone brought me back, and with the way this morning had progressed, I wouldn't have been surprised if it was a job for me.

The caller on the other end was even better than a potential employer. It was Adam.

"You know what?" he said the moment I picked up. "I'm gonna make reservations at the Ritz tonight. Dinner and a room."

"That sounds wonderful."

"Yup," he said, his enthusiasm infectious even through the

phone. "Just get the twins and Ethan situated and then I'm taking you out of there."

"Okay!" I said. "And maybe we can . . ."

I couldn't say any more. It was the alarm that rang inside of me. The alarm that came from my center—that I hadn't heard in a long time.

"Maybe we can what?"

I leaned against the wall to steady myself. "No . . . nothing. The Ritz and dinner will be great."

"You got that right." He paused, more serious now. "Evia, I know things haven't been great, but from now on—"

"I know."

"I love you," he said.

"I love you more."

"I love you best."

I hung up, feeling like I was once again living in the best of times. But then, there was that alarm—what was that about?

I stood in the quiet stillness of our house, just to be sure that I'd really heard it. Closing my eyes, I inhaled, then exhaled—it was probably just the excitement of the morning.

But as I stood pressed against the wall, it was the alarm that I felt for sure. The only thing was, this felt different from all those other times. This didn't feel like a warning, this felt like dread.

I shook my head and pushed that feeling aside. There was no need to listen, because what could go wrong? Even if American Express pulled back its offer again, it wouldn't be like last time. Adam would be hurt, but we had money in the bank. He'd just keep on looking. And me—even if I didn't get a job for another one, two or three years, we would still be all right.

But it was hard not to listen. My heart was singing for all that had happened in the last few hours, but beneath that joy, my soul was twisting and turning.

I went through the next hours doing all that I had to do, preparing dinner for the children, then showering, getting dressed in jeans and a white shirt—Adam's favorite outfit. I packed for both of us for our overnight excursion, filling our suitcase with nothing more than toiletries and what we would wear home tomorrow; we didn't need anything but each other for tonight.

The alarm stayed throughout—soft, but constant, and in those in-between moments, I had to stop and sit and wonder.

I used the TV in the living room, the radio in the kitchen, turning both up so loud that my ears burned. But like a stubborn child, the ringing stayed.

When the telephone rang and I checked the caller ID, I knew this was what the warning inside had been all about.

Hesitantly, I picked up the phone. "Adam?" I whispered.

"It's official; I am now an executive VP with Amex."

I released a long breath, delighted that I'd been wrong. Nothing bad was going to happen.

"You got the kids situated?" he asked.

"Yup, dinner's ready for them, and I packed an overnight for you."

"Great." He laughed. "I can't remember the last time I was this happy."

"I know. And the kids, especially the twins, they'll be happy to see us . . . you know . . . kinda back to normal."

"All the way back to normal," he corrected. "But we'll all be fine now. It's a new day. Okay, I'm pulling up to the house now. I'll be right in, Shine."

Adam hung up, but I stayed still, the phone stuck in my hand.

It was a simple word, a simple name. But he'd called me Shine. Enough days to fill a month had passed since I'd last heard that name. Hearing him call me that filled in all the empty spaces in my heart. It was better, bigger than any diamond he could've placed on my finger.

I was Shine again. That meant that everything was going to be all right.

Then . . .

Adam walked inside, through the front instead of through the garage. He stomped through the door, certainly not the gait of a man who'd just declared that this was a new day. His eyes were dark, his forehead was full of wrinkles, and the tips of his lips were turned downward, aiming for his chin.

What could possibly have happened in one minute?

Not enough time had passed for fear to settle inside me, but with the way Adam glared, panic caught up to me quickly.

He waved a sheet of paper in front of my face. "I was just served with this," he said. "A guy just walked up to me and handed it to me." He opened his mouth, but then pressed his lips together as if he was holding back a tornado of words. Finally, it blew out of him. "She's suing us, Evia! For five million dollars. I told you she would. She's suing us."

The anger that I thought was gone was right there in my face. Adam tossed the paper in my direction, but before I could grab it, the lawsuit floated downward, swirling through the air like a paper jet, until it landed at the pointed toes of my stilettos.

Then Adam glanced at me, shook his head, and stomped away.

Chapter 60

I WAS NOT GOING TO LET this happen.

We'd come too far, we were too close to getting back to being the wonderful couple we'd always been. We needed each other—now more than ever before if we were going to win this legal battle.

Rushing behind him, I followed Adam into our bedroom. "I didn't think she would do this," I said, my voice filled with surprise and panic.

"Well, you were wrong, weren't you?"

"There's no way she can do this. What is she suing us for?" I asked, even as my eyes scanned the papers.

"What do you think?" he asked me, as if I was one of his children. "Breach of contract. She's saying that she paid us the money and we didn't do our part."

"But we can tell the judge that she didn't do her part."

"She did!" Adam snapped. "She did everything she said she was going to do. And so did I."

I had to swallow every bit of pride before I said, "Okay, I'll go back. I'll go back to Ferossity."

When Adam laughed, I didn't know what to do. So I stood there and repeated what I'd just said.

"I'll go back to work for her and she won't have anything to take us to court for."

He stopped laughing long enough to say, "I think it's a little too late for that, Evia."

By any means necessary—that's what I was thinking. I had to do whatever, however, to keep my family together, because we would never survive this lawsuit. Our marriage wouldn't hold up to the way Adam would look at me every day with blame and indignation.

I grabbed the phone from the nightstand. "See," I said, like a child with something to prove. "I'm calling her."

I pressed the phone to my ear as Adam paced in front of me. When Rachel answered, I had no time for niceties; I asked her to put me straight through to Shay-Shaunté.

As I waited, I watched Adam soften; his shoulders relaxed, half the creases faded from his forehead, and a bit of hope shined in his eyes.

He said, "Do you think this will work?"

I nodded. "She wanted to make a point. She wants me to come back there."

"Evia?" Shay-Shaunté said as if she was surprised to hear from me, though I doubted that. "How are you?"

Besides sending my husband to her, this was going to be the hardest thing I'd ever had to do. But I was back to doing for the greater good. As long as I kept that in mind . . .

"We got your . . . the papers. About the lawsuit."

"I didn't know they were going to be delivered today. I'm sorry, but you left me no choice."

"Well, I'm calling to tell you to drop the lawsuit. I'll come back to work"—I took a breath—"tomorrow."

Two beats passed and then, "I'm sorry, Evia," she said sweetly, "but your job is no longer available. I've already found someone to replace you."

"Then why are you suing us!" I screamed.

"Calm down, baby," Adam whispered in my ear. "Calm down."

"Yes, calm down," Shay-Shaunté said as if she was right there in our bedroom. "There is no need for you to get upset."

I clenched my teeth to keep my voice low this time. "Why are you suing us?"

"For breach of contract," she said, like she was surprised I was asking. "You didn't fulfill your part. You didn't stay until I found a new assistant."

This witch was crazy. She was out for blood, out to destroy my family. But I couldn't let her suck the life out of us, so I had to try another way.

"Shay-Shaunté," I began, thinking that maybe begging would work. "I am sorry, but it was hard for me. Adam and I had never—"

"Is Adam there?" she interrupted.

I frowned. "Yes."

"May I speak with him?"

No! rang all through my head. But I passed him the phone anyway. "She wants to speak to you."

It took him a moment to talk over his surprise. "Yes."

It was my turn to pace. Really, I wanted Adam to put Shay-Shaunté on speaker, but I didn't want to interrupt, didn't want to do anything that might upset the fanatical woman on the other end.

I couldn't believe she had us like this. Suing for five million dollars? Would any judge allow that when she hadn't even paid us that much? But how many times had I heard about crazy legal outcomes?

"Yes," I heard Adam say over and over. "Well, I would appreciate that. Anything that we can work out."

Anything that we can work out? What did she want to work out? Was she asking for another weekend with my husband?

I was willing to do anything to save my marriage.

Anything but that.

"Okay," he said with finality. "We'll be there."

He hung up and slid down onto the bed. I sat next to him and he didn't move away from me—that was a good sign.

"What did she say?"

He shook his head slightly. "She wants to meet at her office in an hour."

"Is she dropping this?"

He looked at me. "I don't know. Maybe. Maybe, like you said, she just wanted to make a point." He sighed.

I knew what Adam was thinking—that none of this would've happened if . . . but he had to know that I would've stayed if I'd been able to.

Glancing at his watch, Adam said, "We'd better get moving."

As we strode toward the bedroom door, I glanced at our suitcase, upright in front of the closet, ready to be rolled away for our amazing night of celebration.

"Should we take this?" I pointed to the bag, still hopeful.

Adam paused for a moment and didn't look at me when he shook his head. "Naw, leave it here. We definitely won't need it tonight."

Chapter 61

When I'd walked through these doors almost a month ago, I'd vowed that I'd never return. But here I was, like a boomerang—coming back to Shay-Shaunté.

Shay-Shaunté had requested that we meet in the entry-level conference room. That was a blessing—Adam and I didn't have to walk past curious employees, who would wonder and gossip about the prodigal's return to Ferossity.

As we waited in the empty room, I sat at the head of the eight-seat mahogany table. I'd put in six good years with Shay-Shaunté, and though I would've never called us friends, we'd had a great working relationship. I hoped she remembered those times. There had to be some goodness in her heart that would allow her to call this battle a draw.

Or maybe she would let me come back to work; that's what she really wanted anyway—to degrade me. I would do whatever she wanted—anything from returning to my position, to working in the mailroom. At this point, I would do anything for the sake of my family. Adam and I were just getting it together, so whatever I had to do today to make sure that we didn't go back to yesterday, I would do.

I watched my husband pace from one end of the long room to the other. His head was bowed, his eyebrows were bunched so close together that they were almost connected. But I had no idea what he was specifically thinking. He hadn't spoken a word since we'd left home. I hoped that his silence came from the same place as mine—a need to quietly plot a strategy to battle Shay-Shaunté.

The door to the conference room swung open, and I jumped a bit, startled.

A gray-haired dude entered; then, as if he was presenting royalty, he moved to the side and pushed the door so that it would open wider.

Shay-Shaunté slinked in, sauntering toward us in an emerald-green, turtleneck, knee-length knit dress that hugged her so snugly she couldn't help but take small steps. The pattern on the dress—scales—was straight couture and gave the appearance of a long, lean snake. Her satiny hair was pulled back in a slick ponytail; she was ready for any Paris runway.

I snuggled into my coat, wrapping it tightly around me, hiding my jean outfit that had looked so chic at home.

But then I looked up and caught Adam's gaze. His eyes were on Shay-Shaunté and my stomach cramped.

This was the first time Adam was seeing her, at least as far as I knew. I hadn't thought of this, wasn't prepared.

I tensed. Held my breath. Studied their reactions.

Shay-Shaunté sashayed toward Adam with a smile.

He stared at her blankly.

She lifted her arms, expecting a hug, as if he was a friend.

He stepped back and extended his hand, as if she was a stranger.

She chuckled and wrapped her fingers around his.

He grunted his greeting and gave her no more than a two-second handshake.

She tried to hold him a little longer, but he snatched his hand away from her grasp.

She laughed, a little.

He frowned, a lot.

It was all a relief to me.

Until Shay-Shaunté pirouetted, now facing me. "Hello, Evia," she said, all business, no smiles.

I nodded my hello. She introduced her attorney, Dexter Harrington, then motioned for us all to sit. Adam and I chose the other side of the table—side by side we faced our enemy.

It was Dexter who got the party started. "I understand that you"—he spoke directly to Adam, like the deal had been made with him alone—"would like to discuss the lawsuit."

"Yes." Adam reached for my hand and closed his fingers over mine, and I'd never been more grateful for his touch.

Shay-Shaunté's eyes followed my husband's hands. Then she glanced at me and her lips moved smoothly, easily into her signature smile.

It made me shudder.

Adam said, "We were surprised to get the lawsuit because there seemed to be a breach of contract on both sides—"

"Excuse me." Shay-Shaunté waved her hand, and I noticed the jeweled bracelet on her wrist—a snake that twisted around from halfway up her arm to the base of her hand. On the end, in the place of eyes, were two huge diamonds. She said, "I fulfilled my part of the deal. I gave you five million dollars—"

"Less taxes," Adam said.

She shrugged. "It is not my fault that you weren't clear."

Her attorney interjected, "I don't think we're here to rehash the situation. We're here because my client is willing to discuss a settlement."

Shay-Shaunté nodded.

"And we thank you for that," Adam said.

I wanted to kick Adam under the table. We didn't need to thank her for anything. But we did need to negotiate, so I said, "The only part of the contract that hasn't been fulfilled is my continuing to work."

"Until I found a replacement," Shay-Shaunté said.

"Right. But since you've found someone, I'd be willing to make up for the time when you didn't have the new assistant. I'd be willing to come back for three weeks—anywhere you want to use me in the company."

Shay-Shaunté shook her head as if she was sorry. "I don't think so, Evia. I can't take the chance of hiring you back. You can't be trusted to stay."

"What are you talking about? You trusted me for six years, and it was only because you taunted me with the tax situation—"

"Not my fault."

"And little comments about your weekend with my husband."

"I can't help that you're sensitive."

"And then you saying you were pregnant."

She paused at that one. Took her eyes away from me and looked straight at Adam. "I never said that."

"Whatever," I said, my tone demanding that she turn back to me. And she did. "I would still be here if it wasn't for you."

She shrugged. "Whatever the reason . . . you quit. You forfeited the contract, and now I want that money back."

The only thing that stopped me from climbing up and across the table was Adam squeezing my hand.

"I'd like to know if you have something in mind," Adam said, taking over. "For a settlement. Something's that's fair to all of us."

Dexter glanced at Shay-Shaunté and she nodded before she lowered her eyes. "We will drop the lawsuit for five million dollars, but my client believes that she deserves some of her money back."

I inhaled. This was so not fair. Adam had done his part—which was worth far more than the half that she'd barely given us.

The attorney jotted something onto a piece of paper, folded it, then passed it to Adam. "Here is what my client is asking for."

I leaned over close to Adam to see what she'd written on the paper: 1,575,859.04.

I gasped.

As Adam and I stared at the paper, the attorney continued, "Out of the five million that you received from my client, we feel it is more than fair and reasonable for you to return that amount to Ms. Shay-Shaunté."

I couldn't even bring my eyes up from that paper. That was exactly—less one dollar—what we had left. I shook my head and gathered my strength to face her.

"How did you . . ." The tap of Adam's fingers against mine was my signal to stop. I did—but still I wanted to know how she knew.

Dexter continued, "If you decide to pursue the lawsuit, we would not only be seeking to get the entire five million back—"

"She never gave us five million!"

He continued over my protest, "—but we would be seeking reimbursement of all legal expenses as well. It could be quite costly for you."

Adam had not yet raised his head; his eyes were still on that number that would wipe out our bank account. Slowly, he lifted his eyes and met Shay-Shaunté's.

"We have a deal," he said, not taking his eyes away from her.

She smiled. "That's good." Leaning forward, she spoke only to him. "I would've hated taking you to court," she murmured. "Especially after the wonderful nights we shared."

The scene played out in my mind—it would be a twelve-inch knife. I would stab her in the neck, sever her head. After all, isn't that how you killed a snake?

Dexter cleared his throat. "I have the papers right here. We will expect the check, in certified funds, in a week."

"You'll have the check tomorrow," Adam said.

Shay-Shaunté nodded as she signed the agreement with her standard signature—two giant cursive *S*s.

Slowly, she slid the paper and her pen toward Adam. Still, he didn't look away from her, not even when he pulled his own pen from his jacket. Finally, he broke his stare long enough to sign on the line next to his name.

Shay-Shaunté said, "Don't you think you should read it first, Adam? We don't want another misunderstanding like the tax issue."

He said nothing until he'd signed his full name. "I don't think we'll have any more problems. You've taken everything that we have."

He turned to pass the paper to me, but Shay-Shaunté stopped him.

"There's no need for her to sign." She spoke as if I wasn't sitting there. "This time, the deal is between you and me."

Leaving the papers right where they were, Adam took my hand, helping me stand.

Shay-Shaunté didn't move. She said to Adam, "I'm sorry this didn't turn out better for you."

I couldn't help it. I just had to have the last word. "Well, it worked out perfectly for you, didn't it?"

Now her eyes were on me. "Oh, it did, Evia. It worked out better than you could ever imagine." She took a deep breath that sounded like a hiss, licked her lips, and then did what she did best—she smiled.

I shook my head. Why hadn't I just kept my mouth shut?

Chapter 62

SILENCE. THE QUIET THAT WAS BETWEEN us was like our fourth child. It was always there, and over the past weeks, we'd nurtured silence, allowed it to live, allowed it to grow.

Shay-Shaunté was the cause, and now it was all over. There was no need to let silence stay and separate us any longer; the deal, the dance, the devil . . . it was done.

Yes, we'd walked away with so much less than we'd planned, but the thing was, we'd still received a bit over a million dollars . . . no one could hate on that, right? And we still had everything that was important—Adam and I had each other and our children. Ruby was safe for months, most of our bills were paid in advance . . . and we owned our home. There was no way anyone could look at this and say that this had ended totally badly.

Still, when Adam pulled the car into our garage, shut off the engine, then sat, his eyes straight ahead, I knew I had to say it; I had to help him get to my way of thinking.

"I'm sorry," I said.

Not looking at me, he nodded but didn't say a word. He kept his eyes straight ahead, staring at the garage shelves. I needed more from him. I needed to hear his voice, needed to know what he was thinking.

So I explained, "I read this wrong, Adam. I'd known Shay-Shaunté for six years, and I just knew she would never go public with this."

"I know Shay-Shaunté, too," he said.

Well, I'd wanted to hear his voice, and now he'd spoken. I wondered, though, if he'd meant to hurt me with his words, because he had. The fifty hours he'd spent with her, talking to her, holding her, were far deeper than my six years. Or maybe it was just their connection . . . that man and woman thing that I would've never been able to compete with.

Would Adam always be connected to her?

I shook my head. I needed to leave the paranoia, the jealousy behind. There'd been no connection between them today.

Through my thoughts, Adam said, "I know her and I knew she would sue us. I tried to tell you that."

"I know you did, and I'm sorry," I apologized again, hoping that would make a difference.

Again, he nodded. Said nothing. Just stared straight ahead.

In the silence, I didn't feel the anger toward me that Adam had carried these last weeks. Now he was holding on to something different—disgust, blame, judgment . . . I wasn't sure. Whatever it was, I couldn't let us fall back to the way we'd been. I couldn't let Shay-Shaunté and the silence defeat us.

"The thing is, baby, this is over," I said.

"Yes, it is."

"And now we can put it behind us knowing that we did get something out of this."

Slowly, he turned his head until his eyes were straight on

mine. The question was as much in his face as in his words. "What did we get?"

"Our house," I said because he needed to see that obvious piece of good news. "We didn't walk away empty-handed; we have this house."

For a moment, he gave me nothing more than a blank stare and I swore I heard the sound of crickets. Then he shook his head, opened his door, and jumped out of the SUV.

Quickly, I followed. "Adam, didn't you hear what I said?"

He stopped so suddenly that I bumped right into him. "I heard you—the question really is, did you hear yourself?"

Now I was the one with the blank stare.

He said, "You think the fact that I gave up all that I believed in, all that I promised God, all that I promised you, my integrity, who I wanted to be as a man—you think all of that was worth a house?"

I opened my mouth, but nothing came out.

"Come on, Evia. Would we do this all again—for this house?"

He waited, but I couldn't think of a single word to say. So slowly, he turned and dragged himself into the house—the prize we'd won for Adam surrendering everything that he'd believed in.

Chapter 63

It was over.

But it was not.

We were back to the way we were.

Not as the old Langstons. We were nowhere near the caring, trusting, loving people that we used to be. We were the new Langstons—Adam and me and Shay-Shaunté. Because even though the deal was done, she was still very much a part of our lives.

The day after we agreed on the settlement, Adam went to the bank and withdrew the money to return to Shay-Shaunté. I wanted to go with him, but when I followed him to the car, he turned around, as if surprised to see me.

"No, stay here. I need to do this alone," he said.

I had no idea what that was about. Why would he want to go to the bank by himself . . . unless he planned to leave the bank and take the check to Shay-Shaunté personally. Unless he planned to use this as an opportunity to see her.

I asked him, "Why can't I go with you?"

He heard my wariness—I know he did, because his eyes narrowed and he pressed his lips together. The old Adam would have soothed my suspicions, kidded with me and told me I was imagining things.

But this new man didn't seem to care. He just said, "I'll be back," jumped into the SUV, and drove away.

All I could do was wait for him to return. I counted the minutes as I paced in our bedroom. The minutes turned into one hour. I called Adam's cell. It rang four times, then went to his voice mail.

Then, two hours. I called again. Four rings. Voice mail.

Three hours and I moved my walking marathon into the living room. This time when I called Adam's cell, it went straight to voice mail.

I was still standing, still walking when Adam came home, six hours after he'd left. In that time, so many images had jogged through my mind; I knew exactly what he'd done.

"Where've you been?" I screamed, meeting him at the door.

He looked at me as if I was pathetic. "I went to the office," he said simply. "Remember? I have a job."

I ignored his sarcasm. "I thought you weren't starting until tomorrow."

"I decided to go by today to pick up a few things—is that all right with you?"

I wanted to believe him, tried to believe him . . . but I couldn't.

The days passed and my suspicions grew, mostly because of the silence that stayed between us . . . and because Shay-Shaunté had told me that she wanted my husband.

Every moment that Adam was out of the house, I wondered where he was, even though I knew he was at work. I wondered why he came home so late, even though this was his first week on his new job and he was planting the seeds to becoming one of the top executives. I wondered why he decided to go into the office that first weekend, even though that was so Adam Langston, just trying to get ahead of the game.

But even though one side of my brain gently assured me that Adam's behavior was perfectly normal, the other side screamed, Shay-Shaunté.

I'd told Adam that we should put that deal behind us, but I was the one having trouble with that, though I had a very good reason. It had been more than a month since Adam had returned home and we had yet to unite as husband and wife—and it wasn't because of me.

I told Adam, "Have you noticed, but we haven't made love this year! You haven't touched me since . . ."

His answer was always the same. "I'm just tired, Evia. We've been through a lot and there's a lot on my mind."

Oh . . . kay. When did that ever stop a man?

So, I had to ask myself, if Adam wasn't with me, who was he with? It had to be someone—no man could go so long without sex.

I couldn't keep my thoughts to myself. I had to ask him, "Is it Shay-Shaunté? Is she the reason you can't be with me?"

He would shake his head and say, "Why do you keep asking me about her?" Then he would walk away.

It was the same conversation over and over.

I could've handled all of this much better if Adam had been angry—because I knew that no one could stay angry forever. But Adam wasn't angry. What Adam carried now was regret. And regret was a simmering emotion that could keep you in a state of sorrow forever.

It didn't help that I saw blame in Adam's eyes every time he glanced at me and I felt despair in his arms whenever he hugged me.

There was a saving grace, though—our children. The upcoming party had them too excited to notice the strain in their home, and it kept Adam and me busy enough to push aside my growing distrust.

The party plans were all set—for the dinner, with all the adults, and then the after-party for just the teenagers.

While Adam worked at his new job, I put the finishing touches on the celebration, doing all that I could to lower expenses, now that Shay-Shaunté had taken our last million away. We'd already committed to the restaurant, and though the cost of the party frightened me, this was one place where Adam took the time to reassure me; he kept telling me that we'd be fine.

Still, I worked to lower every part of the budget—I changed the dinner menu from steak and lobster to chicken and rice, I told the live band that our plans had changed and hired a DJ instead.

Neither Adam nor I told the girls about the changes—I figured that in the excitement of the day, the menu and the music wouldn't matter. But I didn't want to wait to tell the girls about their cars—the cars that wouldn't be coming.

Adam didn't want to say a word; I was sure that he was still trying to figure out a way to get the twins the cars that we'd promised. But we had to build our savings; we had to make sure that we never ended up again in the place where we'd found ourselves with Shay-Shaunté.

The twins were going to have their party; everything else, they would just have to understand.

So, the night before the big day, we sat Alexa and Alana down after dinner, and Adam didn't waste any time. "The party is going to be wonderful celebration. But . . . we're gonna have to wait on those cars for a couple of weeks."

It went down exactly the way I knew it would.

Alana said, "That's okay, Daddy. The party is gonna be terrific all by itself." And she hugged him.

Alexa fell out on the floor and asked, "What are we gonna tell our friends?"

But after minutes of Adam promising that he was going to do all that he could do, Alexa finally got up and did the right thing. She hugged her father, told him it was okay, then sulked to her bedroom.

That was last night . . . and all was forgotten and forgiven because now the twins were in the center of the pink and purple haze of the decorated restaurant.

"Oh, Mom," Alexa breathed as she stood in between the tables that would hold the sixty dinner guests. "This is ridiculous!"

I laughed. "I take it that you like."

"Yeah, it's gorgeous," Alana added as she ran her hand over the pink tablecloth on one table and then the purple one on another.

"Hey, sweethearts!"

"Daddy," the twins cried as they ran to Adam when he entered from the long hallway.

I stood back as the girls covered their father with hugs and kisses. My smile remained, but it had certainly dimmed.

Adam had left the house about two hours ago, under the pretense of working with the restaurant manager to complete the decorations. I didn't really have a reason not to believe him—it was just the thoughts that stayed in my head, that made me always doubt him.

"So, you like everything," Adam said as he moved toward me. "Hey," he said and gave me the perfunctory hug that I'd become used to.

"Daddy, this is wonderful!"

Adam grinned; I knew that had special meaning coming from Alexa.

He said, "I saved some of the balloons for the after-party. Y'all wanna see downstairs?"

"Yeah!" they cheered.

Adam led them away and I adjusted the centerpieces, then sauntered to the bar for a glass of wine.

As I sipped on the Chardonnay, I thought about all that this day was supposed to be. Nothing but happiness—our daughters were sixteen.

"Hey, Mom!"

I took a final swallow from my glass, then faced Ethan, who came up behind me with Tamica at his side. I kissed my friend and thanked her for bringing my son, right as the twins rushed into the room. The girls were jabbering with excitement about the room downstairs. But as they chatted, my eyes searched.

There was no sign of Adam.

I ordered another glass of wine.

The restaurant swelled with chatter and laughter as guests arrived and congratulated my daughters. I directed the waiters to serve the hors d'oeuvres.

Still, I searched for Adam; still I couldn't find him.

The twins buzzed around, meeting and greeting, accepting their gifts graciously and excitedly.

Finally, Adam jogged up the steps that led to the room where the twins would be having their after-party . . . had he been down there the whole time?

But I didn't have a chance to ask him because my family busted into the restaurant at the same time.

Wearing a spandex dress that just had to hurt, my mother asked, "How much y'all paid for this?" as loudly as she could the moment she walked in.

I hugged my mother, basically to stifle her. But she went on and on about too much money and spoiled kids.

"It is fancy, though," Cashmere said.

"Yo', sis," Twin began, "is it okay if I smoke?"

Adam answered for me; told him no (especially since we had no idea what he'd be smoking) and then led my sorry family to the head table.

But just as Brooklyn and Cash came in and Adam greeted them, his cell phone vibrated. Adam glanced down, frowned, then turned away from me.

I wanted to follow him, but one of us had to stay with the girls. My eyes remained on him, though, as he pushed himself into the far corner of the room. His fingers were moving feverishly against his phone's keyboard, texting, then stopping, then, texting some more.

"So," Brooklyn said, forcing my eyes from Adam. "Just wanna warn you, we gave the girls a check for a thousand dollars."

Okay, she had my attention. "Get out of here. That's too much."

"Well, Cash thought they might wanna put some rims on their new cars." She laughed, but when she noticed that I didn't join her, she asked, "What's wrong?"

"I'll explain later," I whispered. Then, to everyone else, I announced that they could take their seats.

I moved among the crowd, directing our friends, conversing and laughing, my eyes on Adam the whole time. It had been minutes now, and he was still in that corner—doing whatever he was doing.

Who could he be talking to? Certainly not anyone from work. Adam wouldn't stand for work interfering with his daughters' day. It wasn't a friend—everyone we knew was here.

It had to be Shay-Shaunté!

This wasn't going to happen. Not today.

Pressing my way through our friends, I kept my smile, although my heart was pushing through my chest. When I was just steps away, Adam felt me—he looked up and shoved his phone into his jacket.

"What are you doing?" I hissed, while trying to keep a smile.

"Nothing. Is everything going okay?"

I ignored his question. "Who were you talking to?"

He shook his head. "I have to make a quick run."

No!

He said, "I have to take care of something. I'll be back in five minutes."

Before he could move away, I grabbed his arm. "Adam, please don't do this. It's the girls' birthday."

"I'll be right back, Evia."

"Please." I wondered if he knew that tears were burning behind my eyes. "Not in front of our friends."

He looked at me, his expression sorrowful, but determined. "Get everyone settled," he directed. "I'll be back before they start serving."

He rushed away from me, toward the back door. Without a glance back, he was gone. I stood for a moment, watching, wondering what was happening.

I was losing my husband and there was nothing I could do.

"Mom?"

The voice was quiet, tentative, and I had to stick my broken heart back into my chest before I faced Alana. The smile that I wanted her to see was on my face, even though I knew for sure she wouldn't feel it.

"What's wrong?" she asked with tears in her voice.

"Nothing, sweetheart," I said, finding my happy tone.

"Why did Dad leave us?"

I didn't know the strength I had, because it took amazing power to hold back my sobs.

She had no idea what she was saying. She had no idea that in days or months, she might be asking me that same question again.

"Mom?" Alana called me again.

I said to Alana, "Your dad will be right back. He had to go . . . he forgot something special." Then I added, "For you and Alexa."

"Okay." I could tell that she wasn't sure if she should believe me. But when I said, "Go back in there. You're the birthday girl," she did as she was told.

But I didn't follow her. At least a minute had passed since Adam had left, but I was hoping that somehow I would be able to find him. Not that I had a real plan—I was just going to get in my car and drive . . . maybe catch him at a light, or in traffic.

I pushed the door open . . . stepped outside . . . and froze.

He hadn't even gone to meet her somewhere else. Right in front of me, in the parking lot where our children were celebrating their special birthday, the man I'd loved all my life was holding another woman.

Shay-Shaunté.

"Adam!" Through my scream, I released all the hate I had for her, all the grief I felt for my marriage.

Adam backed away as I bolted down the steps, my stilettos not stopping me. I tore past the cars to where the two were standing.

"Evia, wait," Adam said, grabbing me by my waist. "Wait."

"What are you doing here?" I screamed at Shay-Shaunté. Then, in the same breath, I asked him, "How could you do this?"

"I didn't do anything. I haven't done anything."

"You call being out here with her nothing?" I cried.

"I was trying to stop her from coming inside. I told her not to come here," Adam spoke quickly.

"You've been seeing her!"

"No! Never! She texted me out of the blue today. Told me she was coming here with cars for the girls."

I paused, noticing for the first time where we were standing—between two Range Rovers, the stickers still on the windows.

My eyes moved between the cars and Shay-Shaunté. She stood in the center, just a few feet from us, her arms folded, her hair flowing, her perfection so apparent, even beneath the ankle-length red belted coat she wore. She smirked, posed, as if she was ready for her close-up.

I had her close-up for her, all right.

But Adam held me so tight that I couldn't move. Not that he had to hold me anymore. Because if he had let me go, I was just going to sit down on the ground in defeat and die.

"I just saw you," I whimpered to Adam. "Hugging her, holding her. You were probably kissing her."

"No," he said softly in my ear. "I wasn't. I was trying to get her away from me."

"Oh, Adam," Shay-Shaunté finally spoke. "Why don't you tell her the truth? Let's not hide it anymore. Let's tell her what's going on."

"What are you talking about?" he growled.

Shay-Shaunté took a step closer. Looking down at me, she said, "Your husband loves me."

I moaned.

"Don't listen to her," Adam said, now trying to pull me away. To her, he screamed, "You're a liar!"

"Come on, Adam. Why are you denying it? Just tell her."

"I don't know what you're trying to do," Adam rumbled,

"and I have never laid my hands on a woman before, but I swear—"

"Please," Shay-Shaunté waved her hand. "If I'm lying, then how did I know about the cars?"

I closed my eyes. She was right—the proof that she spoke the truth was right in front of me. Adam *had* been with her.

I pushed my elbows against Adam's chest, forcing his arms to drop. And then, it was the wine—and the taxes, and the pregnancy, and the taunting—and the wine . . .

I went after Shay-Shaunté.

She screamed.

I screamed.

And then my daughters screamed, "Mom!"

I was from Barry Farm; I didn't fight like a girl. My punches landed right where I wanted them—first an uppercut to her jaw, then a jab to her eye. But the thing was, Shay-Shaunté gave back as good as she received. I felt like I was fighting eight people with her punches landing on me from every where.

Adam grabbed her from behind and locked her in a choke hold. While he held her, I planned to take her down. But in one instant, she slipped from his arms, and in the next, Alexa was by my side.

"Mom," she screamed as she started swinging. She grabbed Shay-Shaunté's hair, yanking her head back.

"No! Alexa." My focus turned to my daughter. I tried to pull her away, but we were in the middle of confusion.

So many people: Adam, Cash, Brooklyn, Tamica.

I could hear Ethan's cries from far away.

But I couldn't do anything for my son because I had to save my daughter.

I heard my mother's shout. "Get off my daughter."

Then Twin was there, and with a single punch, he took Shay-Shaunté out.

She hit the ground, and at the same moment two police cruisers sped into the lot, lights flashing, sirens blaring.

It was complete chaos as four officers ripped us apart, settling the brawl, questioning the guests, most of whom stood on the outskirts, shocked witnesses.

"I want to press charges," Shay-Shaunté said as she rose from the ground as if she had not just been knocked down.

"Please," Adam begged. "Don't do this."

She ignored him. "I want to press charges . . . against him and her."

I was horrified—Shay-Shaunté had pointed to my brother . . . and my daughter.

"No," I said, wrapping my arms around Alexa. "She didn't do anything. It was me."

"She attacked me!" Shay-Shaunté said. "Look at my face. She hit me and I didn't do anything to her."

"Why are you lying? I did that to you," I admitted.

The officer asked Shay-Shaunté, "Do you want to file against them?"

"Yes! Definitely!" she huffed. "I will go down now and I want them arrested."

"Mom!" Alexa cried, with her arms wrapped around me.

"I'm sorry," the officer said. "I've got to take her down to the station until we get this all cleared up."

Shay-Shaunté straightened her coat and smirked at Alexa, "You're going to jail, sweetheart."

"Mommy!" my daughter wailed.

Cash and one of the officers held Adam back as he leapt toward Shay-Shaunté. But she showed no fear—all she did was laugh.

"Come on, young lady," the officer said to Alexa.

"Mom!" she screamed.

"Please, please, can I go with her?" I cried.

"Me, too!" Alana begged as she grabbed my hand.

The officer nodded. "Both of you," he said to me and Alana, "come on. It's against policy, but you can ride with her in the back."

I cried as we piled into the white and blue car. I cried as I watched our friends and family stand in the parking lot, shaking their heads in amazement, stunned at the pandemonium that had erupted. I cried as I held my daughters and tried to quiet their sobs.

In the other car, Twin was bound in handcuffs, and I was sure that with his record, he'd spend more than a few hours at the station.

My tears were still falling when Adam knocked on the glass and motioned for Alana to roll down the window.

"I'll be right behind you," Adam said with tears tracking down his face.

I nodded.

As the cruiser began to roll away, Adam yelled out, "I love you!"

My sobs deepened. "I love you more," I quivered.

The car had edged away from him, but Adam jogged by the side, trying to keep up. "I love you best, Shine!" he yelled as the police cruiser sped up, leaving Adam, the party, and all of our guests behind.

Epilogue

THE NATIONAL WEATHER BUREAU HAD PROJECTED blizzard conditions with snow accumulation of up to fifteen inches for the Washington, D.C. metro area. At dusk, the streets were almost empty, as federal employees had been sent home to safety hours before.

The wind whipped across the nation's capital as the temperature plummeted . . . and Shay-Shaunté headed west on Independence Avenue, the Capitol building in her rearview mirror.

As she rolled down the street, a police cruiser edged behind her with his lights flashing, and he turned on his siren. She slowed, and the officer pulled up next to her.

"Ma'am," he said, sounding panicked, as he jumped from his car. "Do you need help?"

Shay-Shaunté peered at him over the top of her sunglasses. "No, I'm fine."

"But the top to your car." The policeman paused and gazed at her devil-red Jaguar convertible. "It's down."

Shay-Shaunté turned her head from one side to the other, taking in the snowflakes that fell around her. She twisted in her seat to get a better look at the officer. "Is there a law against that?"

The officer paused, stumped. "No, not really. I mean, it's freezing and you're gonna be cold—"

"Officer, do I look cold to you?"

Through the snowfall that was thickening, he peered at the woman, movie-star beautiful, her head wrapped with a lightweight red scarf and her eyes framed with red-rimmed sunglasses.

He frowned for a moment, wondering what else was wrong with this sight—and then he got it. Why wasn't there any snow on her scarf, on her coat, on the seats?

She must have one hellava heating system in that car.

Aloud, he said, "Well, if you're sure you're all right."

"I am." She curled her fingers in a wave and sped off.

It all felt marvelous to her. The snow was no bother every flake melted before it got within inches of her skin.

She waited until she was out of the jurisdiction of the district and on the road before she hit her Bluetooth. Using voice dialing, she called out the name, then waited for the phone to connect.

"Shay-Shaunté, how are you, my dear!"

"What's up, Uncle Michael?"

"It's all wonderful here!" His voice boomed through the car, ricocheted off the interior and when his echo hit the concrete of the road, it became thunder. "So, what have you been up to, my darling?"

"Nothing much. I've just been going to and fro, walking back and forth."

"Ah, I remember those days," he said. "So where are you now?"

"Actually, I just left Washington, D.C.," she said, her eyes on the sign that welcomed her into West Virginia.

Shay-Shaunté's uncle laughed. "Oh, lots to see and do there. With all of those politicians, I'm sure your work was easy."

"Actually, I wasn't assigned to anyone in government. This was a young couple—Adam and Evia."

"Ahhhh," he moaned with pleasure.

Shay-Shaunté smiled, knowing that she'd taken him back down memory lane.

He said, "There was this time . . . and this garden called Eden . . . and this man and woman . . . did I ever tell you what I did to them?"

Shay-Shaunté laughed. "You've told me many times, Uncle Michael."

"Oh, sweetheart, I'm sorry if I keep repeating myself. I love to reminisce about the good ole days."

"I know."

"So, tell me about your time in D.C."

"Like I said, I was assigned to a young couple, who said over and over that they loved . . . you know, Him. They went to church, tithed, did all of that stuff that all of those people do, but the thing was, they never really loved Him. Money was always their greater love."

"Isn't that always the case?"

"Uh-huh. Uncle Michael, it was so easy," she said as she gazed at the sign that brought her into Kentucky. "All I had to do was apply a little pressure and they snapped. I didn't even have to resort to the things that money couldn't buy." She shook her head. "I didn't have to make anyone sick, I didn't make anyone die, there was no major catastrophe in their life. I just took away a little money and they lost a lot of faith."

"That means all your goals were accomplished?"

"Well, I think so," she said as she glanced at the sign welcoming her to Missouri. "I'm still a bit new at this, but I completed the trio as you call it."

"Yes," Uncle Michael said, getting excited, pleasing Shay-Shaunté. All she wanted to do was make her uncle proud. "Read them off to me," he said, teacher to student.

"I didn't kill anyone, at least not by taking them out of their physical body. But I did kill their dreams."

"Oh, that's good, that's good. People without dreams are never a threat."

She said, "Their marriage is over, I think; I'm not sure about that. I left them in quite a state, though."

"Don't worry about that. My hope is that they do stay together, and, because you killed their dreams, they will always be miserable."

"And so will their children," Shay-Shaunté said, still delighted with the final blow she'd given to the Langstons yesterday. She hadn't gone to the police station, so of course no charges would be forthcoming. But she'd done enough to traumatize the children—especially the twins.

"Yes! Yes, Shay-Shaunté. You touched their kids!"

"I did. They let me in—they let me get to their children. Three of them—two girls and a boy."

"Oh, a boy! I love it. The children will see their parents' misery and internalize that," Uncle Michael said, releasing a laugh that came through the phone as a roar. "They will have this curse for generations to come."

She was thrilled now as she sped through the heartland of the country.

"Go on," he panted. "There has to be more."

She laughed. For her uncle, this was far better than sex! Mentally, she wasn't in that place yet—sex was still what she craved, and there was always a multitude of men ready to share their bodies and tie their souls to her. The sex was always fulfilling, always orgasmic, because the men had no clue who they were really bedding.

"The best thing, though, Uncle Michael," she said, "is that I stole their future—whether they stay together or get a divorce. There was so much that . . . you know, that Man had planned for them . . . but they gave it up. They will never become what they were meant to be, and neither will their children."

"So, five people were destroyed—and all the people around them will be affected. Marvelous, Shay-Shaunté! You did it— kill, steal, destroy!" He shouted their mantra.

Her eyes dulled a bit as she crossed over the line into Colorado. "The only thing, Uncle Michael, is do you think it's permanent? I mean, I terrorized the wife and then left her with plenty of paranoia so that she would never listen to or believe her husband. And I told plenty of lies that will have them wondering for a long time. But they could sit down one day and figure this all out. They might work through it."

"Oh, you don't have to worry about that, sweetheart. They'll never be able to work through it because they'll never forgive each other. Those people want . . . Him . . . to forgive them, but they carry so much blame, and judgment, and unforgiveness in their hearts that they're blinded, so they can't even do what would be right for their family. They'll never be able to see their way through."

"Good," she said, congratulating herself a little.

"I cannot tell you how proud I am, Shay-Shaunté. So, where are you headed to now?"

"Well, after a lot of thought, I decided to go to the City of Angels."

"Do you know that Los Angeles is one of my favorite places!" he breathed heavily. "What made you choose that city? Oh, I know," he said before she could answer. "All of those angels. You wanted the battle." He laughed.

She laughed with him. "You know I love a good fight," she said, thinking back to yesterday, and how, alone, she'd gotten the best of Adam, Evia, and their offspring. "But I figure in Los Angeles, I can destroy a lot of dreams, coerce thousands into doing things they'd never thought they'd do." She sighed, a release of pleasure. She was in Arizona and the desert heat made her yearn for home. "But there's one other thing, Uncle. The real reason I chose the home to all of those people who call themselves stars."

"Oh, I can hear it." He shivered, emotionally aroused. "I can hear it in your voice. This is big."

"It is," she said. Taking a breath, she told him, "Los Angeles is the perfect place for me to have my baby."

"You're pregnant!"

"Yes, Uncle!"

"You stole his seed! This is fantastic. Our nation grows. And you're going to make one helluva mother!"

Shay-Shaunté laughed. "This, I know!" she said, eyeing the famous landmark that was now in her sight. Embedded in the hills that had come to represent glamour and success, nine forty-five-foot-tall letters welcomed Shay-Shaunté to her new home.

H-O-L-L-Y-W-O-O-D.

Acknowledgments

I HAVEN'T DONE ACKNOWLEDGMENTS IN SEVERAL years because the last time I did, friends and relatives couldn't wait to call me to tell me all the people I'd left out. Sheeze! My feelings were hurt. I mean, all I was trying to do was say thank you and folks took the joy out of that. But then I said, why should I let a few mess it up for the many. So I'm back—but with professional acknowledgments only—you never get a call from anyone in the industry telling you that you forgot someone. So I'll stick with them. But I will say this about my friends and family— you know who you are. And if you really know me and if we're really related, then you also know that I love you. And that includes all of you! So there! (Try to call me now! That was a universal thank-you, if you didn't know.)

Now to the professional folks . . . first, my team at Touchstone: Trish Todd—I didn't have enough time with you! Thank you for continuing to stretch and push me. I learned so much from you and am really sorry our time is ending. Shida

Carr—everyone in the literary world and beyond knows how I feel about you. I don't know how you do it, but every year has gotten better. You are the best publicist . . . period! To the woman who makes sure that I'm where I'm supposed to be, Kym Fisher—your reputation precedes me. Across the country, people tell me that I have the best personal assistant ever—ain't that the truth!

This book was so much fun to talk about, even before it was written, and I have to give a tremendous thank-you and shout-out to Dr. Paula and John Orr—the couple who told me this could very well happen to them. Well, not really, but you know what they were saying. Anyway, how many hours did we spend in the Bahamas talking about this? OMG! It was the best brainstorming session I've ever had. (What are you guys doing next Tuesday, because I have another book to write.) Thanks, Sharon Paige, for helping me talk through the ending! To all my author friends who walk this walk with me, this is not the easiest road, but I have a feeling that if we keep on writing, we'll keep on moving. And my favorite acknowledgment is to all the readers. I don't even know what to say because those two words—*thank you*—seem so small compared to what you've done. My heart is filled with gratitude because if it weren't for you, I wouldn't be here with my tenth adult novel. Thank you for not only supporting me by reading about these people who grow inside my head, but thank you for the other crucial side of this—and that is helping me to spread the word. It is because of you that I am here . . . it is because of you that I do what I do.

Touchstone Reading Group Guide

The Deal, the Dance, and the Devil

High school sweethearts Evia and Adam Langston have been together forever. But when Adam loses his job in the wake of the recession, the Langstons find themselves quickly drowning in financial troubles and unable to support their family of five. Evia and Adam have no idea what to do until Evia's boss, Shay-Shaunté, makes a proposition that sends the Langstons' world spinning out of control. Shay-Shaunté, the owner of a multimillion-dollar hair-care enterprise, makes the couple a proposition that at first seems easy to refuse. But ultimately temptation proves too much to resist, and the Langstons take a trip down the rabbit hole with turns they could never expect and an outcome they could never imagine.

For Discussion

1. How did the author establish Evia's moral center and personality in the opening pages? Did you find it effective? Did you feel as though you'd gotten to know Evia in this introduction? Why or why not?

2. Shay-Shaunté is portrayed to be the villain of this story. Describe your first impression of Evia's boss. How did your opinion of her change, if it changed, throughout the novel?

3. Why do you think the author had Evia drive through her childhood neighborhood and visit her mother on her way home from being offered the fortune from Shay-Shaunté? What did her drive and visit add to the story, and to your understanding of Evia?

4. Shortly after readers are introduced to Evia's husband, Adam, he teaches their children about the value of money and the importance of budgeting. What significance does this scene have for the novel? What impression did this introduction give you about Adam?

5. Beyond their very human love of money and comfort, the Langstons are intrigued by Shay-Shaunté's offer because it seems a solution to many problems. List the hardships the Langstons have endured both before the novel's start and in its beginning chapters. Do these hardships make you feel the Langstons' money problems more deeply? Ulti-

mately, how does knowledge of their suffering influence your thoughts about whether or not they should accept Shay-Shaunté's proposition?

6. Brooklyn and Tamica, Evia's friends from childhood, are still a regular part of Evia's life. Were you surprised that it was Brooklyn, the first lady of their church, who encouraged Evia to take Shay-Shaunté's deal? Why or why not? Discuss the various opinions on the situation and the characters who deliver them to Evia and Adam throughout the novel.

7. Because of their financial situation, Adam and Evia ultimately agree to Shay-Shaunté's five-million-dollar deal. Do you think that if they hadn't been threatened with foreclosure on their home, they still would have taken the deal? What do you think influenced their decision more: the lure of easy money, or the need to protect their family from embarrassment and hardship?

8. In the minutes and hours after Adam leaves for his weekend with Shay-Shaunté, Evia finds that she cannot cope. She keeps imagining them together and wonders what's keeping Adam from calling her: Shay-Shaunté's money or her looks. Do you think Evia was being paranoid, or did she have reason to be worried? Discuss how you think you would cope if you were in her position.

9. On page 259, Evia says, "The last fifty hours had made me see that five million dollars was hardly worth anything." Do you think she really means that, or is she just emotionally distraught at that moment?

10. How do you feel about the legal trick Shay-Shaunté played on the Langstons? Which was worse, the financial deception or the lies she told Evia at work after the weekend together?

11. When Adam and Evia are cheated out of part of the money, Shay-Shaunté says, "You would have done this for whatever I offered. Two million, three million. I was just being generous when I offered you five million" (page 276). Do you think she's right? Is the amount as important as the fact that the Langstons were willing to sacrifice what they believed in?

12 After that weekend, Evia seems to be increasingly suspicious of Adam. She finds every reason to not trust him. Identify and discuss the reasons she finds or creates to suspect he's still having an affair with Shay-Shaunté. Did you think there was a real threat, or is Evia coloring the daily activities with her own imagination of what could be happening?

13. Adam fulfills his part of the deal, but Evia refuses to continue working for the agreed-upon six months. Do you think Adam has a right to be upset? Should Evia have continued working, or was she right to leave even after the worst offense was already done, the bigger sacrifice already made?

14. Throughout the book, the twins are excited about planning their sixteenth birthday party. The finale of the novel takes place at the party . . . where Shay-Shaunté shows up with more drama. Why do you think the author chose this setting for the last conflict between Shay-Shaunté and the Langstons?

A Conversation with Victoria Christopher Murray

Although it's not obvious from the beginning, *The Deal, the Dance, and the Devil* is a contemporary retelling of the traditional "deal with the devil" story. Did you find inspiration in any other similar stories?

Interestingly, the idea for this novel came from Facebook. I asked a simple question—would you give up your husband for five million dollars. Whew! The answers flowed in—all kinds of responses . . . funny and serious ones. I never thought about this as a book, but when it came time for my next contract, that Facebook status came to mind—and *The Deal, the Dance, and the Devil* was born.

In *The Deal, the Dance, and the Devil*, you've managed to set up a solid, almost perfect marriage and family; weigh it down with some financial trouble; and ripen it for the temptation that will bring it down. Have you seen temptation of this sort break families and marriages before? Was this story influenced by real people you know or know about?

I never write about people I know for two reasons. One, I believe and pray that God has given me more of an imagination than that; and two, my friends would kill me! LOL! However, I've seen people broken by their circumstances, and I didn't have to look far. Every day, I struggle with not looking at what's going on around me and keeping my eyes on God. So I didn't have to look beyond my own backyard for the thoughts of how someone could break and fall to temptation under the most stressful of circumstances.

You're the author of several African American novels that preach God's love. Do you consider your work Christian fiction? Why or why not?

Oh, the question of the hour—every hour! First, I hope no one sees me as preaching anything. About God, I write what I know—and I know about His faithful, merciful, graceful, never-ending love. But as far as writing Christian fiction, that was never my intention. I wanted to reach readers who may never step into a church, and having never read Christian fiction before (and I hardly read it now) I wasn't trying to write into any genre. Even now, I hate being given any kind of label—I just write what's on my heart. Labels, like in all other parts of life, limit us.

This book was published during a period of almost-recession and high unemployment. A lot of readers will be able to relate to the temptation of easy money. Is there a lesson here specific to this time and place in our history that motivated you to write this book?

Nope! Truly, I am not that deep. I write contemporary novels, and so this one is just taking place during this time. I do think that this time in our lives provides an interesting backdrop.

Some of the scenes in the book take place at church, where Evia is touched by sermons that seem to speak directly to her. Do you find that such is often the case not only with your characters but in real life? That messages delivered in places of worship often speak personally to individuals?

I think everyone who attends church regularly has experienced this—where you are absolutely sure the pastor walked through your life with you that week and then prepared the sermon just for you. The first few times when it happened to me were scary. But then I accepted it for what it was—God speaking to me in all kinds of ways.

Many first-time authors write semiautobiographical novels. Now that you've written several, how much of your own life still ends up in your novels?

Like I said before, I leave my life and my friends out of these stories. LOL!

You must hear stories quite often from readers who associate with your characters and books. Is there one in particular that you'd like to share with us, something that continues to inspire and encourage you in your work?

You know, over the twelve years I've been writing, I've received thousands of emails and letters from readers letting me know how my novels have impacted their lives. There is not one that stands out; it's the message of all of them that is important to me. And the message is, though I think these books are fiction, these words, these story lines can make a difference in a reader's life. And that's why I keep writing.

This novel takes place in the Washington, D.C., area. Do you research the settings of your novels or did you use places that you already knew from your own life? What importance did the city play in the book? Would you have considered setting *The Deal, the Dance, and the Devil* in New York or Los Angeles, as with some of your other novels?

The District of Columbia didn't play as much of a role in the book as I would've liked. Because the novel takes place in the winter, it was hard to put the characters outside to do anything. I chose D.C. because I wanted to get my characters out of L.A. and New York. I prefer to choose cities that I know a little about—I think writers can make the cities/settings an additional character in the book, but it didn't happen for me this time.

You are both a Christian and an artist. What role does God play in your creative process?

This is probably one of the best questions I've ever been asked. God plays a role in every single part of my life, so His hand in my writing is no different. From the bottom of my heart, I want to please the Lord. So, as I'm writing—or doing anything—I'm always aware, always praying that what I'm doing is pleasing to Him. I tell people that for me, being a Christian is not an adjective, it's a verb—it's in every thing I do.

As far as the books specifically, there have been times when I know for a fact that I've put words down on the page that have come directly from Him. With this novel, I know that He was behind the plot—the way the story twisted and turned—because the entire second half of this book was not in my head when I started. This book was nothing like I thought it was going to be. I thought it was going to be a light, humorous story, and it turned out to be something completely different.

When we last see the Langston family, they're on their way to jail and they've been humiliated in front of each other and before all of their dearest friends. Do you imagine that Evia, Adam, and the kids will ever be the strong family that

they were before? Or has the temptation destroyed what they had forever?

You know what? I don't know, that's why I left the story where I did. My prayer for them—if they were real—is that they figure all of this out and that they are able to find their way back to each other. But it would be a tough road—every part of their marriage was touched, and they would have to fight to put their life back together. Which is why we all need to be careful with every decision we make.

Was it important for you to set up a situation where most readers would fall for the tempting offer? What would be your advice to those faced with such a decision?

It was very important to set up a scenario where most readers would say, "You know, I just might do that." Then, it was just as important for readers to know that you can dance with the devil if you want to, but you're gonna get burned! I believe that there are many people who don't believe that the devil is real and I hope this novel will give readers something to think about. The devil is real and he's roaming to and fro to kill, steal, and destroy everything that God has for you. I hope this book opens up a few eyes—it certainly opened up mine!

Enhance Your Book Club

1. In some ways, this could be seen as a retelling of *Faust*, the theme of making a deal with the devil. Can you think of other stories that you've read, watched, or heard that also deal with the temptation of sacrificing your beliefs for something you want and then regretting it? Briefly outline the elements of these plots and compare them to *The Deal, the Dance, and the Devil*.

2. Make your next book club meeting a movie night. Rent one or more movies that employ the "Faustian deal" such as *Doctor Faustus, Damn Yankees!, Bedazzled*, or *The Devil's Advocate*. Afterward, discuss what it might take for you to "sell your soul" and compromise your beliefs, and consider why this "deal with the devil" theme is so enduring.

3. Put yourself in Adam's and Evia's shoes. Imagine that you or your spouse were laid off and had to find a way to cut corners—to avoid a deal with the devil. What would you do to make ends meet? Are there certain items you could live without, or another job you would consider (part-time, seasonal, odd jobs) to help? If you have children, how would you explain the need to sacrifice during tough times to them? Is there a particular Bible verse that you would consider sharing to help your family cope with the hardship?

4. Victoria Christopher Murray has written a number of popular books. If you've read some of them, discuss how they are alike and different from this one. Take some time to visit and browse the author's website at victoriachristophermurray.com.